The Stranger Within

BY G. C. Johnson

Dedicated to my grandpa, my PaPa, who searched for days to recover this book when it went missing on my sixteenth birthday. If it wasn't for you, I don't even know if this would be here right now. I love you.

Prologue: Olivia

Freshman orientation.

I had been preparing for this all summer. This was the moment where the graduated middle schoolers were officially bumped into high school.

After my stepmother signed us in, we migrated to the gymnasium where Principal Marco would give a speech and present the teachers who would direct us to our homeroom. They would then assign our lockers and classes.

I sifted through the hoard of students, trying to find Tammy, a girl I had befriended over the summer. I had been too excited when we found out we were attending the same high school. But instead I found a person who made me stop abruptly in my search.

Sam.

He was here.

My heart started thumping anxiously against my ribcage. I didn't understand why it was even doing that; I haven't seen or heard from him since the beginning of the summer. I always assumed he had moved and couldn't keep in contact. It was much easier to accept than the other option...

Nevertheless, he was here at *this* school's orientation. Brushing a stray piece of hair behind my ear, I swallowed any bit of nervousness and stepped towards him until I saw the people he was hanging with.

Or more specifically, the gang members he was hanging with.

I stopped suddenly again in confusion, heartache, and dread. Sam had dumped me for *them*?

As if sensing someone was watching him, he turned his head in my direction. He stared at me blankly, not a smile, not a wink. There was nothing. It was like he didn't recognize me. I opened my mouth to say something, anything, but I couldn't speak.

Sam, my best friend, my first crush, the one who was breaking my heart in this very moment, just turned his chin and lifted a lit cigarette to his lips.

Freshman orientation had been three years ago, and nothing has been the same since.

Chapter 1: Olivia

"Where did the time go?" I asked leaning against my locker for the new school year. "I mean, it was like just yesterday we were getting out of this place," I said miserably. "Good thing it's senior year."

One of my best friends, Maya Hilty, opened her locker and sighed. "I know what you mean. I wish summer didn't end so quickly. I was supposed to go to California, but no, the board decided to start school early."

"I was supposed to go to that computer science camp in Washington D.C. but I gave it to Max. He'd enjoyed something like that."

"I don't know how he likes computer science."

"He's a genius, that's how."

Maya fluffed her brown hair, checking it out in the mirror she'd placed in her locker. She was a bit obsessed with her looks, but not too much. "I didn't choose badly, did I?" She referred to the short haircut and blonde highlights she'd gotten last week.

I shook my head. "You look fine." I smacked her hand to prevent messing it up. "Stop worrying."

The sound of clicking heels and smacking lips distracted me from my train of thought. Maya and I looked over to see what it was- or more specifically, *who* it was. I rolled my eyes. It was Anya and her posse. Anya Cambridge, the most popular and richest girl in school, had just returned from Paris. How did I know this useless knowledge? Well, she sent a text to every living being with a cell phone that her parents had surprised her with plane tickets to go to a fashion show. They paused by their lockers on the opposite side of the hall and watched as Anya started playing with her hair, a flirtatious look on her face. I glanced over to see what she was looking at and who her next target might be. My heart caught in my throat.

Sam Wayne.

He's the leader of the infamous Under-Twenty street gang. His members ranged from sixth graders to seniors. This is his second year in reign. To other people, Sam seemed intimidating, but to someone who's dealt with his attitude for the past three years, his devilish smirk and cold glares never made me back down. But if people trapped us in a small isolated room, we'd verbally kill each other.

Maya scoffed which knocked me out of my thoughts and into reality. "I hate this part of the new school year. Everyone wants to be friends with them, and it's sickening about how many girls want to date them."

"Tell me about it," I muttered.

Sam had black hair, dark as the nighttime sky, and fair skin. Despite our rivalry, I couldn't deny that his eyes were beautiful. They were emerald green; a mesmerizing, deep color, and there were moments where they flashed bits of blue and gold. I always compared them to the ocean. They had mysteries hidden beneath the waves.

Other than his eyes, everything else sickened me. He drank and smoked; he played girls with no remorse. His gang was involved in many perilous activities: arms trafficking, arson, vandalism, burglary, and trespassing.

While I added the finishing touches to my locker, Maya kept staring in their direction. "I hate to admit this, but Sam has gotten way cuter!"

I snorted and shut my locker, pushing the lock into place. "Yeah, right."

She shook her head. "He really has."

"How does someone get more attractive?"

Maya rolled her eyes. "Olivia, you and all females know that it is possible with Sam Wayne."

"Oh shut it," I said.

She held her hands up defensively. "Take one look at him. It won't hurt you."

I sighed irritability and looked over. Sam was leaning against the lockers with Anya talking about her trip no doubt. He rested a hand on her lower back and said something to her, causing Anya to giggle hysterically.

"They should get a room," I said bitterly.

An uncomfortable knot sat in the pit of my stomach, the same knot I'd get when girls were all over him.

"Forget her. Look only at him," she ordered directly.

I followed her instructions and regretted it. He was

way better looking than last year. His black hair was spiked and looked freshly cut, bangs no longer covering his forehead. Even from across the hall, I noticed the depth of his jawline, the curve of his neck, the dimple in his grin. He wore dark jeans, a white cotton v-neck that showed his toned arms, and black sneakers. I shamefully averted my eyes, refusing to look at Maya.

"I told you!" Maya boasted.

I pinched the bridge of my nose. "But there are other guys that are-"

She cocked an eyebrow. "Yeah, we both know that's not true."

I gave her the dirtiest look I could muster because it was true. Maya failed at stifling her laughs. "AP Science. Wish me luck!" And then she was off cheerfully, which was ironic since she had complained for hours yesterday.

I glanced back towards them again, and wished that I hadn't because Sam just so happened looked up at the same time. Our eyes met across the hall. His cocky smirk broke out onto his face, and instead of turning away, I stared back at him, assuring him that I wasn't like others who shriveled under his hard looks. He finally replaced his sights on Anya as she messed with the collar of his shirt. I rolled my eyes at their inappropriate behavior and headed towards first period.

It was the first day of senior year and I was already annoyed. Great...

SAM

I leaned against the lockers after Anya and her 'minions' (as Ace likes to call them) walked off in a different direction. Ace, my cousin and fellow senior, was flirting with one of the new students and she seemed so interested that she recited her number almost immediately. I taught him how to talk to girls and how to get their attention very quickly. Sweet talk them, make them laugh... All that good stuff.

"Hey man!" Ace called after she disappeared from sight. "She agreed to go out with me Friday night. It's only eight in the morning and I'm already scorin'!"

I chuckled and patted him on the shoulder. "Chill, dude. There'll be plenty of girls to go around."

"Are you gonna ask out that chick you were checkin' out earlier?"

My eyebrows shot up. "Huh?"

"The chick across the hall."

I glared at him. "That *chick* was Olivia Jenkins- and I was not checkin' her out!"

"I was just teasing, man."

I sent him a harsh look anyways. I ignored the urge to stick my foot out when my least favorite teacher, Miss Kay, started walking through the halls with her always present scowl on her face. She was my Geometry teacher this year, and I had her for first period which is bound to be torture. I picked up my backpack off the floor and swung it over my shoulder, following her to the classroom, and I took a seat next to some freckled-face girl with round glasses. I sent her a kind grin and she almost hyperventilated. Miss Kay wrote her name on the board in cursive, put today's objective, and the date. She then proceeded to turn around and lifted a sheet of paper.

"First things first, I have arranged a permanent seating arrangement for this class. It will be used for the entire year and there will be no exchange," she declared.

The class responded with a low groan. I just sat in my seat; waiting for whatever loser I would be stuck with this year. Whenever we got partners in class, we normally end up working with them for group assignments. Mostly all my partners throughout the past few years were girls so I could just wink at them or promise them a date and they'll do all the work.

Miss Kay called out a few names and I didn't even bother to pay attention until her dark, beady eyes rested on me. "Sam Wayne," some stiffened, others sighed, "will be sitting next to…" It was almost like she was waiting for that dramatic effect. I looked at her impatiently, pushing myself up to move. "*Olivia Jenkins.*"

I stopped abruptly, muscles freezing.

Not her. Please, not her.

Let it be a mistake.

The class was uncomfortably silent because the student body knew of our rivalry. Without a second thought, I snapped my head over my shoulder to see Olivia perched in her seat, avoiding my gaze. I gritted my teeth in anger while collecting my books in a slow trance, thinking of ways for my teacher to *accidentally* disappear. I stood up and walked over to our table, using all my self-control to keep my anger in. I sat down next to her, making sure to keep my distance so neither of us would accidentally bump into each other.

I can definitely see violent words being thrown in the near future.

OLIVIA

Out of all the students, why did she put us together?

It was hard not watching him move, and I scowled at the air, noticing the obvious discomfort between us. Miss Kay finished reading off names and went straight into the rules concerning homework and punishments. I barely paid attention because of a certain gang leader sitting next to me. It wasn't like I was afraid of him or anything. I could count on one hand where I've actually been scared. Most of the time, we would be spitting in each other's faces and threatening to hurt one another.

That wasn't how it used to be though.

We used to be best friends…

It was after middle school graduation. He suddenly stopped returning my calls and texts. He ignored my IM's. He never came over anymore. He started hanging out with older guys and his attitude changed extremely. He started partying and smoking. He joined Under-Twenty then eventually became its leader. He abandoned friendships; he broke promises and spread rumors.

I couldn't help but wonder what happened to the nice boy inside him.

The boy he used to be.

The rumors, the betrayal, the distance, everything probably wouldn't have hurt as bad…

If I wasn't in love with him.

Chapter 2: Olivia

Yep. I'm in love with Sam Wayne.

I know I must be naïve, but after being friends for almost ten years and growing up together, little things started having more meaning. Trust me; I really hated the fact that those feelings were alive. I hated having them while he sat and allowed rumors being spread and never tried stopping any of them. I hated having them when our rivalry started last year and the spitting of venomous words began.

But despite all the wrong he's done, I couldn't stop it, and they had continued to grow until I finally had to admit it.

To clear up any nonsense, I'm not in love with the heartless gang leader Sam Wayne. I fell for the Sam Wayne I grew up with- my best friend, the boy who'd jump in a freezing lake so I wouldn't be sick and alone for a week. A part of me believes that he's still in there somewhere, and maybe one day he'll allow it to come back.

I'm praying that the day will be soon.

Out of nowhere, someone flicked me hard on the arm, and I jumped embarrassingly in my seat, knowing that I spent too much in my thoughts. Miss Kay crossed her arms above her chest, looking at me with an eyebrow raised.

"Miss Jenkins," she said in her strict tone. "Would you like to share with us what distracted you from my class?"

Sam, not so conspicuously, was laughing underneath his breath. I resisted the urge to kick him in the shin. I licked my lips, trying to figure out a good excuse. I really didn't want to share what I'd been thinking. Miss Kay tapped her foot impatiently against the hard classroom floor, the sole of her shoe making an irritating noise.

"I was thinking of a solution for that problem," I pointed at the board and smiled to make it seem more believable.

"Miss Jenkins, if you were paying attention, you would have known that I haven't even got to the problem of the day. I'm telling the class what kind of projects you should be expecting for the next semester," Miss Kay explained.

I bit my lip, dreading what could spill out of her mouth in the next minute. "It won't happen again," I promised. "I'm sorry."

She pursed her lips. "Well, since it's the first day and you were the top student last year, I'll just give you a warning. But no more day-dreaming in class! That goes for everyone!"

As she returned to her desk, Sam whispered, "Teacher's pet."

I stifled a snort. I've got that name hurled at me plenty of times. He'd have to do better to get a reaction out of me.

~~~

When the second bell rang for class dismissal, I was finishing the final problem she gave to check how our math skills were and what we remembered from last year. After turning in the sheet, I started to walk out, but Sam blocked me from exiting the classroom. I huffed out of aggravation. I just wanted to get away from him.

"Get her to switch us," he demanded.

A confused scoff slipped past my lips. "What makes you think I'm able to do that?"

"Teachers favorite you," he said like it solved everything.

"Well that doesn't help me with Miss Kay. No one questions her chart or rules. Believe me, if I thought there was a way, I'd do it. You're not the only one upset about our pairing together, Wayne," I retorted bitterly. I went to leave again, but he mimicked my action and stopped me by pressing his forearm to my stomach. A set of butterflies fluttered their wings and I wanted them trampled.

"I'm not upset." He leaned in and his breath blew across my face, the hardness in his eyes unrelenting. "I'm *pissed.*"

"Deal with it," I snapped, and when I finally managed to step around him, I found myself tripping into the doorframe. I pinned him with a sharp glare and he arched his eyebrows innocently as if he hadn't done it. "Must you always be an inconsiderate jerk?"

"Must you always be an insufferable know-it-all?" He shot back.

If I wasn't afraid of being suspended, I'd smack him. My best friend from freshman year, Tammy Brooks, appeared on my left and grabbed my arm. I stomped over to my locker and threw my math textbook inside, fuming with rage.

"You guys don't waste any time, huh?" Tammy asked sarcastically.

I slammed my locker shut. "He's so rude and selfish and I want to slap that arrogant smirk of his!"

"And to think you're in love with him," she whispered low enough so that no one else heard. "Maybe you should avoid him, Liv-"

"I can't!" I clenched my hands into fists to avoid yanking my hair out. "I'm stuck with him as a partner for the entire year and he's acting like it's my fault." Tammy sighed, rubbing her forehead. "I just wish there was a way to get rid of these feelings."

"I know." She patted me on the shoulder sympathetically. "Just try not to cross any dangerous lines."

A memory triggered at her words.

Sam pressed me against the wall, his emerald eyes enraged; I was burning with fury. He had been teasing me to a point where I finally had it. We began shouting back and forth, and I yelled something about us being friends before and well, it worsened the situation.

"Why don't you just shout it over the intercom?!" Sam asked venomously.

I'll admit; I was hurt by his words. "Do you regret being friends with me?"

He ignored the question, but in a way he answered it. "Do you think I want everyone knowin' I was friends with you?"

"Just leave me alone!" I shoved him in the chest.

"Well, kitty likes to scratch," Sam smirked, lifting a dark eyebrow. "Who knew little Miss I-Do-Everything-Perfect had an aggressive side to her?"

"Just stop," I muttered, feeling claustrophobic.

"Now why would I do that?"

"Because if you have any sort of compassion-"

He snorted indignantly. "Do you honestly think I have that?"

"I don't even know who you are anymore," I whispered. "You're an absolute stranger to me." He glanced in the opposite direction, his jaw firm. "Why did you change?" The words came out of me before I could stop them. The question I've wanted to hear the answer to for years.

He turned back, rolling his bottom lip in between his teeth. "I had reasons."

"Everyone struggles. Including me." I saw a glint of empathy in his eyes and I smirked, using this as bait for a side comment. "Aw, who knew Mr. I'm-So-Big-and-Bad is sensitive?"

Sam pushed me harder against the wall, my shoulder blades digging into the groove. "Shut up."

As another fight was getting boosted, a teacher came running over and breaking us apart, exclaiming about PDA and "this is a high-school hall, not your bedroom" but Sam and I were too busy glaring at each other to acknowledge her. The teacher gripped onto Sam's upper arm and dragged him down the hall away from me, towards the principal's office.

But before they disappeared from my sight, Sam had turned his head with an expression I couldn't read.

I jumped for the second time that day when Tammy poked me on the arm a few times. "What lines are you talking about?" I asked, returning to our conversation.

"Telling him."

"Like I'm going to tell him," I scoffed at the thought. "The world would have to be ending- you know what? Maybe not even then."

Tammy grabbed my arm, pulling me out of my thoughts for the second time today and looking genuinely worried. She glanced at the ground. "I'm sorry."

"For what?" I asked confused.

"For what he's become."

"I've almost accepted it," I confessed. "He just keeps hurting me over and over again. He keeps disappointing me."

She pulled me in for a hug. "Maybe one day, they won't be there anymore."

A part of me wants them gone... but the other part

wants him to return them as well and go back to the way we used to be.

I don't know what I wanted more.

SAM

The second we entered our garage, Ace crashed onto the couch. He told me all the events that happened today and I didn't blame him for heading straight to sleep. I would join him, but I had to fix my truck before anything else. My mom and I didn't have any extra money to pay for a mechanic so Ryker and I have to fix it.

My best friend and second in command, Ryker Smith, stood next to me fumbling with a lighter. I rolled my eyes and grabbed it out of his hands, lighting the cigarette that was already in my mouth. I threw it back to him and took a long drag.

"Now I don't have to wait forever," I said, breathing it out in his caramel- toned face. He narrowed his eyes and smacked me upside the head.

Daniel Rodriguez, another member and friend, sat on the arm of the couch. Based on the racket upstairs, the middle schoolers must have gotten home. "You do know that smoking is bad for you. It could give you lung cancer," Daniel said taking a bite of an apple.

Ace rubbed his eyes with sleep and yawned. "It's true. I had to do a stupid report on it in tenth grade."

I gave them a blank stare. "Do I look like I give a crap?" I replied letting the smoke emerge from my mouth again. Daniel crinkled his nose in disgust. I jumped on the hood of my Uncle Hector's old and non-running '68 Mustang. "So guess what?" I didn't wait for a reply. "I'm Geometry partners with Olivia-I'm-so-freakin'-smart-and-perfect-Jenkins for the entire year!"

Ace and Daniel winced then my cousin fell back onto the cushions. "You're not alone, man. One of my exes is partnered with me for the first semester in English. I thought senior year was supposed to be all about fun."

"It'll get better," Daniel encouraged.

Ryker paused in the middle of checking my truck's engine out and shot me an interested look. "Wait, did you say Olivia Jenkins- as in your childhood best friend?" he prompted.

"Yeah," I said reluctantly, scowling. "Your point?"

He handed me a rag and gestured to the engine. I dumped the rest of my cigarette, taking his spot and screwed off the oil cap. "Well..."

"Your point?" I insisted loudly.

He leaned on the '68. "Wouldn't that cause some issues?"

"Why would it?"

"Didn't you have feelings for her?"

"*What*?" I shot up so quickly, my head hit the top of the hood. "Uh-huh, we were- ouch- only best friends!"

"Denial!" Ace sung from behind me. I threw him a dirty look.

Ryker shrugged one shoulder. "I'm just askin' because she's hot and has brains and is also your childhood best friend-"

"What are you gettin' at?" I demanded, slamming the hood down.

"Maybe it'd cause you to ask her out."

I spun around, eyebrows raised. "Are you screwin' with me?"

"Talk about *weird*!" Ace laughed and I chucked a pillow at his face to shut him up. Daniel failed at hiding his amusement.

"Why would I do that?" I questioned curiously.

My best friend lit another cigarette. "Just thought you might 'cause of feelings, but since those don't exist..."

"You don't have to worry about it."

Daniel threw his apple core in the trash. "Besides, she doesn't date. She's like focused on college."

"And when guys do approach her, she doesn't take 'em up on it. I wonder why."

"How do you two know this? Why do you even care?" I asked.

Ryker sucked in a deep breath of nicotine. "We're bored. We pay attention."

"Well I don't and did you ever think that maybe someone ruined it for her?" *And maybe that someone was you,* a voice, otherwise known as my irritating conscience, muttered. I dismissed the thought. I had reasons why I walked away and she couldn't use me as a reason to not get close to someone. I glanced down at the floor, chewing on my bottom lip. My phone's alarm started ringing obnoxiously, and I pulled my leather jacket over my shoulders. "Well, I'd love to keep up this lovely conversation, but we have to leave."

Ryker stomped on his cigarette. "I'll get Santiago."

As he hopped upstairs, I tied the black and blue U20 bandana around my neck.

~~~

We parked in the development across the street, under the shaded beam hidden from street cameras and wandering eyes. After putting the vehicle in park, I was about to step out when the top headlights from a police car caught the corner of my eye.

"We got company," I announced.

Ryker groaned, thumping his head against the seat. "Ditchin' or rollin'?"

"We should roll. I'm in no mood for a jail cell," Santiago commented.

As the guys conversed, my eyes narrowed, a smirk stretching on my lips. I wasn't afraid of the authorities. "Well, we shouldn't let our gasoline go to waste, now should we?"

"What are you-"

Before Ace could finish his statement, I got out, the

smack of my boots echoing through the empty lot. I propped open the trunk, grabbed a tank of gasoline, and swiftly moved across the asphalt, carrying it over my shoulder.

"What are you doin', man?" Ryker hissed.

"Lighting 'em up."

I reached the police car and ducked slightly to peek inside. Both sets of seats were empty. Ignoring the chance of the officers coming out of the warehouse and catching me, I stepped onto the hood and poured the slick gasoline. It drenched the windshield, the top, and slid to the trunk, copper liquid dripping off the edges. Once the tank was completely empty, I kicked it away and jumped off, venturing to the sidewalk. I leaned against the lamppost, arms crossed and eyes trained on the entrance of the warehouse.

When I saw the door crack open, I whistled three times sharply, barking out an, "Hey!" The officers stopped short, spines straight and in alert. "I applaud you for bustin' on this building. I also wanted to thank you for letting me use the gasoline for a much better place."

I flicked open the lighter that I had twirling in my fingers and threw it in the car's direction, ducking behind one of the nearest lot's pillars. A sudden loud explosion of shattering windows and wild roaring fire thundered my eardrums. In the midst of all the noise, I heard several yells and excited curses from my members. Brushing off any debris and ash, I stood back up and rolled my shoulders. The officers were lying on the opposite sidewalk, their arms covering their heads. With an arrogant smirk, I stalked over to stand near the burning vehicle and held out my hands, adapting a sweet tone.

"Next time, I'll torch the place with you still inside."

Even though I was lying straight through my teeth, I felt a surge of pride at their nods and fearful gulps.

Then I turned my back on the heated flames.

~~~

I opened the door to my apartment, instantly smelling the sensations of burning garlic and steaming vegetables. Mom had gone to culinary school in her early twenties.

"Honey, is that you?" she shouted.

"No," I replied, dripping with sarcasm. "It's a burglar."

"Oh, shush."

I shut and chained the door behind me, setting my backpack on the couch and walking into the kitchen. I leaned against the doorframe, watching my mother cook. Despite all the challenges in her life, Leah Wayne was an exceptional woman and I was proud to call her my mom. Her long, brown hair was pulled into a nicely pinned bun and her apron was double-knotted around her waist. She was standing at the stove, mumbling about which ingredient to add next.

"Hey Mom," I greeted kissing her on the cheek.

"Hey honey." She smiled then crinkled her nose, leaning over to press it against my collar. "Why do you smell like smoke?"

My eyes widened a fraction, stumbling over an explanation. I didn't even think about that. "Uh…"

"Were you smoking again?"

I nodded urgently, wanting to avoid any confrontation. Mom turned to check on the stove. I grabbed an apple out of the fruit bowl and jumped onto the counter, taking a bite out of it. I realized I was sitting next to a giant bowl of marinated chicken.

"What are we havin' for dinner?" I asked, the apple's juice running down my chin.

She grabbed the chicken and successfully dumped them into the pan with the sizzling garlic. "Teriyaki chicken with a side of teriyaki noodles and vegetables."

"I don't like vegetables," I complained, sliding down onto my feet when she made a gesture for me to get down.

My mom wiped her hands on her apron and walked over, softly running her fingers through my hair- which she thought I looked so much better with my new haircut. "Too bad. I cook it, you eat it. I mean, unless you want to live off that junk you eat from those fast-food restaurants."

"Hey, they're not all bad."

She nodded, agreeing with me. "I know, but sometimes I like seeing my son enjoying my food. I think that you don't come home to avoid my cooking."

I laughed. "Mom, I love your cooking. You should know that. I'm just not always here to eat it."

I saw her eyes glisten with sadness. "Because you're doing that dirty gang work. Sam, one day, you're going to get hurt-"

"Mom, not this again-" I began to protest, but she cut me off.

"I don't want my son to come home beaten or have a police officer knocking at my door, waiting to tell me something horrible that I don't want to hear!"

"Why are you so worried?" I asked.

"How dare you ask me that?" She pulled at my hand and looked at me with sad eyes. My stomach tightened at the expression. "I worry because I care about you. You're my son, and I don't want anything to happen-" Her voice gave out on her and she let go of my hand and returned to the stove, turning the chicken around.

I saw the tear stains on her cheeks. I pushed myself away from the counter and trailed over, wrapping my arms around her, pulling her into a hug. My mother began to protest about burning the food, but I tightened my hold and she relaxed, gripping the leather material of my jacket.

"I'm a big boy. I can handle it," I whispered burying my nose into her hair. I noticed some grey strands starting to stand out.

"Sam, you're my son," she replied softly. "I just don't want to lose you." She backed away from the hug when the vegetable pot started to boil over.

I began to walk away from the kitchen when I turned my head and said, "Do you think I actually like some of the things I do? In fact, sometimes I hate it," I admitted. I knew she was listening, even though her eyes stayed glued to the stove. "But there are times in life where you have to do what you have to do and deal with it."

And with that, I ended the conversation and went to my bedroom.

Chapter 3: Sam

I was leaning back in my chair comfortably, my arm draped across my eyes to block the blinding light. Why did schools have to have such bright lights? It was not necessary. I know some would argue that they're there to keep students from falling asleep, but that's what a hood and sunglasses are for- to block out light.

Geez, I'm tired.

A loud drop beside me caught my attention, and I cracked open an eye. "Who knew there'd be a day a teacher's pet would be late to class? I mean, I was here before you."

Olivia rolled her eyes, her tone aggravated. "I had to take my brother to school and I'm not late. Even if I was, I'd have a legitimate excuse unlike 'I partied too hard' or 'I drank too much'."

"Ouch," I hissed sassily. "You might want to watch that judgment, sweetheart."

"I don't have to watch my judgment when it comes to you," she snapped.

I pressed my lips together in a hard line. "You might also want to make sure your perfection is up to par. Wouldn't want that reputation to be tarnished."

I glanced at her out of the corner of my eye and she didn't seem too fond of my comment. Well I didn't care for hers so we're now even.

For the rest of the period, we were silent.

~~~

Ryker stood next to me as we leaned against the lockers in the semi-crowded hallway. Everyone was getting ready for the pep rally. Ace was chatting with the girl who agreed to go out tonight. Anya walked over in her black and red cheerleading uniform, smiling sweetly and running her finger across my bare forearm. Her face was covered with inches of make-up, which honestly bothered me. I hated when girls covered up their natural beauty, but like always, I kept my opinion silent.

"I heard you were messing with Olivia," Anya said with a hint of disgust.

I was confused. "Uh, when was this?"

"In math class." She put her finger on my chest territorially, her blue eyes boring into mine. "You're *my* boyfriend. She does not deserve your attention."

Ryker grunted an indulgent, "I'm outta here", and smacked me on the shoulder. I shot him a desperate look. He ignored it.

Sighing, I replied, "Anya, you can chill. It didn't mean anything."

She pursed her red-coated lips and cocked her head to the side. "Well, I still don't like it. She's not important enough to have my boyfriend's attention. I don't care whether you were joking or not."

I laughed. "You don't own me."

"But I am your girlfriend and you should respect

me."

"That doesn't mean you get to tell me what I can and cannot do."

Anya put her hands on her hips, raising an eyebrow. "I'm not telling you what to do," she retorted.

I clenched my teeth together and said slowly, "Of course you aren't."

"What's *that* supposed to mean?"

"It seems like it."

Anya put her hands on my upper arms and stroked them softly; I shrugged them off. "I just don't want to lose you, baby."

I rolled my eyes. Ace appeared in my side view. He stopped short when he saw that Anya and I were in the middle of a conversation. "Somethin' wrong?"

"No," he answered and pointed to the gang lingering near the gym doors. "Do you want us to go ahead?"

"Yeah, go. Save me a seat!" I called. I turned back to Anya after they disappeared behind the doors and she was checking her nails. "Look, I don't see the big deal. I did it last year; I have to do it in senior year. It's my last chance."

"What bothers me is the attention you give her," Anya crinkled her nose, jealously evident. "It's more than you give me."

I tried not to laugh. There is no way that's possible. "It's just to mess with her. It doesn't mean anything,

Anya."

"Whatever," she muttered then her whole attitude changed. "Let's just forget about it, okay? Let's do something tonight."

You're the one who brought it up, not me. "Uh, the guys and I have stuff we have to do tonight, but maybe tomorrow." We started walking towards the gymnasium.

"You can't take a rain check?" Anya asked, lacing her fingers with mine.

I shook my head. "I can't. It's dealing with-"

"You can't skip off one night to hang out with your girlfriend?" She paused in her spot, thrusting her hip to one side.

I turned around to face her, seething through my teeth. "I'm the leader, therefore I need to *lead*." She rolled her eyes and I rubbed the crease between my eyebrows. "You know it is hilarious how when you're busy, I'm understanding, but when I have plans, you give me a hard time."

Anya scowled. "Maybe because you're always off giving them-"

"*Attention?*" I offered sarcastically, scoffing and running my hands through my hair. "Ah, know what? This isn't workin'. You're too freakin' needy."

"Fine!" Her voice echoed down the hall. "I don't want to date a dude who's not willing to spend time with me anyways!"

I would totally retaliate, but I was too relieved.

Even though I had just dumped her; I grabbed the handle of the door and opened it for her. She glared at me and made her way towards the cheerleaders, adding more sway to her hips. I snorted at the desperation.

I dug my hands into my pockets as I walked past the bleachers; feeling stares and glares. It came with the territory. I lifted my head to search for my group; instead I caught the familiar sight of my *favorite* person. A smirk slid easily onto my face as I trailed over to them. A girl I vaguely recognized as Tammy Brooks smacked Olivia's arm, getting her attention.

She was wrapped up in a book. What a surprise.

"What are you doing here?" Olivia insisted.

"I go to school here," I answered sarcastically, my smirk widening. She sent me a dry look, clearly not amused by my response. "What are you doing here?"

She sighed, marking her book. "I meant, why are you bothering us? I'm not in the mood for pompous guys or did I not make that clear yesterday?"

"I've never seen you so heartwarming," I remarked.

She opened her book back up. "Leave us alone, Wayne."

"Am I seriously that much of a bother? I mean, what if I just came over to chat? No harm done."

Tammy and her other friend scooted a little ways from us and our growing argument. Olivia decided not to answer my question and once again returned to her book.

"What are you readin'?" I tried to see the title, but Olivia snapped the book shut, and before I could ask her why, put it in her backpack and zipped it.

"None of your business," she retorted.

I raised my eyebrows and scoffed. "It is that hard to tell me the name of a book? It's only a simple question."

"And?" I still didn't see the big deal. "I'm not about to let my guard down and let you have what you always get out of girls," Olivia said.

I crossed my arms above my chest, enjoying her second judgment of me. "And what is that exactly?"

"Like you don't know."

I straightened my shoulders, staring curiously. "C'mon, Jenkins. Try me."

"Sleep with them."

My skin prickled at the accusation. Did I really seem that low? I opened my mouth to deny it, but Ryker walked over and slapped me on the back. Chocolate brown eyes locked with mine for several seconds before their owner glanced at Tammy, who was laughing at something in the book she was reading. Ryker began to pull me over to where our friends sat.

"Oh, Olivia," I called out sweetly. She looked up, annoyed. "Nice judgment. One thing you got wrong though; I don't sleep around."

For a second, she looked apologetic then it went away as soon as it showed. Tammy shot me an awkward smile and looked at the textbook in her lap, copying some notes down. Ryker and I walked up the stairs, bumping our newest additions of our lovely group. I sat down next to Ace and grabbed his water bottle, taking a swig out of it. Olivia seriously knew how to piss me off. That was her second judgment today. As if she's perfect.

"Man, she sure knows how to tick you off," Ryker commented.

I swallowed another gulp, muttering, "Of course she does."

I leaned my head against the wall, focusing on Olivia and her two friends. She was sitting with one of her knees propped up with the book open on her lap, entranced with the printed words on the beige-colored pages.

The teacher was speaking about the big game tonight. The cheerleaders which included Anya and her minions were making hand motions and doing flips behind her, making the crowd clap and roar.

They continued to talk about the game, introducing all the players- old and new, bringing the football coaches up. The school year may have just started, but they've been practicing for weeks for this game. It was a big deal.

I showed support by playing hang-man with Ryker.

We kept passing the sheet back and forth, using words our fellow students would be surprised we knew.

Despite their belief, we weren't dumb. Ryker paused, taking his phone out to text his auburn-haired and blue-eyed girlfriend; Beth. Being the daughter of a corporate business man, she attended a private school on the other side of town. I only met her a few times, but I could tell she was the best pick for the guy. How Ryker managed to get her father's approval though had shocked all of us.

"What were you and Olivia talking about?" Daniel asked frowning when Ace beat him at another thumb-war.

Ryker joined the growing conversation. "Somethin' must have been said because you looked pissed."

"I asked her a simple question and she went off, saying that one question could lead to sleeping with a girl," I explained. The head coach continued to talk, losing my interest fast. "I mean I know I'm far from innocent, but that's a low I wouldn't even reach, man."

"What about Nikki?"

I turned in my seat slowly, my face stoic; Ace's had gone pale. My voice was cold and calm, too calm for comfort. "Don't mention her again."

"I won't," Ace squeaked.

One of the teachers shushed us and I stuck my tongue out. I fell back against the wall, pushing Nikki far from my mind. She was a big mistake. The cheerleaders were about to do a performance. I looked around the gymnasium while they did their obnoxious routine, and my eyes drifted to a certain someone who was still interested in her book.

Like she could feel someone's gaze on her, Olivia turned her head charily and caught me. Throughout the routine and even while the crowd applauded, neither one of us broke the stare. Surprising her and myself, I wiggled my eyebrows playfully, a soft smirk curled on my lips. Olivia might have been a few bleachers away from me, but I could see the smile in her facial expression.

It wasn't there on the outside; it was on the inside.

OLIVIA

I felt like someone was watching me intensely so I reluctantly turned my head and I was shocked to see that it was Sam, sitting a few bleachers away with his gang.

I almost gasped when we didn't break it for several minutes, and when I saw him wiggle his eyebrows, I haven't seen it in such a friendly way in a long time, my heart swelled. He'd always do it to make me laugh. The memory of our friendship made me smile in the inside, but on the outside, I tried my best to keep it blank. I didn't want him knowing I missed our time together.

I didn't want him knowing I missed him.

I pulled away finally, not wanting to look at him for another second. My book lay abandoned, my mind being swallowed by our past moments. Sam's eyes were the worst memory.

They were the same pair of green eyes that betrayed me.

The same pair a gang leader wore.

Tammy rested a hand on my shoulder. "I know you miss him, but he's changed, Liv. Stop hurting yourself."

I grabbed one of my backpacks straps and pulled it over my shoulder. "Look, I don't wanna talk about it anymore." My friends didn't take offense. They knew the subject was getting old and extremely sensitive. The teacher had already dismissed us, giving us permission to leave any time. "I have to get Parker. See you later."

I walked out of the gymnasium, trailing past other students and through the many hallways of the large building. I made it to my locker, opening it to grab the few things I needed. After collecting the textbooks, I leaned my head against the locker next to mine, pulling the book out of the front compartment of my backpack. There was a reason I didn't let Sam see it. A picture of him and I was tapped to the back of the cover. It was a photo from my eleventh birthday, and we were smiling happily into the camera with red icing on our cheeks from our cake fight, which I had won fair and square. There was also a note written in his messy handwriting.

"Happy Birthday, Liv! :) You're finally my age, hah! Mom said I had to get you something special for your birthday so I got you a book. I just so happened to pass a book store and I know how much you love reading! And yes, I actually went in there for you. I think I'm traumatized. Anyways, I'm so happy to have you as a friend- wait, scratch that, MY BEST FRIEND! I can tell you anything and you're always there for me. Thanks for being awesome. I hope you have a great birthday. Well, duh,

you'll be with me so of course you will ;) – Sam

By the way, can't wait for our Disney marathon and best friend sleepover tonight! :D

Oh, and I love you."

I smiled. I remembered tackling him in a hug for writing such a sweet message. I turned it back to the cover and ran my fingers over the thick letters. I closed my locker, slipping the hardback into my bag. I walked out of the school and slid inside my car, turned the engine on, and rested my hands on the wheel.

Maybe one day we'll be able to be friends again.

Maybe something more.

Chapter 4: Sam

We ditched the building, the place already erupting into flames; the fire roaring to life with the added gasoline. I dumped the empty container on the side of the street, not caring if authorities collected it for evidence. I stopped abruptly as a gunshot crackled through the air. I closed my eyes momentarily, listening carefully to see which direction- a hand clamped down on my shoulder and I looked up; Santiago was pointing to his right where the shouts and gunfire were coming from.

"Think we should check it out?" He asked, his hand clutching his Glock's hilt.

"Yeah," I said. "Ryker! Ace! You're coming with me. Daniel, Santiago, take the others and get out."

"Wait, wait, let me go," Santiago argued.

"I gave you an order and I expect you to follow it," I told him sternly. I retracted my gun from inside my jacket and gestured to Ryker. "Let's see what this is."

Together, we maneuvered to where the gunfire ensued, being aware of our surroundings. It was dark and eerie; silent besides the sound of gravel crunching under the soles of our shoes. It seemed like whatever was happening was over.

"Yo, U20!" someone greeted in a hush-toned. I ventured over to put a name and face to the voice, my finger nestled near the trigger for precautions. I wasn't about to put my guard down. "Dude, glad you're here."

The figure came into view and I recognized him as Bryce- friend, ally, and leader of the Filipino *Vipers*. He slapped me on the back in greeting. The side of his face was dried with crusty blood and the skin around his left eye was turning black.

"Man, what's goin' on?"

"Turf war with The Royals." He coughed into his hand and a tooth landed on his palm. "You'll come in nicely to beat 'em."

"Good thing we were close," I said.

Bryce chuckled. "Yeah. Speaking of," he pointed at the orange and red silhouette in the sky, "that you're doin'?" I smirked. "Nice," he appraised our work. "C'mon. I'll direct you to-"

Suddenly shots rang out and bullets rained down around us. I dropped to the ground, as did the others, and crawled to the Vipers' defensive line. Ryker, Ace, and I were stationed behind rows of coverage, and I peered through the space that enabled us vision to the enemy, targeting a perfect hit.

I pressed down, not risking being fired at to see if I had hit or not. By the angry cry of outburst, I did. Sweat beaded down my forehead and the back of my neck. Bryce literally slid beside me, dodging a bullet, and Ryker cursed when one grazed his arm. Ace had hid himself in between two large orders of wood and was firing every few seconds, taking no time to reload.

"We're outnumbered!" Bryce spat. We were sitting

with our backs against the tightly bound stacks of boards. "You got any ideas?" he directed towards me.

"One," I breathed out. "It's risky though."

He grinned and wiped away blood from his mouth as he traded in a new magazine. "What's not in our world?"

I inclined my head. Taking in a deep breath, I stood from protection and raised my gun, aiming mindlessly at our enemy's line. I ran hunched over with Bryce following, my barrel never tearing from its line of fire. Cries of agony and loud groans traveled through the air from both sides. I never took my finger off the trigger and never faltered except from crashing to the ground to avoid getting hit.

In the distance, I heard the wails of familiar sirens, and it didn't take a long complicated math equation to know they had responded to the arson and shooting.

Bryce and I shared identical looks.

We needed to abort.

"U20! Let's go!" I shouted, informing my guys to pack up and leave before we're arrested for both charges: arson and involvement in violent activity.

Bryce thanked me for our participation, and I scrammed when the police showed up, not wanting to be spending the night in a jail cell.

What I wasn't expecting was being ambushed by The Royals.

Something slammed into me, forcing me into the brick building on my left and a fist connected to my right eye. The sting of a sharp blade penetrated my shoulder, and I grabbed the assaulter by the waist, and ignoring any pain, flipped him over my body.

I couldn't check to see if he was dead or unconscious because another person wrapped their arm around my neck, pulling me into a tight headlock. I reacted violently; bringing an elbow to their stomach repeatedly and twisting his wrist to break it.

Instead of letting go and surrounding, he brought me down in an attempt to struggle.

I surprised him though by putting the barrel of my gun to the spot under his lungs, knowing I had no other choice. The body went limp underneath me. I stood up, breathing heavily and holding a palm to the wound on my shoulder. I nudged him, making sure he wasn't dead.

I didn't have enough time to check his pulse before I was shoved into the ground, gravel digging into my side. I grunted loudly, not expecting that. I twisted, striking the person in the face, and I rammed them in the stomach with my knee, gritting my teeth in anger when they didn't budge. I finally reached my gun where it had landed a few feet away and smashed the hilt against their head, knocking them unconscious.

I crawled out from under the dead weight and staggered off, running towards my parked truck. I heard the police shouting in the distance, apparently they've caught sight of me, but I kept on, ignoring the sharp bursts of pain in my shoulder. I made it to my truck and didn't even bother putting on my seatbelt; I just pressed down on the gas and sped out of there.

After ditching the police and reaching the highway, a realization hit me and it throbbed worse than my injury.

How am I going to explain this to my mother?

~~~

When I stepped into the apartment, the kitchen overhead light was still on. My mom was either finishing some bills or waiting for me to return, which is highly unlikely due to the fact she's used to me coming home late in the night or not at all. I walked over to where the kitchen was, wincing loudly. My mother looked up from the electrical bills and gasped when she saw the position I was in. Busted lip, a black eye, a cut across my cheek and holding my side. Nothing compared to a gunshot wound, but she didn't know about that- and she was never going to know.

She gestured for me to sit down. I did exactly that with no argument. She always kept a first-aid kit in the kitchen and bathroom. Mom slammed the kit on the dining table, turning around with a hand to her forehead. I knew she hated seeing me like this. I glanced at her, groaning as I pushed myself out of the seat. I put a hand on her shoulder and she slapped it off, almost as it stung her.

"This is too far, Samuel." I winced again. The full

name. "You promised you wouldn't involve yourself in drug trafficking."

"It wasn't a drug deal," I assured her.

She shot me a look. "How am I supposed to believe that when they're always on the news? I'm always left wondering if that's you!" She yelled.

I grabbed both of her hands. "Mom, I'm tellin' the truth."

"You've told me plenty of lies before. Why should I believe this?"

"Do you *honestly* think I would lie about this?" I shouted curtly. She gripped the handle to the freezer, opening it to get some ice. "I've told you we don't participate in those things." I slumped back in the chair. "There was an issue downtown with The Royals and we helped. We just… got into some trouble," I explained.

Mom didn't look at me as she cleaned the cut on my cheek, making me squirm under her touch. She lacked any gentleness. I carefully slipped off my shirt to give her more access to the stab wound on my right shoulder. She dabbed the peroxide onto a rag, gently applying it. I hissed and put my fist to my mouth in case I tried to yell at her or do something I'd regret. The peroxide stung at first then slowly went away. Her eyes flickered over the soft bruises spreading across my ribcage, but I informed her that they were nothing to worry about.

After everything was cleaned and patched up, she set the icepack on the table and retreated to her bedroom without a good-night or anything. I grabbed my shirt off the table and made my way towards my bedroom. It was small, the walls painted dark grey and navy blue, and clothes were scattered everywhere; abandoned homework strewn across my desk. I collapsed on my bed after rechecking that my gun was safely in its drawer and stared at the blank ceiling. The ceiling started getting boring so I turned my head into the mattress and drifted to dreamless sleep.

~~~

"What did your mom do when you came home Saturday night?" Ryker asked dropping next to me on the floor.

"She was ecstatic," I answered dryly. I chewed on a piece of gum, ripping apart a piece of scrap paper in boredom. I threw it on the floor, ignoring the flier tapped on the locker that said *no hall littering*. "She thought I was into drug trafficking with all these stories on the news. She thought I was lying to her. What about you?"

Ryker shrugged, only to grasp his side.

He told me he'd also got attacked and was slammed into the wall pretty roughly. "Elaine didn't seem to notice." Elaine was his foster mom and barely acknowledges him.

Ace sat down in the empty spot next to me. "Hey man." We bumped fists. "Guys, I found a new set of wheels for us." I beckoned for him to continue when he paused. "Uncle Hector got a really good deal on them and he's givin' them to us for no cost."

"What are they?"

He grinned. "Motorcycles. They should be in the garage. I told him just to drop them off. Hopefully he remembers to shut the garage door behind him this time."

"If he's anythin' like you," I put my arm around his shoulders and poked him in the side, "he'll forget."

Ace glared at me. "Hey, he's your uncle too!"

"Yeah, but I'm not uncoordinated or forgetful," I grinned.

Miss Kay noticed us sitting on the floor in the hallway and pointed at us with a wrinkly index finger. "Get off your lazy bums, you little hooligans!" She yelled across the hall. We quickly pushed ourselves up without trying to worsen our injuries. I slid my backpack onto my good shoulder.

"I'm about sick of your games, Samuel Wayne."

I raised an eyebrow. "What'd you call me?"

"Don't use that attitude with me! I've had enough of it!" Miss Kay stomped off. Normally, my reaction to people who use my full name, unless it was my mom who had every right to- I mean, she carried me for nine months and has been a great mother for eighteen years, but anyways, I would punch them in the face or threaten to hurt them. I hated my full name. As much as I dislike Miss Kay, I wouldn't because one, she was a woman and two, I'd be killed by my mother. And besides, I would get expelled for punching a teacher no doubt.

"Enlighten me: what did I do?" I asked to no one in particular.

Ryker shrugged one shoulder. "Who knows? She might be blaming everything that goes wrong in her life on you."

I snorted. "Probably."

I trailed towards first period which I had with two of my enemies. Could this year get any worse? When I entered the classroom, Olivia was already perched in her seat, her math textbook and notebook laid out. Why did she have to be such a suck-up?

Rolling my eyes, I walked to the desk, inwardly guarding my injured shoulder. Images of Saturday night flickered through my head. I didn't mind helping Bryce, but I wasn't expecting to get into fights. It comes with the territory I guess.

Olivia watched me as I lowered myself down into my seat. "All right, I know I'm attractive, but all this staring is ridiculous." Maybe my comment would hint that she could stop gawking at me. "What?" I asked sharply when it didn't. She fiddled with the pencil in her hand, turning it clockwise.

"You look…" she began.

I looked at her, interested in what she had to say. "Like what?"

Olivia shook her head, deciding not to voice it.

"Never mind."

"What?" I grabbed her wrist.

"Don't touch me," she hissed.

I chuckled darkly. "What is the pet gonna do?"

She jerked her wrist out of my grip and of course, that had to be the abused shoulder. My face scrunched up as I used all my strength to not allow the painful moan escape my lips.

I bit down on my tongue and the familiar sour taste of blood filled my mouth. Olivia scoffed like I was being overdramatic until... yep, there's the pity.

Her eyes widened. "Sam, are you okay? I'll go get-"

I stopped her. "Don't. It's nothing."

Olivia sighed, debating on whether or not to get Miss Kay. "Are you sure? I'm really sorry. I didn't-"

"Know. Yeah, yeah, I hear it all the time."

She looked like I had stolen her favorite book. "At least I mean it."

"I don't need your pity," I spat viciously, glaring at the board with the horrific math equation written on it. "Get to the lesson, nerd."

Olivia picked up her mechanical pencil. "I rather be a nerd than a selfish jerk."

Selfish... That word made my skin boil yet made me want to curl up in shame. Forgetting my previous thought, I grabbed her wrist again. "What'd you say?"

Olivia leaned in closer, her breath on my face. "I

said I rather be a nerd than a selfish jerk."

I was about to give a rude comeback, but unfortunately, Miss Kay saw the way we were acting and not paying attention to the lesson.

I could hear the nervousness in the entire classroom as she walked over to our desk. Olivia looked up at our teacher with a fake smile, and I muttered a few nasty words.

"May I ask what is going on back here? You two have been at it all morning long," she announced. Way to state the obvious.

I leaned back into my chair, adapting my cocky persona. "Do you honestly think you'll get it out of me?"

Olivia frowned. "Sorry about interrupting, Miss Kay."

"If I have to come over again, both of you will get detention." Miss Kay returned to the front of the classroom, reciting an equation.

After she was out of ear-shot, Olivia smacked me on the arm and I gave her a look like *was that supposed to hurt?* "I swear if you get me in trouble-"

I laughed. "Do you think I care?"

"You may not, but I do," she corrected herself. "Some of us actually have plans for the future," she remarked.

"Talk about being selfish." Olivia took a deep breath, but didn't reply. I leaned in real close and she froze at the distance between us.

"I know you act like you care, but deep down, I think you want to disobey the rules for once in your life. Let me know whenever you want to," I nuzzled her cheek. "I'm dangerous. I don't mind being the good girl's dirty little secret."

Olivia scrambled out of her seat and to act like she meant to do it, she went to the front and asked if she could go to the restroom. On her way out, she sent me a harsh look and I smirked suggestively, winking at her.

~~~

"Sam! Go. Now!" my father's firm voice ordered before the leftover door collapsed and he disappeared under the rumble.

I was clutching onto my mom's hand as she held Tyler in her arms. He was squalling loud, but the screams of people and the roar of the fire drowned him out. My mother tried to pull me away from the raging fire; I struggled against her. I wanted my dad.

"Samuel!" she screeched, getting my attention. Tears streamed down my face as well as hers. "Honey, we need to get to safety."

"But Dad-"

She tightened her grip on my hand. "Baby, he's gone."

My bottom lip quivered. I glanced back at the orange flames, my entire body shaking. I dropped to the ground, releasing the grip from my mother. I heard her crying my name, but her voice was drowned out by the screams of trapped citizens and the growing flames.

I didn't realize until an older fireman grabbed me and hoisted me up that I was racking with heart-wrenching sobs that no six-year old should be experiencing.

My father had just died saving my life.

There was a knock on my bedroom door, waking me from the nightmarish memory. I let a small groan escape my lips, dragging my head off the pillow and emerged from underneath the warm covers. I strolled to the door in my blue basketball shorts, cracking the door to see who it was. Light flooded into my room from the living room, blinding me for a mere ten seconds. My mother stood there in her light pink nightgown and hair curled up in those cheap rollers from the convenience store. I leaned against the doorframe, waiting for a conversation to start.

"I just wanted to make sure you were here," she said. "Safe and sound."

I nodded, knowing there was another reason for her visit. "No parties tonight."

Awkwardness took advantage of the silence. "I'm sorry," she whispered after a minute. "I shouldn't have thought you were lying to me. That was wrong of me."

"I have lied to you before about the stuff I do, but I wouldn't lie to you about this," I said honestly. "Drug deals aren't something we do," I informed her.

My mom ran her fingers through my dark hair. "I know. Fear and worry just got a hold of me. I am a mother after all." She looked at me with sad eyes. "I have an incredible and handsome son who is lost in a world he doesn't understand."

I sighed, looking down at the ground. "Mom."

"I'm not." She raised her hands and smiled. "Goodnight, sweetie. I love you."

"I love you too," I replied shutting the door after she retreated to her bedroom.

Chapter 5: Sam

I relaxed on the seat of my new motorcycle, courtesy of me and Ace's uncle. It was black with blue flames across the cushion with *Under-Twenty* engraved in the fire. It was an awesome gift and I liked it even more because it was free.

Anya purposely passed by me in a pair of tight jeans and her cheerleading crop-top as they marched to the school. I averted my eyes from areas her jeans seemed to snug. I held back a grin when Olivia and her friends walked past us, laughing about something random. *Oh, what the heck?* I whistled loudly, getting their attention. Olivia's caramel-brown hair was pulled into a braid over her shoulder. Her brown eyes scanned over the bike. I held my arms out, introducing my new baby.

"What do you think of my new ride, ladies?"

Olivia frowned. "I've seen better."

I slid off the bike and walking over to Olivia, who had her arms crossed stubbornly. I stopped when I was a mere few inches in front of her. "Better?" I scoffed. "Heck, I doubt you've even rode a motorcycle."

"And who says I haven't?"

I noticed we started gathering a crowd. I knew Olivia didn't want or like people seeing her vulnerable and I could work with that. I chuckled, glancing over at Ryker and Ace. My cousin cocked his head toward the motorcycle. I grabbed the extra helmet out from under the seat and handed it to her.

"Why don't we go and find out?" I asked, tossing one leg over each side as I mounted the bike. A grin was on my face when I watched her reaction. "Unless you're too scared, Jenkins." I slid my helmet over my face.

Olivia looked at her friends, and both of them shook their heads. For a minute there, I thought she was going to walk off in the opposite direction and leave me alone for the rest of senior year. My luck wasn't that great. Olivia slung her backpack off her shoulders and put the extra helmet on. I grinned in victory. I knew she wasn't going to seem weak in front of a crowd. She wrapped her arms loosely around my waist as the engine sputtered on.

"You might want to hang on tighter," I suggested.

She scoffed. "Like I'm gonna do that."

I bit my tongue. Tried to tell her.

I pushed my foot off the ground; her hands clutched my shirt as the engine roared and I drove off. The crowd watched with wide eyes. I stopped at the STOP sign at the end of the road, checking the traffic before turning to the right, purposely revving the engine and going a bit over the speed limit. The high school began to drift in the background as I took a sharp left, earning a yelp from Olivia and I chuckled to myself, laughing for real when her fist connected to my right shoulder. Pausing for a second, I remembered a shortcut that has a quicker route to our destination for the day.

Her head was buried in my back when I stopped

the engine in the parking space. We were back at the high school again, the small crowd we aroused already in classes. The other motorcycles surrounded us. I turned the machine off, waiting impatiently for her to get off.

"A word of advice: it'll be much easier to get off if your arms weren't wrapped around me," I said sarcastically.

Olivia then jumped off the back, standing a few feet away from the vehicle. She zipped up her jacket and crossed her arms, watching me. I took my helmet off, resting it on the seat. I didn't need to worry about stealing.

"I knew you wouldn't let people see you weak," I broke the silence, "but I honestly believed you wanted to take a ride with me."

She rolled her eyes. "In your dreams, Wayne."

"Definitely in my dreams," I retorted.

Olivia turned to walk away, but I latched onto her wrist. She spun with an irritated huff. "Why can't you just leave me alone?"

"Now I can't do that," I answered.

"And why not?"

I stepped towards her, leaning close enough to let my lips touch her ear. "Because you're way too easy to tease." And with a cocky wink, I grabbed the strap of my backpack and walked off, leaving Olivia standing in the parking lot alone.

OLIVIA

I'm *easy* for him to tease? It took a large amount of restraint to not let my palm smack his face. What an arrogant piece of work.

I walked through the halls in free period, waiting for my older brother, Max, to respond to my text. He was attending MIT for computer science.

He was at the top of his class, one of the brightest students they've had in a while. My parents were extremely proud of him and reminded me and my younger brother, Parker, every day about our intelligent sibling. It was hard being compared to him. He was perfect in their eyes. He never made mistakes; he never had a hard time getting something done.

I, on the other hand, am a different story. Parker was young so my parents never really got onto him. Me, being the only girl and having a brilliant older sibling… it's hard. They always expect me to have everything together, a hundred-and-ten percent. It was exhausting trying to impress them all the time. And when I got in trouble (which is mostly because of Sam Wayne), the world was thrown off its axis in my parent's eyes. They would yell or simplify my work to Max's. I loved Max, but he doesn't know how hard it is being compared to him.

My parents want and expect me to be just like him. Computer science was an intellectual talent, but I enjoyed drawing landscapes and capturing emotion of people's faces. I'm an artist. They don't accept my dream. They're the ones who bought the tickets to Washington D.C. I fibbed when I told Maya about looking forward to it.

Tom and Melanie Jenkins were incredibly hard to impress.

My phone vibrated and I didn't waste a second to reply. Max had left for school early this summer due to a job he found that had great paid and was close to the campus. I've missed him so much. He's supposed to come home next week for a short visit and I honestly couldn't wait.

I was so engaged in our conversation that I wasn't paying attention to where I was heading, and before I knew it, I smacked into somebody. I was shocked that someone else was roaming the halls at this time. Normally during free period, students would either be out on the courtyard or playing basketball. I crumbled to the floor, landing hard on my right wrist. I winced and clutched it to my chest, looking up to see who I ran into.

Oh, you've got to be kidding me.

"What are you doing out here?" Sam asked, raising a dark eyebrow. "I thought you'd be in the library or somethin'."

I waited for him to hold out his hand to help me up, but then the logical part of me reminded myself that this wasn't the Sam I knew years ago. I pushed myself on my good arm, holding the other close to my chest.

"You're gonna need to have that checked," he said.

I gave him an amused look. "No kidding."

"Come here."

I stayed put, not knowing why he was being nice.

"Just come here, Jenkins. Stop over-analyzing."

I decided to take this soft side for advantage. I stepped forward and rested my arm in his open palm. Sam grabbed my forearm and ran his fingers over the sensitive area. He moved his fingers so gently that I barely felt them touching my skin. He let go of my wrist and I returned to its place, propped against my chest. I was having trouble wrapping my mind around his act of kindness.

"Nothing horrible. A bruise most likely, but I would still get it wrapped," Sam pointed in the direction behind us. "Nurse's office is down the hall and to the-"

"I know where it is," I interrupted him.

He hummed, crossing his arms. "What're you doing out here anyways?"

"I have free period-"

"I meant in the halls, genius."

I gave him a weird look. "You don't need to know my business."

"Is it that secretive to keep from me?" Sam questioned, his beautiful yet mysterious eyes stared me down.

I sighed, rubbing my temple. "I was texting my brother and wasn't paying attention to where I was going."

"Do you need a ride?"

I took a step back, caught off guard by his sudden question. "What?"

"Do you need a ride?" Sam repeated. "To your house."

I held up my good hand. "Yeah, yeah, I got that. I just... what?" He rolled his eyes. "Why are you offering me help? We hate each other, remember? Or did you forget that?" I remarked, glancing at the fresh cut on the corner of his eyebrow.

"You know I'm not really doing it for your benefit. I'm doing it for mine," Sam answered smirking. "I get out of school if I take you home."

"How nice of you," I responded dryly. He grinned. "Besides, who says I'm going to take you up on it? My *friends* are always available."

"I offered."

"And? It's just so you can get out of school," I poked him in the chest. "And besides, aren't you a big, bad gang leader?

You can just waltz out of school without being caught."

"Your point being..." Sam gestured for me to carry on.

"I'm not accepting."

His eyes flickered to something behind me. "You

may want to get to that nurse's office. Teacher's coming our way. We're not supposed to be roaming the halls without a pass. Free period or not."

"Why do you care?"

He snorted. "I don't care if I get caught. It's for your perfect record." Sam winked then moved past me, his shoulder brushing mine.

I turned my head, contemplating on whether or not to grab his attention or to let him get into trouble. However, I didn't have a pass so technically speaking, I was also breaking the rules. I caught the familiar glimpse of a teacher and the words left my mouth before I could do anything to stop them.

I'm going to regret this.

"Sam!" I called.

He spun half-way around. "Hmm?"

I prayed that I was doing the right thing. "You gonna take me home or what?"

Sam's grin made my heart stop in its track before returning to its normal pace. I began to walk towards the nurse's office again with Sam at my heels. There was an awkward silence surrounding us. Suddenly the teacher caught sight of us.

"Excuse me! What are you two doing out here?" she asked, her pencil skirt swirling around her knees. She crossed her arms above her chest. It was Miss Rudy, the single woman who taught ninth grade Honors Science.

I could already hear the rumors spreading around. *Sam Wayne and Olivia Jenkins were caught in the halls. Hmm, what do you think? Rivals in love? Enemies for show- lovers for real?* "Uh-"

"Well, I just came back from the office and Olivia was exiting the bathroom when we bumped into each other. She fell, hurt her wrist." He lifted my wrist and added a slight pressure, making me flinch in discomfort. "She's going to the nurse's office and I'm going to take her home afterwards."

Miss Rudy nodded at the end of the explanation. "All right. I won't write you two up." She turned to me and patted me on the shoulder. "I hope you're okay."

"Thank you," I replied with a smile.

Sam grabbed me by the elbow and pulled me towards the direction of the nurse's office. After Miss Rudy was out of sight and out of earshot, I yanked my arm away and glared at him. "You're so sweet, you know that?"

"Oh, thank you, babe!" Sam exclaimed, wrapping an arm around my shoulders.

I shoved him with my good hand. "Stop being annoying."

"It's all part of my charm," he protested. I scowled at him again, quickening my pace, and he just chuckled. "You really don't like me, do you?"

"What on earth gave you that impression?" I snapped back sassily.

"Obviously your sparkling personality."

I let the nurse's door hit him on the way in.

~~~

"Down this road," I directed him, scratching the spot behind my ear nervously.

Being in Sam's truck instead of being on the back of his motorcycle was awkward. I mean, granted it was silent and I was comfortable being in my own seat and all, but it was downright awkward. I was stuck in a moving vehicle with no way out unless I wanted to seriously injure myself.

Since I wasn't in the mood to do that, I was stuck in a truck with a gang leader who happened to be my ex-best friend.

Sam, unfortunately, looked really good in his white V-neck. He clicked on the turning signal and turned. "I think I remember where you live." I was taken by surprise. He never brought up our past friendship. It was always me.

He continued to drive until we pulled into the driveway of my two-story house. It was light grey with navy blue shutters. The wrap-around porch had all its furniture; my favorite being the swing, and white stairs led to the front door. The backyard had a trampoline and a large swimming pool. It had a two-car garage which we never use besides Dad's tools and my stepmother's workout machine.

Sam seemed out of place. I lived in a wealthy town with rich parents while he lived with his mother and brother in downtown. His worn-out jeans and rough leather jacket wouldn't fit in around here. You had to have the newest item in stores or the greatest of everything. I didn't fit in here. My parents had the money, not me.

Melanie's silver convertible and my dad's black Hummer were parked in the driveway, informing that they were indeed home, and I prayed that they wouldn't become interested to see who was pulling in. Sam had enough room to park his black truck, which also stood out in the wealthy neighborhood. I glanced out the windshield, checking to make sure that my parents weren't looking through the window or were anywhere nearby. Sam shifted in his seat, gripping the steering wheel.

"Thanks," I said grabbing my backpack off his floorboard.

He patted the steering wheel. "You don't need me to walk you to your door, right? Because I'm not."

I gave a small laugh and shook my head. If my father saw him, it would make things even more complicated. I got out of the truck, shutting the door behind me. I looped around the front of his truck and walked up the steps to reach the porch.

When I glanced back at him, Sam was already busy pulling out of the driveway. I watched for a minimal of five seconds before walking inside silently, and with a frown, went to my bedroom, ready to be neglected by my parents.

Chapter 6: Sam

I smashed the gun against the officer's face, making blood spurt out onto the ground. He fell on his back with his hands tied. I checked the magazine to see if there were any bullets inside. There were none. The officer struggled against the ropes but I walked over and pressed the barrel against his temple, a taunting expression on my face. Sweat drenched his forehead as his terrified eyes flicked about.

"You kids aren't ashamed of your actions?" the officer asked.

I looked to my left and Santiago chuckled. "Well, if I'm being honest, not really. We don't harm the innocent. But hurting you, on the other hand," I shook my head, the action finishing my sentence. "Think we wouldn't recognize you, Brad?" His eyes widened. "Boss knows who you are. You're the undercover cop sending in excruciating amounts of goods. Not that I care much about that, but Boss doesn't like thieves- thieves who steal his source of power. So, you know who I am?" I asked rhetorically. "Your worst nightmare."

After knocking him out hard, I handed the empty gun to Santiago.

Entering the main compartment of the weapon stockroom, I watched as Ryker grabbed the guy he knocked unconscious by the collar, dragging him to the closet that stored the other security guards. The boss needed more supplies and it was our job to retrieve them.

We were assigned to getting guns and ammo for the boss and exchanging them to other crews. Sometimes we'd gambled to get more earnings. The boss was in charge of downtown Manhattan, and we were the youngest group. People underestimated us until they saw us in action and how well we were trained.

"Yo, Sam!" Ryker called.

I walked over to where they stood and looked at the bags surrounding the circle we formed. There were three rules on our supply runs. One: no members under fourteen. Two: always have a getaway vehicle. And three: don't turn your back unless you've dealt with the situation already.

"Maybe we should leave before more security comes," Daniel offered. I glanced over at Ryker and he handed me a spray can and I shook it up.

"First, we'll have some fun."

We bent down at the walls, vandalizing them and adding our signature touch to the graffiti.

Diego was the artist in our circle, always making our so-called *vandalism* better than others. Not even five minutes later, I heard the shouting of the extra guards and policemen outside the warehouse. I stood from my crouch and grabbed one of the heavy duffle bags, heaving it over my good shoulder. I slammed myself against the door and tumbled out of the area, gritting my teeth at the pain shooting in my previously injured shoulder.

Flashlights blinded me before my fist connected to one of the officer's face, hearing his nose break under my knuckles. Santiago, Daniel, and Diego ran out of the building, heading to where the motorcycles were being watched. Ryker and Ace appeared by my sides, my two right-hand men, and together, we tried to take down as many police officers and security guards we could. The less we had, the better chance of getting out of here.

Santiago whistled sharply from across the lot. He and the others were about to ride off and I gestured for him to go ahead.

"Go!" I yelled.

One of the officers reached for the gun in his holster, but I tackled him, stopping him instantly. Ace was struggling with one of the guards, but with an elbow to the nose, the guard fell to the ground in a heap.

Ryker and I ambushed two other ones before running towards the bikes. "Let's get out of here!" I ordered. "NOW!" I barked when I saw one of the newest members stiffen and stare in wonderment.

Santiago mounted his bike and drove off in the opposite direction of where a few guys went. We tried to separate during runs to make it harder for police to catch us. I revved the engine, strapping the pack around my waist and hurriedly pulled out of the parking lot.

I drove out onto the main street without paying attention to other vehicles or stoplights. A few drivers honked at me, others cursed and flipped obscene gestures. The guys emerged from other roads, slipping by fast and slow cars. Ryker appeared on my left and nodded, confirming my thoughts.

We'd lost them.

~~~

When I entered Geometry right before the tardy bell rang, my breath left me. I stared at the lesson in horror. I glanced towards the back of the room, noticing that Olivia was already in her seat, flipping through a notebook. I ignored the side views from chicks and sneers from dudes as I sat down. I looked at the board, trying to figure out what the first equation said with no luck.

None of them stayed in their correct positions, and if they did, I couldn't tell. I was pretty good at controlling my dyslexia; however, there were lessons that reminded me of my problem with numbers.

I hated asking for people's help, but I needed it in this situation. I tapped Olivia's shoulder. She didn't react. I sighed and did it again. She turned her in my direction with the pencil in her hand in the same stance as earlier.

"Yes, Wayne?"

"What-" I paused. Olivia raised an eyebrow, waiting for me to continue. "What does the problem say?"

She pointed at the whiteboard with her eraser. "If you can't see, go up and-"

"No, I mean, what order are the numbers in?"

Olivia looked like she was about to respond, but her expression changed. "Oh, that's right. You're dyslexic."

"Wait, you remember?" I asked in shock. There were only a handful of people who knew, not because I was embarrassed, but because it wasn't somethin' to make a big deal about. Therefore I only tell people that need to know.

Golden swirls blazed in her eyes before returning to her unfinished problem. "I remember everything about you." She didn't look back at me.

My eyes scanned over her. Her caramel-brown hair was pulled halfway up with the rest cascading down her back as she focused intently on her work. Olivia turned to hand me a piece of paper but stopped. Her brown eyes locked with mine. In her irises, I could see the little girl I hung out with when I was younger.

The girl who used to be my best friend.

A memory, things that I tried desperately to hide away, appeared in my mind. We were eight years old, running through the crowded park. She wore a purple and white dress with a white hair band in her hair. She was hiding behind a tree, smiling at me as I ran towards her with icing on my cheek. It was on Easter and our families would spend it together each year. It was tradition.

WHACK!

Miss Kay slammed her attendance folder on our

table. I jumped out of the memory and pulled away from the stare, acting nonchalant. I leaned back into my chair, looking at our teacher who I severely disliked.

"If you two are done, we can continue the lesson," she said with a sneer.

I smirked. "Well, we're done now. Thank you for holding up for us. You may continue." Olivia stared at me with wide eyes and jaw dropped. I mouthed, "*Hot.*"

She quickly closed her mouth and glared at me. "We're sorry, Miss Kay."

"Mm-hmm," she muttered then returned to her desk.

Olivia huffed. "What was that?" she hissed, venom in her words. "You're such an idiot!"

"Thank you for the kind words, sweetheart," I remarked sarcastically. "It's not the end of the freaking world. My sarcasm's not going to harm your perfect record. I'll even take the blame for you 'cause I'm so nice."

It seemed like she wanted to punch me- plenty of people have gave me that look, my mother included, but she bit her lip and stayed quiet. She handed me the piece of paper. I checked it out and it had all the problems on it.

I muttered thanks and began working, knowing it would be a while.

Ah crap.

Word problems. Yay.

~~~

I walked into my apartment building, balancing the large pizza box in my hands. My mother and I hardly ever got this, and this was one of the days where I got extra money. I opened the door to our apartment, kicking the door closed and announcing that I was home. I trailed into the kitchen, putting the pizza over my mother's head and setting it on the bill-covered dining table. She jumped when the pizza appeared and I wrapped my arms around her torso, kissing her on the head.

"What is this?" she asked, smiling at me with joy.

I grinned, shedding my jacket. "A pizza. Extra cheesy for my mother who I adore so much."

"What'd you do?" she eyed me.

"You have so much faith in me." I stuck my tongue at her.

She smiled warmly. "I do, but every time you bring home something sweet or special, such as this, you normally have failed a test or got arrested."

I grumbled an agreement. "I swear this is not like that. I just wanted to do it," I answered honestly.

Mom opened the box and the smell of pepperoni, mushrooms, and cheese filled my nostrils. I grabbed two plates and got me three slices. She took a bite out of her slice and sighed happily. "This is wonderful, Sam."

"You're welcome." I grabbed her free hand and smiled genuinely. "Watch this." I took a mushroom off a slice and threw it in the air, leaning back and catching it in my mouth. I fist-bumped the air. "Yes!"

She laughed, taking another piece. "Do we have any coke left?"

"Uh, think it's flat." I opened the refrigerator and tasted it. "Mm, yeah, it's flat."

"Shoot. Well, I guess that all that matters is we have something to eat. I've just been so busy with work and taking care of the bills and-"

I shushed her. "No need to explain it to me, Mom."

After a minute of two, I stood up from the chair and wiped my hands on my jeans, ignoring my mother's glare. "I'm going to bed."

"It's only seven-thirty."

"I'm a teenage boy. We all need our beauty sleep, especially me," I teased winking at her. I leaned down to kiss her cheek, and afterwards, took all the bills and threw them in the coffee table's drawer.

"Honey, I need to finish those."

"No. You're gonna finish your pizza and then go to bed. You're stressed, Mom. You need sleep," I ordered.

She frowned. "Samuel, you don't need to worry about me. I'll be fine."

I grimaced at the sound of my full name. "I hate that name," I muttered leaving the subject alone. I bid her goodnight and headed to my small bedroom. *Samuel.* That was the name my father picked. Now I can barely stand to hear it.

It reminds me of the fire. It reminds me that I couldn't stop it or save him.

It reminded me of the good days.

Chapter 7: Olivia

I stared at the stars, watching them light over the entire city. I lay on my back, my thumbs fiddling with one another. Sam, my best friend since kindergarten, lay beside me. We were ten years old, lying on his rooftop, gazing at the stars. He was entranced by the stars' glittering lights and I didn't want to ruin the night with the agonizing thoughts in my head.

"Stop thinking so loud," Sam nudged me in the shoulder, a grin on his face.

I gazed into his emerald eyes, tears forming in mine as my lips trembled. I couldn't say it. Sam sent me a small smile as I felt his fingers intertwine with mine.

Tears streaked down my cheeks as I whispered, "My parents are getting a divorce."

Sam's expression went from shocked to disbelief. He must have known I couldn't say anything more. I started to feel my stomach give in and I sat up, holding a hand to my mouth. I never cried. And he knew that. I felt his arm wrap around my shoulders, pulling me into his side. I dug my head into the crook of his neck; the salty tears escaping. He rubbed my back, whispering soothing words into my hair. I clutched his T-shirt, not wanting to let go. It didn't seem real. It couldn't be real. My stomach churned in knots and I wept pathetically, but it seemed to be the only option for it to become less painful.

"I'm sorry," I muttered wiping at my cheeks.

He laughed, pulling my head from his neck. "Why are you apologizing? You needed to get it out. Divorce is a really hard thing to go through."

"At least it was in front of you and no one else," I said pressing my nose against his neck.

"Everyone has their moments, Olivia. I think people would understand why you were crying," he told me, rubbing my back some more.

I swallowed the lump in my throat. My chest ached. My entire body ached. Sam rested his head on mine. Our hands stayed intertwined. I wiped my nose with my sleeve, leaning against his shoulder. He poked me in the ribs to get my attention. It did.

"You know I hate that," I grumbled.

He shrugged. "You know I'll always be here for you, Liv. Don't ever forget that."

"What if we drift away from each other?" I asked not wanting to ever lose him.

"You sound like we're dating," Sam laughed.

I punched him in the gut. "You know what I mean."

He grinned. "I do. And I do mean what I say. Nothing will ever separate us."

"Now you're sounding like we're getting married," I joked.

He shoved me and I did a victory cheer mentally when a blush edged onto his cheeks. "Just always know you can come to me with anything. I'll always be here for you. No matter what happens."

My brother pounded against the door, waking me from the sweet memory of the Sam I used to know. That was the Sam I wanted more than anything.

held me when I was down. The one who agg

poking me in the ribs. The one who would c

keep me safe and unharmed. The one who

that he would always be there no matter whaι.

gotten of ʲ

I peeled away the blankets as I trampled over some leftover pencils and avoided sketches lying lackadaisically on the floor. When I opened the door, my brother stood in the doorway, all dressed for school. He had straggly brown hair and brown eyes, which we inherited from our father. I was the only girl amongst two boys. There were some moments when I wished there was at least one more girl, but I enjoyed having an older brother to protect me.

"Mom said to come get you. She doesn't look too happy," Parker said.

"She never is," I muttered under my breath.

I trailed down the stairs with Parker behind me. I entered the kitchen, knowing that my parents would be in here. My real-estate father, Tom Jenkins, typed away on his computer, probably emailing a client while my step-mother worked her magic cooking. I didn't really like my step-mom. I can't come and talk to her about anything or she'll think I'm up to no good or make it into a bigger deal.

Melanie stood at the stove, sliding the greasy bacon off the skillet and onto a plate. She wore a knee-length, black pencil skirt with a burgundy blouse and black high heels. She works at a law firm and was named one of New York's finest lawyers. She was also a cook, but she hasn't paid to do it yet. Melanie flipped the pancakes out the pan and placed them on a large platter, putting them on the counter. I leaned forward, resting my arms on the island, waiting for her to start the conversation.

"Olivia, I have a question for you."

"What is it?"

Melanie finished the pancakes and wiped her hands on the apron. She looked at me with her soft blue eyes. "I saw a boy dropping you off two days ago. I've never seen him before."

"Oh, it was no one. He offered to drop me home after I hurt my wrist." I held up my wrist in an ace bandage. "No big deal."

She took a drink of her water. "What's this boy's name?"

"I think I heard the door," I made up quickly, wanting to get out of this situation. I started to turn around until my father's stern voice stopped me.

"Answer your mother," he said strictly.

I shrugged, trying to act nonchalant. "Sam."

They both paused and looked at me with wide eyes. I clenched my teeth, preparing myself for the yelling.

"Sam? As in Sam *Wayne*?" he shouted, standing up from the laptop and running his fingers through his hair. He looked at me like I was stupid and it burned a hole in my chest. "Do you know how dangerous that boy is? He could have easily taken you somewhere-"

"He's not like that-"

"He's a criminal!" Melanie interrupted. "I should know. I've looked over his folder plenty of times knowing you're going to school with him."

"He's treacherous, unthankful, a bully. I don't want you nowhere near him," my father ordered.

I sighed, becoming aggravated. "That's going to be kind of hard considering we're partners for the year!" I snapped.

Oh crap, I shouldn't have said that.

"*What*?" they shouted simultaneously.

My dad picked up the house phone and started slamming down buttons. I was afraid he'd break it. "I'm going to call that school and-"

"You're overreacting-"

"Overreacting?" Melanie scoffed. "Olivia, Sam is the *leader* of a *gang* and you put yourself in a car with him!"

"He's not going to hurt me," I assured her, then grimaced at my choice of words. At least he wouldn't physically.

"Olivia-"

I slammed my palms on the counter despite my small bruise. "He offered to take me home," I said through gritted teeth. "I agreed because of my wrist. I couldn't drive home." The nurse had said I needed it to rest for a day or two then it'll be good.

"You could have asked Maya or Tammy. Anyone but him," my father argued.

I crossed my arms and glared at the granite countertop. "Like I said, he offered. Trust me, he's not gonna offer his help again. He just happened to be there."

Melanie stabbed a bite of her pancake. "Okay, I'm done with this conversation. I don't want to hear his name mentioned again in my house." Sure. Like that's going to happen. "I don't want him bringing you home. I don't want him near my house."

"It's not just your house," I corrected her.

"Watch your tone, young lady."

I fought the urge to salute them.

"You're not hanging out with him beyond school walls. I don't want you involved with this boy," he said.

"I'm not going to get involved."

"Don't argue with your father," Melanie retorted, brushing her bangs behind her ear. "Listen to what he says and do it."

I walked towards the exit of the kitchen but before doing so, I said, "Don't judge him. I did that once and I was wrong."

And with that, I left.

~~~

"I can't believe they overreacted like that," Maya commented taking her attention away from her English textbook.

I bit into my apple as Tammy said, "My parents would have told me not to hang around him or his friends, but not yelling."

I sighed. "I know they don't like him, but they shouldn't judge him like that. I actually feel bad for accusing him of sleeping with girls. I mean, I know he's the leader of a gang, but there has to be a reason behind it," I said honestly. "I don't think a person could change that drastically without one. Sam wasn't the kind of guy who would hurt others on purpose."

Tammy hummed, gathering her honey blonde hair up into a ponytail. "You don't know though. Maybe he wanted to change."

"That's what I'm afraid of," I admitted, messing with the zipper on my jacket.

~~~

I was leaning against a tree in the yard of the school. We were allowed to eat lunch or hang out here during free period. I usually chose this place to relax and read in my free time. This was one of those moments. I wanted a break from everything that happened this morning.

My parents always overreacted when it came to Sam. Whenever I mentioned his name, they'd go bizarre. They didn't know about me being in love with him nor will they ever know. Who knows how they'll react?

I let out a deep breath, closing my eyes in the warmth. I blocked out all the thoughts of my parents and

Sam Wayne. This was the only place (minus my room when the door was closed and could shut out all the crap) that I could get away from the stress of prideful parents.

School was the one place where I could shine. The place I could be someone special. People see me for who I am and I'm not compared to anybody. It felt nice. The sun shined on my face, making me sigh in happiness.

Then, causing me to frown, it disappeared.

"Hey sweetheart."

My eyes snapped open at the familiar deep voice and before me stood the one and only, Sam Wayne.

"What do you want?" I asked crinkling my nose. "You're blocking my light."

"Most people would want the sun to be blocked."

I groaned, wanting to go back to my relaxation mode. "I'm not like most people."

"We finally agree on somethin'," he said taking a seat in the grass next to me.

I stared at him like he had two heads. "What are you doing?"

"Being a good sociable student." He cracked a sarcastic grin. "Why, what's the problem? Don't want any company?"

"Actually I don't," I retorted. "Especially from you, so why don't you go and annoy your girlfriend?"

Sam chuckled, resting an arm behind his head.

"What girlfriend?"

"Oh look!" I acted surprised and brought my hands to my cheeks. "Sam Wayne doesn't have a girlfriend. Who will be his next prize?"

"Well I've dated most of the girls in our year and the year below." He looked over at me. "None of them are right for me."

Did he really think I wanted to hear this? I turned away from his gaze. The sun was now blocked by a few clouds. I frowned miserably. I missed my chance of being absorbed in the wonderful heat.

"So... why are you out here all alone?" Sam inquired, interrupting yet again.

"Why does it matter you?" I sneered.

"Ouch," he hissed. "I was just wonderin'."

I glanced up at the sky, waiting for the sun to come out from behind the clouds. I wanted to have some sunshine before I go back inside. I let out a disappointed sigh. When I felt a hand on my arm, I jumped, remembering that I wasn't sitting alone. Sam stared at me with those beautiful and mysterious green eyes. They were the only physical reminder of our past friendship.

Although this may be true, those same captivating pair of eyes reminded me of the rumors, the teasing, the gang leader.

I don't know what was worse.

"What?" I snapped.

Sam raised an eyebrow. "Are you okay?"

"I'm fine," I lied straight through my teeth.

He pursed his lips. "No, you're not." Fabulous. He chooses now to act all concerned and whatever.

"Why do you care if I'm fine or not?"

He shrugged, his eyes scattering across my face, avoiding eye-contact. "It's nice to ask people if they're okay."

I laughed without an inch of humor. "Who thought you were actually nice?" I retorted, pulling my arm away from his touch. Pathetically, I missed the warmth coming from his hand. Sam looked at the ground, his jaw set. I scoffed, packing all my things and grabbing my backpack. "And why do you care anyways?" Venom drenched my words. His head tilted up, suddenly interested. "You stopped caring when you abandoned me after eighth grade!"

Wanting to leave the conversation, I stood up and walked away from the scene. I wanted him to leave me alone for the rest of my life, excluding math class.

I wasn't that lucky, I guess.

Sam grabbed my arm from behind, turning me around to face him. "What is your freakin' problem?"

"What is my- what is your problem?" I yelled acrimoniously in his face. I shoved him in the chest. "*You* were the one who turned your back on *me*!"

We stood there in the middle of the schoolyard, glaring at each other. His hand was still wrapped around my forearm; his touch spending sparks up my arm. I peeled my arm away from his grasp, not wanting him to ever touch me again. I may love him, but I've decided that doesn't change anything.

"You hurt me. You b-broke-" I stopped myself from saying anything else. "You lied to me. You said you would always be there... Now look at where we are."

Sam stood there, his arms by his sides, fists clenched.

"Where is my best friend?" I asked stepping closer to him. "What happened to you?" He didn't flinch. "I don't know this Sam Wayne. You're somebody else. You're a stranger." *No response.* "You promised that you weren't going to hurt me. Well, newsflash, you're hurting me more than anyone else."

Sam glanced at the ground then back at me, with an unknown emotion glittering in his eyes. "Olivia, you don't understand. You *wouldn't* understand why-" His voice cracked and he curled his lip in distaste. "Why I'm in the gang in the first place."

What *had* happened that made him turn out this way? Maybe it was finances. Maybe it was peer pressure. Maybe it was something much, much worse.

"Then tell me!" I whispered in a hoarse voice. I'm tired of all the fights and the lies and the pain.

He sucked in a harsh breath. "Forget it."

Sam moved past me, his shoulder bumping mine as he walked towards the school building. I stayed there, breathing heavily and tears emerging in my eyes. I've come up with another conclusion: he will never be the Sam I fell in love with.

Chapter 8: Sam

I sighed, drumming my fingers against the hard interrogation table. I leaned back into the chair, crossing my arms and balancing myself on the two back legs. As I examined the scar stretching across my knuckles, the door opened with a loud buzz, and a cream-colored file appeared in front of my face. I leaned forward, seeing the name on the side tablet. *Samuel Wayne.*

"Open it!" commanded the officer.

I scowled at the air before opening the file at my own pace. My picture was in there along with information such as my full name, DOB, age, parent's names, etc. I looked at my list of charges. There were only two. The first time I got arrested for involvement with crime behavior and the act of distribution. Ryker and I were tricked into a drug deal. We weren't booked considering Under-Twenty's former gang leader told the police we were innocent. The second time I had been caught trespassing onto private property, but luckily the owner didn't press any charges.

The officer sat himself in front of me, and I held his gaze easily, not shaking under his icy cold stare. He tapped his fingers against each other. "So Samuel-"

"Sam," I corrected.

He raised an eyebrow. Police officers hated to be interrupted. Yeah, well I hate having to be brought into the intimidation room for doing absolutely nothing. "Samuel, do you have any idea why you are here?"

"Not at all," I answered honestly. I was pulled over for my left taillight being out, then next thing I knew I was being put into the back seat of a police car.

"You had alcohol in your system while driving," he informed.

I shook my head incredulously. "You got to be kidding me!"

"Did you even think before you got behind the wheel? Or better yet, before drinking illegally?" He smacked the table. "You're putting innocent lives in danger!"

"I'm not heartless. I wouldn't drink and drive."

"You had alcohol-"

"I'll admit I had a drink with a friend. It was like an hour before I even went behind the wheel. I was coherent, I wasn't stumbling around. It was safe," I told him. I brushed invisible dust off my leather jacket's sleeve. "I have a question: why do cops act like they're better than

anyone, yet they're not? I bet you've screwed up multiple times in your life," I counteracted, resting my arms on the table.

He seemed surprised by my disrespect. He's not the first. "Mr. Wayne, my personal life is not open to the likes of you-"

"To the likes of you? Are we going old English here or somethin'?" I tried not to laugh. This was too easy.

"Mr. Wayne," I could tell he was trying to keep his cool, "you better learn how to keep your mouth shut or I'm gonna-"

If anyone knew me, I wasn't the one to keep my mouth shut. That is why Boss lets me handle the authorities. "You're gonna what?" I leaned back into the chair, a devilish smirk curled on my lips. "You can't charge me. I wasn't impaired, I was aware of what I was doing. I'm also definite my BAC will come back clean. You only arrested me 'cause you recognized my bandana."

The officer glared coldly at me.

"So what'd I do?" I asked. "Offend you somehow? Date and dump your daughter?" A muscle in his cheek twitched and I chuckled. "Ahh… that's it."

Right when it looked like he was about to bust my lip, the door buzzed and opened, bringing in the odd smell of a police station. I turned around as a female officer entered the room. "Leave him alone, Valt. He can have his one phone call now."

She gestured for me to stand up and I grinned at Officer Valt. She led me out of the room and to the phone, releasing the cuffs on my hands. Blowing out a breath, I dialed my mother's phone number and waited, wrapping my fingers around the cord and tapping a random beat on the wall.

"Hello?"

I closed my eyes. "Mom?"

"Sam? Oh, sorry, honey," she laughed. "I didn't recognize the number. Where are you calling from?"

I bit my bottom lip, wincing. "Don't freak out."

"*Sam.*"

"I'm at the police station."

The call ended.

The female cop directed me to a single holding cell and I flopped onto the steel seat, lying on my back and throwing an arm over my eyes.

About thirty minutes later, I heard my name being called out and I sat up, my mother coming into view. She was wearing her nicest dress and trench coat. It contrasted against the dark atmosphere.

"His BAC was clean so the charges are being dropped," the lady cop said.

Despite the good news, my mom looked at me with so much disappointment in her eyes that I had a sudden interest in the grey floor.

This was going to be a long night.

When we finally made it home after the silent car ride, Mom collapsed into a chair at the small dining table and dropped her face into her hands. This happened the last two times she's brought me home from the police station. I knew she was criticizing her parenting, blaming herself for my mistakes. She was thinking *why didn't I raise him better*? I didn't know what to say but apologize, which I had repeated on the ride home until she silenced me. I never said sorry to anyone but my mom.

She was the one who kept getting hurt. Not me.

"Mom-"

"Sam, as happy as I am to know you weren't drinking and driving, I still hate picking you up from that place," she told me.

"I know. It wasn't my fault though. He arrested me 'cause of my bandana-"

She stood up. "Exactly! All Under-Twenty has done is screw your life up. I'm tired of you coming home with bruises and cuts and blood on your knuckles. I'm tired of being judged by everyone in this building. I'm tired of this gang crap!"

"This *gang crap* is helping us live here!"

"You know what, just go to bed. I can't deal with this anymore," she said walking to her bedroom. I watched her take off the few pieces of jewelry she owned and set them on the coffee table next to her childhood Bible. She didn't meet my eyes. I kept watching her until she shut the door without a 'sweet dreams'.

I trailed to my room, closing the door behind me. I tugged off my combat boots as I stripped out of my shirt and fell on the bed. It creaked under my sudden weight, as usual. I pulled open the drawer of my nightstand, wanting to get my pack of hidden cigarettes. I halted to a stop. The corner of a picture caught my eye.

It was hiding underneath the pack of cigarettes, my gun and extra magazines, and a few sheets of abandoned homework from junior high. An eyebrow raised, I took out the pictures out of the drawer, and immediately wished I hadn't.

The first was a photo of Olivia and me at the beach. My arm was wrapped around her waist as was hers. We were caught right in the middle of a laugh. Waves were crashing in the background. I remembered the day like it was yesterday. We were celebrating graduating elementary school. Well, actually, my family took a vacation and it just so happened to be after we finished fifth grade.

The second photo was another one of me and Olivia; a close-up this time. We were sitting on the couch in my apartment; my arm around her shoulders, Olivia pressing a playful kiss on my cheek and my tongue was sticking out. We were thirteen years old, the summer after seventh grade.

The last photo made my stomach churn with a huge knot of guilt. I swallowed the lump in my throat. It was at eighth grade graduation. I sat in my blue graduation cap and gown with my little brother, Tyler, sitting on my lap.

We were both grinning into the camera. I remember being extremely happy about finishing middle school; I remember him exclaiming about getting ice cream with the Jenkins afterwards.

I threw the photos back into the drawer quickly like it had burned me, slamming it shut. The picture of my brother and I floated around my head as I drew out a cigarette out of its pack and climbed out onto the terrace, quickly lighting it.

I leaned against the railing, trying to find something that would distract me from thinking about Tyler. Sirens wailed in the distance: police, ambulances, fire trucks, and I closed my eyes, lifting the butt of the cigarette to my lips. The constant loudness of Manhattan drowned out the unwelcomed thoughts and memories.

After a few drags, I dropped the cigarette and returned to my warm bedroom, climbing underneath the covers and burying my face in the cushion of my pillow.

~~~

Miss Kay was assigning us a project.

With our partners.

What was she thinking?

I took that moment to look over at Olivia and she didn't look like a happy camper. Her lips were set in a firm line; her hands closed in fists. I honestly think Miss Kay was handing us a first-class ticket to murdering each other. Well, come to think of it, neither one of them would have to deal with me anymore. Maybe this was an evil plan that they both created. Who knows? Who cares?

I have to work on a project with Olivia Jenkins!

It's bad enough to be her math partner in school, but to work with her after school just sounded awful. Worse news: I'd actually have to work.

I rested my head on my arms. I mean, it probably wouldn't be a problem with anyone else 'cause I could get them to do the project by themselves. With Olivia, that's a different situation. She would literally strap me to a chair and force me to work. I highly doubt I could get out of this.

I could ask Miss Kay for a different partner.

What the heck did I drink last night?

Olivia breathed out deeply, swallowing the fact that she hated being my partner during school and now she has to work with me afterwards too.

Wait a minute, maybe this could be fun.

She cleared her throat. "Whose house do you want to work at?"

I shrugged. "Your house, I guess."

"Uh… that might be a problem."

"Why?"

"My parents hate you," she stated bluntly.

I laughed, not expecting anything else. "Not surprised."

"Can we just work at your house?" Olivia asked. "It would be a lot easier since there's only your mom and brother-"

"Just my mom," I corrected uncomfortably.

She looked confused. "But-"

"Why don't we work somewhere other than our houses?" I quickly changed the subject, searching for a place mentally. "The place where you nerds go?"

She snorted. "You mean the library, Sam?" I grimaced, but nodded anyways. "Do you think you can handle being in a library with books and silence and-"

"I get it, I get it." Olivia laughed, gathering her materials. "How about we go to my hang-out?" I suggested, standing from my seat and shouldering my backpack.

Olivia froze. "Where your gang hangs out?"

"Yeah," I responded slowly. "What? You scared?" I teased, smirking.

She shook her head stubbornly. "No, but isn't that like private property?"

"I'm the leader; I can invite anyone."

Olivia seemed hesitant but eventually agreed, grabbing her bag. We left the classroom and walked off in opposite directions.

~~~

After last period dismissed, I ventured over to Olivia's locker and leaned against the one closest to hers as she traded in random work materials for a sketch pad and her math textbook. I waited impatiently, drumming my fingers to a beat of a catchy song that kept replaying in my head.

"What vehicle do you have today?"

I grinned. "What do you think?"

She groaned. "Your bike."

"You know it's awesome."

Olivia shut her locker and faced me. "Keep telling yourself that, Wayne."

"Hey Liv!" Tammy greeted happily but paused hesitantly when she saw me.

Maya appeared from behind her, an irritated glare edged on her face. "What is he doing here?"

I feel so loved.

"We're partners for a project," Olivia answered.

"So I'm going to have to steal your friend here for a few weeks," I said entering the conversation.

"Don't corrupt her," Maya spat.

I chuckled, gripping the straps of my backpack. "I'll try. Not keeping any promises though."

"Okay, let's go," Olivia said. "I want to get this done." She grabbed me by the sleeve of my jacket and I followed her out of the school and into the parking lot where my bike was located.

"Hey, your friend Maya is pretty hot," I commented wanting to see what her reaction would be. "I wonder if she's a good kisser."

Olivia spun around so fast and yanked me by my shirt collar. "Try anything with her and I won't hesitate to-"

I chuckled, surprised by her reaction. "Whoa, I'm just kidding."

"Sure you were," she stalked off.

"Olivia-"

She gestured to the motorcycle. "Let's just go."

I grumbled down a few not-so-nice words and mounted the bike, ignoring the thought of dropping her off somewhere and having her hitch-hike.

~~~

I opened the door to the garage, Olivia following me inside. A few of the guys were already there. Ace and Daniel were lounging on the couch, laughing at something on Ace's phone; Ryker was working on one of the cars; Santiago sat on the bottom step of the stairs, cleaning out a Glock. Olivia sat next to Ace who greeted her in a friendly matter. She looked out of place being in a gang's place, but Ace was keeping her company for the time being.

"What are you doing here?" he asked her.

"Math project."

"Three weeks of torture," I added under my breath. I trailed over to where Ryker was standing. "'Sup, man?"

"Nothin' much. But can you finish this up for me? Beth's on her way over and I have to get ready," Ryker said, jumping over Santiago and heading up the stairs to the second floor.

I shrugged off my leather jacket and began finishing the work on the engine.

The guys decided to stroll upstairs, leaving me and Olivia alone, something I wasn't comfortable with. The heated argument from Friday repeated in my head and I remembered every single question. The last thing I wanted was it being mentioned.

I was busy twisting one of the loose bolts when Olivia appeared by my side, a surprising pleasant look on her face. "When are we gonna start the project?"

"Whenever you want to. I need to do this," I replied checking the battery.

She lifted her eyebrows. "Um, I'm not doing the project by myself, Wayne."

"I never said that," I said. "I'll help you when I'm done with this."

"Good, because I'll let Miss Kay know that you didn't help and she'll fail you," Olivia smiled sweetly.

I returned it. "Aren't you the sweetest?" I pretended to gag and clutched my throat. "Too sweet. I'm about to suffocate."

"You're so- UGH!"

"Very well put."

"Shut up, Sam."

I grinned at her obvious aggravation. "And I will help you. I'm just busy at the moment," I told her for the third time.

"You can at least help me pick out a topic."

"Just use one of the easiest topics, unless you want to me to epically fail at explaining and understanding a hard one," I expressed.

She crossed her arms across her chest. "You know, if you actually put effort into doing homework and paying attention in class, you might understand it better."

"Honestly, Jenkins, I'm not worried about getting good grades like you are, so it's not that important to me to do well."

"Whatever then," she muttered. "Anyways, I'll search for something that you can comprehend and something I can do without losing brain cells." Olivia smirked and patted me on the cheek. I tried to bite her hand.

About an hour later, I was finished overlooking the engine and changing the front tires. The radio was on, playing a mix of hip-hop, pop, rap- anything that played in today's society. I bopped my head to the beat of one song, singing along under my breath. Olivia sat with her knees propped with the textbook in her lap, threading through the pages for an idea.

The project was nothing to me. I don't give a crap about it. It's just another grade. It's not like I'm going to college. I need to stay here and take care of my mother, especially when she enters her older years. I rather to stick with the life I have now then leave her. Leaving her wasn't an option.

Wiping the back of my neck with a rag, I collapsed next to Olivia, who now sat cross-legged and I looked over her shoulder as she studied one of the pages intently.

"What topic do you have in mind?" I took a sip of my water.

She tapped her pencil on the page. "I'm thinking about this one. Is that all right with you?"

"I'm fine with anything," I replied simply.

"Figured."

I laughed, peering over her shoulder again to look at the lesson. The light breeze from the fan made me catch a whiff off her shampoo. I found myself leaning closer for a better whiff. Coconut. The same kind she used when we were younger. I used to love the smell of it. It was up there with my mom's homemade cinnamon buns.

"What are you doing?" Olivia's voice sounded alarmed.

I realized that while I'd been lost in my thoughts, I had reached over and brushed the loose strands from her braid behind her ear, my hand wrapped around the corner of her cheek. Her face looked as shocked as mine must have been. Her eyes were as wide as saucers. We stared at each other, my mouth open in embarrassment. I pulled my hand away from her hair, resting it on my lap, and I settled on the words the textbook had printed. Olivia excused herself, heading straight for the bathroom.

I leaned back into the couch, thinking...

What did I seriously drink last night?

Chapter 9: Sam

I leaned against the lockers, watching Ryker escort his girlfriend around. Beth decided to pay him a visit since her school was out today. He was explaining to her what classes he was taking and she listened interestingly. I smirked at him because Beth wasn't the kind of girl who showed affection in public- maybe a kiss or two and holding hands but nothing too extreme. Ace walked over, knuckle-punched me, and I threw my backpack over my shoulder and started stalking the halls with my cousin.

"Hey, is Olivia coming over tonight?" he asked.

I gave him an odd look. "How am I supposed to know?"

"Well, you guys are partners, right? Shouldn't you know where to meet?"

"No. I don't work on projects," I answered. "But I either work with Olivia on the project or risk her telling Miss Kay which results in failing. I much rather deal with Olivia's wrath than Miss Kay's."

Ace nodded, agreeing with me. "So, what's up with you two?"

"Why do you care?" I smirked and threw an arm around his shoulders. "Oh, that's right." I poked him in the stomach. "You have a crush on her!"

"I used to," he corrected immediately. "I don't anymore."

I laughed, dodging the punch he aimed for my gut. "How defensive!"

He pushed my arm off his shoulders. "Seriously though, what's going on with you two?"

I stopped in my tracks and spun on the balls of my feet to face him. "What do you mean?"

"I mean, you guys seem to be getting some-what closer." At that, I raised an eyebrow in confusion. "You're not gettin' up in each other's faces. You're not yelling at each other. People think the world has flipped because it seems like an alternate universe."

I snorted. "I think you're exaggerating a good bit."

Daniel appeared from behind me, shoving a chocolate-sprinkled donut in his mouth. "No, it's true." He must have been listening in on our conversation. "Everyone's talkin' about you two not ripping each other's faces off. I find it a little shocking myself."

Ace pointed to the guy next to me. "If he's noticing it, everyone else is."

"Well, they should keep their noses at of other people's business. Nothing is going on between us. *Nothing*. I still hate her, and she still hates me. End of discussion."

I turned around, leaving Ace and Daniel to inform the student body that accurate information. Nothing is going on. What happened in the garage was nothing. I had a drink the previous night. Maybe that had something to do with it. There was nothing between me and her.

Nothing.

OLIVIA

Maya sprayed her water everywhere after I finished telling her what happened between Sam and me. Tammy was just shaking her head with a mischievous smile. I looked at her suspiciously. She didn't elaborate what that creepy smile was for.

"You had a moment with *Sam*?" Maya shouted.

I covered her shrill mouth. "Just tell the entire world, why don't you!" I glared at her before taking my hand off. "I don't think he wanted me to tell anybody. I mean, if it even counted as a moment for him. He probably doesn't. He has all those pretty girls worshipping him."

"Are you jealous?" Tammy asked, nudging me teasingly.

I started to laugh. "Are you kidding me? No way. I may really like him, but I want no part of his game. He's a player and a jerk. Why would I even want to put myself in that position, anyways? All he's going to do is hurt me in the end. It's just a waste of time."

Maya took a small sip of her water. "I don't want you to end up with him."

"I'm not going to," I said, not voicing the thought that crossed my mind: *unless he changed.* We were sitting outside, enjoying our lunch at a picnic table when drama entered. Sam and his gang exited the side door of the school, guffawing and yelling as they did. I glared at my lunch. There was absolutely no escaping him.

I glanced up to see what direction he was headed

when he turned his head and caught me staring. I saw the familiar glimpse of his smirk before I looked back at my lunch. My Subway sandwich looked delicious. Maya glanced behind her then groaned, probably cursing in her head. I heard footsteps coming closer and I made a mental note to make sure he never caught me again.

"Hello girls," Sam greeted with his deep voice. My eyes didn't look anywhere. "Leave." I knew exactly who he was talking to.

Tammy laughed. "Why should we? We were here fist."

"It's not kindergarten, Blondie," Sam patted the top of her head and she flinched. I felt his emerald eyes on my figure. Don't look. Do not look. Show restraint. "I want to talk to Jenkins here. Alone."

"Just give us a few minutes," I said looking at my best friends. Their expressions clearly read they didn't want to, but they gathered their stuff and left. Sam sat down as his gang filed away, leaving us in an awkward silence. I met his eyes and crossed my arms above my chest. "What do you want?"

"I just want a friendly conversation between partners," he answered sarcastically with a grin.

I scoffed, not in the mood for his games. "What do you want, Wayne?"

"I want to bring something to your attention," Sam leaned forward on the table. "Everyone seems to be talking about us. Supposedly, we're friends now."

"And you're here why?" I inquired, missing the part where I'm involved.

"Have you been telling people we used to be friends?" Sam asked, his green eyes glaring into mine.

"No. Why would I? Those memories are long gone. They're history, according to you." I smirked and faked an innocent expression. "Why? Have you, the fearless gang leader, told people that you and I, the biggest nerd, used to be friends?"

"I haven't told anyone," he said through gritted teeth, "unless you count your best friends because I know you tell those chicks everything."

I leaned in closer. "Those are my friends. Not just some 'chicks'. You can make my life miserable and treat me like crap, but leave them out of it."

"My, my, kitty does like to scratch."

I rolled my eyes. "Are we done?"

Sam stood from his seat, his beautiful green eyes hiding secrets and emotions that would tell his story. "I wish we were." With one last glance, he began to walk away.

"Hey! Where are we meeting?" I called, grabbing my backpack from the ground.

Sam turned around and winked. "I'll just see you after school, Jenkins."

I stared after him, wondering and dreading what

that could possibly mean.

~~~

There was a knock on the door, breaking my concentration on the book in front of me. *Six of Crows* had that way of grasping your attention and keeping you entertained and wanting more, especially when you wanted to escape reality for hours. Parker ran for the door, probably knowing I didn't want to leave the clutches of my book.

"Olivia!" he shouted. "A boy is here to see you!"

A boy? I raised an eyebrow, slightly confused. "Who?"

"I don't know, but he said something about a project!"

I shot up, my book forgotten. About three seconds later, any shock left my body so I stood up from the couch and walked over to confirm my suspicions. Sam was leaning against the doorframe, clad in his leather jacket and dark jeans with a roguish smirk on his face. His blue and black bandana was wrapped around his neck. My brother looked at him for examination before shrugging and running off to the living room. I crossed my arms, feeling a bit exposed in my lazy shorts.

"What are you doing here, Wayne?"

"Here to work on our project, partner," Sam answered, his eyes scanning over my appearance.

"Do you have a problem with what I'm wearing?

Not enough skin showing for your liking?" I asked, even though my legs were dead visible.

Sam chuckled then looked over my shoulder. "You gonna let me in or what?"

I glanced over to where my brother sat, watching the television show *Danny Phantom*. The gang leader switched to one foot to another; impatient written all over his figure. My parents weren't home yet if they walked in and saw Sam, they would skin him alive and ground me for an indefinite number of days. But we need to work on this project. I'm not just going to put his name on it and turn it in; I refuse to.

I sighed, rubbing the crease on my forehead. "Come on in," I said moving over so he could enter.

I led him to the living room where he sat his backpack next to my father's desk. My brother turned down the volume on the TV and looked at Sam with interest.

"What's your name?" Parker asked.

"Sam," the senior answered.

He lifted an eyebrow. "Olive, is he the Sam Dad and Mommy don't like?"

I sighed and bit my lip. "Yes, but we're working on a project so we need to work together. Melanie and Dad will just have to accept that," I said.

"Are you sure it's okay that I'm here? I don't want your parents calling the police or anything," Sam said. "I'm really not in the mood to deal with them."

I shrugged. "What they won't know won't kill them." Parker must have decided we weren't entertaining and returned his attention to the TV screen.

"Ah, rebellious. Feels great, doesn't it?" he winked.

Scoffing, I announced, "I'll be right back. I'm gonna get my books."

When I reached my room, I dug through my backpack and grabbed the math textbook and my book of notes; I also grabbed a box of pencils from my desk. A sudden knock on my door made me jump and my books dropped to the floor. I turned around quickly to see Sam standing there, glancing around. He stepped into my room, not bothered by the fact we're alone.

"It's different," he mumbled almost silently.

My eyebrows shot to my hairline. "*Huh*?"

"From the last time I saw it," Sam rubbed the back of his neck, indicating he was nervous. "The colors were different." At eight, my walls were purple and white. Now they were ocean blue.

I was surprised. "You remember?"

"Don't flatter yourself, Jenkins."

Sam walked over to where I was as I knelt down to pick up my books. He slid his hands in his pockets as his eyes were glued to my desk. The hardback from my eleventh birthday sat on it. He leaned over and grabbed it, opening the cover page. My eyes widened and I almost stopped him. I was too late. He was silent while reading the note. He closed the book and set it back down on my desk. Sam looked at the carpet before lifting his eyes. We didn't say a word to each other.

I stood up and adjusted the books, clearing my throat. "Um, we should work in the kitchen. I have to keep an eye on my brother."

Sam nodded, shrugging. "I don't care where we work. I just want to get it done."

"We finally agree on something," I responded, brushing past him and exiting my bedroom. I realized with a wince those were the words he said to me last Friday.

An hour later, we were sitting at the island. Sam busied himself with taking on the notes while I designed the poster board. Being artistic had its benefits. I chewed on the tip of my pen, contemplating on what to do next.

Sam's laughter, though, distracted me. "What?" I questioned.

He pointed at the utensil in my mouth. "You always did that. Whenever you would concentrate on something, you would have the end in your mouth and eyebrows in a weird angle."

I retracted the pen. "I thought you forgot everything about me."

"That's kind of hard considering we were friends for many, many years," he replied scribbling down an equation.

"Do you remember everything?" I was interested on how much he remembered.

Sam laughed. "From the time you threw up in kindergarten to the time on the roof where you told me about your parent's divorce."

I shifted uncomfortably. "You haven't told anyone, have you?" He lifted his eyebrows. "The reason behind it," I clarified. My stomach froze in nervousness and the back of my neck felt clammy.

"No. Why would I? It's not my secret to tell."

I thought he would tell a million people for leverage against me. Maybe deep down, he did have good in him; he just didn't share it. "Thank you," I whispered. He didn't do anything to acknowledge the fact that he heard me, but I knew he did.

"Sam!" Parker said coming into the kitchen.

Sam turned his head in his direction and smiled. "'Sup, little man?"

"Can you play a game with me?" Parker asked holding up a remote control.

Sam sighed. "I would, but your sister is holding me hostage."

I glared at him. "I am not!"

"Can I borrow your boyfriend?" my brother inquired.

I choked on my spit. "He's not my boyfriend."

"Yeah, never."

"We're acquaintances," I corrected. "Partners."

Parker shrugged, not caring either way. "Whatever. Can I still borrow him? I hardly have anyone over."

In other situations, I would say no, but I felt bad. He barely has any friends at school, and Sam could use a break from all the equations and notes. I smiled at my brother, ruffling his brown hair. "Go ahead. Half an hour."

"Yes!" Parker grabbed onto Sam's arm and pulled him out of the chair.

Sam took the controller. "What game we playin'?"

"*Mortal Kombat*!"

I decided to take a break also. I put down my pen and followed them into the living room where the game was already set up. I know Parker have missed his older brother just like I did so I'll let them play for a little while. I leaned against the wall as the duo sat on the floor. Sam assured that he'll go easy on him, but Parker snorted and challenged my fellow senior. I watched in amusement.

"Olive doesn't like to play video games. She rather read and draw," he said. "Oh, and nobody knows this, but she has underwear with polka dots. I found them in her room." *WHAT?* I stashed those away the day Melanie bought them.

"Oh really?" Sam looked back at me and smirked.

I glared at him though my cheeks betrayed me. "I'll be in the kitchen."

About forty minutes later, my partner returned, and as I dug my nails into his skin, I whispered, "You mention that to anyone-"

"But babe, that's perfect blackmail footage," Sam winked.

I smiled wickedly. "You don't want to do that."

He laughed. "And why not?"

"I remember a time where you were so excited about your *Toy Story* birthday cake that you jumped out of the pool so fast, you slipped and fell on top of Ella Fernfield! That was the talk for weeks in sixth grade."

If Sam was embarrassed, he didn't show it. "What about the time where Tony Davis dumped that drink with freezing cold ice down your shirt in fourth grade?"

"Third grade; someone put worms in your lunchbox and you screamed like a little girl," I retorted.

He rolled his eyes. "Fifth grade; you told Peter Carnage that you had a crush on him during the talent show." That was a dare and he knows it.

"Seventh grade; you kissed me."

"Olivia!" Thirteen year-old Sam called after me.

I giggled and stopped by our tree. "You're running too slow!"

"I just ate!"

Laughter bubbled in my throat as we chased each other. Life couldn't get better than this. Sam was still my best friend, despite the rumors about us being more than friends. Despite physical and emotional changes, we were inseparable. We were Batman and Liv, no matter what.

After he tackled me to the ground and tickled me on that spot on my ribcage, we busied ourselves by talking about the day's event, and I broke a stick out of anger as I retold the stories girls would make about me in the locker room. He listened carefully to every detail, frowning when I mentioned how much prettier they were compared to me.

"What?" I asked as the expression lingered longer than necessary.

He shook his head. "Nothing."

"What?" I repeated nudging him with my shoulder.

"You are pretty."

I snorted in amusement. "Yeah, sure. I totally agree," I deadpanned. I'm one of the least attractive girls at our middle school. "Now be honest."

"I am being honest."

"I think you're confusing me with Ellen," I argued.

Sam rolled his eyes. "Olivia, just take the compliment. You're so stubborn."

"But-" My sentence was cut off because Sam had grabbed my face and kissed me. HUH? Since we were both inexperienced, I didn't know what to expect. One thing I did know; my brain turned into noodles and the small crush I had on him doubled- no, tripled in size. He pulled back, our faces close and breaths mixed. His eyes shined a radiant green.

He licked his lips, eyebrows furrowed. "Uh…"

"What just happened?"

Sam rubbed the back of his neck, blushing red. "I kissed you."

I shoved him, smiling at his ignorance. "I know that, silly, but why?"

"I wanted to," he shared bluntly. Surprised by his answer, I rested my chin on my knees and my cheeks turned a rosy color. "Uh, sorry if-"

"No," I stopped him instantly. I didn't want him thinking I was rejecting him because that was the last thing I would do. "I kind of liked it." I glanced up to see his expression.

Sam raised an eyebrow, looking slightly confused. "You liked it?"

"It was awkward," I said honestly. "But it was nice... for my first."

The corners of his mouth lifted into a smile. "Yeah," he agreed. "It was nice."

We stayed silent for several minutes.

After that afternoon, we never brought it up again. We never spoke of it with our parents; we never spoke of it to each other. It was like it vanished from history. But I remembered it. That was when I knew I had strong feelings for him, not just that little crush you had on your hot older neighbor.

Sam pursed his lips. "Don't speak of that. I was delusional back then."

I scoffed. "I'm surprised I didn't go and boil my lips afterwards. You kissed awfully." *No, he didn't.* I pushed the thought back.

He clicked his tongue. "Is that what girls say about

me? Man, I thought they talked about how good I am at it. They always seem to enjoy it in the moment," he wiggled his eyebrows suggestively.

I stepped backwards. "You're disgusting."

"Say whatever you want about me," Sam spat. "I don't care what people think. I am who I am, and I don't have to please everyone unlike some people."

"I'm not a people-pleaser."

"When did I ever mention you? Who's conceited now?"

"You stated it directly at me. I'm not stupid."

"Are you sure about that?"

It would have hurt less being slapped in the face. "Get. Out." I said through gritted teeth.

"Thanks for the lovely hospitality, Jenkins," Sam replied and hooked his backpack over his shoulder, pushing past me. I stood there, clenching my fists and debating on whether or not to throw my textbook at the back of his head. "Should I leave a note apologizing to your parents for the lovely mood you're in?"

"Get out of here, Wayne!" I yelled feverishly.

The last thing I heard was his laugh and the closing of the door. While biting back the tears wanting to escape, I retreated to my bedroom, and tucked myself under the sheets, wanting more than anything for this deep ache in my chest to be gone.

~~~

When next Thursday morning rolled in, I rested my head on the closed fist of my hand and waited for Sam to enter, tapping the end of my pen against the textbook. The project was due this Monday coming up and there were things that needed to be done still. I had been jealous when I had walked in and three posters were already finished because normally I would be one of the first ones to hand it

in early, but with Sam as a partner, I'm surprised that we've come this far.

"Hit the books too hard last night, Sleeping Beauty?" Sam inquired, resigning in his seat. I shook my head and like my body was working against me, I yawned. He lifted an accusing eyebrow.

"I stayed up late studying," I admitted, waiting for the bell to ring, informing that class had started.

He chuckled, leaning back in his seat. "Aw, your nerd is showin'."

"Shut up." I reached over and flicked him in the ear.

He snatched my hand in his before I could fulfill the action though, and I realized how well our hands fit together in that small moment. His skin was warm and calloused; mine was cool and smooth. Sam retracted it just as the second bell rang, looking distraught. It was obvious he hadn't meant for that to happen for a mere second before adopting a smirk as Miss Kay collected homework.

For the rest of the period, slight tension was in the air. We had to work on a thirty-question quiz with our table partners, and while I explained an easier way to dissect word problems, Sam had knocked my entire box of pencils, pens, etc. across our work area, creating a mess.

Instead of yanking bits of hair out of his scalp, I just laughed it off and picked up the cluttered utensils. When he gave me the ones he'd collected, our hands touched again and I swallowed a rosy blush as our fingers brushed each other's and discreetly focused on the calmness Sam presented because it hadn't even crossed his mind. Glaring at his textbook, he dropped his head on the table and groaned.

"This is torture!"

"No, it's not. You're not trying hard enough," I said.

He leaned back in his chair and crossed his arms, scoffing. "Excuse me for not understanding it. I have dyslexia so sometimes numbers and words-"

"I know what dyslexia is and does," I interrupted.

He narrowed his eyes. "Then stop patronizing me!"

"I'm not-" I stopped to choose my words carefully. "I'm trying to help."

Sam sighed, rubbing the crease between his eyebrows. "Word problems have always been my enemy. I've tried to avoid them."

"If it makes you feel any better, word problems aren't my favorite either," I confessed in a whisper. "There have been moments where I've skipped over them."

His mouth dropped and he brought a hand to his

heart, if it'd been on the right side. "The world has ended."

"Shut up," I warned. "And your heart is on your left side, idiot."

And *no*, I didn't smile because of his absolutely adorable grin.

~~~

After gathering tonight's homework, I left the classroom, searching for the Under-Twenty gang leader, otherwise known as my partner. I needed to know when we were gonna finish the project. I strolled over to them when they appeared from the left corridor. One of the gangsters patted Sam on the arm, causing him to turn around, his emerald eyes meeting mine, and I was reminded of our hands touching in math class and how right and amazing it felt. He raised a dark eyebrow as I stopped, not intimidated by the members floating around.

"We need to finish that project, Wayne."

Sam smirked cockily. "We'll do it whenever I'm free."

"Uh, no."

"Uh, yes."

I quirked an eyebrow. "Do you honestly think I would let you pick when we're gonna do the project? I'm not stupid."

"Are you sure about that?" questioned a sophomore-looking member.

That stung. Those were the same words Sam said to me in my kitchen a few days ago. "I want a good grade on this project."

"Don't you want a good grade on everything?" Sam rebuked.

"Well, excuse me for actually wanting nice scores," I shot back.

He set his jaw firmly and dismissed his friends, ordering a few to meet him in weight-lifting class. "My place. Tomorrow afternoon. I got plans tonight."

"Ah," I nodded, knowing somehow it had to deal with the gang. "Just don't do anything that will make me end up doing your work."

"Not making any promises," he smirked. "Try not to worry too much about me, kay, babe?" His eyes glinted with humor. "I can handle myself."

I blinked, keeping my expression blank. "I'll do my best."

He grinned then turned heading towards the gymnasium. I watched him for a minute, finding it amusing how easily he could irritate me and make me want to punch him repeatedly for everything he's done in the past three years, yet there were moments where I felt a warm and tender feeling when he smiled for real or looked at me with an expression that sent shivers down my spine and tingles to my toes.

He'd be the death of me someday. No doubt.

Chapter 10: Sam

I sat in the getaway car's driver's seat, patting a beat on the wheel in irritation. After looking at the stopwatch on my wrist, I slipped out a curse and Ryker stopped sliding in a new magazine in his gun to look at me with a surprised eyebrow. "They're screwing it up. They've been in too long."

"Want me to get 'em?"

"Nope." I got out of the car, keeping the door open. "I should not have to babysit them and hold their hand."

I ducked into the underground armory, minding my head to the fat slick of asphalt in the opening. When I reached Ace, Santiago, and the others, I whistled loudly to get their attention. "Get moving! Cops will be here in less than two minutes."

Returning to the car, I slammed the door shut. "I may be a chill leader, but this is seriously pissing me off."

"Ace and Santiago should have known how to handle it, that's for sure," Ryker commented.

With thirty seconds left until the police showed, Ace jumped into the backseat and assured me all the supplies were secured. Keeping one hand on the wheel and the other on the gear, I pushed down on the gas pedal.

"Drive faster, will ya!" Ace shouted, smacking the back of my seat.

"Let me see you do it!" I looked in the rearview mirror and scowled at the sudden flurry of police cars.

"Where's everyone else?" I asked, glancing at the speed monitor. Eighty MPH.

"Stayed behind."

"All right," I licked my lips. "Keep an eye out on those cars," I ordered. "Tell me when they've passed the gate."

"Why?" Ace questioned.

I rolled my eyes. "Just do it!" I pressed harder on the gas and quickly passed over the ninety.

"Why did I even agree to this? I hate road trips!" my cousin whined.

I jerked the car into another gear. "Distract him or he'll puke."

"Hey, Ace, when we were younger, Sam would always be the one driving the getaway car," Ryker said, referring to our freshman year. "Boss wouldn't allow anyone else even though he was a newbie. Sam just had no fears, man. He did what he thought was best, and Boss liked that."

"Maybe that's why he chose me," I mumbled.

"They just passed the gate," Ace informed weakly, bringing his head in between his knees.

I let my foot off the gas slowly. "Perfect."

"Prepare yourself," Ryker directed to Ace.

When I calculated it was the right time, I let my foot off the gas completely and slammed down on the brake, tires squealing sharply. The police cars tried to stop, but ended up crashing into another and into the wall. I straightened the wheel abruptly, shifting the gear again. I pressed on the gas, revving the engine and heading straight into the glass security gate. It shattered upon impact. I spun out onto the road at an angle to avoid causing any wrecks. I headed towards the ramp for the highway, leaving the state of New Jersey and back home to Manhattan.

I just wasn't expecting the police to catch up with us so quickly.

Guiding swiftly between the other vehicles and avoiding the bullets breaking through the glass, I handed my gun to Ryker. I depended on them in moments like these. Ace, gaining his composure, positioned himself safely yet in perfect range, firing off at perfect timing. We had plenty of ammo stored, considering what our job concerned, and I cursed as a bullet ricocheted off the dashboard and into the seat cushion inches from my leg.

Taking matters into my own hands momentarily, I ordered Ryker for my gun and clicking a bullet into place; I rolled down the window and glanced in the rearview mirror, noting that a police vehicle would be coming up on my side in seconds. With one hand on the wheel and the other on the trigger, the tires were blown out. Ace whooped, but ducked at the sound of gunfire.

Adrenaline and fury bubbling in my veins, I threw the wheel to the right, surprisingly missing other innocent vehicles, putting good distance between the police and us. Ryker and Ace traded in their old magazines for new ones, and while speeding in the process, I shifted to another lane, getting as far as possible on a three-lane highway.

Finally entering the state of New York, Ace exhaled a relieved gasp. "I know why Boss chose you for getaways now."

I sent him a cocky smirk.

~~~

Daniel spit out his water and it sprayed on the students in front of us as we finished retelling last night's event. The student who got the most of it turned around to say something, but I raised an eyebrow and the glare he got from the rest of the gang made him swallow his words and return his attention to the coach. No matter their social status, people didn't mess with us. Most kept silent, others were terrified, and the brave ones were blessed with a kiss from my knuckles.

"Wow," Daniel said. "I missed out on a fun night."

Ryker chuckled beside me. "There'll be other times."

"Why do we keep having pep rallies?" Ace asked, appearing next to me. He had to make up a test from the other day. "I mean, I know its homecoming, but is this really necessary? It gets boring after a while. Wake me up when it ends." He threw his hood over his head and leaned against the wall. The buzzer from the scoreboard rang and Ace jumped, surprised by the sudden noise.

"What the heck?" he screeched.

All of us started laughing hard before we were shushed by various students and teachers. Ace glared at us, not amused by any of it. On the gym floor, the cheerleaders got into a stance until an annoying pop song started blaring through the speakers. Oh, just be done already... Searching around the audience for something more entertaining, my eyes landed on Olivia.

She and her friends were sitting on the set of bleachers next to us, their attention captured by the performance yet I was aware of the earbuds plugged into Olivia's phone, no doubt playing better music into her ears. Her waves were cascading down her back and a bit in the front; the caramel-brown color popping against her black shirt.

Shaking the observant thoughts of Olivia out of my head, I watched the cheerleaders in so much enthusiasm that I took out my phone and played an exciting game of *Temple Run* until we were dismissed.

~~~

Ryker threw a toffee-colored arm around my shoulders as we walked behind the rest of the gang. "Who knew you would be such a good leader?"

"Thanks for the support, man," I said smacking him on the back of the head.

He chuckled. "I'm serious; Boss chose well. Even as a regular member, you outshined us all."

I shot him a rare smile. "Thanks, I do my best."

"Everyone thinks highly of you," Ryker shared.

"Don't be getting all mushy on me now," I teased.

Out of nowhere, a hand gripped the back of my leather jacket, and I was pulled back roughly. I turned to realize it was Olivia. Her arms were crossed over her chest with an impatient expression. Ryker glanced at me and I inwardly prepared myself.

"What's up, sweetheart?"

"We need to work on the project," she stated rolling her eyes.

"Okay."

She sighed, irritation written over her features. "It's due on Monday."

"And?" I lifted an eyebrow.

Olivia scoffed and turned to look at my best friend. "Is there any way I could steal him away from you for an hour? We need to finish our project, whether he likes it or not," she said scowling at me.

Ryker nodded then pushed me towards her. I skidded to a stop before I toppled over her. "Go ahead and take him. I can handle the gang."

"I hate you."

He grinned. "No, you don't." He raised his hands in surrender. "See you later, man!"

Then he left me standing in the middle of the hall with an angry Olivia.

I turned to look at her. "What's the big deal about this freakin' project?"

"The big deal?" she asked. "If it's not clear enough, I actually want to graduate high school," Olivia explained. "I want to pass this class. I want to get into a good college and get a good career out of it. I understand to you gangsters, you probably don't care about this stuff, but to others it's a big deal."

I swallowed any insults or rude comments down my throat, deciding to follow her wishes for a change. I grabbed my car keys from my back pocket and swung them on my fingers. "C'mon then. Let's get it done for your perfect record."

"Thank you."

"Yeah, well don't expect this all the time," I told her. "And for your information, I want to pass this class too. I rather fail Spanish or English than have Miss Kay again."

"I think everyone feels that way. Besides, I think she'll pass you anyway if you did fail. She doesn't want to deal with you anymore than she has to."

I shot her a dirty look, grabbing my notebook from my locker and Olivia innocently smiled in return. We exited the school, walking side by side towards my truck. "My house fine with you?" I asked unlocking the doors.

"Better than mine," she replied.

"Yeah, I don't really feel like getting killed tonight," I said as we climbed into my truck.

She laughed. "I don't feel like cleaning up my living room either."

"Oh no, your dad will kill me right on the doorstep. I won't even be able to put a foot down before he came out with the shotgun," I winked.

We drove out of the school parking lot with Olivia messing with the radio. She switched to channel to channel until she stopped on a song I immediately recognized.

"Oh my gosh, you listened to this every day for like two years," I blurted out before I could stop myself. *Miss Independent* by *Kelly Clarkson* was playing and it was her favorite song when we were younger. I tried to keep our childhood memories from resurfacing, especially from my words or actions, but there were moments where I'd slipped up. "You'd break out in the middle of whatever if it came on."

Olivia smiled sheepishly, a light blush on her cheeks. "It was an awesome song!" She defended. "Still is, in fact." A faded image of Olivia dancing on her bed, singing along carelessly and acting foolish as I sat on the floor laughing entered my mind. "And if I remember correctly, your weakness was *Simple Plan*."

"How can you not like them?" I asked rhetorically. "They're great!"

"Not disagreeing," she said. "But no picking on me because I have plenty of blackmail footage, Mr. I-Must-Sleep-With-A-Nightlight-Until-I'm-Eight."

I glared at her, suppressing the blush wanting to

show. "That information is strictly classified." She laughed at my response. "There are reasons-"

"Monsters?" Olivia teased, wiggling her fingers.

I shoved her in the shoulder, breaking her into more laughter. "No. My mother didn't want Tyler in complete darkness, despite me being in there," I said. At the mention of my brother, my stomach dropped with a large, uncomfortable knot.

"Speaking of, he'd be a freshman this year and he's not..." I could hear the confusion in her voice.

"He lives with his aunt in Florida. He was enrolled in a school there and our aunt offered to take him in until he graduates. Tyler didn't hesitate to agree because of his love for beaches."

Olivia nodded, saying a simple reply. An awkward silence emerged between us, the radio playing randomness in the background. The past couple of weeks I've been noticing we've been sharing moments. It almost seemed as if we were getting along, and dare I say it, flirting with each other.

At that thought, my foot slipped on the brake. Olivia and I were both jolted at the abrupt stop. She looked at me with wide eyes.

"Everything okay?"

My phone began to ring obnoxiously, saving me from a battle with my thoughts, and I dug it out of my pocket, seeing it was Ace.

"Sup?" I asked.

"Another drug deal gone bad."

I slammed the wheel in anger without thinking and Olivia jumped, surprised yet again. "How many?"

"Four."

"Why don't they listen to me?" I hissed.

"I dunno know, man, but it's getting out of control," Ace said.

"Tell me about it," I glanced over at Olivia, who seemed concerned so I waved her off. "Keep the kids out of the loop. It's bad enough that older ones aren't listenin' to me," I growled. "They're gonna keep getting themselves killed."

"Why don't you just tell them why we don't do drug deals?"

I pinched the bridge of my nose. "I *have* told them! They just don't listen." I stopped at a stop-light. "Get a meeting set up. Tomorrow night."

"'Kay, boss."

"Get Ryker on the phone."

I heard him hand the phone over. "Yah?"

"I know there's someone working these jobs behind my back. I mean, this is the third time in the past month we've had members walk out on us and end up dead." I slid the phone to my right ear. "I may have to tell Boss what's going on."

"If someone loyal is behind this, he'd already

know."

"Either way, I still think it would be good to consult with him."

"On it. Oh, and sorry about interruptin' your little study date."

I glared at the windshield. "Shut up. Call me if any new information comes in."

"Will do." He ended the call.

Olivia turned her head, eyebrows raised. "What was that all about?"

"Gang stuff," I answered tentatively.

"Is your hand okay? You slammed it pretty hard," she observed.

I gave her a genuine smile despite my inner protests. "I'm fine, babe. Stop worrying about me. I'm a big boy."

"Yeah," she muttered then smirked, "boy is all I see."

I frowned. "I'm wounded. You gotta cut those kitty claws soon."

"I'll get an appointment this weekend," Olivia said. "Just for you," she added sweetly, mimicking those cheery girls at school and I laughed at her accuracy.

When we got to my apartment complex, I parked my truck and shut the door behind me, throwing my backpack over my shoulder and retying my bandana around my neck, signaling that I was here. Olivia followed me, taking in her surroundings. She smiled at the kids that wore the same shirt twice a week. They returned it brightly, sending a greeting in my direction. These kids had crazy talents: drawing to rapping to dancing to singing- you name it. They're the ones that'll make it through all the hard times and come out smiling and stronger than ever.

I held the door open for the single mother of five children. Her husband decided to walk out on her for another woman, right at the same time she got pregnant with the fifth child. She smiled up at me and ran a hand through her youngest child's hair. I shot back a grin and high-fived the kid.

"WELSH!" I shouted when I entered the lobby.

My tenant, Scott Welsh, appeared from behind the check-in desk. "WAYNE!" He threw me the package I received every month. It was the money I got from the gang business. "Nice to meet you." He tilted his head at Olivia.

She smiled. "You too, sir."

"Manners," he winked at me. "I already like her."

I rolled my eyes then held up the package. "Thanks."

"No problem. Can you do me a favor?" He gestured for me to come closer and I did so. "I don't want uh, your *friends* around here. Try to keep it on the down low."

"I will," I promised. The renters in this building

knew who I was from news articles or TV and obviously what I was involved in. They weren't too fond of it.

I trailed up the steps with Olivia on my heels until we reached the third floor. I unlocked the door to my home and entered, holding it open as she came inside. She walked into the small division where the living room and kitchen didn't meet completely. Olivia smiled fondly at the apartment, probably remembering all our movie nights and sleepovers, all our memories. It was strange seeing her here again.

It reminded me of the past. The place I never wanted to step back in.

OLIVIA

It's been years since I've been here, and I instantly felt like I was at home. It was seeing all the kids playing with years old toys and enjoying them instead of taking them for granted. It was seeing everyone treating each other with respect and love, and seeing Sam help that woman with her child, it just made my heart flutter, if that was possible.

His house was small yet spacious; it was comfy and warm. I remembered when Sam and I were younger and we would have sleepovers. We would make a tent in his room and make images with flashlights on the sheet covering. We would go out onto his terrace and stare out at the stars. We would prank Tyler and make it up to him by inviting him to watch movies with us, which I was still surprised that he'd moved to Florida, but I remember the financial problems Sam would mention so I guess it was a good idea.

The best thing about this place was that I could come over and let my real self show. I didn't have to hide behind a mask.

Ever since I was young, I wanted to live in a place like this. No three-story houses. No fancy furniture or decorations. No designer clothing. No rich and hard-to-please parents. Just a small, comfy house with smiling parents who would listen to me talk about my problems and give me hugs every day. That was my dream.

I entered the kitchen to see his mother and one of my favorite people in the world, Leah Wayne, standing at the dining table and searching for something in her purse. She must have heard the door open because she turned to greet her son but stopped when she saw me.

"Mom, you remember Olivia Jenkins, right?" Sam asked, coming from behind me. He threw his stuff lackadaisically on the floor and kissed his mom on the cheek. He jumped onto the counter, taking a bite out of an apple. I believed I was seeing a glimpse of his life beyond the gang and school.

Leah gasped. "Olivia?" I waved sheepishly. She ran over and embraced me. I wrapped my arms around her, being ambushed by how much I've missed her. She had been there when my mother deserted me. She had been the only one who knew about my crush on her son in junior high. I hugged her tighter. "My, how you've grown!" She pulled back to look at me. "Oh, you've gotten so beautiful!" Leah gave me that proud stare I've wanted for years. "I've missed you so much, sweetie."

"I've missed you too," I smiled. I never felt this happy at home.

Sam took another bite of his apple. "Mom, you're suffocating her."

I scowled at him, not wanting to be free from motherly love. "I'm sorry, hon. I just missed seeing you around here." Leah glanced over at her son who seemed more interested in the zipper on his jacket. "What exactly happened between you two?"

Sam's head snapped up and his emerald eyes seemed agitated. I would love to know too. "We went separate ways," he finally said after a while. He jumped off the counter and rummaged through the fridge, crinkling his nose at some things.

Leah frowned but it disappeared as soon as it showed. She grabbed her purse off the table and took her jacket from the coat rack. "I would love to stay and talk, but I need to get to work." She gave me another hug. "Rules while I'm gone. One, behave yourselves. I don't want any funny business-"

"Don't have to worry about that, Mom!" Sam informed her.

"Like I would ever do anything with this pig."

He glared at me. "Likewise, nerd."

Leah's face saddened at our behavior. I gave her an apologetic look and she smiled in return. "And two, don't burn my house down!" Her eyes narrowed on her son. Sam laughed and promised that he'd try. "See you later honey," she addressed to me before departing.

Deciding not to bark at him for lacking a heart, I grabbed my backpack from the living room and sat it on a free chair, unzipping it. I opened the poster and laid it on the table, holding the corners down with big erasers. We

needed two more examples and we're finished. Sam stood at the counter, making himself a sandwich. I watched as he supplied a hunk of mayo, plenty of meat, and other little things. He chewed on his bottom lip, checking to see he had everything. I got too lost in my thoughts to notice he had turned around until his deep and raspy voice sung in my ears.

"Checking me out, Miss Jenkins?" I could practically *hear* the smirk on his face.

I scoffed, meeting his eyes instead of backing down. I decided to play along and I smiled endearingly. "Who wouldn't?"

"Knew you had something for me," Sam winked before sitting opposite of me.

I felt my cheeks redden against my will. "You wish," I retorted. "Why would I like you?"

He tipped back his chair. "You don't think I'm good-lookin' or anything?"

I stood my ground and lied straight through my teeth. "No."

"Gotta hand it to you. You're one of the only girls that would ever stand up to me and not give in."

"Do I get a prize?" I asked sarcastically.

Sam chuckled, finishing his sandwich. After throwing away his plate and dusting off his hands, he leaned on his elbows at the edge of the table; eyes flickering over our work. The muscles in his forearm stood out and I wondered how many girls had run their fingers over the tan skin.

Shaking my head to dismiss the thought, Leah's question lingered unforgettably. *What exactly happened between you two?* What did happen? I've never got a straight-up answer from him. He always distances himself or changes the subject whenever I ask. My brain was clouded with the question that I could barely focus on the project.

"Earth to Olivia." He waved a hand in front of my face and I blinked rapidly, retracting from my overriding thoughts.

"What?" I said guessing he asked a question.

"You seem distracted."

I rubbed my temples, feeling a headache brewing. "Because I am." I decided to skip right to the point. "Sam, I have the same question."

He gave me a bemused look. "Huh?"

"What your mom asked," I explained cautiously, knowing I was crossing into dangerous territory. "About us."

"Why do you keep bringing this up?" he asked exasperatedly.

"Because I deserve an explanation."

His eyes hardened. "There's nothin' to talk about."

"I think there is."

"About what?" The poster was forgotten. "There's nothing to talk about, Olivia. I was honest with her. We went separate ways."

I stared at him in disbelief. "No, you went *your* separate way," I corrected him. "You abandoned me." He cursed under his breath and leaned his forehead on the table, putting his arms behind his head, exhaling sharply. I didn't stop. I wanted to see if I could get some reaction out of him. I deserved something. "Sam, we were best friends. Since kindergarten we were inseparable. We were finally done with the dramas of junior high, and we had plans for the entire summer.

"Then I get a phone call from your mom saying that they're all canceled. They're just gone. You were gone. You distanced yourself from me and then at open house, I see you've joined *Under Twenty*." I stopped to catch the shaking in my tone. "One second you were there, and then the next you weren't." He peered at me through the opening of his arms, his eyes angry. "You started smoking, hanging out with criminals, getting arrested and becoming a ladies' man. And before I could even take a minute to register it, you became a gang leader. People don't change like that just because they wanted to," I expressed. "I know there's a reason behind it."

"What makes you so sure?"

I inhaled deeply and released it. "The drastic changes in personality and practically everything else. You, the *real* you, wouldn't have done this." Sam seemed dazed, but regained his composure quickly. I was finally getting to him- it might've been small, but at the moment I didn't care. "Sam, you can trust me. You know I won't tell anybody." By his silence and mute responses, I firmly believed something in fact did happen. The question is, what was it?

His eyes dodged mine, reminding me of the aching pain in my chest when he avoided me that summer. The muscle in his jaw surfaced. "There's nothing to talk about!" He suddenly barked, causing me to jump.

I had ambivalent emotions, but anger filled me to the rim. Grabbing all the materials, I stood from my seat, wanting more than anything to leave. Sam raised an eyebrow as I stuffed everything into my backpack. He grabbed my wrist and I jerked away from him, slamming my elbow into the wall.

"Do you honestly not see how much pain you put me through, or are you just that oblivious?" I insisted weakly, not expecting an answer.

"Olivia-"

"Let go of me," I protested, not wanting to hear his response.

He grabbed a hold of a strap from my bag. "What are you doing?"

"What does it look I'm doing?" I spat rhetorically. "I'm going to finish the project. I'll put your name on it so we'll both be done with this," I said hoping that he'll let me go. "We can go on hating each other in peace," I said sarcastically.

He shot me a bewildered expression. "What is up with you?" I jumped at the rage in his voice. "I mean, one minute we're fine and working compatibly together, then you open your *big* mouth and start interrogating me!" Sam yelled.

"Well excuse my big mouth for deserving an explanation!"

His eyes were a dark shade of green. "If you keep bringing this topic up and not leaving it alone, I *promise* you things will never go back to where they were."

Slick, went another slash to my heart. "Why can't you-"

"Olivia, just shut up about this! How many times do we have to- I mean, did you ever stop and think, maybe I just ditched you for no reason? Maybe I just didn't want you in my life anymore?"

Another *slick*. My stomach clenched tighter, my chest ached uncomfortably. I had never really thought of that. Was that what happened? "I-"

I couldn't get another word out. I slammed the door shut behind me and clambered down the stairs, hiccupping from shoving down my tears. My steps thundered in my ears as *I'm done, I'm done, I'm done,* rang repeatedly through my mind.

"Olivia." A pair of calloused fingers threaded around my wrist. I shook my head and shoved my palm against his chest. "Olivia, stop. Come back inside."

I turned around. "Why?"

"I didn't mean to say that, okay, Jenkins?" His green eyes were less foggy, the anger not as apparent. He struggled for his next words. "I didn't mean it."

"Is it that hard for you to apologize?"

He released a slow, deep breath. "Let me make it up to you. I'll help finish the project. We only have a couple things left." I looked at the ground considerably, chewing on my lip furiously. "I know how important grades are for you. I promise we'll get an A."

I was seriously debating it. As much as I wanted to turn and walk away, I needed a top grade to please my parents. I crossed my arms and sighed, meeting his eyes. "I better not regret this."

The corner of his lips twitched in what seemed like relief.

~~~

A little bit later, Sam was jotting down the rest of the notes onto the poster as I designed some extra symbols. I wanted it to look nice and not too bare unlike the posters that were turned in early. Sam clicked his pen as he cocked his head and read over his notes, fixing any mistakes he could. His handwriting was proof to Miss Kay that he indeed *did* help.

His phone buzzed, making the table rumble. He picked it up and his eyebrows rose and a look of confusion stretched across his face.

"What is it?"

"Bailey, one of my exes, sent me a picture of her dress shopping with one of those ridiculous poses girls do. I think it's called the back-breaker."

I stifled a laugh at the pure horror on his face. "You look like you've seen a ghost."

"There's a reason why I broke up with her. She doesn't pull off short dresses."

Laughter bubbled in my throat and I couldn't stop it. He set his phone down, not even bothering to reply. "If you're broken up, why is she sending you photos?"

"You're a girl. You tell me."

I scrunched up my nose. "I don't know. Dating isn't one of my strongholds."

"Yeah, I've noticed," Sam commented. "You haven't dated much."

I refused to correct him: I haven't dated *at all* because of a certain black-haired, green-eyed, gang leader.

SAM

I was supposed to be finishing the examples on the poster, but my eyes locked on something else, or more precisely, *someone*. Olivia was interesting as she worked and I watched as her eyes darted over our project and her facial expressions, varying from her eyebrows coming together to biting on her bottom lip to her eyes glowing in satisfaction.

The question came from our previous conversation, and I don't know why, but I wanted to know. For some odd reason, something kept tugging me to ask it. I scowled at the air because there was a good chance it would cause more strife. However, instead of fighting myself, I licked my lips and took a giant leap.

… And that is where everything changed.

OLIVIA

"Can I ask you a question, and can you answer as honestly as possible?"

I looked up from the textbook. "It depends on the question, but sure."

"If I wasn't who I was and we didn't have this mess of a past…"

I waited expectantly. "Mhmm?"

"Would you date me?"

My eyes widened so much, they ached. *"What?"* I

replied loudly. "Where did *that* come from?"

He rolled his bottom lip in between his teeth. "Curiosity."

"Why do you want to know?"

"I just answered that. I'm merely curious."

I hesitated, searching for a reasonable answer. Why is he even asking this question? He has made it very clear nothing would ever happen between us so why the heck was he asking?

"You're hesitating," he muttered incredulously with narrowed eyes.

In desperation for a reply, I stupidly settled for, "I don't know."

"You're hesitating because you're afraid to admit it."

I raised an eyebrow, dampness on the back of my neck. "Admit what?"

"That you would."

My first instinct that someone might have told him about how I felt, but then realized that this was Sam Wayne; a player and heart-breaker. He would say anything to get he wants. My mouth opened to protest, but no words came out as I lost myself in his eyes. They reminded me so much of the ocean. The getting lost in the ripples of the waves, and the different colors: green, blue, gold. They were beautiful. There were things deeply hidden. Mysteries I couldn't solve. Maybe things I wasn't ready to see.

Sam lifted his hand and rested it on my cheek. I swallowed the lump in my throat as his thumb ran over my skin. My heart was anxiously flopping all over the place. This *couldn't* be happening… He leaned forward and I could feel his hot breath on my lips. I shyly leaned in as well and before I knew it, Sam Wayne's lips were on top of mine in a heated kiss that completely changed everything.

SAM

If someone asked what came over me in that moment, my reply would be this: I have absolutely no freaking idea.

It was like something snapped and suddenly I was kissing her.

Olivia's lips met mine and I was surprised by how we both reacted. I returned to that time in seventh grade where we kissed under the tree. Her lips were soft and warm back then, and they were now. I've had plenty of kisses since then, but Olivia had a rareness that only we shared.

Any worries about someone walking in on us were abandoned as I kissed her again. Her waves were tied up with a rubber band, so I pulled the band out and her hair tumbled down. Her arm encircled around my neck and played with my black locks. One of my hands curled beneath her knee, pulling her closer to me while the other cupped her chin.

Something ignited inside me, and I refused to acknowledge it.

Olivia pulled back from the kiss and mumbled, "Sam-"

Instead of letting her continue, I said, "Shut up," before knocking my forehead against hers with a crazy grin and capturing her lips in another fiery kiss.

THIRD PERSON

Ace and Ryker climbed the stairs of Sam's apartment building, laughing as they did. Welsh had granted them permission due to Sam's list of members allowed inside.

"I sure hope Sam doesn't mind us barging in," Ace said.

Ryker shrugged. "Well, we need to go over this new information. He won't care, but Olivia might be over since they're working on that project."

"Shouldn't they be done by now?" Ace glanced at his watch. "It's five o'clock. She may have already left."

When Ryker and Ace opened the door to Sam's apartment, they were expecting him to be sleeping, watching TV or digging through the refrigerator. What they weren't expecting was to see their gang leader kissing his math partner and so-called enemy:

Olivia Jenkins.

Chapter 11: Sam

The awkwardness filled the room as Ryker and Ace stared at me with their mouths open as I sat in my seat, elbows on my knees with my head resting in the palms of my hands. Olivia had already left. My best friends were having a hard time speaking, staring at me with bewildered expressions. I breathed out heavily, the scene replaying in moving images. I couldn't wrap my mind around what happened.

I heard the door open, but I was too preoccupied by the kiss and my brain had gone elsewhere. Olivia was the one to pull back and gasp when she saw who it was. I took a second to look at our surroundings. My fingers somehow, in the moment, got tangled in her hair and her arms were wrapped around my neck, but now rested by her sides. Olivia stood up quickly and started shoving things into her backpack. She mumbled something in my direction which I didn't quite catch before pushing past Ryker and Ace, who spun around looking at her, and then back at me with their eyes wide. The door shut behind her, leaving me stranded.

"What was that?" Ace exclaimed.

"What?" I asked, trying to act dumb. I wanted to avoid the topic.

"Why were you kissing Olivia?" Ryker questioned. Those words jumped around in my head. *Kissing Olivia.*

"I don't know," I answered honestly. "It just happened."

"You know how bad that could have been if someone else walked in?" Ace said.

I groaned. "My mom could have-"

"Dude, your mom wouldn't have cared!" Ryker said.

"What if another member came in?" Ace threw his hands up in the air. "I mean, they could tell the boss. You could get in serious trouble."

"It was nothin'!" I retorted.

Ryker scoffed, shaking his head. "Man, that wasn't nothing, that was *somethin'*."

I dropped my head in my hands. "I'm gettin' a headache."

"You know what the boss could do-"

"We're *not* in a relationship!" I interrupted him instantly. "It was... I don't even know how it started. It's sort of fuzzy."

"I can see Olivia made an impression," Ryker teased.

I glared at him. "If another member caught us, I would have to explain the situation to the boss. She's just another girl. She's nothing serious."

There were only two rules the boss enforced. First, stay loyal and do not turn your back on the gang. Second, don't get involved in a serious relationship. The second rule was occasionally broken. Ryker, Daniel, and I all have. If the boss ever found out, we would be in trouble. I don't know the reasoning behind the rule, but it's important to him to keep anything serious out of the business. I've only had one serious relationship, and that was when I was sixteen.

"Don't mention this to anyone," I ordered. They both nodded.

Ryker sat down in the seat opposite of me. "What's gonna happen between you and Olivia?"

"No idea," I said, balling my hair in my fists. I knew that stupid question would make things end badly. I ended up kissing her- the girl who I was enemies with, the girl who used to be my best friend. "Hopefully, we can forget about it and go back to avoiding and disliking each other."

"Go back?"

I looked up with an eyebrow raised. "Huh?"

"Go back? Have your feelings changed-"

"No!" I answered too quickly and I winced at how obvious it would sound if it was me asking the person.

Ryker shot me a pointed look. "I beg to differ."

"I don't have any feelings for her," I stated angrily, standing up from the chair. I walked over to the kitchen sink and gripped the edges, staring at the busy streets of New York. Her image appeared against my will: her wavy caramel-brown hair, her chocolate brown eyes. I found myself, for like the first time in my life, confused about how I felt towards a girl. I had no idea what I felt. She was annoying and bossy yet funny and, at times, sweet. But there was so much baggage between us, and I couldn't allow myself to reconcile with her because that would mean explaining things I wasn't ready to share with anyone; things that damaged me too bad that I could never be the same again. Despite those previous thoughts, I squeezed the counter tighter until my knuckles were white and whispered in the silent room, "At least I think I don't."

They left without a single word.

~~~

I walked down the hallway with Ryker on my left, talking about the English essay that was due in two weeks.

I haven't seen Olivia yet, considering first period hasn't started. We stopped by our lockers. The air outside was starting to get chilly, and I mentally thanked the person who turned the heat on inside. I threw my leather jacket in my locker and took out my stuff for math. After getting what I needed, I slid to the floor, still processing that I freaking kissed Olivia Jenkins Friday. Ace sat next to me, studying for his history test. Santiago strolled over to me with a small envelope in his hands. By the no return address, I immediately knew it was the boss.

Santiago and a few others departed for their first period classes. I opened the sealed envelope and pulled whatever was inside out. I had contacted his second-in-command Saturday about the recent activity of drug trafficking, the loss of members, and the chance of someone organizing it on their own. By his reply, I knew that what was happening.

*Keep stocking up. The runs are becoming short-handed.
I'll be coming in the winter. You find out who it is, do somethin'
if able to. Otherwise, I'll handle it myself.*

~~~

As Ryker and I walked towards our first periods,
we chatted about the drug deals and what exactly needed
to be done to end them.

"I don't know. I say leave the boss to it," he said. "I
mean, we can wonder and everything, but maybe it's just a
gang acting up. He can handle it."

I shrugged, gripping the strap of my backpack. "I
know he can. I just..."

"You feel responsible for the gang."

I nodded. "We're like a family, and you protect
your family. I'm the leader and I feel responsible for who
joins."

"How many have we lost?"

"Eleven."

Ryker sighed. "It's their decision to leave. You
didn't kick them out or force them to leave. They left
because they chose to."

"I know."

"Then stop blamin' yourself."

I glanced down at the floor. I can't *help* it. They're
my responsibility.

"Okay, before you go into that classroom, we need to talk."

"Aw, you're not breakin' up with me, are you, Smith?"

Ryker held my stare, just with a lot more seriousness. "It's about Olivia."

I straightened my shoulders, narrowing my eyes. "What about her?"

"I know you say nothin' is going on, but there have been too many occurrences for you to just ignore it. There is something between you guys."

Un-freakin-believable. I scoffed in disbelief. "There isn't-"

"Look me in the eye and tell me that's not true," Ryker dared. I swallowed hard, waiting for an argument to rise out of me, but nothing came. I couldn't say it. He nodded triumphantly. "Sam, she isn't some chick you've picked up in the halls or a classroom. You have a past with her. And you can call me a freakin' idiot, but you had feelings for her once- which is why you couldn't leave her alone. Why you've picked on her and messed with her all these years."

I stood there, breathing heavily.

"Now I think they're back." My hands and back of my neck were clammy. "And as your best friend, I'm telling you if you wanna be with her, then be with her. Nothing's stoppin' you!"

"There is!" I shouted, causing students on the opposite end of the hall to pause and stare. I waited for them to turn their nosy ears before turning back to him. "Ryker, I can't. It's not a possibility."

He lowered his voice. "Then do yourself a favor: kill it now."

And with that, Ryker smacked my arm and walked off, leaving me stranded with an assortment of thoughts and feelings.

I realized, with an urge to throw my fist in a wall, that Ryker was right. Though the things I felt were so small and barely noticeable, it had to be killed now. We can't be together. Being with her is just not an option, not a possibility. My jaw and head ached from grinding my teeth together so hard.

I finally regained my composure, rolled my shoulders, and entered math class. A pretty blonde shot me an interested smile. In an attempt to distract what was just conversed minutes ago, I threw on a smirk and walked over since I had time to spare.

"What's your name, gorgeous?" I asked.

She looked a little shocked that I came over here. "Mia."

"I think I've seen you around. I'd remember those legs anywhere," I winked.

Mia blushed; obviously a little nervous by the way she fumbled with her thumbs. Most girls were nervous around me. "Rumors say you're back on the market."

"Maybe," I said grinning. "Why? Know anyone who's interested?"

She shrugged not so conspicuously. "I might."

I leaned onto my elbows on the table, bringing my face close to hers. "Well, I might consider this hot blonde in my math class," I looked in her eyes, meeting a nice shade of blue. *But they weren't brown…* My brow furrowed at the thought and I tried to ignore it bouncing in my head.

"She might be available."

"Mm, maybe I'll call her and find out."

"Here," Mia slid a piece of paper into my hand.

I leaned closer to brush my lips against her cheek. "Thanks."

"Let's find our seats," Miss Kay ordered, coming into the classroom.

I turned on my heels to head to my desk and I stiffened when I saw Olivia already there. The kiss replayed in my head.

Avoiding any signs of interaction, I sat on the edge of my seat and made no effort to start a conversation.

Miss Kay wandered over to us with a smile on her face. That's a first. "Excellent job on the project." Olivia must have turned it in right when she got here. "A plus."

"Thank you," Olivia replied happily.

"Yeah, thanks," I said.

Our teacher quickly lost her smile and glared at me.

When she turned to walk back to her desk, muttering about how disrespectful teens were these days, I stuck my tongue out. Olivia laughed beside me and I glanced over at her. "What?"

"Your expression."

I chuckled. "I've wanted to do that for the past two months."

"Finally got it out of your system?" she asked, raising an eyebrow.

I nodded, drawing a small box on a blank sheet of paper. "Yep. Now I feel great." I then remembered the number Mia gave me. I took out my phone and added it to my contacts.

"Another phone number?" Olivia snorted. "How many girls' numbers do you have?"

"Only a few," I admitted. "I delete most of them after I dump them."

"Nice system," she said sarcastically.

I grinned. "I know right?"

She scoffed. "You're so-"

"Hot. Funny. Irreplaceable."

"Annoying."

I made a face. "Now that's just mean."

She rolled her eyes. "Leave me alone, Wayne, so I can do my work." Olivia pushed me in the shoulder and scribbled down an equation to answer.

We were silent for a long time as a new lesson was taught, and I didn't really like it. The kiss and my conversation with Ryker had overridden my thoughts and I kept glancing over at Olivia, wanting her to put the pencil down and talk to me. Wanting her to tell me that we could go back to normal and never speak or think of it again.

So when Miss Kay wasn't looking, I took initiative and tapped her on the shoulder, and when her attention finally averted from the board, I handed her a piece of paper. Olivia lifted an eyebrow but willingly took the note. I waited, bouncing my knee up and down. I wrote down

the homework in desperation to distract myself. This was agony! Then, after what seemed like hours, she gave it back to me.

After the bell rang, she gathered her materials and hurriedly departed from the room. Yeah, things were gonna be awkward for a while. Unless we'd agreed to wipe it from history and never let it happen again. When I opened the note, underneath my messy handwriting saying, 'we need to talk.' Olivia responded with, 'meet me in the courtyard right after class. ' I picked up my things and darted out of the room, finally being able to speak with her.

Now let's get this over with and resume hating each other.

I should seriously stop wishing for stuff.

OLIVIA

"What do you want?" was the first thing I said when he appeared from the school building. Okay, maybe snappy wasn't the best way to go. He probably wanted to talk about the kiss.

Sam sighed. "We need to talk."

"About what?"

"You know what," he simply replied, his emerald eyes fierce.

I already knew where this conversation was going. I didn't want to speak about it. The feelings I felt for Sam were becoming harder to handle. They wanted to control me; they wanted to come out. They were pressing against my stomach, but I fought against them, and I was losing.

And now with the kiss... they were jumping everywhere.

Everything would tingle when he looked at me. Butterflies erupted when he smiled. I would get goosebumps when those beautiful green eyes would lock with mine, and I hated myself for allowing these feelings to come alive. I should have fought; I should have told them not him. Anyone but him. Unfortunately, they latched onto him and I couldn't argue and say I felt nothing towards him, when I knew I did.

Without trying to be obvious, I, more or less, checked him out. He wore dark jeans that hung on his hips in a non-trashy way, and an olive-green T-shirt with his leather jacket. His blue and black bandana was wrapped around his neck, like usual. His black hair was windswept and it had grown in the past two months; his bangs almost touched his eyebrows when it wasn't gelled.

"What is there to talk about?" I avoided the burning hole my feelings were causing in my stomach.

Sam's eyes were cold and hard. "We can't ever let that happen again."

"Why? Because your reputation would get ruined if people found out you kissed me?" I sneered bitterly.

He ignored the comment, glancing down at the ground. "I just want to forget it and move on."

"What if I can't?" I blurted out without thinking.

Sam's head shot up. "What?"

I got a burst of confidence, knowing that it was now or never. "What if I can't forget it?"

"Then learn how!" He stepped closer, his eyes boring into mine. "Because it doesn't matter whether you do or not, Olivia... It's never happening again. And we're gonna forget it and act like nothing changed, because it hasn't."

"Sam, look at me, and tell me nothing has changed," I dared.

He sucked in his bottom lip, looking unfairly attractive. "It hasn't."

"Something *has* changed!" I argued. "Ever since that kiss happened," I took a deep breath. "Maybe even before then..." I let the sentence trail off as I gathered my thoughts. Sam stayed silent, even though his head must be whirling. "I do know..."

He seemed in a state of compunction as he said, "Do know what?"

"Things have changed," I confessed, "on how I feel about you."

SAM

Things have changed on how I feel about you...

Everything turned silent. We stood there, facing each other. I felt the world drop from underneath me. She was feeling different towards me?

No.

No. It can't be. I must have heard her wrong.

"What do you mean?" I'm surprised I found my voice. I prayed that what I heard was only my imagination playing with me. Please. *Please.*

Olivia stared at me, seriousness etched on her features. This was no joke. "Sam, that kiss did something. And I can see in your eyes that it's not just nothing."

I instantly closed my eyes. Please be lying. "Olivia, please tell me you're lying."

"I'd be lying if I said I was."

I choked back a nasty word, choosing to release a deep sigh. "So you have a crush on me," I spat.

"Sam," she shifted uncomfortably, "it's much more than that..."

My world stopped on its axis as the realization sunk in.

Olivia wasn't crushing on me.

She's in love with me.

Chapter 12: Sam

I stood there, letting the words sink in.

Olivia's in love with me.

No.

There's no possible way. Remembering what Ryker had said, I shoved whatever was rekindling towards her so far down, no light of day could shine on it. I couldn't feel anything for Olivia. I don't care how close we used to be in the past because it was the past. Everything between us was in the past. A place I can't return to.

"Olivia," I said licking my lips. I chose my words carefully. "You can't be in love with me."

She took a step forward and I retracted backwards, seeing a flash of disappointment cross her face. "It's too late, Sam."

When she moved closer to me again, I held up a hand in an attempt to stop her. "Olivia, listen to me!" I hissed. "You CAN'T be in love with me!"

The look on her face told me she wasn't expecting me to react this way.

Well, how else was I supposed to react? Did she want me to tell her I loved her too, when I don't? Did she want me to be happy and excited, when I'm not? I didn't love her- heck, I barely even liked her. We're two different people, looking for two different things. We're complete opposites, and there's too much baggage between us that I would have to explain everything to her- which is something I'm not gonna do.

"Why not?" The hardest question to answer.

I sighed. "Because…" I couldn't tell her the real reason. "You just can't."

Her eyes yelled hurt. Olivia pushed me away from her, anger fuming. "I don't even know why I told you. You're probably going to tell all your friends and start nasty rumors about me like you did freshman year!"

Freshman year? Wait, she's not talking about *that* still, is she?

"Hey, isn't that the girl you used to be friends with?" one of my new friends, Will, asked.

I glanced over at Olivia, who was chatting with these girls, Tammy and Maya. "Yeah, used to be. She's such a nerd," I smirked.

"You got that right," said another one.

Will winked at me. "She's pretty hot for a freshie."

I laughed uneasily, but they didn't seem to notice.

Evan, one of the oldest members, who happened to be a player, glanced over at her and a big grin came onto his face. "I wonder how many guys she's made out with."

"What do you mean?" Ryker questioned.

"Yeah," I said, raising an eyebrow, "what do you mean?"

He laughed and pushed himself off the lockers with his foot. "I mean, haven't you seen the way she acts with guys?" I shook my head. "She throws herself at them, not that they'd complain. She does have a nice body, and I wouldn't mind getting to know her better." He wiggled his eyebrows suggest-

ively. I knew it was lies. Olivia wasn't like that.

A part of me wanted to stand up and defend her, but I didn't.

So that's when the rumors about Olivia obviously flirting with guys started, and it eventually flared to hooking up, but I had no idea who said that. I didn't even know how to react to it myself. It dimmed down after a week when the principal found out and her parents said they were going to report the school for verbal abuse, but Olivia didn't speak to me for months. She would barely look at me.

"I didn't start those rumors," I said.

Olivia scoffed. "But you didn't stop them!"

"I had no control over it. What was I supposed to do?"

"Are you seriously asking me that question?" Her eyes flared. "Defend me! Not just stand there and go along with it!"

"I didn't go along with it! I had no-" I groaned, feeling a headache brewing. "Do you want me to change my reaction? Oh wait, I can't. It happened three years ago!"

"Oh, so you're telling me I can't be mad about rumors going around saying I slept with guys?" Olivia shouted.

I rolled my eyes. "I didn't say that! I'm saying I can't go back and change what happened. It *wasn't* even my fault! Why can't you just forget it?"

"How can I?" she retorted. "That ruined my freshman year! I was teased and bullied and stared at every day until summer came. Maya and Tammy were the only ones who stood by me that year while my best friend stood there and *let it happen*!" Olivia shoved me in the chest, making me stumble backwards. "That was when I knew you changed because the Sam I loved wouldn't have let that happen!"

Her voice cracked at the end and she became silent. I didn't say anything because I didn't have anything to say and I was still in shock by her admittance.

"I'm done. I am done," she declared venomously. I looked up and saw her eyes. They glistened with tears, and I almost reached out and touched her because Olivia was strong. She never let anyone see her at her weak moments, but I refrained myself from doing so. "I might love you, but that doesn't change the fact that you're a jerk and a bully; you're selfish and a liar. You can't imagine how much heartache you've put me through." *There are different types of heartache.* "Now do me a favor and leave me alone!"

After she finished, Olivia sent me one last look before moving past me; bumping into me roughly. I turned my head over my shoulder, watching her as she walked away. My fists were still clenched and I realized if I hadn't have done that, I probably would have hit her. Red dots filled my vision and I knew I was angry. I could feel it burning through my veins. Olivia disappeared from my sight as she entered the school building.

Letting out a frustrated yell, I kicked at the trashcan and it toppled over, its contents falling out. I ran my fingers through my hair, dropping to the ground in exasperation. That conversation couldn't have gone worse. I was hoping she'd totally go for the 'move on and forget' option, but instead, she had to go that route.

I yelled into my palms, wanting to get rid of my anger, my confusion; wanting to forget what had happened; wanting to get rid of these conflicting feelings dancing in my mind.

Punching in a message to Ryker, I typed,

Cancel meeting. Bring something strong. Need to relax tonight- S

On it -R

~~~

"I'm done, man," I drawled, stretched out on the garage's couch with one leg dangling freely. Ryker lay on top of one of the car's hoods, taking a long drag of cigarette. "I'm just done."

He chuckled. "You've said that before and you've kept on."

"No!" I sat up abruptly, pausing to stop the spinning in my head. "I want *nothing* to do with her anymore."

His toned face was surprised. "You serious, man?"

"I'm tired of this tug of war," I said harshly, staring at the liquor bottle in my hands. "So yeah, I'm serious. Absolutely nothing."

And with that, I swallowed the last drop and wiped my mouth.

Chapter 13: Olivia

I sat on my bed, hugging my knees to my chest and flipping through my favorite book. The papers were old and raggedy, considering it had been my mother's copy.

I'm emotionally drained. First, Sam Wayne, and the huge fight we had in the courtyard. Second, my brother forgot to tell us he had plans last weekend so that's why he didn't show up, and is deciding not to come until next weekend. And third, my parents were inviting some of Dad's co-workers and their wives over for dinner.

Yay...

"Olivia?" someone whispered in the silence. I looked over and my brother was poking his head inside. "Can I talk to you?"

I nodded, patting the spot in front of me. "Come on in."

Parker shut the door behind him and walked over. He poked me on the elbow. He knew I hated that, but I made no effort to scowl or say anything against it. "What's going on?"

"Are you okay?"

I forced a smile on my face. I didn't want my little brother worrying. "Yeah, I'm fine. Why you asking?"

"You just seem sad," he said wrapping his arms around his knees. "Ever since that Sam guy came over, you've been different. I mean, you haven't even had ice cream the past few nights. I know you're upset when you ditch ice cream."

I laughed softly. "Senior year is proving to be harder than I thought. I'm okay though," I ruffled his hair. "Thanks for checking on me."

"You're my sister. It's my job," Parker grinned.

"Well, let's talk about you. How are you doing?"

He shrugged, picking at my blanket. "School's alright. I don't think my teacher believes in recess. She's always forcing us to stay in longer."

"That's messed up. Recess is supposed to be your break."

"Exactly!" Parker exclaimed.

I leaned back against my pillow, placing my book gently beside me. He continued messing with the blanket, eyes glued to the floor. "Why is Dad always working?" He asked suddenly.

"I don't know, kid. He's been like that since I could remember. He really likes to work. He wants to support his family."

I hated making excuses. I've done it my entire life.

"But he never spends time with me," he said solemnly.

A frown dipped my lips. "I'm sorry, bud."

"I ask him to play video games or Legos, but he never does it."

"I'll play with you sometime," I offered.

Parker's face brightened. "Really?"

"Yes," I promised.

My bedroom door opened and we both turned our heads. Our father waltzed in, wearing black slacks and a sky blue button-up. "There you two are."

We both shifted uncomfortably, and I was wondering if he had overheard any of our conversation. "What's up?"

"Our guests are here. I'd appreciate it if you guys would stay up here."

"I have Minecraft loading," Parker said.

I rubbed my wristbone. "Tammy's coming over."

"Alright."

With no wave or a *"have a good night"*, our father left my room.

~~~

Tammy's eyes widened as I finished explaining the entire Sam fiasco. The pieces of popcorn dropped out of her mouth onto my carpet. *"What?"*

I shushed her, covering her mouth. My father's co-workers were downstairs and they hate to be interrupted. "I'm not even supposed to be telling you this!"

"Yeah, like Sam doesn't tell his buds everything," Tammy took a bite out of the Cookies 'n' Cream tub.

I sprayed some whip cream into my mouth. "Probably only Ryker," I replied with my mouth full. Some dropped out and Tammy laughed, wiping it off my chin.

"What's going to happen between you two?" she asked.

I shrugged. "I hope he actually listens to what I say. I'm done with him, Tammy! After graduation, I'm leaving New York and never seeing him again. I want to get out of here. Like now."

She nodded, eating a cherry. "Yeah, I know you hate it here. With your parents and the Sam drama."

I didn't respond. She took that as an agreement.

"You know, Sam used to be my getaway. Whenever I went over to his house, it was like these chains left; I was free. I could be myself. And then I would go home, they would always reattach. Sam knew what to do to get me cheered up. He knew what to do when I was hurting-emotionally. That's the Sam I miss," I paused, his image floating in my head. "I hate the new him."

I heard my voice crack. Tammy grabbed my hand in a sisterly, encouraging way and I smiled at her. She would always listen to me while I vented. She and Maya were the only people who saw pieces of the real me. The one hidden behind fake smiles and tough, guarded walls. But there were still some things left unsaid…

"I just hope he doesn't spread it around," Tammy said.

"Are you a mind-reader?" I teased.

She laughed. "Not that I can recall. I don't have other people's thoughts floating around in my head."

"I'm praying that he won't," I referred to our previous conversation. "That would be a whole new level for him."

She sighed. "I guess we'll find out Monday."

"It's going to be nagging me if I don't find out though," I admitted.

"Call him."

I frowned. "What part of 'I am done with him' don't you understand?"

"It was all I could come up with."

I sighed, rubbing the crease between my eyebrows. "I know. I'm just stressed out."

"Why don't we kick back and relax? Forget Sam. Forget your parents. Forget homework," Tammy leaned back on her bean-bag, blonde hair bouncing free from her messy bun. "Let's eat junk food until we puke and watch horrible television until we die of laughter. Hey, let's even have Parker join in on the fun."

I turned on the TV. "The perfect night."

"Indeed it is," Tammy smiled before jumping up and leaving to retrieve my little brother from his world of Minecraft.

~~~

I'm going to be totally honest.

When I walked into school Monday, I expected Sam to be at my locker, waiting to pick a fight with me or something, but there was nothing. He was chatting with Ryker on the other side of the hall. With a laugh, he glanced around the school and his eyes landed on me. Instead of striding over or smirking, he dropped his gaze and stalked off in the opposite direction.

That was a first.

I couldn't decide if I was relieved because he was finally leaving me alone after all this time or heartbroken because I had lost him for good.

Tuesday and Wednesday it was the same. He ignored me in the halls and was never in Geometry. I knew he was ditching because I would see him in the courtyard with Ryker and Ace at lunchtime and free period. Miss Kay must have been enjoying not having Sam in her class because the homework load had been decreased. I was grateful for it, and I'm positive other students were as well.

Sam finally showed up Thursday, escorted by the principal himself. The tension was so incredibly thick. He was grouchier than ever with Miss Kay, and I just wanted to sprint out there in embarrassment. We never spoke, not for a murmur or an insult. We kept a monumental space between us, enough room to not bump elbows and our workload didn't cross into each other's.

When Friday came, I was counting down the hours to the weekend. Waiting for first period to start, I was standing at my locker, reading a book as Maya and Tammy talked in front of me. Maya was telling us about how awesome her week has been, and I barely engaged in the conversation. The halls were buzzing with anticipation considering Under-Twenty wasn't roaming the halls yet.

When I looked up from my book to give my eyes a much-needed break, I immediately froze. Why did I always have bad timing? Sam and his friends were entering the building, laughing and chatting amongst themselves; his black and blue bandana wrapped around his neck as he talked with Ace. I watched as a girl- I recognized her from math class; the one who gave him her number, walked up to them and ran her hand across his arm and Sam grinned. He wrapped an arm around her waist and kissed her.

After the girl practically skipped away, he glanced in this direction with a cocky smirk and I realized he knew I'd be watching. It was an act of revenge. I sent him a disbelieving look and Sam stared back coldly until Ryker tapped him on the shoulder, breaking the connection.

"Olivia, Olivia..." I heard someone say in the background.

Maya snapped her fingers in front of my face. I jumped. "What?"

"What were you looking at?" She turned her head and sighed. When she faced me again, she had no emotion in her face. "Olivia, why are you wasting your time with him?"

I was taken back by her sudden harshness. "Excuse me?"

"You heard what I said," she snapped. "Don't play dumb with me."

Tammy looked confused as I was. "Maya, what-"

Maya scoffed, not allowing her to finish. "Tammy, stop defending her. She can fight her own battles." We were both too shocked to reply. "I'm sorry, Olivia, but I wouldn't be wasting my time on a guy who is never going to change back to the way he was. The old Sam is gone. If you wait for him, you're just going to get more hurt."

"Where is all this coming from?" I asked, still in shock.

"I've been thinking about it for a while and I'm finally telling you. You shouldn't wait for him anymore. He's *never* coming back. The Sam you fell in love with is not here. He is gone."

Tammy stared at her in disbelief. "Maya..."

"What?" She turned to look at Tammy and I took that moment to catch my breath. She was supposed to be my best friend so why- I gulped down the large lump in my throat. Why was she treating me like this? "I mean, think about it! If your best friend changed and turned into someone completely different and treated you like you meant nothing to him, would you want to be with him?"

Tammy didn't answer.

I decided to speak up. "Maya, I've already thought about that. I don't want to be with him the way he is now. I don't care how much I love him or the fact that we have history," I informed her.

"Olivia, you're stupid to *ever* get together with him, even if he did change. All he'll do is hurt you."

I bit the inside of my cheek, trying to block off the tears. "I thought you were my friend," I whispered, not having enough strength to go any higher.

She just continued to tear into me. "I never thought I'd see you so incredibly pathetic and *desperate*!

Tammy gasped. "Maya!"

"So this is how you really see me?" I asked, my head starting to spin.

Maya scoffed, ignoring me. "I guess it shouldn't surprise me. You've always been like that. I mean your own mother left to get away from your desperate hands."

My chest crushing from the pain in my heart, I began to back away slowly.

Ditching my backpack, I headed straight towards the doors. I started to pick up the pace when Tammy began shouting my name. I ran into people, maybe even teachers, but I didn't care. My head was pounding; my knees were shaking. I pushed past the gang members and their leader, my throat burning. Tears desperately fought to leak out. I couldn't break, I couldn't break.

Not here. Not here.

"Olivia!"

I recognized the deep voice, but I didn't look back.

"*Olivia!*"

Keep running. I needed to get out of here.

As I burst through the doors and towards my car, sobs were racking through my entire body. Everything with Sam and my parents and now Maya was getting too much for me to handle. I couldn't do it anymore!

I hated everything. I hated the love I had for Sam. I hated Sam for causing me so much grief and heartache. I hated my parents for neglecting me. I hated my brother for

being so perfect. I hated myself for not being the perfect child, the perfect friend. I hated myself for loving Sam. I hated myself for helping my mother leave.

I just hate myself…

My chest ached with all the overbearing feelings.

I began to sink to my knees beside my car, allowing the hatred and sadness and anger and pain and rejection wash over me. Tears streamed down my cheeks, and I did nothing to stop them.

But before my knees touched the asphalt, strong arms wrapped around me, pulling me into a warm embrace and against their chest. The person brought me to the ground, my head buried deep into their T-shirt.

"I can't, I can't," I repeated with hiccups. "*Please* I *can't-*"

And just like that, I snapped and let myself break.

I sobbed manically. I couldn't stop the tears. They just kept coming and coming. Everything that I've had bottled up for years came tumbling over me and giving me more excuses to cry. I curled my fingers in the person's shirt, yanking them closer and drowning in the feeling of someone comforting *me*; someone finally seeing how *broken* I was from being neglected to losing my best friend and possibly having to accept the fact that he could be gone forever.

After what seemed like hours, the tears finally stopped. My throat was dry and burning; my cheeks were red and puffy. When I realized that I was sitting in someone's lap, I tensed up, wondering who it was.

Who was it that saw me at my weakest moment?

Shyly, I glanced up to get an answer. The sun blinded me, but I caught glimpse of a blue and black bandana, black hair like the nighttime sky, and beautiful emerald eyes filled with concern.

Sam.

The gang leader who used to be my best friend, who betrayed me and caused me most of my stress, was cradling me against him.

He just let me cry. Let me get it all out.

And I was so grateful.

Chapter 14: Sam

I don't know what came over me.

But when I saw Olivia running out of the school with tears pouring down her face, I knew something was wrong. She never let anyone see her cry. She was too strong.

Instead of watching her like everyone else was and doing nothing to help, I felt something stirring inside of me, telling me to go after her. Comfort her.

That is exactly what I did.

I threw down my backpack and chased after her; not caring if people saw or started asking questions. I came into contact with the sun-soaked parking lot and my eyes caught her nearing her car. I started to sprint, and when she was about to collapse, I wrapped my arms around her tightly, pulling her close against me.

I sat down with her in my lap, her body trembling against mine. She kept saying *I can't* until abruptly, she started sobbing uncontrollably; heart-wrenching sobs muffled by my T-shirt. Olivia buried her head in my chest, letting her guard down and allowing herself to let it all out. I've never seen her cry like this.

After a while, Olivia managed to stop the tears, but her body was still shaking from the aftermath. Almost shy like, she looked up and the sun shined into her brown eyes, lighting them up. Her cheeks were puffy and her eyes were swollen, but she still looked beautiful- wait, what?

Why did I just call her beautiful?

I shook the thought of my head, mentally pinching myself. She stared at me for a few more seconds before taking a deep, shuddering breath. She slid out of my arms and onto the concrete next to me.

"Thank you," I heard her mutter after a moment of silence.

I looked over to see her playing with her thumbs, avoiding eye-contact. She wiped at her cheeks. "What happened?"

She sighed. "You wouldn't want to know."

"I wouldn't have asked if I didn't want to know."

Olivia sighed again. "Maya and I got into this argument about..." She took a hesitate breath. "Um, she just said some pretty hurtful things. I've been having a rough past couple of months, and the dam just broke today."

I sucked in a breath through my teeth. "Well, that sucks."

She gave a weak laugh, rubbing her eyes. "Yeah, it does."

"Do you want to do somethin'?" I prompted suddenly.

"Like what?"

I shrugged. "Anything."

"We have school-" she began to argue.

I shot her a look, immediately shutting her up. "You just had a very intense moment, which people will be talkin' about." Her face paled. "I don't think school is the best option for you right now. And besides, you need some cheering up."

"And you plan to do that?" Olivia asked, raising an eyebrow.

I grinned, pushing myself off the ground and standing above her crossed-leg form. "I'm the freakin' best at it." I held out my hand, waiting for her to take it. Her eyes looked at my hand reluctantly. "You have two choices. Go to school and get asked several questions or go somewhere to get your mind off of things."

"But tomorrow, people will-"

I bent down, meeting her eyes. "Would you rather deal with it while you're still emotional or deal with it when you've thought about what to say?"

Olivia bit her lip, contemplating what I just said. If she goes to school now, everyone will want to know what happened and trample her. If she waits until tomorrow, it gives her some time to think about what to tell everybody.

She took a deep breath and slid her hand in my palm. I stood up to my full height, pulling her up with me, and we stood facing each other. We were only inches apart and I could see puffiness around her eyes from her breakdown. A few strands came loose from her braid and I reached forward, brushing them behind her ear. Olivia smiled faintly and I was slammed with the thought of *she's in love with me.*

She broke the stare, grabbing her keys from her pocket.

"What are you doin'?"

"Getting my keys," she deadpanned.

I rolled my eyes. "I know that, genius. But we're not taking your car."

"Then what am I going to do with them?"

A smirk made its way onto my face.

~~~

The wind blew through my hair as we rode through the somewhat empty roads of downtown Manhattan.

Olivia had my helmet on, and normally I would have two, but considering that I don't have a girlfriend at the moment, I only had mine. Mia is hot and stuff, but she's not girlfriend material. She's too clingy and way too girly for me to handle, which is weird because I thought she wasn't like that. Maybe I need to get my girl-odometer checked.

"Do you think Ryker will get the note and key?" Olivia asked when we stopped at a red light.

I nodded. "He should. He goes to his locker almost after every period."

"Why'd you leave it with him?"

"I trust him the most that he'll return your car exactly the way it is. Ace will write something on your windows. Trust me, I would know," I chuckled at the memory.

She laughed. "I'm not even going to ask."

"I wouldn't."

She tightened her arms around my waist as we went through the intersection. "I hate intersections," she muttered.

"Why?" I asked.

"I'm always afraid that someone won't be paying attention and run into me," Olivia replied.

"Don't worry, Jenkins," I patted her on the hand when I stopped. "I'll protect you."

She slapped me on the back. "Shut up, Wayne."

"Even if I do, I'm more of a man of action," I grinned.

She groaned, pressing her forehead into my shoulder blade. "Why me?"

"You love it," I teased but that stupid, annoying thought rang through my mind. *She's in love with you, man.* I cleared my throat, trying to past the awkward pause. "Where do you want to eat?"

"I'm not really hungry."

I heard my stomach rumble. "Well, I am so I'm stopping by Mickey's."

When I parked in the lot, Olivia hopped off and together, we walked into the crowded restaurant. The lines weren't long, but there were plenty of people. I saw a few elderly couples and two sets of parents staring at me with judgmental eyes. One of the dads lifted their child onto his shoulder.

I knew why too. The U20 bandana was tied around my neck.

After I ordered enough food to feed an entire

population- Olivia's words, not mine- the beautiful girl beside me ordered a large drink and two blueberry biscuits with extra icing. Okay, I'm not gonna lie. Olivia is obviously a beautiful girl. She just didn't show it off. She doesn't have to wear designer clothing or wear make-up to look pretty unlike other girls.

In the last four years, I've never actually took the time to look at her. I've always tried to put the past behind us- and most of the time, it just came and slapped me in the face- and I've tried to forget the small crush I had on her in sixth grade. Ninety-eight percent of the time, I can push it away and forget about it, but sometimes, I could feel it return. It doesn't control me because I get drawn to other girls, and because there's too much history between us. I couldn't ever be with her.

But now that I'm looking at her, I really saw her. Like every little thing. The few dark moles on her neck and the slight arch of her eyebrows. The curve of her upper lip and how her eyebrows were darker than her natural hair color.

"Sam?" Her voice broke my train of thought.

"Huh?"

Olivia handed me my tray and after I got what I wanted to drink, we sat at a booth, and I ate a few bites of my hashbrown before stabbing a bite of pancake.

"So anything you prefer to do?" I asked.

"I don't want to go home," she answered, taking a sip of her drink. "I don't want to face Dad or Melanie."

"We could go to my house," I offered.

"Will Leah be there?"

"Nah," I shook my head. "She's at work."

She wiped at her hands with a napkin, taking another sip. "I guess we could still go," she said after a minute. Olivia glanced up at me and I noticed the gold swirls in her eyes. "Yeah. Let's hang out at your place."

~~~

I parked in an empty space, shutting off the engine and waving at some of the kids playing on the sidewalk. Olivia slid off the back, stepping onto the ground. Two of the kids who weren't enrolled in school smiled at me. I returned it, ruffling their hair and chuckling at their protests. My pal Abby, who was seven years old and incredibly smart for her age yet doesn't act like a know-it-all ran over to me with a sheet of paper in her hand.

"Sam, I got a hundred on my spelling test!" she squealed, jumping up and down.

I laughed, fist-bumping her. "Good job, squirt."

Abby giggled. "Thanks."

"What're you doin' outta school?"

"I had a dentist appointment, but Mrs. Hall allowed me to take my test before I left. I'm about to go back."

"Don't let any boys mess with you," I tapped the tip of her baseball cap. "No makin' them go home with bruises," I winked.

"I'll try my best, only 'cause you said it."

I grinned. "See ya later, babe."

I walked into the lobby, and one of the college students who lived here with his sick mother was talking with Welsh, and I patted him on the shoulder.

"How's your mom, man?" I asked genuinely. He was going through a rough patch, and pretty much everyone who lived here were like family. At least to my mother. Most adults couldn't stand me.

He shrugged. "Doing better, I guess. She can stand, but only for a few minutes."

I didn't know what else to say besides I hope she gets better and not to hesitate for any help. He shot Olivia a nice smile before leaving.

Welsh quirked an eyebrow. "Shouldn't you be in school?"

"Rough morning." I didn't clarify if it was me or Olivia.

As we trudged up the stairs, she said, "I have a question for you."

"Shoot."

"Why are the kids here so sad?" she asked, not trying to sound rude.

I sighed, ruffling my hair. "Because these kids don't get a lot compared to rich kids," I glanced over at her and saw her messing with hem of her T-shirt. "Every person that lives here, besides the elderly, have to work for a living. Some have absolutely nothing. Others are passing by. Some are struggling." I stopped for a second to fish my keys out of my pocket. "My mother and I, for example, are one of the families struggling."

"Is that why you're in a gang?" Olivia inquired.

I stiffened; staring at my apartment door's faded numbers. By the silence, we left the subject alone.

I unlocked the door, walking straight to the kitchen. Sam's hungry, and he's hungry now. Yeah, I know I ate not only ten minutes ago, but I skipped dinner last night. Bad mistake. I heard the door shut behind Olivia, and I searched for food in my fridge, my stomach jumping for

joy at the sight of leftover homemade chicken soup. It was the most appetizing thing in here besides an old jar of jelly and milk, which I don't drink. I mentally added grocery shopping to my list of things to do as I grabbed two water bottles from the bottom of the fridge. I closed it, turning around to throw one at Olivia, but froze, inwardly cringing.

Seeing her at the dining table, in the exact same seat, caused me to visual the kiss. Her lips on mine and hands tangled in my hair; me pulling her closer. I blinked repeatedly to get the image out of my head. I busied myself by pouring myself a small bowl of soup and heating it up. The aroma from the broth filled the kitchen. After it was done, I sat down at the table, avoiding eye-contact as I handed her a water bottle. I could feel her watching me.

"You okay?" she asked.

I nodded, taking a bite of the soup. "Yeah."

Olivia cleared her throat and I looked up, hating myself for doing so because I caught a hold of her brown eyes. "Thanks," she said, "for everything."

I nodded again. "You're welcome." I then leaned forward, resting my left elbow on the table and stirring my soup with the other hand. "So, can I ask you somethin'?"

"You just did," she remarked.

I rolled my eyes. "I'm being serious."

"So am I."

"Do you have to be your usually annoying self right now? I'm tryin' to be nice-"

"You being nice? Never knew that was even in your nature."

"You know, I didn't have to follow you." Her eyes softened, like she remembered what happened. "I could have left you alone... but I didn't," I crossed my arms, leaning back into the chair, looking away. "Now I'm thinkin' I made a mistake."

Olivia went silent, probably hating the fact I was right. "What is it?"

I scoffed. "Don't do it 'cause-"

"I'm not." She shook her head. "I want to know."

I bit my lip. "You mentioned earlier," I began, "that you've had a lot on your mind. I was just wondering what it was?"

She looked taken back. "You want to know what's been going on in my life."

"Yeah."

"Just a little bit of everything." She was trying to brush the conversation off.

"Olivia," I said ignoring the soft tone in my voice, "Tell me what's up."

"Sam-"

Our eyes locked; green on brown. "Tell me."

She looked down at the table, tracing the different shapes on the cover. "Things are going on at home. Max's at college, and my parents are just shoving comparisons in my face every day," she said bitterly. "Max has these grades, has these credits, and has this, has that..." Her voice sounded different. I released my hardened expression, adopting a much more relaxed one. "My parent's just don't understand that I'm not him, or understand that I don't want the same life." She closed her eyes.

"I have college applications to finish filling out, tests I need to study for, projects to work on, essays to be finished. I'm always one step ahead, to make sure I don't mess up, because I can't afford to mess up. My parents aren't even going to put a dime towards college funds. Why? Because Max got a scholarship!" Olivia said sarcastically.

"I just have so much stuff going on at home and with school, and then add you and your gang making my life more complicated. With all the crap you give me and the rest that's thrown in my face, sometimes it just gets too much for one person."

Olivia finished her speech, and I sat there, going over everything she told me... *it just gets too much for one person.* I've known that feeling.

I didn't know exactly what to say. I'm not the person known to say 'I'm sorry' and I wasn't about to start now. There were only three people I've ever told those words to: my mom, my cousin Kerstin, and my brother, Tyler.

"I know what you mean."

Olivia's head snapped up. "How?"

I licked my lips, choosing my words carefully. "Not really with the whole school complications, but more with having to deal with what life throws at you."

"How would you know that?"

I stayed quiet. *Experience.*

"You know you can tell me anything. I know we're not really friends, but we're not strangers either," Olivia said.

I stood up from the table, grabbing my empty bowl. I put it in the sink and gripped the edges of the counter.

"Do you mind if I take a nap?" she asked, changing the subject. "I need to get out of this emotional stage."

"Go ahead," I whispered, not caring if she heard me or not.

I heard her get up from the table, the bottom of the chair scraping against the floor. I turned my head to see her grabbing the blanket off the side of the couch. She lay down on her side and pulled the blanket over herself, resting her head on the throw pillow. A smile tugged on the corner of my lips as she yawned, gripping the soft material to her chest. In less than thirty seconds, she was fast asleep and breathing softly in the silent room.

Our conversation replayed over in my head. Honestly, I didn't know how much trouble she was having at home. I mean, I've always known that she's had problems with her parents, and living up to an older brother who happened to be perfect in their eyes must be hard. Now add me into the situation…

I know I'm rude and mean and many other things, but there's a reason behind it. There's a reason why I am who I am. Olivia was correct in one area: I didn't use to be like this. I didn't use to be a player or a bully. Before the summer after eighth grade, you wouldn't catch me hanging out with gangsters or near their neighborhoods. I would avoid them. I'd have nothing to do with them.

But things change. People change.

Pushing those thoughts out of my head, I stood there, watching Olivia as she slept. Her hands were balled up to her chest and her face was free of stress. There were moments where she would move into a new position. Our couch isn't the best thing to sleep on, considering it being old and all that.

I maneuvered my way across the kitchen, entering the living room and heading into the direction of my bedroom. However, on the way there, I took the blanket off her and bent down, sliding my arms under her neck and knees, gently lifting her off the couch. She was as light as a feather.

I sat her down on my bed, giving her a more comfortable place to sleep. Olivia softly grunted, scowling in her sleep, and burying her nose into my pillow. I laughed quietly, trying not to wake her. Watching her decide whether or not to stay asleep or wake up was strangely adorable. I felt sort of like a stalker, but it ended quickly as her eyes fluttered open; her brown orbs searching around before locking on my kneeling figure. She smiled, her eyes sparkling from sleep.

At that moment, I didn't see the genius who was a teacher's pet and didn't like being wrong; instead I saw a beautiful and broken girl, who happened to be my former best friend nevertheless.

Something clicked inside of me when I lifted my hand and caressed the side of her face; my thumb stroking her cheek. Olivia closed her eyes at my touch. She muttered something that I didn't quite catch. My hand moved until it locked under her chin. I knew I leaned in, but I didn't realize what I was doing until my lips touched hers, making that feeling I had in sixth grade come alive and take over me.

OLIVIA

His lips on mine sent so many emotions soaring.

Sam kissed me again, harder this time, and I reached up, putting my hands behind his neck and brought him closer. His lips fit perfectly against mine, like a missing puzzle piece or a missing shard from a broken plate or window.

Suddenly, Sam pulled away, and his eyes stared back at me in shock. "I can't do this. This is wrong." His voice was strained like he was trying to convince himself.

Those two familiar words floated around in my head. "Why not?"

"I just can't," he whispered so softly that I barely heard him.

"Sam, I don't understand," I said utterly confused. "One moment you're telling me that I can't be in love with you and then you're kissing me!" He seemed lost from the world. "You're kind of sending me mixed signals."

He sighed, running his fingers though his hair. "You can't be in love with me."

I gritted my teeth. "Then why are you kissing me?" I hissed.

Sam glanced down at the ground. "I don't know," he sounded truthful, but a part of me couldn't help thinking that he was just playing me.

"You don't know?" I repeated. He nodded. "That doesn't explain any-"

"You *can't*, Olivia!" Sam snarled. "It's hard to explain, but you-me-we, we can't be together."

"WHY?" I asked.

He ignored the question. "I'm not right for you."

"Why are you so afraid to tell me?" I was getting aggravated.

His eyes turned cold. "I'm not *afraid*. You're not gonna like the answer."

"I don't care." Before I could stop myself, I ran my hand through his hair. Sam roughly grabbed my wrist; his fingers warm against my skin, and set them down on the bed covers. He shot me an irritated look.

"Sam..." I whispered, needing to know. His eyes flickered to my figure. "Why can't we be together?"

He let out a deep breath. I prepared myself for the answer. "There's a rule that forbids the gang, including their leader from having serious relationships. Our business could put them in serious danger. Possibly get them targeted and killed."

That just made me even more confused. "Then how come Ryker and Daniel have girlfriends?"

"They sneak around."

He's not making any sense. "Why can't we do that?"

"Olivia-"

"Just tell me!"

"I'm not in love with you!" Sam shouted, slamming his fists on the bed. Those words punctured my heart. "I don't feel what you feel towards me."

"I don't believe that," I said, swallowing the lump in my throat.

"Well, you should," he retorted, "because it's true. I don't love you."

"Couldn't have said that a little less hurtful?" I asked softly.

Sam shook his head. "You wouldn't have heard it." He stood up and walked out of the room, balling his hair into fists.

He wasn't telling me the entire truth.

I knew those eyes better than anyone else.

He may not be in love with me, but I knew he felt something different.

Chapter 15: Sam

A groan slipped out of my mouth as I traveled up the steps, trying to stay upright. The gunshot echoed through my ears. I had everything under control until that stupid bullet nicked my shoulder and something slammed me in the back of my head. I knocked weakly on the door, leaning against the brick wall beside it, my head pounding. I already double-checked to make sure that no one had followed me. No one should know where she lived.

The door opened. "Sam?"

My vision blurred. "Help..."

"Sam, what happened?"

"Bullet nicked... head hurts..." was all I managed.

"Let's get you inside..."

I didn't hear the rest. I collapsed to the ground.

"SAM!"

~~~

When I regained consciousness, the pain had lessened, but it had numbed my arm and it was stiff. My eyes fluttered around, taking in my surroundings. The small living area was painted a nice burgundy and pictures hung on the wall. A TV was playing a random cartoon and a fire was burning nicely, enveloping me with warmth.

I was lying on a couch, covered with a thick blanket. I tried to sit up, but my arm started to sting in pain, causing me to moan. I looked at where I was nicked, seeing the wound covered with a white bandage. My shirt was on the ground, stained with blood. I would just throw it out. My mom shouldn't have to worry.

"Sleeping Beauty awakens," said a feminine voice from behind me.

I rubbed my eyes with my good hand. "How long was I out?"

"Well, from the time you passed out on my doorstep- thank you for freaking me out by the way, and you need to stop eating so much. You're pretty heavy. You've been knocked out a few hours. I called Leah and told her you decided to visit. She sounded concerned but I covered for you. Again. Which by the way, this is like, the twelfth time I've helped you. Now pay up."

"Can I give you hugs for payment?" I grinned, looking over at my cousin, Kerstin, who shook her head.

"Nope. Sorry, bud."

I frowned, and not only because she didn't agree. Kerstin walked over, helped me sit up comfortably, and handed me a cup filled with water and a few aspirin after I situated myself.

"What mess did you get into this time?" she asked, sitting on the coffee table.

I swallowed the pain medicine before answering, "Tried to get some supplies and got shot in the midst. I don't know where it came from. They got my head pretty good too," I probed the swelling knot.

"Why did you decide to come here and not a hospital?" she inquired, sounding angry. "What if they followed you?"

"They didn't. I made sure of it," I assured her. "And hospitals aren't the best thing for me. I'm known around the neighborhood. They'll call the police."

Kerstin sighed, rubbing her forehead. "When are you ever going to learn?"

"Easy for you to say."

"What's that supposed to mean?" she asked, raising an eyebrow. Her grey eyes stared back at me.

"You live in a perfect world. Don't have to worry about financial struggles. Don't have to worry about making it to the next day. You don't have to worry about anything! Your husband left you with enough savings to survive!" I hissed, venom drenching my words. I wasn't angry at her. I'm just mad in general. This past week has been intense and long.

She gave an emotionless laugh. "Yeah. Great life, huh?"

"Kerstin," I began and she hushed me.

"No. No need to apologize. I get why you're mad."

I reached over and grabbed her hand. "I didn't mean to get mad at you."

"It's not a big deal."

"You forgive me?"

"Do I have a choice?" Kerstin teased, winking at me.

I grinned. "I knew you had a soft spot for me."

"It's getting smaller and smaller."

Hours later, we sat by the fire, wrapped in its warmth. My head and arm was still throbbing, but with the pain medicine and the excellent work by my cousin, the pain was bearable. It was silent, besides the crackling fire. Kerstin stared at the fire; the flames causing reflections on her face. I poked at the coals, thinking of my mother. Since she knew where I was, she wouldn't be fretting over whether or not I was safe.

"So, what's been going on?" Kerstin asked, pulling her knees to her chest. "A girlfriend? Any secrets you want to share?"

"No girlfriends. No secrets. Nothing's been really going on."

"What's her name?"

I was taken back by her question. "Who?" I asked, raising an eyebrow.

"The girl you like."

"I don't like anyone."

Kerstin shook her head, scoffing. "It's in your expression. What's her name?" When I didn't comply, she frowned. "C'mon, Sammy. I need to know. We've always told each other our crushes and things."

"There's no one," I answered. *Quit denying it.* I ran my hand through my hair, trying to get the annoying voice out of my head.

"Either you're denying it or it's my imagination."

Denying it. "Your imagination."

She didn't seem convinced, but she ignored it. "How's Ace doing?"

"He's alright."

"Is he still wrapped in the gang business? I haven't heard from him since last August."

I sighed. "Yeah."

"I was afraid of that," she whispered.

I noticed the sad tone carried in her voice. Kerstin stared at the cup in her hands, not bothering to carry on with the conversation. She let out a deep breath and looked over at the flames. I saw the outline of picture frames on the coffee table, and using my good arm; I pushed myself up and walked over to pick one up. It was a picture of all of us; Kerstin, Ace, and me. We were taking a summer vacation back when I was in seventh grade. We looked alike with our matching black hair; despite the fact Ace and Kerstin weren't actually related. We had different color eyes though. Ace had pale blue, Kerstin had grey, and I had green. Kerstin was six years older than me, but even with our age difference, we all used to be super close.

That was before a death separated us.

"Can you believe it's been two and a half years since Ethan's death?"

I swallowed the lump in my throat. "Yeah I know." I set the picture down; the memories flooding away from me. "A year since Erica's."

"And three and a half years since Tyler's," Kerstin muttered.

We were a broken family.

Ace's sister died in a hit-and-run.

Kerstin's husband died in the army.

And Tyler…

I stiffened at the memory of my little brother, stumbling to slam that door shut. Kerstin watched me sympathetically and walked over to squeeze my hand. I turned my chin and attempted a grateful smile.

"Let's watch a movie," Kerstin suggested tugging me to the couch.

I followed willingly, eager for distraction.

OLIVIA

"MAX!" I screamed when the front door opened and my older brother walked inside. He threw his bags down and wrapped his arms around me in a tight hug. "I've missed you so much!"

"I've missed you too, Liv," Max said holding me closely.

"You're… crushing… me…" I managed to say.

He chuckled and released me. He patted me on the head. "You've gotten so big."

I gave him an amused look. "I haven't changed that

much since June."

"You have to me."

I rolled my eyes, but secretly enjoying his playful comments. "How's college?" I asked, grabbing one of his bags. "Tell me everything."

"Great. A ton of awesome classes, the teachers are incredible, and there are plenty of pretty girls. First year of college is going even better than expected. How's senior year?" I must have made a face because he raised an eyebrow. "What happened?"

"Nothing," I answered too quickly.

He shot me a look. "Olivia... does it concern Sam?"

Max was the only family member I had confided to about my feelings for Sam. He hadn't once been judgmental, but totally understanding and a shoulder to lean on until he left for college this past summer.

I bit my lip. "We'll talk about it later. Right now, I want to enjoy spending quality time with my brother," I said smiling at him.

"Okay, but we're talking about it."

I shifted nervously. I really didn't want to explain everything.

After beating him at poker and watching our favorite movie, which we had the best popcorn fight ever, Melanie had returned home from work. She began making his favorite dinner, chicken stroganoff, and Max insisted on helping her. I sat at the dining table, listening to their conversations about dicing mushrooms and boiling chicken while I typed my History paper. Max said that he had to learn the basics of cooking since he lived in a small apartment close to the campus. He sometimes had girls over and impressed them with his cooking skills.

Parker was so excited to see his older brother. After my father talked with Max for a few minutes, Parker dragged him outside to jump on the trampoline. I transported my laptop outside to watch them interact. We always took advantage of this time, because after he left, it was hello to-

"Olivia!" Melanie shouted, popping her head out of the window. "Come set the dining table!"

"Could ask me a bit nicer," I mumbled under my breath before entering the kitchen with a fake smile plastered on my face.

When dinner was finally ready, we sat at the dining table and enjoyed the meal. Parker was chatting to our father about his latest invention with Legos. Max, Melanie, and I were involved in a conversation about Max's classes. He was part of a great class that supposedly had the greatest of teachers and remarkable lessons. I'm proud of my brother, but Melanie would wink at me, hinting that one day this could be me, and all I wanted to do was frown.

"All right, enough about me. Olivia, how's senior year treating you?" One of the reasons why I loved Max

was because he didn't like having the attention for long periods of time.

I took a bite of chicken, stabbing a few mushrooms along with it. "It's been fine. I'm acing all my classes, including extra-curricular. There are still annoying cheerleaders and perverted boys, but I honestly believe you'll never get rid of them."

He grinned. "No boyfriends I should know about?"

"No boyfriends."

"Olivia's been focusing on her schoolwork rather than fraternizing with hormones," my father added, sipping his iced tea.

I shoved another forkful of food forcefully in my mouth.

"Parker!" Max poked him in the shoulder and our little brother giggled. "How's Mortal Kombat? I've been practicing."

"I have been too. It's been way easier since Sam showed me a better way to learn the skills."

Everything went silent, even the clinks of utensils against plates.

"Sam?" Melanie repeated, her eyes locked on me. "As in Sam Wayne?"

Parker nodded. "Yeah! He's an awesome opponent!"

"That's great, buddy," Max commented awkwardly,

sending me a sympathetic sideward glance.

Melanie continued to stare at me with disappointment and anger. "You brought him to my house? You brought him near your brother?"

"I didn't have a choice."

"*You didn't have a choice*? What kind of excuse is that?" she demanded.

I shrank back in my seat. "I really didn't. We had a math project due and I-"

"You couldn't have done it anywhere else?"

"He showed up on his own. I honestly didn't plan on it."

"It doesn't matter! You disobeyed me!"

"It was for school-"

"Olivia, just shut up!" My father's baritone rang in my ears, smacking the table and making us all jump. "I am so tired of your excuses!"

I saw Parker's eyes water and lips tremble and I mouthed *go*. If I could at least save my innocent little brother's ears from harsh words, I'll take it.

Max laid a supportive hand on mine. "Dad, listen to her-"

"No, I'm so tired of her disrespect!"

"From what I can tell, she hadn't planned on it."

Our father scoffed. "That is a lame excuse. I want you to apologize."

"But I-"

"Apologize to your *mother* now!"

THAT'S IT.

"She's not my mom!" I stood up from my seat. "I'm sick and tired of this family's constant arguments. And I'm getting freaking tired of you calling Melanie my mom when she isn't!' I looked at my step-mother. "I'm done with you always ordering me around and treating *me* with disrespect because I'm not perfect like you or Max!" I glanced at my brother, trying to say with my eyes that I didn't blame him. He gave me an apologetic look. "I'm sorry I can't have it all together all the time. I hate that you don't see that I'm trying so hard to impress you every day!"

I turned towards my father, fury boiling in my veins. The hurt and hatred from years ago returned. I clenched my fists. "You don't even see how hard I'm trying to forgive you." My voice cracked. "I've been trying to look at you like I did when I was younger, like the hero I always thought you were, but I can't do it... because all I see now is a man that cheated on my mother and drove her out of my life. It was your fault she left, not mine so stop treating me like I was the reason!"

After those words surfaced, I silenced. The night of the roof, seven years ago when I told Sam about my parent's divorce, appeared in my mind.

"Just always know that you can come to me for anything. I'll always be here. No matter what," Sam whispered, wrapping

an arm around my shoulders.

I sniffled, wiping at my cheeks. "Thanks, Batman."

We sat there on the roof for a little while longer. Sam was admiring the stars, occasionally telling me a name and poking me to cheer me up. I stared at my hands, rubbing them together, trying to pre-occupy myself to stop the images. My mother crying, my father upset, their yells, and the truth being told.

I didn't know that Sam was looking at me until he brushed my bangs out of my face. His green eyes met mine and I could tell he was worried. "Are you all right?"

"No," I said dryly.

He bit his lip. "I know that. You just seem really pale." He brought his hand up to my forehead. His hand was cool against my hot skin.

The tears returned. "I'm thinking of the reason why."

"Do you mind telling me?" he asked softly.

I took a shuddering breath. One word floated around my head. "Pregnancy."

"Pregnancy?" he repeated. I nodded. "Is your mom pregnant? If she is, then I don't-"

"No, my mom is not pregnant."

Sam looked even more confused. His eyebrows furrowed. "Well, I don't think your father can-"

"My father cheated on my mom!" The words escaped. Tears began to fell. His eyes widened. "And he thinks the girl is pregnant."

Sam pulled me against his side, resting his head on mine, and whispering soothing words into my ear. "Why'd your dad do that?" I couldn't answer because I don't even know why. "I mean your parents... I'm so sorry, Olivia."

Even though we were ten, we both knew the definition of cheating and how it was wrong to get someone else pregnant that wasn't your wife.

About a month later, we found out that he was not the father of the baby and that someone else was. Yet that didn't stop

my mother from backing up her bags and leaving. My father tried to talk her out of it, but she didn't want to take a chance of this happening again. No matter how hard he begged and said they would go to marriage counseling, she still left.

I haven't seen her since I was ten years old.

I returned to reality when Max placed a gentle hand on my arm. I shoved it off and walked away, running up the stairs to my bedroom. I heard footsteps behind me and my no excuse-of-a-father calling my name. When I made it to my bedroom, I slammed the door shut and locked it. Parker sat on my bed, thumbing through one of my books.

"I'm sorry."

He faintly smiled and jerked his chin to the window. "Go."

I yanked my jacket from the back of the desk chair and zipped it on quickly. Pushing the window open, I hooked one leg over the ledge, hurriedly pulling the other one over when I heard loud knocking and Parker rushing to stall whoever it was. I landed on the garage's roof and easily climbed down the large tree beside it.

When my feet settled on the ground, I instantly started running. I didn't look back, not wanting to take a chance of my father seeing me.

I was tired of putting on a mask and pretending everything was perfect when all I wanted was affectionate hugs and warm smiles and parents who cared. Parents that asked me about my problems and helped me get through crazy high-school life and prepare for college.

Was that too much to ask?

After I declared that I was a good distance away from my house, I felt the familiar weight of my phone in my pocket. I scrolled through my selected contacts, contemplating who to call. Maya? No. Tammy? Maybe. Ace? No. My eyes stayed glued to one of the names I could never delete from my contacts, no matter how I tried. It was calling out to me; repeating itself over and over again in my head.

Swallowing the knot in my throat, I dialed the number and pressed the speaker against my ear.

"Hello?" His deep, rough voice said into the phone.

"Sam," I breathed out, grateful that he answered, "I need a favor."

Chapter 16: Olivia

I sat on a park bench, shuddering against the cold as I waited for Sam to pick me up. I was expecting him to decline and hang up, but he asked me where I was, and when I told him, he was already on the road. The stars were out tonight, reminding me of the night on the roof.

His familiar truck pulled up next to the curb and I pushed myself off the bench, walking over. I opened the passenger side's door and climbed inside his warm truck. Sam sat in the driver's seat, clad in jeans and a hoodie. His hair was messier than usual, but his eyes were as light as ever.

"Did I wake you?" I asked, taking in his appearance.

He gave a wave of his hand. "Nah, I was watchin' a movie."

Even though I didn't really believe him, I pulled the seatbelt over me. I rubbed my hands together to get warm. My fingers were freezing. The jacket I was wearing didn't do justice against the cold. Out of nowhere, Sam's black hoodie appeared in my lap. I glanced over to see him only wearing a long-sleeved V-neck.

"Sam-"

He turned on the heater on the highest it could go. "Put in on. Don't worry about me, Olivia. I'm fine."

"Thank you," I muttered pulling off my light jacket and switching it for his warm one. It was a little big, but I didn't care. I snuggled into the material, bringing my hands to my chest.

He pulled out onto a normally busy road. "Fine with my place?"

"Yeah," I mumbled, resting my head on the window. I watched as the lights passed. "Just get me away from here."

Sam flipped on his turning signal as we sat a red light. "Everything okay?"

"No," I answered chokingly, debating on whether or not to tell him. I did call him. I guess he deserved to know why. "My brother's visiting, and my family... w-we started fighting," I said, unsure on how to continue.

"About me?" I gave him a look that questioned his assumption. He shrugged reluctantly. "From all the times you've mentioned that your parents hate me, I figured it was about me."

"There were other things as well."

He turned onto a road, resting his arm on the seat behind him. "Anything you want to get off your chest?" I looked at him skeptically. "I promise nothing will leak out to the student body," he added with a crooked grin.

A smile tugged on the corner of my lips. "I kind of lashed out."

"Seriously?"

I brushed some hair out of my face. "Yeah, and I mentioned that I haven't forgave my dad for what he did."

"You haven't?"

"I've been trying to," I confessed, "but I ... just can't." Those vivid images of my mother packing her things and leaving in a NYC cab flashed in my head. "He hurt me so bad, Sam," I said softly, staring out the window. "He's never apologized, he's never- never asked me how I feel about Melanie. He didn't ask me if I was all right with him marrying her!" My voice crackled, warning me I was getting emotional. "He did what he wanted, and never thought about me or Max." I stopped to catch my breath. "It doesn't even affect Max anymore. He's used to Melanie and besides, he's never home. He doesn't deal with them like I do."

Sam looked over at me, his eyes scrolling over my figure. I brushed back my hair, moving it out of my face. He didn't need to say anything. All that mattered was someone was actually listening.

"Sorry," I said, meeting his emerald eyes.

He shook his head, glancing at the road once again. "Don't be. Everyone has a breaking point. And honestly, it's nice to know you trust me with something."

"Well you're the only one who knows all the details," I shared bluntly. He sent me a look of surprise and I gave him a genuine smile, one that brightened my mood. Rubbing my hands together some more, I timidly announced, "Can you... uh..."

Sam raised an eyebrow. "Can I what?"

"Can you hold me?" He seemed reluctant and my chest burned with emotion that I stumbled out a, "Please."

After glancing over and seeing my expression, he lifted his arm in a hugging gesture. "Come here."

I undid my seatbelt, scooted over and rested my head on his shoulder; warmth spreading through my body. He wrapped his arm around me, his hand resting on my back. He used his left hand to drive.

"Thank you," I mumbled into his shoulder, using the advantage to take a whiff of his aftershave.

"Yep," Sam murmured, watching the road.

I'll be honest: I never thought I would enjoy being in his arms as much as I did.

When we pulled into his apartment complex, I was almost asleep. The breeze of the heat blowing on my face, the gentle hum of the tires against the road, and with Sam's heartbeat thumping under my cheek, it created a lullaby. A nice, soft lullaby.

He pulled into an empty parking space, but instead of getting out, we sat there, letting the heat absorb us. The radio was playing softly in the background. It couldn't have been more perfect. His arm was still wrapped around me; I was snuggled up against his side. I never felt safer in my entire life.

I shut the car door behind me and stepped onto the sidewalk, heading towards the entrance of the building until I heard Sam gently say, "Wait."

I turned around to see him standing near the front

of his truck, his hands in his pockets. He sighed, letting out a smoke of air, and cocked his head to the side. "Can I show you something?"

I buried my hands deep into the hoodie's pockets. "Sure."

Sam held his hand out, a serious look on his face. I hesitated a mere second before taking a step forward and sliding my hand into his. His calloused skin rubbed against my soft palm and my cheeks warmed at the touch. He began walking towards the back of the apartment building. I was confused on why he was taking me back here, but I continued to follow him, trusting him exceptionally much.

Sam stopped in front of a familiar ladder against the side of the building. He pointed at it and I grasped the first bar, stepping onto the bottom step. I continued to climb with him behind me. My hands were sweaty and clammy and I swear I heard the ladder creak. I whimpered, hoping that Sam wouldn't hear me. He must have because he put a hand on my waist, steadying me. The warmth in my cheeks returned.

I finished climbing and my feet stepped onto solid ground. I realized with a jolt of happiness and appreciation that we were on the roof- the same one from all the times we snuck up here during our childhood. The sky was bright with dozens of stars and the city wore its usual attire for the late night. New York City was the city that never sleeps.

Sam walked over to the ledge and sat down, not afraid of the height. It didn't seem to bother him. As kids, we never went close in case of accidents. I wonder how many times he's been up here since then.

"Get over here, Jenkins," he said in the silence.

I lifted an eyebrow, wondering if I heard him correctly. "Do what?"

"I'm not gonna bite," Sam glanced behind him with an adorable grin. I was standing a little ways from him.

I took a deep breath, ignoring the list of multiple ways I could die. I walked over and sat down carefully beside him. My hands were shaking. Sam had grabbed my arm on the way down to help me, and his fingers strolled down my arm, stopping at the top of my hand before flipping it over and lacing our fingers together. My stomach erupted into flames and I swallowed the nervous knot in my throat. He had no idea how he makes me feel.

I looked up from our intertwined hands and Sam was staring at me with those beautiful emerald orbs. I bit the inside of my cheek, feeling bittersweet. I saw the corner of his lip tug up into a little smile. Even in the dark night, I could see his face and all his features. His thick dark eyebrows and nighttime colored hair. His slightly unshaven cheeks and the few scars on his face.

We continued to look at each other for whoever knows how long, and I didn't realize our foreheads were pressed together until a horn from whoever knows where broke my concentration. Sam awkwardly pulled back and faced the city, retracting his hand from mine. He rubbed the back of his neck, averting his eyes.

He retrieved a blanket from a secret stash, hinting he came up here on cold nights, and I pulled it around me, hating the winter weather. I looked over at Sam, and his eyes were glued to the bright lights. He was lost in his thoughts.

"So, how many girls have you brought up here?" A slight discomfort tugged at my heart. I wanted this to just be our roof, not a place for dates with other girls.

Sam chuckled, despite the slight awkwardness, and glanced over at me. "Actually… you're the only one."

Something swelled in my heart. "Really?"

He nodded. "This place is where I think," he confessed. "Thought it might help gather your thoughts."

"What do you think about?"

"Everything," Sam answered. "Life. The gang. The future."

I scratched the place behind my ear like I always did when I didn't know what to say. "Well, I'm honored," I said. "It's always been so beautiful and special."

"Yeah," he murmured.

Not knowing how to continue, I stared at the city, wondering what I should say or do. Should I leave? Should I start another conversation? I didn't know.

"Olivia," Sam spoke up in the dead silence and I noticed he was already looking at me, "do you want to hear stories about the gang?"

SAM

I turned my head to see her reaction and she looked shocked by my sudden question. To be honest, so was I… but for whatever reason, I wanted to share the stories. The stories about why people wanted to join.

"You can't tell anybody though," I said strictly.

Olivia nodded, her brown eyes meeting mine. "I promise."

I cleared my throat, debating on which member to start with. "Any requests?"

Her eyes told me the answer.

I shied away, hiding the door to those horrid memories.

"What about Daniel?"

"Daniel…" I licked my lips, searching through the stories. She ogled the view of the city. "He joined sophomore year, wanting to be apart of something. His parents abandoned him when he was young and was raised by his aunt, who most of the time is drinking," I sighed sadly. "During last summer, he asked about what we did, and when school started back he joined." I cracked my knuckles. "His story isn't very long. It's actually the simplest."

"What's Ryker's?"

I looked at the billion stars in the sky. "Ryker was twelve when his mother died from a brain tumor, and after her death his father turned into a drug addict. He was abusive, a bully, and Ryker couldn't run to anybody because his family is either criminals or serving time. He felt like nobody cared about him.

"He joined freshman year along with me, thinking that no one would care if he did. He met his girlfriend, Beth, who showed him what life really had to offer," I bit my lip, wondering if I should continue. It wasn't necessarily my news to share, but this was Olivia. She

wasn't a blabber. "He's gonna try to leave," I admitted, "and when you're in a gang, you can't get out easily. We're a family. You don't walk out. And if you leave, they'll most likely put a hit out and..." I cleared my throat. "But he wants to do it. He's going to. After graduation, he's gonna do one last run then leave. Change his identity. Move somewhere with Beth. Start a new life."

"Wow," Olivia muttered. "He's very brave. I'm sure you're going to miss him."

"Yeah," I nodded. "It'll be different."

Her shoulder brushed mine as she wrapped her arms around her knees. "Why'd Ace join?"

I shifted uncomfortably. "His sister died in a hit and run."

"What?" she gasped out.

I closed my eyes. "Two years ago, Erica moved up

here for school and Ace followed her. Their mother allowed it because they were really close." I ran my hand through my hair, remembering the call from the police. "She was out late one night and a driver swerved her car headfirst into a tree. He took off without a care in the world and there were no leads. Unfortunately, there wasn't any chance of saving her. Ace joined two days after the funeral."

Olivia looked brokenly at the view. "I never knew."

"Only a few people know," I replied. "He hated talking about it."

"I don't doubt it."

I leaned back onto the roof's surface, resting my hands on my stomach. The stars twinkled beautifully. I loved coming out here. It was relaxing after reckless weeks of putting your life in danger. Olivia didn't say anything else and I took it as we were done. The night was cool and silent except for the occasional honks and screeching tires.

"What kind of stuff do you guys do?" Olivia asked.

The answer rolled off my tongue instantly. "Boss has us in charge of weapon stocking and burning down the warehouses once we've hit them clean."

"Weapon stocking?"

"Guns and ammo, sometimes other things, depends on the order. We have to turn them in by a specific date. If not, I could get into trouble."

"Like serious trouble?"

"Not bullet-worthy trouble, but I get a *friendly* visit from the boss's guards. Maybe get a cracked rib or two. Like I said, depends on the order. Some are more valuable than others."

"And you don't participate in drug deals?"

"No, we're not a part of that." I paused in my gaze across the star-crossed sky to look at her with a cocked eyebrow. "What's with all the questions anyways?"

Olivia shrugged, sighing. "I just always thought gangs, specifically U20, to be only…"

"Dangerous? Intense? Scary?"

"Yes," she shared honestly. "But now I realize you're more than that."

My interest was definitely piqued. "What are we then?"

She glanced over her shoulder, pursing her lips as she thought. "Peculiarly meaningful." My eyebrows touched my hairline at the odd choice of words. "With the commitment and risks you're taking, you said it yourself; it's like a family. You protect and rely on each other. It's meaningful because it means a great deal to the members involved, and it's peculiar because you bond over committing crime. You use it as an outlet and to be a part of something. I'm sure there are a few that join only for the name, but by the stories of Ryker and Ace, I'm positive more join because they need a place to belong and to have some sort of family. To have a place of no judgment."

Leave it to Olivia to find a beautiful way to look at us.

"Now I'm sure it's not true for every gang, but for U20..." Her rich chocolate eyes flickered up to mine and I couldn't look away even if I wanted to. "You're not all monsters. Not all of you want to cast out murder and drugs and whatever else gangs are into. So therefore, you're peculiarly meaningful."

Despite my inner protests, my head began to swarm with thoughts about her. Her natural beauty, her flaws, her bright smile, her tantalizing eyes. Her voice, her face when she's angry, amazed, frustrated, confused, and her deadly talent to look hot when she's yelling at me...

Gosh, my thoughts were gonna kill me.

I mindlessly reached over and took her hand hostage, entwining our fingers and running a thumb over her knuckles. She smiled softly, her cheeks flush from the cold and I grinned. I knew she wanted to hear my story, but I couldn't bring myself to tell her. I'm not ready to speak about it. I pushed myself up, our shoulders brushing, and rested my forehead on hers.

I'd never admit this to her, but right then and there, I realized I felt something extremely strong towards her.

She was something else. I've met every kind of girl. Clingy, shy, obsessive, flirty, wild- Olivia was different from all of them. As we gazed into each other's eyes, it seemed like hours passed by. It was silent except the whirring from the heater and our mingled breath.

"Sam," she whispered in a way that drove me crazy.

Ignoring the invisible tugs on my arms, I cupped her face and leaned in, my nose slightly bumping hers. The action caused her to smile even brighter than usual and I closed the distance between our mouths. Olivia wrapped one of her arms around my neck, fingers knotting in my hair, and her other hand hooked onto my shirt. I deepened the kiss, loving the way her lips molded against mine. We continued to kiss until we physically couldn't anymore. I pulled away, my breath heavy and emotions reeling.

The realization slammed into my chest, the force strong.

I wanted to tell her.

I swallowed the giant lump in my throat.

I'm not ready yet.

If I can't trust Olivia, then who else can I trust?

It'll ruin everything. She'll find out and betray you. She'll tell everyone.

Her breath hit my face; our eyes locked. Rich and beautiful.

Don't do it. She won't understand. She'll be judgmental-

I *needed* to tell her. It was aching to get out. Pushing, clawing against my chest. I'd been drowning in it for years, and I was losing hold of almost everything of who I once was. I kept burying and burying that person down inside, desperate to hide the brokenness, and instead of releasing what's been torturing me, I've been covering it with a mask.

It was becoming harder and harder every day to reach the real me.

"Olivia," I muttered, taking a hold of her hands.

Her eyes- *focus on her eyes*.

I can do this. Just get the words out.

"Olivia, I'm ready to tell you my story."

Chapter 17: Sam

I'm ready.

I searched for the right words to begin with.

Olivia stayed quiet. My throat clogged up and my hands began to sweat. She tightened her hold and my bottom lip quivered from the nervousness. "Well, you know after my dad passed away, I took over the man-of-the-house position. My mom was working double shifts and I had to help take care of the house and Tyler," I winced at the name. She rubbed her thumb over my knuckles, not realizing that in less than a few minutes she'll never look or touch me again. "So when I was fourteen, two weekends after middle school ended and summer was starting, my mom needed me to run an errand..."

The memories swallowed me.

"Sam?" my mother called.

I walked out my room and into the kitchen where she was. I was finishing my entry for this summer's skateboarding competition before going to Olivia's tonight. It had to be turned into tomorrow or I couldn't participate.

"Yeah?" I replied. She shot me one of those motherly looks and I held my hands up in a teasing way. "Yes ma'am?"

She smiled and handed me a sticky note. There were a few items written on it. I raised an eyebrow, wondering why she was giving it to me. I already did my chores this afternoon. "Do you mind running to the store to get some milk? The others aren't necessary, but I would like you to get them. I need milk for tonight's dinner."

"Uh-"

"Oh, and can you get some more macaroni and cheese? I forgot to write it down."

"Um, Mom, I'm in the middle of something-"

"I think it can wait a few minutes."

"I need to finish this before I head over to Olivia's tonight," I said.

Mom put her hands on her hips. "Does it have to deal with life or death?"

"No," I said confused, "but-"

"No buts. I asked you to go to the store."

"I'm busy!"

"Don't interrupt me while I'm talking to you!" she shouted. I shut my mouth. "I just need some milk and I think our dinner is more important than whatever you're doing."

"But Mom-"

"Do what I say!" my mother ordered.

I bit my tongue and forced my next sentence down my throat. I turned around to head back to my room, and when I shut the door to change my sweatpants for a pair of jeans, I faced Tyler who was lounging on his bed. He was playing with his Nintendo DS that he won in a spelling contest.

"I need you to do me a favor," I said grabbing some spare dollars from the inside of our shared drawer.

Tyler looked up from his game. "Go to the store?"

"How'd you know?" I asked.

"I heard you and Mom yelling at each other," he stated plainly.

"Well, I need to finish my entry for the boarding competition tonight. I have to turn it tomorrow."

He shrugged. "Mom asked you to do it. She doesn't like me going out after six."

I sighed then sat down next to him. "Please, Ty. This is the only time I'll ask you to do this for me. Just for tonight."

Tyler stared at me with brown eyes, inheriting them from our mother. He paused his game and held his hand out. "Fine, I'll go."

"Thanks, little man," I ruffled his hair and placed the bills in his hand.

After he exited the room, I sat down at the desk and began answering the basic info about yourself and etc. On the third

question, I heard my mom call me again. And not in the nicest way.

"Samuel Wayne!" she screeched.

I flinched. That didn't sound good. I walked out of the room and back into the kitchen where my little brother sat at the dining table and my mother faced me with an angry look on her face. I looked around the room and slowly stepped in, my arms hanging by my side. I decided to play the innocent and dumb look. She must have seen right through it.

"I told you to go to the store, and instead you're going to send your little brother!" Mom yelled, eyes blazing. I glanced at

Tyler and he had an apologetic look on his face. I wasn't mad at him. "You better tell me the truth. You're already in enough trouble," she said.

I bit my lip. "I asked him to do it." Maybe if I'm honest, I won't be punished.

"Because you didn't want to stop doing your stupid project?" she asked. I didn't reply because sometimes I couldn't control my tongue. "You're grounded-"

"For what?" I yelled.

"For asking your little brother to get something when I asked you to do it."

I rolled my eyes. "It's just milk!"

"Don't you dare roll your eyes at me!" she shouted. "You're grounded for two weeks. No friends over, no TV, and you're staying home tonight."

"What?" I asked in disbelief.

"That's final."

"Do I still have to go get the milk?"

"Yes."

I sighed, pinching the bridge of my nose. "Why can't Tyler do it? He's almost eleven years old. I was going out way before his age."

She hesitated. "I just don't like him going out."

"Why?" A sharp sting pierced me in the chest. "Because you like him better?" I asked angrily, and deep down I knew she did.

"Sam!" Mom shrieked.

"WHAT?" I growled. "I know you do! You barely ackno-

wledge me, and if you do, it's to tell me to do something or order me around. Tyler never has to do anything! And I'm getting freaking tired of it!"

"Sam, honey-"

"No!" I said, not wanting to hear her sympathy. "He needs to take some responsibility in this family." And with that, I stormed off towards my room, slamming the door behind me.

"It's not that I didn't love Tyler or I didn't have a good relationship with him, I just did everything. I did the dishes, took the garbage out, cleaned the house, and got groceries. Since my mom worked double shifts, she wasn't home during the day and she was tired on the weekends. And I was angry that she grounded me for a stupid reason."

Olivia continued to stay silent, listening intently as I told the story. It was getting to the hard part.

The part where we found out what happened.

There was a knock on the door, but I thought it was my imagination since Mom didn't head to the door herself. I was sitting on the couch, playing Tyler's game, waiting for him to return. I just got done apologizing to my mom for my behavior and she accepted, apologizing as well. She was standing at the stove, stirring the vegetables in the frying pan.

The knock repeated, much louder this time. I lifted an eyebrow. I guess it wasn't my imagination. I stood up from the couch as my mother walked over to the door, wiping her hands on her apron. She grabbed the handle, opening the door to reveal two police officers. We glanced at each other, thinking the same thing: why are they here?

"Are you the family of Tyler Wayne?"

My mom nodded slowly, afraid to answer. "Yes. May I ask what's going on?"

"Miss," the older police officer stepped forward, looking saddened. "I don't know how to tell you this... but your son was shot." Those words echoed in my head. "I guess he was returning home and someone drove by and struck." The officer looked down and took a deep breath before continuing. "Miss, your son is dead."

... Is dead. I froze in the middle of the living room. My heart stopped, my lungs collapsed, my legs shook. I couldn't breathe. I couldn't move.

"What?" my mom asked. I could hear the trembling in her voice. Her bottom lip was shaking. "Please. Please, tell me it's not true."

"Miss," the second officer said, "I'm sorry-"

She shook her head, wanting it not to be true. Tears were streaming down her cheeks. She kept trying to speak, but there was no sound. I stepped towards her, my legs still wobbly, and took her into my arms. She began to sob horribly into my chest and I tried my best not to break down myself. The officer took her from my hold and I became dizzy.

Somehow I made it to my bedroom, and before I could reach the bed, I collapsed to the floor, my knees not able to support my weight. I started hyperventilating, gasping for breath. I leaned forward, my forehead touching the carpet, and I didn't care who heard or saw me, I started crying, shouting, cursing, wheezing; I was losing myself. If I hadn't argued and acted selfishly and told him to go, he would be alive. He would be here. He died because of me. I held my stomach tightly, trying to stop the knot from taking over. The knot of guilt.

Tyler was dead.

And it was my fault.

I stopped talking.

My throat was clogged and I couldn't continue.

Olivia grabbed my hand tightly. "Sam..." she whispered, "I'm so sorry."

I bit my lip so hard that it began to bleed. "His death was my fault. If I hadn't have yelled at my mom or told him to go, he would still be here." I was letting everything spill. No more secrets. No more lies. "If I went, I might have had a chance of surviving. Maybe it wouldn't have happened. I don't know! All I know is that I told him to go. I argued with my mom. I was selfish. I sent him to his death!"

"Sam-"

"Olivia, *I sent him out!*" I yelled. I let my guard down. The tears I've been holding in for years came running down my cheeks. "He died because of me. All because of me..."

Tears filled my eyes, desperate to get out. I've never told this story to anyone, and I was envisioning everything again. I dropped my head into my hands; hiding my face. I knew what Olivia thought. She blamed me too. Everyone blames me.

I felt hands tug at my wrists, but I fought against them. She hated me. She had to. Olivia eventually locked onto my wrists, bringing me close to her in the process. Instead of keeping it together like I've had for the past three and a half years, I broke.

Olivia cradled my head to her chest, allowing me to release it all. I wrapped my arms around her, sobbing into her shirt. All the guilt clouded me and I wanted to fight it off, but I was too broken to do it. This is the first time I've ever broke down since that night. I've locked away all of the emotions, and tonight, everything crashed onto me. It felt like a tidal wave had grabbed a hold of me. I was caught in the impact zone and I couldn't resurface. I was drowning.

Olivia whispered soothing words into my ear, running her fingers through my hair. She didn't do anything to stop me. She just sat there and held me as I did a couple days ago when her breaking point shattered.

After what seemed like hours on end, I swallowed the large lump in my throat. My cheeks were dried with tear stains. It was so hard talking about this, but I had to finally tell somebody. And for some reason, I felt a tug to tell Olivia, the girl who stuck by me when my father was killed in the fire. The girl who was my best friend for years. The girl who I had turned my back on when said events occurred.

"Sam, listen to me. It wasn't your fault."

"Yes, it was." I didn't want to hear those lies. His

death was on me.

Olivia lifted my chin and forced me to look at her. How could she stand to look at me, knowing what I had done? "No, it wasn't. You had no idea that was going to happen. No one did."

"But *why him*? Why him, of all people? Why'd it have to be my brother?"

"I don't know," she whispered. "But I do know something. His death was not your fault."

"How do you know that?" I asked, wanting to believe it, but I couldn't...

Olivia's fingers touched my lips, smiling brokenly. "I just do."

I closed my eyes, taking deep breaths. Olivia moved her fingers away from my mouth and rested her hand against my cheek. I leaned into it, loving the feeling of her skin against mine. She didn't release me, and we sat there in silence, underneath the stars. That night was so vivid in my mind. I couldn't get rid of it.

"Why did you join the gang?"

It took me a minute to gather my thoughts.

"I lost my way," I answered honestly. "I thought the guilt would go away if I drank and smoked. That summer was so freaking hard for me, Olivia. You have *no idea* how hard it was," I explained, my voice cracking. "I joined the gang because my mother fell into depression, and I was too young to get a job. I had to take responsibility for everything." Her eyes softened. "And at the beginning of junior year, the boss offered me the leader position and I accepted."

She waited patiently for me to finish. "If you did it to take care of your mom, then why did you change?"

"The guilt. I thought maybe smoking and girls would take it away," I said. "I changed to play the part. It just became permanent after a while."

Olivia looked down at the ground, fiddling with her thumbs. "Why didn't you tell me?"

"I didn't know *how*!" I whisper-cried. "I didn't know how people would treat me knowing the truth. I thought it would be better to change than having to explain it all."

"I'm really sorry, Sam."

I rubbed my eyes with my knuckles, suffocating under the guilt and aching pain in my chest. "Don't tell anybody. Please," I begged sorrowfully.

"I'm not," she promised. "Sam?"

I looked up with coarse eyes.

"Thank you for telling me," Olivia touched my arm softly.

I shivered against the cool breeze. "I should be thanking you."

She smiled warmly.

"Olivia?"

"Yes?"

I focused on her face, seeing the scars I had left behind her smile. "I'm sorry for hurting you."

"What?" she asked, shock evident in her voice.

"I'm sorry for pushing you away. I'm sorry for everything. Everything I've done to you. It was stupid, it

was wrong. I'm sorry about the rumors, the lies, the fights... I'm just so, so sorry," I apologized, feeling horrible for the things I did.

Olivia gasped softly. Our eyes had stayed attached the entire time. "Thank you."

I allowed a rare smile to show; I've never felt happier in my life.

I leaned in slightly and with her beautiful smile on her face, Olivia slid an arm around my neck, rubbing the back of it. I placed my hand underneath her chin and tilted her head. I leaned down and pressed a soft kiss on the base of her throat. I felt the thump of her heartbeat against my lips and I smiled.

Sometime later, we were lying on the roof's surface with her head on my chest and my arm wrapped around her waist, keeping her close. Olivia eventually fell asleep to the hum of the heater, but I lay awake.

I tried to stay away from her, but couldn't bring myself to do that.

Now one question remained:

Was her life in danger because of me?

Chapter 18: Olivia

The sunrise was so beautiful.

I sat on the roof, mesmerized by the beautiful sight in front of me. The sky was a variety of different colors: pink, light purple, soft blue. I never got to see the sunrise. I was usually getting ready for school at this time in the morning. Sam was fast asleep next to me.

My head was still whirling from last night. I mean, I guessed that something drastic had happened, but never had I ever thought his brother was so tragically taken away. As a cool breeze blew by, I wrapped my arms around myself, relaying everything again. It wasn't easy seeing how much pain and guilt Sam had buried himself into these last three years. He had fallen apart right in front of me, and all I could hope for now was that I said and did exactly what he needed last night.

It wasn't easy thinking that my best friend blamed himself for three years for a death that simply occurred at the wrong time.

Speaking of, Sam shifted in his sleep and I leaned down, hovering above him. His emerald eyes fluttered open and I smiled at him, still waiting for someone to pinch me awake. This had to be a dream.

"Morning, Sleeping Beauty," I teased.

He snorted. "You and my cousin are a lot of alike."

Sam looked even more handsome in the morning than in the day. His hair was messier, his eyes were clouded with sleep, and his voice was huskier.

"Did I wake up a grizzly bear or somethin'?" he asked, rubbing the crease between his eyebrows.

I blushed. "No."

He reached up and brushed a few locks of my hair behind my ear. "Mornin'." He yawned then grinned at me.

I didn't stop the smile edging onto my lips. "What?"

"We stayed out here all night."

"And?"

"Won't your parents put out a search warrant?" Sam asked.

I rolled my eyes. "They're probably not even worried," I played with sleeves of his hoodie. "What about your mom?"

"She's used to it."

I pointed towards the sunrise. "It's quite beautiful."

"Eh, I've seen somethin' better."

"What?"

"I'm looking at it," Sam said, winking at me.

I pushed him playfully in the chest. "Never thought the Sam Wayne would pull for such a cheesy line."

"I can be cheesy, and occasionally romantic," he smirked.

"How so?"

He shrugged. "Gift the girl with sweet things and compliments and she'll fall head over heels for you."

"That's not true for all of us," I retorted.

Sam raised an eyebrow. "Are you like that?"

"No. I like affection," I said sheepishly.

"In what way?"

"Cuddling," I answered after a minute.

He pushed himself up then proceeded to scoot behind me and wrap his arms around my torso, pulling me against his chest. I leaned back into his touch, failing to hide my smile. He tightened his hold and I laced our fingers together, secretly loving this. Sam rested his chin on my shoulder, and I shuddered from the heat of his breath blowing on my skin.

"Hey, Sam?" He hummed a response. "Are we back?" I leaned my head back to rest it in the crook of his neck.

He kissed me on my jaw. "I think after last night, I say yeah. Yeah, we are."

"Are we together?"

He laughed against my shoulder. "Do you want to be?"

I don't know why I was nervous to answer. Maybe because I was waiting for someone to wake me up, for someone to say nothing happened. I'd wanted this for so long, but I was having a hard time wrapping my mind around it. I turned my head, and as I lost myself in his green orbs, an image of the old Sam resurfaced in my mind. Specifically, one afternoon under the clouds. We were trying to determine what shapes they made, avoiding homework and chores. Sam was twelve, I was eleven, and we had just entered the most awkward three years of our lives: middle school. That afternoon was when I realized I liked him. His flaws, his corniness, his smile, his gazillion ways to annoy me, and his beautiful emerald eyes. They were the reminders of our childhood.

"I want to," he said, "but only if you're okay with it."

After he said those words, the nerves disappeared and I could answer.

I turned sideways and allowed a giant smile to break onto my face. "I would love to be your girlfriend." Sam grinned. "So I'm taking it as we can't tell anyone?" I asked.

"Not right now. Maybe one day." He lifted his hand and caressed the side of my face. "Are you sure about this?"

I nodded. "There's nothing I want more." A thought came to mind. "Do you promise not to dump me in a week for another girl?"

Sam chuckled and rested his forehead on mine. "There's no girl better than you."

I smiled, a blush creeping its way up my neck. After a small argument with myself, I cautiously leaned in and kissed him. If he was caught-off-guard, he didn't show it. He pulled me closer and I gripped the collar of his shirt, my fingers clinging to the fabric in happiness. My heart clenched with glee at this precious moment that I would cherish for the rest of my days.

"You want me to take you home?" Sam asked, getting up from behind me. I copied his actions, stretching my arms above my head.

I frowned, acting sad. "You're already tired of me?"

He laughed. "Nah, I just wanted to make sure you won't get in trouble."

"Maybe I need to get in trouble," I said walking over to the ladder's railing. "Maybe that'll my parents realize that they're neglecting me."

Sam shrugged one shoulder. "So do you want me to take you home?"

I shook my head. "I'm staying, if that's all right with you."

"Doesn't matter to me," he said then added with a smile, "but I'm glad you're staying."

I gestured to the ladder. "Men first."

"I think the correct term is ladies first."

"This thing scares me. If we fall, I'll at least land on something soft," I poked him in the chest. "And besides, I'm not a fan of heights."

He gave me an amused look. "We just spent the night on a rooftop."

"I didn't like sitting on the ledge," I admitted. "You made me, you big bully."

After my feet touched solid ground again, Sam opened the door to his apartment building and I walked into the lobby.

His doorman, Welsh, sat at the main desk and greeted both of us. Sam engaged in a conversation with him for a minute and collected a brown package, which I concluded it had to deal with the gang. I crossed my arms and looked around the lobby, smiling at some of the residents. A newspaper stand sat in one corner. A couch and two chairs surrounded a small table covered with magazines. A coffee machine sat close to the entrance. The walls were painted a faint dark blue.

"Let me know who wins!" Sam called out to Welsh, coming to stand by my side.

"Wins what?"

"Welsh loves watching basketball games and he pulls for whoever has the greater chance of winning, and me being the annoying resident, I pull for the opposite team. I usually win," Sam laughed.

"You're crazy," I said.

He shrugged. "I love picking on him." He shot a little girl a wink and she giggled. I recognized her as the girl who told him her grade on her spelling test. She sent me a toothy smile, and I returned it, causing hers to widen.

Sam unlocked the apartment door, allowing me to walk in first. I entered the small hallway where coats and shoes were collected, and after slipping off my sneakers, I went into the living room, collapsing on the couch. Instead of joining me, Sam leaned against the doorframe, crossing his arms and staring at me with an expression I couldn't quite put my finger on.

"What's that look for?" I inquired curiously.

"Because I'm still in disbelief that you're not running away."

A soft smile curled the corners of my lips and I got up to stand in front of him. I cupped his cheeks with my palms. "I'm not going anywhere."

The minute I slipped out those words, Sam's lips met mine.

~~~

"What'd you do this weekend?" Tammy questioned Monday morning.

I dropped my backpack to the floor and opened my locker. "Nothing really."

"Did Max come home?" I nodded in reply. She raised an eyebrow. "I thought your family always did something when he visits or whatever."

"We decided to get into an argument instead," I said sarcastically, grabbing my books for Math and

English. "I hardly spoke to any of them this entire weekend. I was so angry, and a bit disappointed. I wanted to have a great time because we never see him and... it went all downhill."

I left the greatest part out. Sam told me his entire

story and now we're together.

"Oh," Tammy muttered. "Ah, great, here comes trouble."

I watched as Sam and his gang entered the school building, and he was talking with his best friend, laughing and nudging each other. Ace threw an arm around Sam's shoulders, dragging him away from Ryker, probably complaining about the homework they're going to be stuck with tonight. On their way towards their lockers, Sam happened to glance over and caught me staring. I blushed against my will and he winked at me, his adorable grin stretching across his face. I bit my lip, trying to hide mine, but it was no use.

"Ba-what- HUH?" Tammy exclaimed, eyes wide as saucers.

I broke the gaze and stared dumbly at her. "What?"

"He just smiled a-at YOU!" she gasped loudly. I blinked; giving her a blank look. She looked in between the two of us. "Did you reconnect or something?"

I snorted. "No. What made you think that?"

"You know me," Tammy shrugged. "I come up with strange ideas."

"This is your strangest one yet," I patted her on the shoulder. Sam and I both agreed to not let anyone know of our relationship. If the wrong people found out, we'd be in danger.

~~~

I was finishing the problem of the day when someone tapped me on the shoulder. I looked to my right and Sam sat in his seat, very close to mine.

"We can't act like we don't hate each other anymore. People will get suspicious," he whispered.

"You know how to act?" I teased, winking at him.

He shot me a look.

"Wayne, could you *be* any closer?" I started the beginning of a beautiful argument.

He laughed. "As a matter of fact," Sam scooted his chair to be hip to hip with me. I ignored the butterflies in my stomach. "I can."

"Move over," I hissed.

"Don't feel like it," Sam retorted.

Miss Kay entered the classroom and I vaguely heard her ask the students to take out their homework. She went around the room, checking to see who did it or not. She passed by our table, collecting my papers and raising an eyebrow at Sam. The gang leader just smirked and leaned back into his chair, putting his arms behind his head.

"Mr. Wayne, I'm guessing you didn't do the assignment?" Miss Kay asked, probably already knowing the answer.

He shook his head. "Yep. I had other plans to attend to."

I rolled my eyes. I bit the inside of my cheek, knowing that I had to say something smart to make it more realistic. "Miss Kay," I began, "Sam rather do be a part of illegal activities than do his homework."

"Shut up, teacher's pet," he snarled rudely.

Miss Kay held her hands up. "Enough both of you! I've been dealing with your arguing long enough. Next time it happens, I will send both of you to the principal's office. Understood?"

"Yes ma'am," I agreed. Sam grunted in response.

She eyed the dark-haired boy beside me. "Tell your mother she should expect a phone call from me."

He snorted, his green eyes glinting with humor. "You honestly think that will get me to do the homework?"

Miss Kay's eyes shined with anger. "Okay, Mr. Wayne, if you want to be disrespectful and talk back, how about you go visit the principal? Maybe he won't be as nice as I've been these past few months."

"Oh, but Principal Marco loves me," he smirked.

She pointed to the door. "Don't forget a hall pass."

"I have one encrypted in my brain," Sam replied, pushing himself out of his seat, and after plucking one from the wall because of Miss Kay's repeating statement, Sam disappeared from sight as the door closed behind him.

I slouched in my seat, thinking *when will that boy learn*?

After first period ended, I strolled the halls with Tammy beside me, heading in the direction of second period when Sam and Brett (another member; junior) slammed into us, making me lose the grip of my backpack, and since I forgot to zip it, everything- all my books and materials fell out onto the floor. I glared at him.

Sam stepped closer to me, his arms crossed. "Stop pushin' my buttons, Jenkins." He leaned in; his breath hot on my face. His eyes locked with mine. Gold and blue speckles flickered in them, making my throat clog up and my hands clammy. "I'm not very forgiving."

Tammy defended me, scoffing. "Okay, seriously, you have to have someone other than Olivia to irritate. I'm sure there are plenty of girls that would love to have you near them."

"Actually, all my other slots are enabled. Your friend gets the entire experience."

"Well, you better stop."

He quirked an eyebrow; the corner of his lip lifted in a smirk. "Or what?"

Tammy backed down. She was strong and independent, but she didn't like playing games with Sam. No one did. "I-I-"

Brett chuckled. "Do you have a stuttering problem?"

"No," Tammy scowled.

Sam grinned. "You really wanna challenge me?" He glanced over at me and through our gaze, I pleaded with him to back down. He subtly jutted out his chin in an okay. "That's what I thought."

Then Ryker came over and clamped him on the shoulder, pulling him away.

"Olivia, I'm so sorry," Tammy apologized while helping me gather my stuff.

"Why?" I asked. "It's not your fault."

She sighed. "I know it's not. I just hate the fact that you're constantly being bullied by him and I can't do anything to stop it."

"I've dealt with it for three years. I think I can handle it the rest of senior year. After graduation, I don't have to deal with him or Under-Twenty anymore."

She handed me the leftover books. "I still hate it."

"Don't worry," I said standing up. "I'm a big girl. I can handle him," I reassured her. But on the way to our next class, a question lingered through my head: *what will happen after graduation?*

SAM

At the back of the school, I held an unlit cigarette between my fingers, debating on smoking it or not, and leaned against the wall, waiting for Ryker to show up.

"I have to tell you somethin'," I said when he appeared around the corner.

He looked at me with raised eyebrows. "Why you look so freakin' serious?"

"Because it is," I rolled my bottom lip in between my teeth. "It's about Olivia."

"Olivia?" A smirk lifted on his lips. "What about her?"

I ran a hand through my hair, and after making sure there wasn't anyone near us, shrugged in nonchalance. "You were right."

He didn't even hesitate; he barked out in laughter and clapped his hands loudly, making me scowl at him unamused. "Say that again."

"Shut up."

"I freaking knew it! So you two together yet?"

"Yes, but we're keeping it silent."

Ryker nodded. "Got it. I won't say nothin'." I inclined my head thankfully. "So…" he crossed his arms, not bothering to hide his cocky grin. "How does it feel knowing I was right?"

I narrowed my eyes at him and shoved him in the shoulder roughly. "Get out of my way." We headed towards the parking lot and noticed Olivia and Tammy exiting the front doors. "Uh, I gotta get going."

"Yeah, yeah, be with your girl," Ryker pushed me forward.

OLIVIA

"Do you need a ride?" Tammy asked. School had just been let out, and my car was at home. Max drove me to school before going back to Columbia. We had a good conversation and enjoyed a nice breakfast to make up for this weekend's fight.

"Nah, I'm good," I answered.

She unlocked her car, tapping the roof. "Are you sure?"

"Go. I'm fine."

She blew me a kiss before getting into her car. I waved goodbye and when her car vanished from sight, I shouldered my backpack and started walking. I could have called my parents to bring my car or to come pick me up but I wanted to enjoy the beautiful nature. The weather was nice for the first week in November (in New York, nonetheless). Fall was starting to kick in. The leaves were starting to change colors; green to red to orange to yellow and finally resting on the ground for all of winter. I continued to walk, letting the sun shine on my face, and closing my eyes as I breathed in the warm fresh air.

I jumped slightly when a honk broke my stride, and I turned around to see Sam pulling up next to the sidewalk. He rolled down the window. "Want a ride?"

"I don't mind walking," I said beginning to walk again.

He drove at a slow pace to stay by my side. "Olivia, stop being stubborn and get in the truck."

I glanced over at him with a smile. "Ask me nicely."

"*Olivia*," Sam coated the word with sarcasm, "please do me the wonderful favor of allowing me to drive you home."

I snorted in laughter. "I accept." I opened the door and climbed inside easily, buckling my seatbelt before Sam accelerated. "Thanks."

"The least I can do for my girlfriend," he teased, flipping on the turning signal at the end of the road.

I beamed at the word. "You know, we're very good actors."

He chuckled. "Indeed we are. I almost believed it."

"Did you get in trouble?" I referred to his visit with the principal.

"Nah. Principal Marco's very chill. When he saw

me, he just marked up a detention slip and gave it to me," Sam shrugged. "Nothin' horrible."

"Most kids would love to be you," I glanced out the window. Grey clouds were starting to brew and I frowned, not in the mood for rain. "He's strict."

"I guess he's used to it. He knows that there's no other punishment, considering that I don't care if he calls my mother and I don't show up for Saturday detention," he stopped at a red light, "so taking away free period is the only solution. I'm already at school and I like talkin' with the teacher. He's funny."

I shook my head, laughing at his comment.

"Anyways, did that shove hurt?"

"No," I answered. "Though I wasn't expecting all my stuff to fall out."

"The glare was real then?"

"Yep."

He laughed. "My place?"

"Sure."

Sam reached over and entwined our fingers so naturally, I had to bite back a giant smile.

"Does your mom know about this- or more precisely, is she *allowed* to know about this?" I inquired.

He sighed, releasing my hand to make a sharp turn. "She knows I'm dating somebody, but doesn't know who." Leah was the one person I knew wouldn't have a problem with us dating. She made plenty of comments when we were younger. "I was thinkin' we could surprise her… which is why I'm bringing you to dinner tonight."

My eyes widened. "Sam, I-I'm not dressed-"

"You have clothes on. I'm pretty sure that says dressed to me."

I gave him the stink eye. "You know what I meant. I don't want to meet your mother while dressed in-"

"It's not the first time you're meetin' her."

"As your girlfriend, I am."

Sam sighed loudly, breaking my rambling. I raised an eyebrow. He looked over at me and stroked my knuckles with his thumb. "Olivia, she loves you. She won't be judging you by your appearance or whatever you girls fret over." He grinned. "And besides, you look beautiful."

My cheeks betrayed me. I glanced down, looking over my appearance. I wore dark jeans and a light dirty-yellow jacket with a simple white tee and tied it off with grey converses. My hair was pulled into a messy bun; loose strands falling in front of my face. I didn't wear any

make-up (I was blessed with amazing acne go-away cream) and my hair wasn't glamorous. How can he call this beautiful?

When I asked him, his emerald eyes met mine; series of colors swirling in his irises, and Sam simply answered with a shy grin, "Because it's you."

I smiled bashfully, trying and failing to hide my blush. A minute later, he pulled into the apartment's parking lot, and shut the engine off as I unbuckled myself. We emerged from the truck and began walking to the front door. A comfortable silence floated between us, our hands intertwined. Abby, the little girl that he was friends with ran over and tackled Sam with a hug.

"Hey, squirt!" he greeted after setting her down.

Abby giggled. "Hey."

"How was school?"

She lifted her hands in a shrugging gesture. "Could have been better, could have been worse."

"Any bullies that I need to interrogate?" Sam asked.

She shook her head. "Not today."

"Good," he turned her baseball hat the other way and stood up to his full height. "If they ever bother you again, tell them-"

"That I know somebody that will make you run faster than seeing the Boogeyman," Abby finished, turning to look at me with a twinkle in her eyes. "Is this your girlfriend?" she asked innocently.

"Yes," we simultaneously said. She giggled and we looked at each other and had matching grins on our faces.

"Well, I gotta go finish homework. See ya, dude." They did a fancy handshake, or at least tried. She bid me goodbye and raced, well more like, skipped inside.

We entered the lobby, waving at Welsh and ignoring the looks from other residents. They knew of Sam's reputation and what he was, and by the gleam in their eyes, they were warning me. Warning me to be careful. I pushed it away. I was different from other girls. I knew of his past and the reason why he joined. I knew the real him. They saw a masked boy, who was involved in the wrong crowd, and they judged him by what the police or other people say. They should look past that and get to know what's hidden from everyone. They would be surprised.

As we clambered up the stairs, I thought of the person Sam keeps locked up. He wasn't merely a gang leader; he was also lost and broken. He wasn't just tough and blunt; he could be tender and sweet. The real Sam was hidden behind a heavy wall of brick and stone, but there were things that had stayed the same. His sarcasm, the smirk, the small dimples in his smile, his tendency to look extremely handsome when he's confused or excited.

The gang leader and the broken boy were the same person, but were shown at completely different times.

He had someone buried away from the world.

You just had to search and search his guarded soul until you found him:

The stranger within.

Chapter 19: Sam

"The boss will want new supplies when he gets here."

"And how are we supposed to get them? Warehouses will be stocked out."

"We'll find a way."

The gang sat around the circle of different vehicles. I sat on my bike, listening to their conversation while forcing myself to stay awake. They were correct. The boss will want new supplies, but with the warehouses all empty... yeah, we got a problem.

"There's no possible way we'll get them in time," Ryker said. "I checked the logs. Most of them won't be available until next week."

"Then we should have enough by the time he comes!" one of the younger members interrupted. His name was Josh and he joined not too long ago.

Ryker took a long drag from his cigarette, waiting impatiently for Josh to finish. He glared at the boy. "May I finish before anyone interrupts this time?"

The members nodded and I just smirked.

"We need supplies for four months. If availability isn't until next week then we won't have enough. The boss is coming in less than- how long, man?" He directed the last part to me.

"Three weeks."

"So we're in a deep hole of crap. Yay," Ace said.

Daniel threw his empty soda can on the cement. "That's a problem."

Santiago, whose vehicle was parked near me, spoke up. "We may have to-" I already knew where he was getting at before he even finished.

"No," I said through gritted teeth.

"We may need some help with this round-"

I tapped the pocket where my gun was located, indicating that if he said anything more, I wouldn't react lightly.

Ryker crossed over to where I sat. "It may not be a bad idea-"

"*No!*" I shouted, jumping from the seat. "We're not involving ourselves in a deal."

"Why a deal?" Victor asked, a sixteen year old that recently joined. "I thought they only transported drugs."

"You could put in an offer for other things," Daniel answered. "It's not just a market for drugs; it's for whatever you're in need of."

"Exactly," Santiago appeared by my side. I was tempted to deck him right then and there, but decided against it. "It could give us the stuff Boss needs."

I spun around and grabbed him by the collar, pressing the gun into his temple; my finger trigger-happy. "I don't care. I'm not puttin' us through a deal. These kids don't need those horrific images scarring them," I hissed.

Santiago glared at me and after I released him, he stalked off towards his car. Ryker put a hand on my shoulder. "You do know what could happen if we don't get them in time, right?"

I glanced up at the grey sky. "Of course I do."

I could get in a lot of trouble. It was my responsibility to get the supplies. And if I didn't, I had to suffer the consequences.

~~~

I loaded the magazine, moving the slide into place, and I heard the bullet enter the chamber. I raised the gun, aiming it at the cardboard cutout of a person. My finger hovering over the trigger, I listened intently, making sure these thirteen year olds were watching. When I noticed one of the kids whispering to another and laughing at their comments, I quickly tilted the gun and fired at the kid,

missing the top of his shoulder by an inch. The kid jumped, surprised by the gunshot and looked at me with wide eyes. The others around him scattered away, frightened.

"Next time, I'll lodge that sucker *in* your shoulder," I threatened.

He nodded frantically. I went back to my previous position and shot at the cardboard cutout, the bullets hitting the target each time. I smirked, lowering the gun, and handing it to the kid behind me. He copied my stance, looking at me with questioning eyes.

"Don't let your enemy see fear in your eyes," I ordered. "They'll use that against you, and if it's hand to hand combat, never let them get a hold of you first. Majority of the time, you'll lose."

The younger members nodded simultaneously, listening carefully to all the instructions. If they decide to leave, they'll have to survive on their own. After they leave, I'm not responsible for them any longer. I had to keep reminding myself of that...

When the training session ended, we left the underground bunker and headed past the garage to the upstairs lounge/living quarters. I laughed as a few jumped on Ace, who was taking up the entire couch, and he

groaned in surprise. I leaned against the doorframe, watching as the kids gathered on the different sets of seating, turning on the TV and quickly agreeing on the newest episode of a famous TV show. Looking at the scene, it reminded me of how close we all were. We were like a family. We protected each other and hung out together, despite our differences. There are two things that everyone had in common: we broke the law and had secrets.

"Sam," Ryker appeared by my side. "Boss sent us something."

I took the envelope out of his hands and went into the room on the right, opening it and displaying the contents on a table. It was pages of information about the drug deals and the groups included. The boss concluded that they were acting on their own authority, which he handled silently. Being the crime lord of Lower Manhattan earns you major credit and nobody wants to mess with him so they'll agree to anything he suggests. I tore off the note he addressed to me and sighed.

I'm countin' on you. Those supplies need to be delivered.

Santiago entered the room, making me roll my eyes. We haven't been agreeing about anything lately. "What'd he send us?"

"Just informing us that the drug trafficking is taken care of," I answered shoving the pages back into the giant envelope. "But that doesn't make up for the loss of eleven members." I pictured each face mentally.

"Sam, I know you feel responsible, but they chose to leave. You gave them a home and a place to be apart of something," Daniel whispered, placing a hand on my shoulder. "That was their decision, not yours."

I stared at the wall, allowing no emotion to come across my face. "It's done. We can't do anything to bring them back," I said. "Let's just focus on getting the rest of the supplies by the deadline."

Ryker uncurled a piece of paper from his pocket. "There's been an early shipment to that warehouse on fifteenth."

"Go tomorrow night. Pick out the boys, and Ryker, you'll lead this run," I ordered looking at my best friend. He nodded, exiting the room to gather his crew.

Santiago lifted an eyebrow, looking confused. "Why aren't you-"

I gave him a look that warned him something would happen if he finished that sentence and he quickly closed his mouth. "Continue watchin' those gangs for the

rest of the week. Make sure the boss's actions were followed." I turned to leave.

"Yes sir," Santiago said sarcastically.

I stopped abruptly and faced him again, my right hand clenching air instead of the hidden gun in my jacket. His eyes were cold. "What is your problem? You've been treatin' me like-"

"Like what?" he hissed. "Not like the king you think you are?"

I gritted my teeth. "Is this because I didn't allow us to be involved in a deal?" I scoffed. "I'm savin' these kids' lives. They already put themselves in the runs, and besides, I don't choose. Boss gives the deals to other crews."

He rolled his eyes. "Because you told him you didn't want to do any."

"It's been that way for years!" I shouted, anger radiating off of me. "If you paid attention, you'd know that!"

"They've not even that bad."

"Have you been to one?" He reluctantly shook his head. "That's what I thought. So here's some education for ya. It's not a fun get together. You don't sit around and swap stories about hittin' second base with a girl. You risk gettin' killed every second you're on that dock." I shut my eyes, trying to delete the images from my mind.

"You're too soft to be a gang leader."

My eyes snapped open, blood and voice turning ice cold. "*What?*"

"I said *you're soft.*"

I reached inside my jacket, grabbed my gun, and shot a bullet into his thigh without a second's hesitation. He crumbled to the ground in pain. I walked over and knelt down and pressed my closed fist against the wound. Santiago whimpered incoherent words and blood drenched his pants. I heard the door open and loud gasps.

"Call me soft one more time, and I'll make sure that you'll never see daylight again," I growled.

His response was gurgled by spit, and I stood up, placing the gun on the table. I left the others to deal with him. I pushed the door open with my shoulder, scoffing irately. *Soft!* Only in rare situations would I act soft. Anyone who's heard of me or what I'm capable of knows I mean business. Yeah, I didn't kill or do drug deals for money; however, I'm the youngest gang leader in downtown Manhattan, and authorities and rival crews were wary of me. I've earned my title. If he knew what all entails to be leader, Santiago wouldn't survive. He acted too quickly; decisions are based on the safety and numbers, not on one personal opinion. He couldn't handle the stress of juggling not just your own, but other people's lives. You have to bury whatever feelings you feel about something- a trait I'm still struggling with, and be willing to do certain jobs.

It wasn't an easy task.

~~~

I grumbled inaudible words in protest against the annoying flicking near my eyebrow, and I rolled over in my bed, smashing half of my face in the fluffiness of my pillow. I heard an aggravated sigh, and I smirked sleepily.

"You've always been a pain in the butt in the morning," Mom stated.

I groaned. "It's Saturday. Why are you waking me up?"

"Well, I guess if you don't want your girlfriend to come over-"

I lifted my head, hair sticking out in various directions. "What?"

"I was going to ask if you wanted to have Olivia over, but since you're so tired…" she trailed off.

"Manipulation. Maybe you are my mother," I joked tiredly.

She smoothed my hair down, a warm smile on her lips. "I'm going to the store to get stuff for dinner, and if you guys get here before I do, no-"

"You don't have to finish that sentence, Mom," I

blurted. "Olivia and I aren't intimate like that."

"I was going to say no burning down my house," she said.

I laughed, sitting up straight. "No cooking. Got it."

"Want anything special for dessert?" Mom asked.

I scratched the back of my neck then grinned. "Cinnamon buns."

"Should have known," she winked. "Oh, and Olivia said don't worry about hiding the truck. Her parents are at a friend's wedding."

"Thanks," I said.

Stepping out from under the covers, I pulled on a pair of jeans and wandered around the room, searching for a clean shirt. I threw on a random T-shirt, stuffed my wallet and phone in the back pocket of my jeans, and left my bedroom. After brushing my teeth and running a hand through my hair, I slid on my sneakers and grabbed the last can of Coke, taking a drink as I locked the deadbolt.

When I got down to the lobby, Welsh stopped me. "I know you probably don't want to hear this, but some residents are questioning whether their children are safe or not," he said.

I pinched the bridge of my nose. "What happened now?"

"Nothing. I tried to tell them-"

"Tell them this: I don't give a crap about what they

think of me. Their children aren't going to be harmed. The gang knows not to come near unless for necessary reasons. There are only three allowed to come inside and that's Ryker, Daniel, and Ace. They're never armed and I doubt they'd stoop to a level of hurting innocent kids," I informed him. "Maybe they'll listen this time, and if they don't, that's for them to decide." And with that, I exited the building.

OLIVIA

"Hey," I greeted when I opened the door to see Sam leaning against the doorframe, looking comfortable. "Let me just finish this last thing and we'll go." I strolled into the kitchen, organizing the cluster of books, notes, and pencil shavings; my sketchpad lay abandoned on the counter. "Are you okay? You seem distracted."

"Fine." I shot him a knowing look. He sighed. "People at my complex are digging their noses way up into dirty business. I don't know how many times I have to say the same thing over and over again," he huffed.

I gave him an apologetic smile. "People are judgmental. I think it's a trait in every human being."

"Tell me about it," Sam remarked. He cocked his head at the evidence of schoolwork. "What are you working on?"

"Extra curriculum," I answered.

"Your nerd is showing, Jenkins," he teased.

I smirked, shoving a few pieces of lined paper into a folder. "Thanks for notifying me, Wayne."

He chuckled and watched as I finished. I took a seat on a free stool, saving what I had written on the English assignment and documenting the list of materials for a project. Sam came to stand behind me, resting his chin on my shoulder, and I felt a smile edge its way onto my lips.

"I like what you're wearing," he complimented.

I glanced down. I wore black tights and a grayish-blue long tunic with dark ankle boots; my hair was pulled into a messy bun. "Thanks. Just threw it on."

Sam snorted. "I'm not an idiot. You're wearing this because of my mom."

"I am not!" I didn't have to look at him to know he rolled his eyes. "Okay, maybe," I admitted. "This is for bringing me over many times without a warning. I want to wear something nice. Is that a crime?"

He poked me on my hipbone. "No, but she doesn't care what you wear. She loves you even in sweatpants and jeans."

"I know," I logged off my laptop and shut it, turning sideways, "but I want to." He finally gave up, knowing I wouldn't change my mind. "I've been meaning to ask, where'd you get this scar?" I touched the puckered white line over his right eyebrow.

"Last year, we had an incident with a couple of drunken dudes. One smashed the bottle across my face and glass... well, got caught. Three stitches," Sam explained.

"What about this one?" I moved to the scar on his chin.

"Pocket knife; sophomore year."

My fingers lingered on his skin longer than necessary. "Do you remember every time you get hurt?"

"Only the ones that leave reminders."

"Hmm," I murmured. My eyes flickered to his and butterflies entered my stomach as colors swirled and rippled. He had no idea the effect he had on me. There were moments where I felt like taking charge and kissing him, but even after a month together, I'm cautious that maybe it isn't real. That I'm locked in a dream and couldn't leave. I'm afraid of doing something to ruin everything we've accomplished: our reuniting, trusting each other again, the building of our relationship- I'm afraid of it ending because of me.

But then I see Sam smile, and all the worries and insecurities are erased; instead, I'm overwhelmed with the indescribable feelings I have towards him.

~~~

As Sam drove, I switched stations on the radio and decided to shut the music off; wanting to enjoy the silence. I gazed out the window. The sky was gaining cloud coverage and the blue sky was beginning to fade due to a storm brewing. Scooting over, I rested my head on Sam's shoulder and intertwined our fingers. For the past month, we've been having dinner dates at his apartment since the forbidden rule denies access to public restaurants or fast-food places except after midnight. Leah fully supports us, which it feels nice to have at least one person on our side.

Whenever my parents are away for business or are busy, I would sneak away and join Sam on his couch for movie night. Leah had been suspicious when she found us one morning sprawled across the floor with empty popcorn bowls and candy boxes, but after reassurance, she believed that nothing more than sleep happened. Another thing I enjoyed was having a mother figure in my life again. It had been lonely those years without her.

When Sam pulled into the apartment's parking lot, he took the key out of the ignition, but we sat in the lingering warmth from the fixed heater. I brought my knees to my chest, wrapping my arms around my legs. Sam put an arm on the headrest, his fingers brushing the side of my arm. I sighed in content.

I've pictured this moment in my head many times; I never realized that maybe one day it might've come true.

Suddenly Sam was scrambling to get out of the truck. He landed on the pavement and turned to look at me. I gave him a bewildered expression. "Stay in here. Lock the doors. I have to deal with something."

I nodded mutely, grabbing the door handle and slamming it shut. I pressed my finger against the lock button, keeping a watchful eye on him. He walked over to someone dressed in black, speaking in hushed tones. He glanced backwards as the person he was speaking to pointed in my direction, questions evident on his face. I froze instantly, recognizing the familiar blue and black bandana.

SAM

"What's with the limp?" I smirked noticing the different pace in his walk.

"Someone shot me the other day," Santiago answered with a glare.

I glanced around to watch for residents lurking about. "What are you doin' here? You're not supposed to step foot on my residence."

"Ace sent me. He said that another warehouse got stocked early and wanted to know when you'd want to hit it," he said.

I shrugged. "I'll let you know. See when we're free."

He nodded then cocked his head, pointing towards my truck with interest. "Who's the chick?"

"No one, man," I said trying to keep his attention away off her.

"She looks familiar." His eyes widened in realization. "Is that Olivia Jenkins?" I stayed silent. "What's she doin' in your truck?"

"Why do you need to know?" I insisted.

"It's just a question, man. Why so defensive?" Santiago raised an eyebrow. "You two sneaking around or somethin'?"

I gritted my teeth. "No."

"Then-"

"Stop worrying about my freaking business!" I snapped. "There's nothin' going on," I turned around to return to my truck.

"If the boss finds out about this-"

Santiago didn't have time to finish his sentence before I spun and punched him hard, knocking him into the brick wall. I took him by the collar, shoving him. "The boss doesn't need to get involved 'cause nothing's going on," I stepped closer, close enough to make beads of sweat appear on his forehead. "But if she gets hurt, and I mean if there's one scratch on her, I swear *nothing* and *no one* can protect you from the damage I'll do to you."

Santiago chuckled despite the worry expressed on his face. "Nothin' going on, huh, Sam?"

"Leave," I ordered releasing my hold.

I headed back to my truck and gestured for her to unlock the door. Olivia slid out and I grabbed her wrist, pushing her in front of me. Santiago watched as we

walked. I looked in his direction and he stumbled backwards at the deadly glare I sent him. Olivia entered the apartment complex, my hand resting on her back to keep her as far away as I could from his grimy hands.

I collapsed on the couch, replaying the incident in my head. I groaned. If my defensive actions didn't give our relationship away, it was definitely known that we were together by the threat.

"He knows," I announced, feeling stupid for not being more careful. I ran my fingers through my hair, muttering foul names towards myself.

Olivia's eyes widened. "What?"

"I acted foolishly," I said wanting to smack myself repeatedly. "I snapped when he mentioned telling the boss. Man, I'm such an idiot!"

She sat in a chair close to the TV stand. "What does this mean?"

"I don't know," I muttered. "Maybe he won't tell because he knows I'll do somethin', but either way I need to keep an eye on you. Santiago can't be trusted," I looked over at her. Her arms were wrapped around her knees and her eyes stared at the carpet. Hating the fact I'd considered this, I said, "I'd understand if you don't want to keep this going."

My stomach heaved at the thought, but I thought about the danger I'd be putting her in if this continued. I wasn't about to risk her life for my selfish reasons. However, I knew that if we ended, I would completely lose myself and permanently bury the real me. She was the only one that could open the steel door, and I wasn't about to let her go. I wasn't about to lose her again.

But if this was she wanted, I would grant her wish.

I almost thought she was accepting by her silence. "No," Olivia argued firmly. "I'm not ready- I don't *want* it to end."

"Why?"

She looked at me confused. "Why what?"

"Why do you still want to be with me?" I inquired.

Olivia stood from the chair and stopped in front of me, running a hand through my windblown hair. She smiled brightly. "Because I love you."

I love you…

"Why are you still in love with me after everything I've done to you?" I queried.

She took a minute to answer. "From the beginning, there was always a special connection between us. We could be strong or vulnerable. We could annoy each other

to no end yet comfort one another." Her eyes sparkled. "I've never felt more alive than how I feel when I'm with you. Yes, we've had a long journey, but I wouldn't trade it for the world, Sam.

"You know," she pressed her forehead against mine, "there were moments where I wanted to smack you, and there were times where I wanted to get rid of the feelings, but I'm glad I didn't because I wouldn't be standing here today. I can't see myself with anyone other than you. I'm in love with you, Samuel Wayne, and I forgive you." I let out a small surprised gasp. "I forgive you for every hurtful word. I forgive you for the mistakes you made in these past three and a half years. I forgive you for all of it."

Right then.

Right then I knew I'd fallen in love with her.

Taking her face in my hands, I kissed her. Olivia responded enthusiastically, grabbing my shirt collar. After we pulled back, she lifted an eyebrow. "Did that mean what I think it means?"

I swallowed the lump in my throat. The last time I said those three words, it didn't turn out well. The person who abused them turned me into the player I had been for two years. I had to trust her. Olivia wasn't Nikki.

I brushed back strands of her hair that became loose. I licked my lips, staring into her chocolate brown eyes. "I love you," I declared proudly.

Olivia smiled, her mouth hovering a few millimeters from mine. "I love you too." I grinned, leaning in to kiss her again.

THIRD PERSON

He held the photo in his hand, engraving every detail there was possible. The caramel-brown hair, the brown eyes, and the person who happened to be standing next to her: the Under-Twenty gang leader, Sam Wayne.

He huffed in anger, looking up to the face who presented him with the evidence. Santiago stood looking worn from the drive, shifting from one foot from another- his left leg slightly unbalanced from the bullet wound. "You sure this is legit?"

"Yes, sir."

"Not just some fling?"

Santiago chuckled humorlessly. "By the way Sam acted, it's obviously serious."

"Well, we can't have that, now can we?"

The boss handed the picture to his bunker who took it without a second glance. "Take care of this. Make sure he gets the message loud and clear."

Three large guys exited the underground compound, leaving the boss and Santiago alone. The gang member looked up at the seated powerful man. "What are you plannin' on doin'?"

"Makin' sure Sam Wayne knows who he's up against," the boss answered.

Chapter 20: Sam

"I am not about to engage in that freakin' drug deal!" I yelled slamming my fist on the table.

Daniel scooted farther from me. "It's just a suggestion, man."

"How many times-"

"What is with you and deals?" A newest addition asked.

"You really wanna know?" The young ones nodded. "It's a friggin' death trap! That's all it is. We're not sacrificing our lives for people's addictions!" I threw my gun on the table, knowing that my finger is getting a little too comfortable with the trigger. "Boss doesn't want drugs from us, he wants supplies. The others are part of the deals because that's what they're ordered to do."

I sighed, deciding to spill a bit of truth. "Ryker and I have been to one. We were fifteen and somehow got chosen to go. We weren't ready for what went down. We weren't prepared to see people gettin' murdered. We managed to escape with the help of our leader who decided to take pity on us," I explained visualizing the night. It had been dark and I remembered the docks being sticky with blood and dusted with spilled bags of

marijuana, meth, and heroin. "Now, any more questions?" I insisted.

"I say we still do it." And there's my favorite person butting in...

He was seriously making his way up my hit list.

"No one asked you."

"This-" he referred to the table and members sitting around it. "-is a group discussion. Everyone has an opinion."

"I don't care!" I spat. "We're not doing it!"

Santiago didn't seem to like that I wasn't acting on his choices. Too bad. "I understand where you're coming from, Sam-"

"I swear I'm gonna hurt somebody," I murmured.

"-But if you don't-"

"I know the flippin' consequences."

"Oh, really?" He smirked. "Don't you know the one if you get into a serious relationship?"

Everyone shifted their eyes onto me and my hands itched to wrap around his skinny neck and do some massive damage.

"What's he talkin' about, man?" Daniel asked in the dead silence.

"Nothing."

Santiago laughed. "Oh, so no one knows about you and-"

"Shut up."

"I can't wait to see what Boss will do if he finds out. He's gonna love pressin' his gun against her head-"

"Shut up!"

"-And killing her right in front of your eyes-"

"I said SHUT UP!" I shouted, grabbing my gun and pointing it in his direction. The gang scrambled out of their seats, edging to the corners of the room, not wanting to be in the middle of this. I didn't blame them. The tension was overwhelmingly thick.

He chuckled venomously. "Aw, how sweet. You don't want anythin' to happen to Olivia-" A bullet entered the chamber at the mention of her name.

"Finish that sentence and I'll shoot," I growled.

"I really hope nothin' happens, Sam. The boss will hate killing a pretty girl-"

I fired, lodging the metal round in his shoulder, and he roared in pain, slamming into the wall and crumbling to the floor because of the wound in his thigh. I walked over and knelt down to his height, pressing the barrel against his temple, threatening him to try anything. I had control

of the situation so it would be idiotic. "If anything happens to her, I swear *nothing* can stop me from doing the damage I will do to you."

I stood up, but not before I smashed the hilt against his face, knocking him out cold. I turned to face the members, their expressions reading from impressed to terrified to questioning. I dismissed them, not wanting to hear all their comments, and told Brett to gather another group and pick up the newest shipment. Ryker, Daniel, and Ace stayed behind and I prepared myself for their reactions.

"You're dating Olivia?" Ace asked the golden

question.

I leaned forward, gripping the edges of the table. Ace and Daniel were my friends. If anyone deserved to know, it was them. Daniel trusted me enough to tell me about his serious relationship and I've never turned against him. Instead of digging myself out of it and making an excuse, I nodded.

"Why didn't you tell us?"

"We made a pact not to tell anybody. If the wrong person found out, which I'm meaning the boss, I could get in so much trouble with my position and all, and her life

would be in jeopardy," I explained. "It wasn't that I didn't trust you guys, it was for safety."

"Does Olivia know the risk she's taking?" Ace asked.

"Yeah," I said, "but she-"

"She chose to be with him anyways," Ryker interrupted supportively. "When I told Beth about my father and past, it didn't even change her feelings. It brought us closer actually. We trusted each other enough to share our deepest and darkest secrets."

I thought about the night I confessed my story to Olivia. She didn't blame me for what had happened even if I did. She looked past the darkness and found the light, bringing it back to the surface.

"I know what you mean," I mumbled. "She still wanted to be with me." I tried to hide the smile as the previous day's event popped into my head.

"Do you love her?" Daniel insisted.

Their eyes widened at my silence. They took it as an agreement.

"Ahh, our little Sammy is growing up!" Ryker exclaimed, dodging the slap I directed his way. He threw an arm around my shoulders, grinning widely. "Who knew our love-is-for-idiots gang leader would find someone?"

I laughed. "Guess I'm an idiot."

"Wait, what about Nikki-"

I cut Ace off by sending him a death glare. "Why do you always have to bring her up? She's one of the biggest mistakes of my life."

"Sorry, man."

Daniel frowned. "I'm not trying to keep the conversation at large, but does Olivia know about her?"

I shook my head. Nikki had been my first serious girlfriend. We began dating after my sixteenth birthday and dated many months in sophomore year. Our relationship ended badly, which had its benefits, but with that messy break-up came the years of being a player.

Let's just say Nikki hadn't been the person I thought she was.

~~~

"Sam?" Olivia called from my bedroom. After I had picked her up, I had collapsed on the couch in need of cushioning. I turned my head to look at her as she entered the living room, pulling her hair out of the shirt-hole, clad in light skinny jeans and one of my black V-necks that swallowed her petite form. "Sam?"

"Huh?" I replied stupidly.

She smirked. "Were you checking me out, Wayne?"

"Who wouldn't, Jenkins?" I winked grinning.

She laughed before planting herself next to me. I slid my arm under hers, capturing her hand and laced our fingers together. I grabbed the remote and turned on the TV, surprised to see the news channel playing. Mom must have been watching it this morning before work. I couldn't tear my eyes away from the screen as the reporter spoke about the deal that had supposedly gone under last night. Six murdered, two injured, twelve arrested. This was a local's new channel so the guys would see it being distributed. They would now understand why we weren't given these assignments. I've been protecting them from death and prison. If they decided to leave or go with another crew, that's their decision. I can't blame myself for the kids that have already been killed because there was nothing I could do. I switched the channel, trying to find something decent. Shows nowadays were crap.

Olivia nudged me in the rib. I looked over only to be blinded by a bright light. I realized her iPod was in her hands. She giggled as I reached over and squeezed her knee. "No warning, huh?"

"Nope. Its better when it's natural, not staged." She tapped the app icon again, turning to face me. "Now smile."

I grinned. "Why are you taking these?"

"Because I can," Olivia retorted. "And besides, is it a crime to want to take pictures of your handsome boyfriend?"

"Okay then," I chuckled. "Wait, you think I'm handsome?"

She scowled at the smirk on my face. "Don't let it go to your head. Your ego is already big enough."

"I'm wounded! That hit me deep," I complained faking to be hit in the chest and I fell on my side dramatically.

"You're such a drama queen."

I sat up again, fetching the remote and turning the TV off. There was nothing good on and saving electricity was good for the bills.

"I've been meaning to ask, when'd you get this?" Olivia's fingers ran over the barbwire tattooed around my left bicep.

I smiled faintly at the memory. "A bunch of us went and got them. Ryker has flames covering his right side, Ace has his sister's name written in French, her favorite culture and language by the way, and Daniel was too afraid to face the needle."

"Was it for some identification?" She queried, her

hand still on my skin.

"Nah. We were sixteen and uh, disobeying rules," I smirked. "I forged my mom's signature. She wasn't too happy when I came home with it."

"How did you manage that? Your handwriting is horrible!" Olivia stuck her tongue out.

"I will let you know that it took a whole lot of patience to write it out neatly so no picking," I retorted. She laughed, her eyes crinkling at the sides. "Now this," I pulled the collar covering the back of my neck down, tracing the **U20** printed in blank ink, "was for the gang. Got it the summer I joined," I said uneasily. That summer wasn't our fondest memories.

"You'll always have that," she said, her eyes distant.

I shrugged. "My shirt hides it. It's only noticeable when I'm shirtless or purposely showing it off."

Olivia scratched at an inch on her hand. "I've thought about getting a tattoo, but I wouldn't know what to get."

My face stayed serious. "Fairy."

She hit me in the arm and I burst into laughter. "You're an idiot." I grinned. "Something that has value, like a specific date or- I don't know. It's just an idea. Have you ever thought about getting another?"

"I might," I responded. "Don't know yet." I nudged her in the side. "Hey, maybe we'll go and get one together."

She picked at a loose thread on her shirt. "Maybe."

I threw an arm over the back of the couch, edging closer to my girlfriend. I picked up the TV remote, but something caught my eye. It was one of Mom's magazines and the cover was a picture of a child at the park, all smiley and happy. An idea started forming in my head and Olivia noticed my excited expression. "Wanna go somewhere?"

"Where is this-"

"It's a surprise, but I know you'll love it," I assured her.

She bit her lip, hesitant. "I'm not fan of surprises."

I gave her a look only reserved for her. "Olivia, trust me. I promise you'll love it." She eventually agreed with a nod.

~~~

Olivia gasped when I stopped the motorcycle in front of the colorful and memorable children's park. There were hardly any people here so we'd be safe. She slid her helmet off, staring at it in shock. "I thought it was demolished," she said.

"They were going to, but the town fought and obviously won."

"This is the park we played at as kids." She smiled happily. "I haven't been here in years. I wonder if our initials are still here."

We walked to the big oak tree and after tearing

away the bark, I ran my hand over the craved *SW* and *OJ* and the words *best friends 4ever.* "Well, look at that."

"I can't believe it," Olivia said. "How old were we? Like nine years old, right?"

I nodded. "Seems forever ago." In my peripheral vision, the swings caught my attention. "Bet I can still beat you at the jump."

Olivia smirked. "Oh, you're so on!"

OLIVIA

We sat on the jungle gym, facing each other; Sam on one side, me on the other. The sky was clear and blue; the clouds were white and puffy, hiding the sun's rays. His emerald eyes bore into mine as we spoke about anything and everything. I took this moment for advantage. There was no gang business, no drama, no secrets or lies. It was absolutely perfect. Sam opening up and telling me his darkest secret opened so many doors. We were back again just like I'd always hoped.

He traced my knuckles with his thumb, creating goosebumps. "What's the deal with the guys? You've been skirting around runs for weeks."

"It's been complicated. The boss is becoming antsy and I'm trying to hold off as long as I can. I can't believe I'm saying this, but I might need to call in a favor."

I lifted an eyebrow. "A favor?"

"I don't want you worrying about it," Sam leaned his forehead onto mine. "It's gonna be okay."

"Promise me you won't do anything dangerous," I whispered knotting my fingers into his hair.

"Olivia," Sam sighed, "I can't promise that."

I swallowed the lump in my throat. "Can you promise to be careful?"

He tucked a strand of hair behind my ear. "That I can do."

"So, I thought we weren't allowed to be seen in public?" I asked.

"Little kids play here. I'm not really worried," he answered.

I glanced at movement near the swings, seeing a child kicking his feet to go higher. He pouted as the swing refused to do what he wanted. His mother stood near their silver Volvo, talking on her cell phone and practically ignoring her son's efforts. I frowned. The child needed help and she was too busy with her call to push him a few times. I wanted to pull the woman aside and tell her how neglecting a child can emotionally damage them.

"What's wrong?" Sam inquired.

"The boy can't swing and his mother isn't paying attention. It irritates me so much when parents ignore their children," I huffed.

"Let me guess: you want to go push him?"

I smiled innocently. "Maybe."

He gripped the bars above his head, his biceps bulging in a way that made my insides flutter and flip upside down. He pulled himself up then reached down, taking a hold of my hand. Sam, being the rebel he is, walked down the little slide as I climbed down the wall like you're supposed to.

"Hey sweetie," I greeted the little boy with a smile.

He looked up and tried to disguise the disappointed look on his face. "Hi."

"My name is Olivia and this is Sam," I pointed to the teenager leaning against the dark pole of the swing-set.

"Eli," the kid answered.

Sam sat in the swing next to him, carrying on the conversation easily. "How old are you?"

"Eight."

"Ah, the awesome age."

Eli looked confused. "Huh?"

"Eight is the age where you can get away with anything with just a smile or hug. You're at the top of the cuteness factor," Sam explained. "Trust me, when I was your age, my simple 'I love you, Mommy' got my butt saved plenty of times."

Eli laughed- a cute little chuckle that instantly brought a smile to your face. "I like you," he said.

Sam grinned. "I like you too, little man."

"Do you want to swing?" I asked.

"Yeah!" The little boy exclaimed enthusiastically.

I went behind him, pressing my hands on his back. I

pushed gently, smiling as Eli's laughter grew with every push. Sam decided to join him, pumping his legs to swing higher. Before I could do something to stop it, Eli's mother stomped over and yanked on the chain, stopping Eli from continuing. He begged her to stop, but she ignored him, grabbing onto his arm in a tight grip. I noticed other bruising on his arms the shape of fingers and fists, and I had to control myself from attacking her. How dare she touch him like that?

"Momma, stop it!" Eli cried out.

She glared at me and Sam with cold eyes. "How dare you come near my child?"

"We're sorry, ma'am, we were-"

"Not you!" She snapped her head in Sam's direction. "Him! I've seen posters of your gang all over this neighborhood! Your graffiti is everywhere!"

"Ma'am-" I began.

The woman cut me off sharply. "Why would you come near him? Danger lurks around him."

"You have no idea what you're talking about!" I shouted.

"He's a gang leader."

"How about you stop judging him and learn what's on the inside?"

She didn't reply. She fixed her blouse and turned on her heels, dragging Eli with her. I watched as he stopped fighting her, probably knowing it was worthless, and walked along. He looked back, waving goodbye until his mother opened the car door and he climbed inside. After they disappeared from sight, I faced Sam and slid my hands in my back pockets.

"I'm sorry. I know you could've-"

Sam kissed me and his arms encircled my waist, bringing me closer. I wrapped my arms around his neck, fisting handfuls of his hair. We pulled away seconds later and I felt lightheaded. His lips were a definite distraction.

"You're amazing," he breathed out.

"Not that I'm disagreeing, but how?"

Sam laughed. "You defended me, even though I could have done it myself." I blushed, my cheeks heating up. "But thank you."

"You're welcome," I said. Suddenly my phone beeped and I took it willingly, frowning when it read a text from Melanie. *Your dad wants you home. Remember, you're babysitting tonight* –Mel. "Can you take me home? Apparently, I'm on babysitting duty."

He handed me the helmet. "Try not to rip your stepmother's head off."

"She expects me to have no plans and be available every night. I know I'm not the most social girl, but I'm not friendless," I sat behind him, digging my head in his back. I felt his muscles through his T-shirt. "It's getting irritating."

"If I were you, I would have cracked years ago,"

Sam revved the engine, starting it up. "You're stronger than you think."

I tightened my grip in a way of saying thank you.

~~~

I entered my house, kicking off my sneakers near the door, and waltzed into the kitchen, following the scent of dinner. My parents sat at the dining table, probably discussing Dad's latest project and finances. Melanie stood to stir the contents in the frying pan, an awkward silence in the air. Though it's been a month, they were keeping the argument with Max fresh in their minds. I've been treated very unkindly.

"Did you have a good time with your friend?" Melanie sparked a simple conversation.

I nodded. "Yeah."

"Which friend was it?"

"A friend, Dad."

"Was it a boy?"

I shrugged, not answering yes or no. "And what if it was?"

He pursed his lips. "I would like to meet this boy then."

"Why? I'm seventeen years old. I think I can choose friends wisely," I said.

"I just want to know what kind of people you hang out with," Dad replied.

I scoffed. "Oh, now you choose to become a concerned parent?" His eyes flashed with anger. "I'll be upstairs. Let me know when dinner's ready."

When I reached my bedroom, I shut the door and flopped down on my bed. I stared at the ceiling, breathing in the familiar scent from the shirt I wore.

SAM

I parked the motorcycle in its parking space, storing the helmet under the seat. Zipping up my leather jacket, I shoved my hands in the pockets, trying to fend off the cold air. As I began walking to my apartment's lobby, I heard the crunch of rocks, alerting that there was someone behind me. I listened carefully, a plan creating in my head. I slowed down without making it obvious, keeping my steps as soft as possible to rule out how many there were.

Concluding there was only one, I spun around and punched the guy in the nose, breaking it instantly on impact. He was caught off guard and I prepared myself for a fight. However, surprising me, an arm wrapped around my neck from behind and pulled me into a choke-hold. Another guy appeared from the shadows, burying his fist into my stomach. I hissed through clenched teeth and struggled, but I was quickly overcome by pain as hard knuckles smashed against my left cheek. He kneed me in the stomach repeatedly, the last hit forcing me on my knees. I spit blood out on the sidewalk, coughing hoarsely.

"He said you were good, but I never believed it until now. You're a feisty one, Sam Wayne," the leader said.

"What do you want?"

"The boss sent us with a message." He took a hold of my chin and made me look him in the eyes, blue and relentless. "Stay away from Olivia." My eyes widened. "He's not an idiot, Sam. He knows about you and her. He's very disappointed. He thought you'd be the one who'd enforce the rule, not abuse it." The leader smacked me, my neck cracking as my head turned from the sudden pressure. "Do you think Boss is a fool?!"

"Don't-" My jaw ached horribly. "Don't hurt her."

"Aww, that's sweet. You really care about her."

"I swear if you touch her, I will kill you."

The guy smirked. "She's a pretty girl. I'd love to-"

"I'll kill you!" I shouted.

He fisted my hair, lifting me up. I winced, hoping it wasn't obvious. I hated being weak. "She won't be touched if you stay away."

"And if I don't?"

He grinned venomously. "We'll subject her to this."

He smacked our foreheads together, knocking me off balance, and threw me on the ground roughly. My face collided with the pavement and rocks cut into my skin. The thugs took turns kicking their metal-toed boots into my ribcage. Pain shot through my entire body and tears blurred my vision. I coughed out blood, feeling more defeated than I ever had. Their laughter disappeared in the darkness.

No! Stay awake, Sam!

Pushing myself onto my hands and knees, I crawled to the door. I grunted in agony, but refused to stop. I had to get to the lobby. I whimpered miserably, clawing at the rocks to drag my limp body. The searing pain had no effect to the aching realization in my chest. Olivia was in danger, and it was all my fault.

What have I done?

When I reached my destination, I knocked my head against the glass, getting Welsh's attention. He looked up from his sports magazine, glancing around to see what caused the noise. I repeated the action, creating a loud, thunderous thud. His eyes widened at my beaten appearance and he raced over.

"Sam, what happened?" Welsh asked worriedly, dragging me inside. I cried out, my ribs stabbing like never before.

"Talk to me, man. Stay awake!"

Black spots dotted my vision.

"Sam!"

Next thing I knew, my eyes shut and everything drowned out.

Chapter 21: Olivia

The weekend was silent.

From Friday night to Sunday evening, I hadn't heard anything from Sam. I wasn't one of those obsessed girlfriends, but I became a little worried when Leah answered his cell Saturday afternoon and sounded off, like something was wrong. I tried again early morning, but it went straight to his voicemail. I only called him those two times because I didn't want to force myself on him. He would call me when he was ready, and I would just have to be patient.

Yet I couldn't help wonder if I had done something.

Trying to dismiss the thoughts on Monday morning, I entered the school silently and was immediately ambushed by Sam's friends. Ryker hooked his hand around my elbow, dragging me to a private corner behind the lockers. A quick glance around the school told me Sam was nowhere to be seen.

"Have you seen or heard anythin' from Sam?" Ace fired the first question.

"He hasn't answered any of our calls," Daniel said.

I quirked an eyebrow. "Why are you asking me?"

"Oh, we know about you guys," Ryker's lips curled into a smirk.

My eyes widened, and I refrained myself from looking around the school in a nervous manner. "Does everyone know?"

"Ah, no. We found out by… accident."

I brushed strands of hair out of my face, noticing the uncomfortable tension radiating between them. Saving them from any unwanted questions, I said, "Um, we hung out Friday, but after that I haven't heard anything. I spoke to his mom though and she sounded… off."

Ryker took a deep breath. "Something's up. Sam just doesn't disappear. He wouldn't get up and vanish without telling me first."

"I think we should visit their apartment."

"I agree," I said.

In all honestly, I didn't want to wait almost an entire day, but we had classes to attend and if my parents found out I ditched, I wouldn't be able to leave the house unsupervised. We devised a plan to meet up after school and we would head over together. After biding Ace and Daniel goodbye, I found myself being grabbed in a hug by Sam's best friend.

He patted my back sympathetically. "Don't worry. Sam will be fine."

"I know. I just wanna know what's going on," I admitted.

"Me too." Ryker pulled back and squeezed my arms. He stared at me for a few seconds and nodded, a smile on his lips. I gave him a confused look. "You're good for him. He needs someone like you."

A swelling rose up in my heart at those words. I

was glad Sam's friends, especially his best friend, approved of our relationship.

~~~

As I tried to depart from school hurriedly, Tammy latched onto my arm and asked me why I was in a hurry. I licked my lips, thinking of a good explanation. "Uh, Melanie wants me to pick up things for dinner. She can't because of a late meeting tonight at the firm."

"Oh," Tammy pouted. "I was going to invite you over."

I squeezed her hand. "I'm sorry, but I can't."

"Another time?" she asked hopefully.

I smiled. "Definitely."

After telling her goodbye, I exited the school and slid into my car, waiting for Ryker's headlights to flash. I gripped the steering wheel, praying that nothing was

horribly wrong and there had been a misunderstanding. Because his friends didn't have any contact with him either, I knew I didn't do something to make him throw his walls up and avoid me.

When I saw the Jeep's lights do our signal, I turned the car on and pulled out, tapping my left foot impatiently. I turned onto the main road, seeing the Jeep in my rearview mirror, following me at a distance.

I shut the car door, locking the doors as the guys piled out of their vehicle. We walked into the lobby, disregarding the pointed looks, and Welsh smiled heavyheartedly at us. Did he know something? I trashed the thought of being patient and ran up the stairs, practically skipping one step at a time. We jogged down the hallway and stopped at the door, and I stared at the faded numbers, nervous butterflies flooding my stomach. I lifted my hand and pounded my knuckles against the wood. About twenty seconds later, Leah appeared in the doorway. Her brown hair was pulled in a tightly-wound bun and dressed in her work outfit. She didn't seem that surprised to see us.

"I knew you'd be showing up sometime soon," she confirmed my suspicions.

Ryker stepped up to stand by my side, putting a gentle hand on my upper arm. "Where is he, Leah?"

"He is here, right?" I added anxiously.

She nodded. "Yes, but-" Instead of continuing, Leah moved to the side and gestured for us to come in. "Why don't you see for yourself? He's in his room."

The boys allowed me to go first, and I trailed into the living room, trying to ignore the sight of bloodied rags and the rolls of bandages on the coffee table. I swallowed the rising lump in my throat. When we stopped in the open doorway to his bedroom, my eyes watered. Sam was lying on his bed, the sheets pulled up to his waist. He was shirtless, and I gasped at the exposed purple and black bruising across his ribcage. His skin glistened with sweat and a bandage was wrapped around his head. The side of his face was all cut up, and I brought a hand to my mouth shakily.

I've never seen Sam so fragile, so vulnerable…

"Man, what happened?" Ryker asked.

The gang leader grunted as he adjusted himself. "Boss knows."

"What?"

"He found out from Santiago- that little weasel is going to get it. Mark my word," Sam's eyes were fierce, voice emotionless. "The boss sent bunkers after me and well, you can figure out the rest." He ghosted his fingers over his injuries. "Several of them are bruised, one's cracked, and I have a concussion."

I wiped at my cheeks, not wanting him to see me cry.

"What do you want us to do?" Ace asked.

Their gang leader sighed. "I don't know yet. All I know is…" He cut himself off, his eyes meeting mine with an unspoken plea. I walked over without hesitation and knelt by his bedside, lacing my fingers through his. "Olivia, he knows about you. They told me they weren't going to hurt you, but I don't trust them. You're not safe."

"What should we do then?"

Sam turned away the second the words slipped off my lips.

The answer dawned on me. "No," I choked out. "No, I'm not losing you again. Not after all we've been through and accomplished."

"Olivia-"

I snapped my eyes shut as tears filled them. "No! I just got you back and you can't- you can't do this to me again! I'm not leaving you."

"You don't know how hard this is for me."

"Then don't do it!" I yelled. I pushed myself onto my feet, wanting to throw and hit something yet I wanted to fall and cry. I realized the others had left, giving us a moment alone. I knew he was thinking about my well-being, but I was too angry and emotional to really consider anything rational. My heart ached imagining us being the way we used to be; separate and miserable. "Please don't do something drastic again! You saw what happened last time, Sam."

"Olivia-"

"We barely made it! Please don't tear us apart," I begged my voice breaking.

"Liv, come here."

"No!"

"Come here," Sam whispered gently.

I didn't reject him this time. Lifting the covers, I slid next to him and buried my head in the crook of his neck. He rested a hand on my lower back and I squeezed my eyes shut, refusing to cry, though a few traitor tears managed to escape and they landed on his skin. His thumb drew circles on my back.

"I'm sorry," he murmured against my hair. "I shouldn't have suggested that."

"Please just don't do that to me," I mumbled sniffling.

"I won't, I'm sorry. You gotta just promise me one thing, though."

"Anything."

"Don't go anywhere without me or one of the guys. It's not safe," he said. "There's a good chance the boss knows where you live so he'll probably be monitoring the place."

I switched positions; I sat up and faced him. Our hands stayed intertwined. I wasn't ready to let go of him. "I can't stay away from home unless I tell my parents."

"We may not have a choice," Sam remarked.

My eyebrows shot to my hairline and I stared at him incredulously. "You're not serious, are you?"

"Not usually, but right now I am."

"What am I gonna tell them, Sam? I can't just come out and tell them I'm dating you and your boss is targeting me!"

He glared at me. "You have no idea what he's capable of! He's not afraid of crossing over lines. I know the things he runs and he'll do anything to keep the situation underhand."

I swallowed the quarter-sized lump in my throat,

not liking what that could possibly mean. "Underhand?"

Sam's jaw tightened. "He could send a hit out, naming you as a target."

The breath got knocked out of me. My chin dropped to my chest, the words echoing in my head. I could become a possible target for murder. I wrung my hands together, wanting to scrub away the clamminess.

"I'm not even dangerous..."

Sam stroked my knee and I looked up, meeting his beautiful emerald orbs. "To him, you are."

I chewed on the inside of my cheek and continued to wring my fingers nervously. Sam pushed himself up, neglecting my attempts to stop him because of his pained expression. He slid a hand behind my neck and pressed his forehead against mine. I closed my eyes, focusing on the closeness between us and how amazing it felt as his fingers threaded through my hair.

"I'm sorry I got you into this," Sam muttered.

I shook my head. "It's not your fault."

"Yes, it is-"

I pulled on his collar. "No, it's not. You warned me, didn't you? You warned me about the chance of him finding out, and we took that chance. It's not your fault."

"But it is," Sam pleaded. "I acted defensively and Santiago found out. He told Boss about us and if I had been more careful, this wouldn't be-"

"Please stop blaming yourself. You gotta stop doing that," I said, not leaving any room for him to argue by quickly changing the subject. "How bad is your pain?"

"It comes and goes," he answered. "If I move too fast, it hurts."

I tapped my fingers against his shoulder. "Well, I still think you look handsome, bruises and all."

He grinned. "What happened to burstin' my ego?"

"Oh, shut up," I said teasingly, feeling a slight tug in my stomach at the adoration in his eyes.

"Can I ask you to do something?" he queried suddenly.

My eyebrows drew together in confusion. "Uh, sure."

Sam smirked, his hand coming up to caress my cheek. "Kiss me."

I let a laugh bubble out of me before leaning in. I undid the bandage, feeling it slip off his head as I knotted my fingers in his hair. I heard him wince, but he didn't pull back. Deciding that he was okay, I kissed him again and he chuckled against my mouth when our noses brushed. After a few seconds of this, Sam broke apart and leaned down, nuzzling my neck with his unshaved chin and cheeks.

"Hey, Sam-"

Ace's voice came interrupting my thoughts. We moved away from each other at the noise. I looked over to see his cousin and best friends standing in the doorway, Ace and Daniel's heads turned; Ryker grinning smugly.

"What's up?" My boyfriend directed the question to his friends.

"I hate to be the one to break the nice atmosphere, but what are we gonna do about the late supplies?" Ryker insisted. "I mean, Boss is coming next week."

I froze, everything inside me stiffening. "Wait, what?"

"He comes every four months to collect them," Sam informed me. "I forgot he was coming so soon." He scratched his chin, and I could practically hear the gears whirring in his head. "I can't risk being short, guys. I might need to call in a favor."

"What kind of favor?" Daniel asked.

Sam gave them a look that I couldn't decipher what it meant. "Somethin' the boss will enjoy. I'll have it

covered."

At his words, the guys nodded understandably while I sat in ignorance.

"These jobs, you've mentioned them to me before. You said that you could get in trouble if you're late."

"Much worse than broken ribs," Ace said.

"He won't- like-" I made a hesitant finger gun.

"He won't kill me if that's what you're insinuating. Most likely, a hospital visit."

I narrowed my eyes. "A visit in what extent?"

"Look, we're not going there!" Sam hissed, running a hand absent-mindedly down his bandages. "We'll figure out somethin' else."

An idea began forming in the midst of their conversation. "When does the boss normally get here?"

He thought about it for a minute. "Around the evening time."

"What if you weren't here when he came?"

"What are you talkin' about?" Daniel questioned.

Sam glanced at me interestingly. "What's runnin' through that pretty little head of yours?"

"Well, next Friday is the beginning of Winter Break. It gives you a good alibi to disappear and not have to

worry about missing school," I patted Sam on the leg. "It would ensure your safety, and if you get that favor, the boss won't have to see you. He can take his supplies and there is no face-to-face meeting."

"Where would we even go?" Ryker asked.

"My parents own this little cottage down in North Carolina- a wedding gift from the grandparents. It's in a secured area, deep in the forest, and no one could find it without specific directions or by accident. It would be the perfect place to hide out for two weeks."

After the informative explanation, I waited for their responses. They seemed to be taking it all in, thinking about it firmly. Ace leaned forward, resting his elbows on his knees; Daniel pursed his lips, a distant look on his face; Sam was concentrating, eyebrows drawn together in thought; and Ryker sent me an interested smile.

"It would be nice to get out of New York for a little while," Ryker finally commented.

Ace nodded, agreeing with the second in command. "I like it. I wouldn't mind getting away from everything."

Two down, two to go.

Daniel reached over and fist-bumped me. "I say we do it as long as there's food."

"Of course," I laughed, rolling my eyes playfully, "I'll make sure the kitchen is fully stocked."

"Then I'm definitely in," he chuckled.

The four of us turned our attention to the injured gang leader. He stared hard at his sheets, rolling his lower lip in between his teeth uncertainly. It's been his nervous habit since I could remember.

"Your thoughts, Wayne?"

He inclined his head and adapted his infamous, devilish smirk. "Let's do it."

Now that I had all their consent, I had to voice the only problem we faced for this to work. I braided my hair, trying to avoid it for as long as I possibly could. Sam must have seen my shift in attitude because the next words out of his mouth were…

"Jenkins, what aren't you telling us?"

The guys looked at me with raised eyebrows.

"It's just a small little detail."

They weren't amused by my nonchalant tone. "What?"

"I have to get my parent's permission."

Chapter 22: Sam

A week later, I could walk without doubling over and having to have someone always near me every second. My ribs were feeling better with the exceptional help of pain medication and the nursing of my mother. My stomach still had the horrible bruises, which made me cringe whenever I looked in the mirror. It reminded me of my failure of protecting Olivia. It reminded me of becoming weak in front of the enemy.

I couldn't wait to get out of New York, if only Olivia would have the courage to ask her parents. I know I may seem harsh, but I'm not taking the chance of having her here when a cold-blooded killer was. He would come after her, no doubt. I don't trust his guards. They don't have an honest bone in their body.

I knew the boss wouldn't leave until all his goods were in his possession. I had no other choice but to call in a favor. I wouldn't be able to order enough runs to get the usual dose of weapons and ammo. I'd have to get him something else, something special to make up for the lack of supplies- something he'd enjoy better.

I dialed the number and pressed the speaker against my ear, listening to the dial-tone. He was the only person I could trust.

"Who's callin'?"

"Bryce. It's Sam," I said.

"Ah, my trusty colleague. How's supply hunting?"

I shoved my free hand in the pocket of my leather jacket. "That's exactly why I'm callin' you. I need a favor."

"Name it."

"You got any extra goods?" I hated doing this, but it would be the only way to keep the boss from sending more thugs. "Like just a box?"

"Of course," Bryce chuckled. "Time and place."

"Thirty minutes. Alley near Hanley's bar. Come alone."

He snorted. "No worries. I'm bringin' no coverage. I trust you, Sam."

"Seems we have an agreement," I grinned. "I'm out."

The line went dead.

~~~

I leaned carefully against the dark brick wall, watching drunken women and men stumble out of the bar and laugh hysterically at nothing. The music thundered

from inside, and when the door opened to welcome new residents or say goodbye to old ones, it was loud and obnoxious; people dancing and hollering without a care in the world. I used to be one of them, wanting to forget whatever pain I was in; wanting to lose myself carelessly and avoid dealing with life.

"Looks invitin', doesn't it?" Bryce's voice drenched with sarcasm shouted from behind me.

I smirked. "Absolutely." I turned around to face the

other gang leader, my fingers clenching the rolled up bills I had for payment.

He took in my appearance, noticing that something was off. "You're limpin'."

"Yeah, uh, things got rough," I said then quickly changed the conversation back to why we met. "This is gonna save me. I can't thank you enough."

"Don't mention it." Bryce handed me the sealed package and I was surprised by the weight. "Sixty pounds of all sorts in there. That should definitely make the boss happy."

"How'd you-"

"I figured it had to do somethin' with him." I slid the box under my arm and grabbed the wads of bills. He shook his head. "No payment."

"But-"

"If it weren't for you, I'd be dead so consider this as my debt being paid," Bryce clamped me on the shoulder and I gritted my teeth together to keep the wince intact. "I gotta get going. The guys can't run themselves for long."

"I know what you mean, man. Be careful!" I called.

He laughed over the rambunctious music and chorus of yells. "You too, Wayne!" And he disappeared into the moonlit night.

~~~

When I got to the storage unit, Ryker pulled the

door open and I set the package down in the front that way the boss could find it easily. Boxes were stocked on another, differing from sizes and objects.

"He better accept these," I said clicking the lock into place. "If not, I'm screwed."

Ryker shrugged. "I wouldn't worry about it. We'll be gone while he's here."

"Hopefully," I murmured.

"I think he'll like the surprise," he chuckled. "You know he loves his goods."

"More than the gun strapped to his hip," I grinned.

As we headed towards his Jeep, I swore I heard footsteps behind us; therefore, I slowly rested my hand on the weapon stashed in the inside of my jacket, prepared for whatever action I had to take. In the corner of my eye, I saw Ryker do the same. So it wasn't my imagination. I gave a soft, ordering nod.

Together we turned and threw our guns up, sliding a bullet into place. We were surprised to see a young kid- a boy about eight, shivering against the gaining cold. He wore muddy jeans and a black raincoat; his hair was hidden by a snapback. I couldn't shake the feeling that I knew this kid from somewhere.

"Wait a minute," I said stepping closer to get a better look at him. "Eli?"

The little boy from the park looked up at the sound of his name, confirming my suspicions. "Y-yes?"

"It's Sam," I informed him. I put my gun away, seeing the fear in his eyes at the barrel pointed his direction. Ryker took this as an advantage to check out the area, in search of anything problematic. "What are you doing here?"

He licked his dry lips, rubbing his hands together. "I ran away. I couldn't handle it anymore." That's when I saw the bruise on his face, the shape of a handprint. "I

followed a car inside and ended up locked in."

I knew the last thing he wanted to hear was an apology for his home life. "Well, you're safe now. We'll get you somewhere warm and some food."

Eli perched up, happiness glinting in his eyes. "Thanks, Sam."

"Don't mention it." I wrapped an arm around his shoulders, guiding him to the parked Jeep. Ryker sat in the driver's seat, the heat already cranked to its highest. Eli slid in the backseat while I texted Ace to get comfortable clothes and a bath ready. "Here's what's happening, little man. You can stay at our place as long as you like until we find you a new, better home," I told him. He nodded in the rearview mirror. "But you have to promise not to get involved in any dirty business."

"I promise," Eli said firmly.

~~~

After parking the Jeep in the garage, we trailed up to the living area and introduced him to the youngest companions of the gang. They took him in easily, probably sensing Eli's determination to be accepted. He seemed to like the fact of having older kids around him. I showed him to the bedroom he would borrow for the time being,

and his expression as he fingered the cotton T-shirt and blue pajama pants made me realize how hard of a life he'd gone through. I could see the hurt in his eyes; I could see the always-afraid-of-being-rejected look glued on his appearance.

And when Eli thanked me for saving him from life on the streets, I ignored the sharp pain in my ribcage as I knelt down and hugged him. I focused on the revival of life in his eyes instead of the marks on his arms that were branded from the past he left behind courageously.

Eli had fought his way out and won.

OLIVIA

Tuesday afternoon, Sam strolled over to me with a slight limp in his walk. His ribs were healing fairly well, but I knew there were moments where he wanted to throw his fist into a wall. (Sometimes I wonder if, around people he cared about, he tamed the aggressiveness boiling in his veins.) He leaned against the locker next to mine, staring at me with questioning eyes.

I wanted to hide my face in shame. "No, I haven't asked my parents yet."

"Olivia-"

I sighed, looking over at him. "I know, I know. I need to ask them, but every time I'm about to, they get distracted. Melanie's either off doing this or Dad is busy…"

He tapped a random beat on the locker. "Well, I want to tell you that we've already asked our parents and they've agreed. Though if we don't get authorization to use the house, I guess it was useless."

"Yeah," I mumbled then a thought crossed my mind. "You just used a big word! I'm so proud of you, Wayne!"

Sam rolled his eyes. "Shut up."

I smirked and returned to stuffing my locker. "What'd you tell Leah?"

There was a soft chattering behind us and the gang leader glared at the students not-so-secretly watching us. Their attention pivoted elsewhere. "The truth." I shot him an amused look. "I told her I was goin' out of town with some friends and I'll be gone until the weekend school starts back. She didn't seem too into it at first, missing Christmas and such, but I convinced her it was needed. I also promised there would be no parties or drinking. I said I'd be a responsible adult."

"You- responsible?" He winked. "Does she know I'm going?"

"Yes."

"How'd that roll over?"

He shrugged one shoulder. "She didn't freak out. I mean, she knows we've been alone plenty of times, and she's trusts us or at least you," he chuckled. "Besides, she knows that I'm not sleeping with a girl again until-"

"Wait, again?" The word echoed in my eardrums. Again, as in he's done it before. An uneasy feeling entered my stomach. Sam swore under his breath, indicating he hadn't meant for that to slip out. "I thought you-"

"One girl," he confirmed. "Only one and it was a huge mistake. I promise."

I gnawed on my bottom lip, not meeting his eyes. "Oh."

"Olivia," Sam said, "it was a long time ago."

"Who?" *Please not Anya. Please not Anya.*

He shifted uncomfortably. "An old girlfriend."

I shoved my English textbook in my backpack. "Was it serious?"

"At the time."

I looked down at my shoes, deciding I needed to trade these for a new pair. These were all scuffed up. "Was she pretty?"

"Olivia, I'll explain all of it to you, but not today. It's a long story, and I really don't wanna do it here," Sam whispered, propping my chin up with his finger. His beautiful eyes stared into mine, convincing me. "I promise I'll tell you. One day."

I nodded, forgetting for a minute that we were in the halls at school after last period. I snapped back to painful reality, pushing him in the chest- not enough to hurt him. "I'm holding onto that promise."

"Didn't expect anythin' else."

He turned his head to see those nosy students watching us with interest, and Sam sent them a dirty look. They looked frightened for getting caught again, quickly walking away to avoid confrontation. I laughed at their retreating backs and he grinned, his eyes flickering to something over my shoulder. Looking in that specific direction, I was surprised to see Maya standing there.

"Are you ever gonna talk to her again?"

I frowned mournfully as she stalked off without an explanation. "Apparently, we're still not on speaking terms."

"You'll forgive her."

"You sound certain."

"If you forgave me, you can forgive her."

"You know me too well," I said and he agreed. "I have forgiven her. The hard part is talking to her again," I confessed.

Sam nudged me in the side. "You'll figure it out. You always do."

I sent him a grateful smile. "Thanks."

"Well, as much as I'd love to continue this lovely conversation, I have to get going." He threw his backpack over his shoulder. A part of me wanted to ask if he'd want to hang out, but I knew he had to deal with some things involving Under-Twenty. "See ya later, Jenkins."

"Bye, Wayne."

I watched him greet his friends and disappear from my sight, heading towards their vehicles. Remembering the notes I needed for History homework tonight, I opened my locker once again and grabbed it, slipping it into my backpack. I knew I had to ask my parents for permission, but I couldn't bring myself to do it. I felt weak against them. They had a high aura of authority over me and I wasn't fond of that. Just because I lived with them didn't mean they decided every aspect of my life. I felt powerless.

A hand appeared on my arm and Tammy stood beside me, her hair pulled in a fishtail braid over her shoulder. I tugged on the end. "Pretty."

"Thanks," she smiled widely. "Where've you been?"

"What do you mean?" I lifted a confused eyebrow.

"I've tried calling and texting but you never pick up."

"Been busy with homework and college applications," I answered.

"The loveliest part of senior year," Tammy replied, understanding. "So I saw you talking to our *favorite* person."

I laughed. "Yeah, he had some questions about the work in Math."

"No insults?"

"Nope."

She gasped. "The world is ending."

I rolled my eyes teasingly and she hooked onto my arm, dragging me with her in the middle of the hall. "Have you spoken to Maya?"

"I haven't talked to her since that afternoon."

"That was almost two months ago."

I raised my hands. "She ignores me."

Tammy frowned. "Anyways, I wanted to invite you for our annual beginning-of-freedom Winter Break this weekend." Excitement radiated off of her. "No teachers, no Sam drama, no-"

"I can't. I already have plans." The words slipped out before I could stop them.

She stopped abruptly. "But we've always hung out the first weekend of Winter Break. It's tradition."

"I'll be out of town." I hated hurting her feelings but it was necessary. "I'm leaving on Friday after school."

"Oh." Her whole attitude shifted. "Well, I hope you have fun."

And Tammy walked off, upset that I blew her off, but I couldn't forget the danger lurking around just to hang out with her.

"I'm sorry," I muttered, even though it was impossible that she heard me.

I definitely had to ask permission now.

~~~

I stepped into the house, closing the door and throwing my backpack on the stairs. "Dad? Melanie?" I called, entering the kitchen.

"Your father is stuck at the office, Olivia," Melanie informed me. She stood at the counter, a document open on her left and a cutting board on her right. "Is there something you need?" She asked.

I sat at the island, determined to mention the house in the growing conversation. "Uh, do you need any help?" I referred to the vegetables lying un-chopped.

Melanie shook her head. "I've got it. Thank you for asking."

I smiled. "No problem." I recognized the familiar smell coming from the oven. "Are you making teriyaki chicken-"

"And Asian noodles?" She nodded. "Yes. Your favorite, right?"

Something inside me swelled. We haven't had this meal in a very long time. She usually made what the others wanted, and I didn't hide the smile wanting to come onto my lips. I was surprised we weren't at each other's throats. Maybe it was a good day at the firm and she brought the happiness with her. This was the perfect time.

"Do you mind if I ask you something?"

Melanie began cutting the rows of vegetables. "Sure."

"I know its last minute but could some friends and I use the house in North Carolina over Winter Break?" I inquired. "We were trying to find a place to take a vacation and I thought it'd be perfect, but I told them I needed to ask you guys."

She stayed silent, thinking about it thoroughly. "Let me speak to your dad and we'll decide from there."

"Okay," I agreed nervously. Dad would be the hard one to convince. I tapped my fingers against the countertop, awkwardly shifting in my seat with all the tension in the room. "I'll be upstairs," I vocalized, trying to make a hasty exit.

"Olivia, wait," Melanie said softly. I turned to face her, expecting a lecture or another comparison. "I want to apologize, for treating you the way I have. For not appreciating everything you do, whether it's in school or at home. For not accepting you for the way you are. I am proud of you and all your accomplishments," she smiled. "I'm proud to call you my step-daughter."

Without even thinking about it, I had walked over and wrapped her up in a hug, blinking back tears. I had been waiting to hear those words for a long time. "Thank you," I whispered. "I'm sor-"

"Don't," she interrupted. "You had every right to be upset with me. It just took me a while to realize what I'd been doing."

"Thank you," I said again.

Melanie smiled and cocked her chin towards the living room. "Now go do your homework," she joked. I laughed and exited the kitchen, feeling happier in the contents of my home for the first time in years.

~~~

When my father finally returned home from work, they stepped out of the room and into his office, and I had a pretty good idea what they were discussing about. I hid myself in my room, keeping myself busy with homework because I knew that if I didn't keep my mind whirring, I would drive myself to the limit. Besides, my English essay can't write itself. It was due after Winter Break, but I knew I wouldn't have time to finish it, let alone start it if we went to North Carolina.

There was a knock on my door, and as I finished a sentence, my parents trailed in, making the space of my room become smaller. I turned in my chair, meeting their calm stares. I fidgeted, waiting for them to initiate the conversation.

My father tapped his fingers against his arms, his reading glasses perched on his nose. He probably had paperwork to tend to. "Your mother said that you want to go to the cottage, and I think it would be a good idea to get away from drama-"

"Oh, you're taking too long! Olivia, we give you permission to go," Melanie interrupted.

I gasped. "Are you serious?"

"Yes. You're turning eighteen next month and I agree that you deserve a vacation and spend some time away from here," Melanie explained further. "You've also been getting excellent grades and think of it as a gift for doing well."

"Thank you!" I said excitedly. My father grunted a reply and stalked off, but even his grumpiness wouldn't ruin my good mood.

"How many people are going?"

"Uh, five, including myself," I answered.

She pursed his lips. "Any of them being boys?"

All. "A few, but I trust that won't try anything. They're all involved anyway."

"Well, I trust you and I know you'll make responsible choices."

I jumped out of my seat and hugged her. "I can't thank you enough for this!" I exclaimed.

"Just promise to update us every now and then."

I nodded. "Don't worry, I will."

After she bid me goodnight and retreated from my bedroom, I grabbed my phone, and after entering the boy's contacts, I typed two words:

Permission granted.

~~~

The next day we sat around Sam's coffee table, finalizing the plans and deciding what vehicles to bring. I suggested three, but Daniel was afraid it would raise suspicion, leading the boss to unwanted ideas. Sam and Ryker were chosen as the designated drivers so we'd just bring theirs.

"I don't want to listen to all that lovey-dovey crap on the way there," Ace protested against riding with me and Sam. "I get enough of that at school with ridiculous cheerleaders and sappy girls."

"We're not that kind of couple."

"Or are we?" Sam wiggled his eyebrows suggestively, grinning crookedly at me.

I punched him on the arm, shaking my head at his ridiculous comment. I looked at the list in my hands, chewing on my bottom lip. "There's enough food to last us for the entire time minus drinks."

"How do you know the fridge is fully stocked?" Daniel asked.

"We rent it out over the holidays to friends or family, and we order cleaners and everything. I've told them we'll need plenty of food," I winked.

Ace jabbed a thumb in Daniel's side. "Especially with personal garbage disposals coming with us."

"Hey!"

Sam rolled his eyes. "Next is..." He glanced over my shoulder, his scratchy chin tickling my cheek. "Room assignments."

"There's a master suite and two guest bedrooms."

"Sam and I can share, Ace and Daniel as well, and Olivia can have the master suite," Ryker suggested.

"Why does she have a room to herself?" Ace asked.

"Because she's obviously not a girl," Sam replied dryly. His cousin glared at him. "Don't ask a stupid question if you don't want a sarcastic answer."

While they engaged in a foolish banter, I directed a question to Ryker and Daniel. "How do Beth and Rebecca feel about this?"

"Beth is good with it as long as there's plenty of Skype involved."

"Rebecca's out of town this time of the year, but same goes for her."

"Good," I breathed out. "I won't be attacked by jealous girlfriends."

The guys laughed, making me feel more comfortable. They easily accepted me and Sam, and I had been afraid of negativity. They proved me wrong. These past several days, I've learned a lot about them. They've had rough lives and been through traumatic events. They were searching for a way to forget the past. I glanced over at Sam and his green eyes shifted to mine. I didn't know how long we stared at each other, but it was enough to make electricity tingle from the top of my head to the tips of my toes.

"Where are we going to meet?" Ryker queried.

"I was thinking somewhere local," I articulated leaning back on the couch.

"What about Wal-Mart?" Ace offered.

I smiled. "Perfect. The back parking lot. It's less

risky."

"Meet up at twelve," Sam added. "We'll pack everything in the cars and get some lunch before heading out."

By five, we had everything sorted and finished.

Now all we had to do was wait for Friday.

Chapter 23: Olivia

After class was dismissed and the bell rang marking the beginning of Winter Break, students cheered and teachers barked at them for being too rambunctious and loud. Tammy walked over as I shut my locker and hooked the lock on it. She held out her arms, a pout displayed. I stepped into them, wrapping my arms around her. "Does this mean I'm forgiven?"

"I was never mad," she said. "I'll admit I was disappointed and a little upset, but I got over it, realizing it was stupid."

"Good because I don't want my best friend mad at me," I said pulling back.

Tammy smiled. "I can never have negative feelings towards you. It's simply impossible," she giggled.

"I'll see you in the new year."

She grabbed her messenger bag and placed a New Year's hat with sparkly streamers and painted USA colors on her head. "Have fun, Olive!"

With a goodbye hug and a wave of the hand, she skipped off with the rest of our classmates. I turned around and jumped as strong and warm hands caught my wrists. I recognized the calluses on his fingers.

Faking aggravation, I pursed my lips. "What do you want, Wayne?"

He smirked, strands of hair sneaking its way out of his dark beanie. "Oh, come on, Jenkins. I know you're going to miss me."

"Sure will," I said sarcastically. "I'll be drowning in tears and chocolate these next two weeks."

"Aw, you'll miss me," Sam grinned cockily.

"Whatever floats your boat."

"I'm not afraid to admit it. I'll miss you."

I scoffed, not amused.

"Babe, stop fighting it."

I pried his hands off my wrists, stepping back. "You're ruining my good mood."

He wrapped an arm around my shoulders. "I'll cheer ya up."

"No, thanks." I ducked under his grip and walked the opposite direction, waving goodbye to other classmates. Our argument was totally ironic.

The parking lot was almost empty by eleven forty-five. I paced down the sidewalk, seeking warmth. I was waiting for Sam to pull up beside me. When his black truck came around the corner, I glanced for any pedestrians before jumping inside; he accelerated as I buckled my seatbelt.

"So you're gonna miss me, huh?" I nudged him in the side.

"It is gonna be a terrible two weeks," he winked.

I climbed out quickly, jogging up the steps of my house. I trailed into my bedroom, throwing my backpack over my shoulder, and carried the large duffle bag. I left a note for Dad and Melanie, telling them I'd call when we reached the cottage and wishing them a Merry Christmas. Turning off all the lights and locking the deadbolt, I left with a smile on my face.

We reached Wal-Mart with minutes to spare. I watched the boys from inside the warm vehicle pack up the trunk of Ryker's Jeep. I braided my hair loosely for a more relaxed feel and snuggled in the softness of Sam's hoodie. I had already made myself comfortable. Earphones lay carelessly on the dashboard, phone stashed in the waistband of my sweatpants, my perfect-conditioned *Shadow and Bone* novel near my hip- I was all set.

The sound of closing doors entered my ears and Ryker high-fived Sam before parting ways. Sam slid behind the wheel and put the key in the ignition, but didn't turn it on. I reached over mindlessly and took his hand, running a finger across his scarred knuckles. He leaned back against the seat cushion, sighing.

"We'll be okay," I said.

Sam nodded. "Yeah, I know. Are you nervous?"

"Nah."

"Glad to know I'm not the only one." He leaned in and kissed my forehead.

I frowned. "You missed." I tried to ignore the whine in my voice.

He gave me a lingering kiss. "You're startin' to sound like me," Sam chuckled.

I shrugged. "As long as my voice doesn't change, I'm okay with it."

"I don't know. I think you'll be pretty hot with a deep voice like mine," he smirked. I rolled my eyes, but I knew there was a blush on my cheeks. "Isn't that cute? You're blushing!"

I shoved him in the shoulder. "Just drive." I referred to Ryker's headlights flashing- the signal to know when they're ready.

My green-eyed gang leader intertwined our fingers, sending me a shy grin. "Are you ready?" He started the truck, its engine revving.

"I'm ready," I answered.

And with a soft kiss to my hand, Sam pulled out of the Wal-Mart parking lot and began our journey to North Carolina.

~~~

The radio played in the background as Sam and I finished eating. It was about six o'clock and we were a good distance from New York. I tried to get Sam to allow me to drive, but he felt safer if he drove his 'junk-yard on wheels'. About twenty minutes ago, we stopped to eat because of the boy's hunger issues, and not wanting to delay any longer (we had some traffic), we decided to take it on the go.

"How was your food?" Sam asked sparking a conversation.

I took a sip of soda, the wonderful taste of *Dr. Pepper* dancing on my tongue. "It was good. Thanks for paying."

"I'm the dude. I'm supposed to pay for the girl's food."

I laughed. "I know, but I still feel obligated to say thank you."

"Then you're welcome."

He switched channels on the radio as I gazed out the window, the sky turning from its usual blue to a shade of purple as the sun said goodnight, allowing the moon to shine. The highway wasn't heavy since work had ended for the day and people are retiring for the night.

When we crossed over into the next state, the accidental mention of Sam's ex-serious girlfriend slammed headstrong in my mind. I wanted to know what happened between them; I wanted to know how she was so special that he slept with her. It wasn't because I was jealous; it was natural curiosity.

"Hey, Sam?"

"Hmm?" I chewed on my bottom lip, searching for the right words, but none came. "Olivia, what is it?"

"Who was she?"

"Who?" He was so oblivious.

I sighed. "The girl you slept with."

Sam stiffened and his hands gripped the steering

wheel, his knuckles turning white. He inhaled sharply. "Do we have to talk about this right now?"

"Please," I begged. "It's been on my mind ever since you've mentioned it."

"I didn't mean for it to slip out."

"Sam, I want to know," I replied. He glanced at me and his eyes were disturbed. "We're best friends. We're in a relationship. We can tell each other anything." His jaw was set firm. "I just want know who she is."

"Why?"

"Because she's a part of your past."

"It's not important."

"To me, it is. She's a part of the time I wasn't around," I answered. "And besides, wouldn't you want to know about the guy if we were serious enough to sleep together?"

He released his tight hold and relaxed. He was considering telling me. "What do you want to know?"

"Everything," I said reluctantly.

He stared at the open road ahead of us, tapping his fingers against the wheel. He sighed. "I met her the summer after freshman year," he began. "My friends dragged to me a bonfire for the Fourth of July and one of them introduced me to her. Her name was Nicole, though everyone called her Nikki. She attended a private school with some of the girls." His voice seemed strained but he continued anyways. "At first, it was awkward and very uncomfortable, considering we were forced together and our friends ditched us. When the fireworks went off, she said her favorite color was purple, and that simple statement became a three-hour conversation.

"About a month later, I asked her out and obviously she accepted. In the month of October, the boss found out I was involved in a committed relationship and let me off with a warning, but demanded I break up with her. I didn't." Sam flipped on his turning signal and went into another lane. "We continued secretly dating for two months.

"One night, she dropped by my house all teary-eyed and make-up messed up, and told me her dad got a promotion, but it was all the way in California. She asked me if I loved her. At the time, I believed I did and that is when..." He drifted off, clearing his throat. I knew what he was saying: that's when they slept together. "Anyways, what happened was Nikki rebelled against her parents. She did everything they disagreed with, including having sex before marriage. I felt betrayed because she used me. She used me to get back at her parents. She abused my trust and my feelings for her and used it for her own selfish reasons.

"I snapped at her one day and we had a huge fight, resulting in breaking up. She broke out of her rebellious stage, believing that would send me back crawling after her, but I refused to take her back. She even surprised me with a plane ticket to come with her the weekend they moved, but I told her to leave. Leaving me a nasty note about how it was my entire fault," Sam laughed humorlessly, "Nikki moved to California with her parents. I haven't heard from her since."

It was silent for a few moments as I gathered my thoughts.

"She's the reason why I turned into a player. I believed girls were just going to use me so it was easier to date 'em and not have to deal with feelings getting in the way and controlling me," Sam confessed.

"I'm sorry."

"For what? It's not your fault."

I shrugged. "I don't know what else to say."

"It's fine. Besides, I much rather have this brown-eyed beauty instead of having her," Sam grinned in my direction and a wide smile spread across my lips.

"You're earning major brownie points, Wayne."

He laughed despite the previous tension. "Good to know."

I turned in my seat and leaned my back against the passenger door, my legs taking up the free space, and propped my feet in his lap. "Can I ask you a question?"

"Yeah."

"Did you like it?"

Sam lifted an eyebrow and amusement twinkled in his eyes. "Do you really want me to answer that?" I shook my head, fiddling with my thumbs. That was incredibly stupid to ask. What boy didn't enjoy sex? "But I'll be honest... I do regret it."

I looked up, surprised by the comment. He didn't go into explanation which gave me the impression he didn't want to speak about it anymore. "Olivia, you look like you're about to crash," he observed. "Get some sleep."

I yawned, not bothering to argue with him. I scooted closer and leaned my head on his shoulder, otherwise known as my pillow. "Wake me if you need directions."

"I will, babe. Now sleep," Sam breathed into my temple. "Don't let the car bugs bite..."

"Oh shut up," I murmured, letting my hand fall on his cheek as a slap attempt.

Chapter 24: Sam

"Olivia," I muttered in my girlfriend's ear, coaxing her to life.

"Wha'?" She groaned in response, burying her face in my shoulder.

I chuckled. "Come on, Liv. Wake up."

"Shut up, you idiot. Trying to sleep." She pressed her palm to my face in a tired attempt of a slap.

"Someone's violent when sleepy," I teased, getting no reaction from her.

Drifting to drastic measures, I stuck my finger in her ear.

She smacked my hand away. "Don't do that!"

"Then get up," I deadpanned.

Olivia yawned and sat up, rubbing her eyes. "I'm guessing we're here."

"Yeah," I said. Her mouth opened, but I already knew the question that was on her mind. "It's one in the morning."

"I'd ask you to carry me, but I'm not taking a chance of making you worse."

She stepped out of the truck, all cute and lazy in her sweatpants and ruffled hoodie, which I recognized as mine, and smiled at the cottage. There were a few outside lamps, illuminating the walkway to the front door. Even though it was past midnight, I could see the mountains in the distance, a different shade from the sky. I wished we had this in New York.

Olivia had been right about the house being hidden. When I had pulled onto the road, after missing it once, I drove for about five or seven minutes before reaching the brown cottage. Good thing I had directions or I would have gotten lost.

Ryker's Jeep pulled in next to mine and the guys jumped out, looking weary and tired. We busied ourselves unpacking the vehicles as Olivia unlocked the house. She flipped on the outside lights then returned and picked up two duffels, carrying them inside. By one-thirty, we had everything stuffed in the living room, and all of us collapsed on anything with cushion. I looked around the room and it was consisted of two sofas, a loveseat, and a recliner in the corner; there was also a flat screen, a shelf filled with plenty of movies to keep us satisfied these next two weeks, and a coffee table.

"Dude, I'm retiring," Ryker announced.

Daniel shot to his feet. "Good 'cause I'm about to crash."

Ace stalked off towards the bedrooms, claiming the comfy bed. I laughed as the two fought in hushed tones about it. Olivia bid the guys goodnight as did I with a fist-bump or handshake.

"Time for bed," I said.

She rolled off the couch she'd occupied and trailed in the direction my friends had gone. I followed her into the hallway and turned to enter the room I was gonna share with Ryker, but Olivia gripped unto my hand. "Sleep in here with me."

"Olivia, I don't think that's a good idea," I whispered. Lying in a bed with minimal space between me and my gorgeous girlfriend didn't help the attribute the male species lacks: self-control.

Her eyes met mine; green on brown. "I trust you."

"Liv-"

"Please," she pouted. That was the first time I've ever seen *her* pout.

I frowned. "That's not fair."

"Exactly why I used it," Olivia smirked.

I sent her a dirty look and she trailed into the master suite, leaving me stranded in the hallway. I took a few steps forward and leaned against the doorframe, watching

her as she slipped off her boots and discarded her hoodie- or should I say, *my* hoodie, then climbed under the covers. She smiled tiredly at me and I returned it, included with an adorable yawn. Olivia laughed. There was a tap on my shoulder and I turned to see Ryker standing in boxers and T-shirt.

"I'm takin' it you're staying here for the night?"

I nodded. "Apparently."

"Kinda figured," he chuckled. "Night, man. See ya in the mornin', Olivia." She replied with a goodnight. He walked off to the bedroom closest to the master and closed the door behind him. No doubt he'd be making a phone call to Beth before sleep took him for the rest of the evening.

I ventured out to the living room, retrieving black pants, and returned to the bedroom, leaving the door cracked. Kicking off my sneakers near the dresser on the side Olivia didn't occupy, I changed out of my jeans and into my sweatpants in the bathroom. When I was done, I crawled beneath the covers, sighing softly as I felt the mattress lying under my back. Olivia rolled onto her side, facing me. Her hand found mine in the darkness and our fingers entwined. Relief set in my bones. She was here with me, safe and out of harm's way.

"Get some rest," she whispered. I locked eyes with her; the moonlight streaming in through the windows reflecting onto her figure. "You've been driving for almost twelve hours."

"That long, huh?"

She threaded her fingers through my hair. "Yeah. I'll let you sleep in and drag one of the boys to the pharmacy for better pain killers."

"You're the best person in the world," I muttered, resting my forehead on hers.

"Mm, I know," Olivia winked. I lifted a hand and stroked her cheek, my fingertips brushing the softness of her skin. Her eyes were droopy. "I'm tired."

"Me too. I'm going to sleep." I grabbed an extra pillow and held it to my chest, burying the side of my face in the cushion. I closed my eyes, beginning to drift off.

"Are you not comfortable snuggling with me?" Olivia asked in the silence.

I shook my head, dismissing the unwanted thoughts of us being *extremely* close, in a bed nonetheless. "I didn't want to push you into something you weren't okay with."

"We slept on the roof, remember? I don't mind."

I sighed. "This is different. We're in a *bed*."

She tilted her head in confusion and I gave her a look. "Ohh…"

"Yeah. It's a lot easier to be tempted." I scratched the spot behind my ear, wanting to do nothing except break the tension. "Look, I'm not-"

"Sam, I trust you," Olivia said suddenly. "I know guys have trouble keeping stable in a relationship, physically speaking, but I trust you more than myself, and I know you won't try anything. You're not like other guys."

"But I am," I argued. "Yeah, I didn't sleep around with tons of girls, but I still wasn't the purest thing around. Making out was the norm for me. I'd have to stop myself from going too far because I didn't want to be the guy who'd take *that* from a girl and never speak to her again," I confessed. Olivia was the only person I was comfortable sharing this information with.

"That's what makes you different," she pointed out.

"Most guys wouldn't care." I knew that for a fact. There were some members who'd sleep with a girl and never gave them a second glance. "So, please stop being hard on yourself. You have more self-control than you're aware of." I snorted, finding it somewhat hard to believe. "Sam,

I'm being honest when I say you've never pressured me to do something I didn't want to do. You're patient, you don't push me, and what makes you extra special is you regret having sex with Nikki. Not many guys could admit that," Olivia tapped her fingers against my forearm. "Anyways, what I'm saying is I'm fine sleeping in a bed platonically with you, as long as you are."

I smiled. "Have I ever told you that you're amazing?"

She laughed. "You've mentioned it. Now let me sleep. I want to cuddle."

"Then come here." She scooted closer to me and retracted the pillow out of my arms, immediately replacing it with herself. She rested her head on my chest, being aware of my healing injuries.

"Besides, I'd kick your tail if you tried anything."

I chuckled at how Olivia that statement was. "I know you would. Night, Liv," I said into her hair.

She grabbed a fistful of my shirt. "Night, Wayne." And with that said, I fell asleep to the sound of crickets chirping and Olivia's heartbeat against my chest.

~~~

"Up and at 'em boys!" Olivia shouted, waking me up from my peaceful slumber.

My eyes shot open and I sat up, rubbing my eyes with sleep. She entered the master bedroom, clad in navy sweatpants and a white tee. "Time to face the day."

"Mornin' babe," I grumbled falling back onto the mattress, not wanting to leave this amazing masterpiece. It was way sturdier and comfier than the one I had at home, and I was going to miss this thing when we leave.

"Breakfast is served," she told me and I perked up at the sound of man's best friend. "So I got Ryker to go to the pharmacy with me and got you this incredible medicine that should ease two-thirds of the pain."

"Awesome."

"Oh, and also, your favorite drink is waiting for you."

I gazed at her with a grin. "You're a goddess."

She laughed. "C'mon. The guys are already eating."

I stepped out of bed, following her to the kitchen where my best friends sat around the large island, stuffing their faces. I slapped Ace on the back on his head, chuckling at his angry grunt, and prepared myself a plate. I took three pancakes, a scoop of eggs, few strips of bacon, and a piece of toast. Olivia moved to stand next to me, sipping an opened can of Dr. Pepper.

"Who knew you could cook?" I asked, my mouth filled with syrup and grease.

She tapped her fingers on the countertop. "I'm full of surprises."

"Indeed you are," I kissed her on the cheek and Ace groaned at the public display of affection. Shooting him a glare, I stuffed my face.

"That was good," Ace said.

Ryker patted her hand. "Man, this is awesome!"

Daniel nodded enthusiastically. "I'll never be able to eat another biscuit at Mickey's ever again. This is too good."

"Thanks," Olivia smiled.

"What's on the agenda for today?" I questioned, cracking open a can of Coke and letting its taste dance on my tongue.

"How 'bout a movie marathon?" Ryker suggested. "Personally, I want to relax and do nothin'."

"Sounds like a plan," Olivia replied, heading towards the living room. The others trailed after her as I finished cleaning my plate. After placing it in the sink, I sat down on the couch, propping my feet on the coffee table. The guys found their seats; either collapsing on the floor or chairs. Ryker spread himself out on the second sofa, Daniel called the loveseat, and Ace ended up sliding off his seat and unto the floor, kissing the carpet. We got a good laugh out of that.

My girlfriend stood near the DVD section, arms crossed and hip cocked; staring at the titles. "There are plenty of movies to choose from. Any requests?"

We looked at each other simultaneously and shouted together, "No freakin' chick flicks!"

She blinked at the sudden announcement. "Um, I prefer action and thriller."

"Yes!" Ace exclaimed, earning crazed looks from us. "Finally a girl who isn't all about romance and cheesiness!"

Olivia shrugged. "Some aren't *terrible*, but they're not my choice of genre."

"I've decided you're my new favorite person," my cousin declared, sending me a quick teasing smirk. "Sorry, Sam. I'm stealing your girl."

"Better not," I said. "My finger is still trigger-happy." He glared at me and I smiled innocently. "Anyways, stop torturin' her. Let's find a movie!"

"How about-" She scrolled through the alphabetical order, her fingers ghosting over the DVD cases. She grabbed a movie and presented it. "- *The Dark Knight*?"

A chorus of yells broke through the room. Olivia opened the DVD player and put the disc inside, grabbing the remote from the TV stand. She moved to join me on the couch; however, I surprised her by pulling her onto my lap. I winced at the sudden weight added, but refused to release her. I wrapped my arms around her waist, allowing her to lean on me though I was cautious about putting pressure on my ribs. She started the film and it began playing on the screen with the masked villains doing the burglary and the Joker making his appearance.

Around the part where Bruce was throwing the fundraiser for Harvey Dent and the Joker dropped in, the pain acted up again. I could barely watch the movie because of the sharp stabs happening every few minutes. Sleep was overtaking me also, which I didn't know why I was so tired, but maybe it was the pain and the twelve-hour drive mixed together.

"Take those pills on the counter and go take a nap," Olivia whispered. I gave her a bewildered expression. "I'm not an idiot. It's obvious you're tired and it doesn't help that you're injured. Don't worry. I'll tell the guys not to

bother you and to stay quiet."

"You're amazin'," I mumbled, brushing my lips over hers. "Thanks."

"I know." She smirked, pressing a real kiss to my mouth. "You're welcome."

I stood from the couch and entered the kitchen, immediately noticing the medicine bottle perched on the counter. I dropped a few pills into the palm of my hand and got me a glass of water. I heard Olivia informing the guys of my plans and that if they weren't quiet, she'd come after them with a knife or worse, no homemade breakfast for the rest of the time we're here. They agreed quickly to use inside voices.

Not even realizing where I was going, my feet dragged me to the master suite, and I shut the door, stripping off my shirt, and hid myself under the covers to avoid the bright sunlight shining in. I closed my eyes, sleep overtaking me.

~~~

A soft movement on my face woke me up. Ignoring my body's desperate pleas to stay asleep, my eyes fluttered open and they landed on Olivia, who was running her finger across my jaw and five o'clock shadow.

"What're you doin' in here?"

"I could ask you the same thing."

I rubbed my eyes, waking up more fully. "I didn't think you would mind."

Olivia nuzzled her head in the crook of my neck. "Not at all," she mumbled against my skin.

I reached over, taking a leap and moving to lie on my side (that medicine worked wonders), and placed a hand on her waist, drawing little circles with my fingertips. She draped an arm around my neck, untangling knots in my hair. "How long was I out?"

"Three hours," she answered. "The guys ambushed the TV after *Dark Knight* ended. Not that I'm complaining, they had great choices." She turned silent and I listened to her steady breathing, practically hearing the gears in her head shifting. There was something on her mind. "Can I show you something?"

"Mm," I nodded.

We stepped out of bed and I pulled on my discarded shirt, exiting the room with her in front. We snuck past the living room where my best friends laid sprawled, enjoying their movie marathon, and Olivia led me to the sliding-glass door in the back of the cottage. She pushed it open, letting in a whoosh of chilly air, and I zipped on a hoodie before walking out. I stopped in awe.

The backyard had different colored leaves covering the ground, welcoming winter with the bareness of the surrounding forest. Large grey mountains stood in the distance; the sky painted with pink and orange and soft purple from the sunset. North Carolina had to be one of the prettiest states I've visited. I'm sure gonna miss this.

"Thought you might like it," Olivia said.

I peeled my eyes off the scenery and looked at my girlfriend who was standing at the wooden railing, staring at the natural beauty. She wore dark skinny jeans and a tan leather jacket, zipped up all the way to fend off the cold. Her caramel-brown waves were cascading down her back and shoulders, some annoying strands pinned to the side. She turned her head, her mouth open like she was about to say something, but stopped, a shy smile appearing on her lips.

"What?"

I walked a few steps forward, pausing when I was in front of her. Hooking my fingers in the belt loops of her jeans, I pulled her close. Her palms laid flat on my chest; my hands respectively rested on her lower back. "I love you."

Olivia grinned, her chocolate brown eyes sparkling. She grabbed my chin, tracing a finger across my bottom lip. "I love you too."

We decided to sit on the steps, our shoulders and hips pressed against another, not that I minded, and enjoyed the cool fresh air. However, the way Olivia fidgeted with her hands and rubbed her knees, I knew there was something she wanted to talk about.

"What's on your mind?" I asked. She glanced at me with questioning eyes. "I've known you for years, Liv. I think I know when you need to talk."

"It's nothing," she retorted.

I nudged her with my shoulder. "We're best friends. We tell each other everything." She kept her eyes on the ground. "All right, something is seriously buggin' you. What is it?"

"What's going to happen after graduation?" She asked abruptly. There was a sudden change in the atmosphere after those words escaped her mouth in a shaky tone.

"What are you talking about?"

"After graduation, we'll be going separate ways."

I reached over and lifted her chin, not giving her the choice of escaping my gaze. "Where is this coming from, Olivia?"

She took a deep breath, blinking rapidly to stop the

tears welding up. "Tammy and I were talking one afternoon, and she mentioned that after high school ends, we wouldn't have to deal with you or Under-Twenty again. It got me thinking…" Olivia chewed on her lower lip. "When high school ends, what's going to happen with us? Is this some sort of fling or are we for real? My stupid thoughts are telling me that our relationship will end; it'll fade." She turned her head, her voice brittle. "Sam, none of the colleges I've been accepted to are even close to New York. I'm worried that if I go to school somewhere else, I'm gonna lose you."

Her eyes were cloudy with tears and vulnerability, and some broke through her tough shell, leaving soft smears on her cheeks. "You're not gonna lose me."

"How do you know that?"

I touched her cheek softly, wiping away the tears with my thumb. "Olivia, listen to me." She stared at me, our eyes locking; green on brown. "I'm never letting you go. We've gone through that once, and that's somethin' I'd *never* let happen again. I promise you, you'll never lose me. Why would I let go of the best thing that's ever happened to me?" Olivia made a small choking noise in the back of her throat, her face breaking out into a smile. I pressed my forehead to hers, shutting my eyes. "You're everything to me, Jenkins. I don't *ever* plan on letting you go."

And *no*, the kiss she gave me didn't make me forget who or what I was and the boss threatening our lives and the danger lurking after us for that split second of paradise.

"Yo, Sammy!" Ryker's voice called out, making us break apart quickly and he stood in the doorway, eyes wide like a deer caught in headlights.

I tossed him a split glance. "What's up, man?"

"Wanna order pizza for dinner?" Olivia and I both nodded, giving our input. "That's all. You may proceed."

I sent him the stink eye as he dashed back inside. "Best friends. Always come at inopportune moments."

She laughed, stretching her legs out and made an attempt to stand up. "Well, we better head inside-"

"No," I grabbed at her hand to stop her, earning a confused look. "Let's stay out here and talk some more."

"I'm getting the impression you actually like talking to me," Olivia teased.

I sucked in a deep breath, licking my lips. "Busted."

"As much as I would like to, it's getting chillier by the second, and I don't want those boys stealing my food."

"They wouldn't dare. I'll hurt 'em." She lifted an eyebrow as if saying, 'are you serious?' "Well, they can have yours, but mine on the other hand, they won't see tomorrow." I tilted my head and gave her a lopsided grin, knocking my forehead against hers before retreating to the door.

Olivia hoisted to her full height, pressing a hand to her heart. "My hero."

"I feel so honored," I replied smirking. Passing by, she greeted me with a slap on the cheek.

~~~

"Merry Christmas, baby!" Mom cheered.

"Merry Christmas," I greeted her back.

"I've missed you so much and you've only been gone a week..." I leaned against the wall, listening to my mother's rants about how quiet the house was without my sarcastic comments and obnoxious yelling at the TV.

"I miss you too, Mom," I cut her off, meaning every word. It was weird not seeing her every day, but she didn't seem to mind.

"How's Olivia?" She asked.

I glanced to the right where my girlfriend was sprawled out across the couch, her face buried in the pillow she stole from the master room. Our absurd friends were challenging themselves with the task of waking her up. Ace had a feather in his hand, tickling her in the ear. She rolled over, muttering a pissed off *go away*. The funniest thing about it, Olivia was already awake. She wanted to see how long they would go before admitting defeat.

I chuckled, grinning. "She's doing fine."

I could practically *hear* the smile on her face from the other end of the line. "Tell her I said hello, Merry Christmas, and I miss her pretty face."

"Will do."

"You're behaving, right?"

"Not at all. I've been terribly naughty. Like I'm at the top of Santa's list."

Mom laughed. "Okay, okay, I'm stopping." A ten second passage of silence came between us. "When are you coming back?"

"Uh, about a week. We'll be home by Sunday the latest," I answered, scratching an annoying itch on my elbow.

"All right, because when you return, I need to talk to you about something."

I raised an eyebrow. "Like what?"

"I'll speak to you when you get back."

"Why can't you talk to me now?" I asked, a little worried and frustrated that she mentioned this and is avoiding questions. She didn't normally hide things from me.

She sighed. "Sam-"

"Mom-"

"We'll talk when you're home. Now leave it alone, Samuel."

My body stiffened at the sound of my full name. She never used it unless I was in trouble or I disappointed her.

What could I have possibly done being several states away?

"I gotta go. The guys are messin' with Olivia-"

"Sam, I-"

"I love you." I ended the call before she had the chance to reply. I didn't like it when my mom kept things from me. We were closer than that.

Ryker noticed the change in my attitude. "You all right, man?"

I realized I had become silent. "Yeah," I nodded then pointed at the 'sleeping' figure of Olivia. "You know she's awake, right?"

"You gotta be kiddin' me!" Ace exclaimed.

Her eyes popped open and she sat up, scowling at me. "Thanks a lot, Wayne."

"You're welcome, babe," I smirked.

"I hate you."

"Hate you too," I winked at her.

Daniel clamped a hand on my shoulder. "Everythin' okay?"

I released my worries. "Mom's hiding somethin' from me. I can hear it in her tone and she's never distant like she was today." I sat down next to Olivia, crossing my arms and propping my feet on the coffee table. "Just hope it's nothin' bad."

"It'll be fine," Olivia smiled. She stood and retreated to the kitchen, exclaiming about her stomach wanting food. I chuckled at how she's becoming like me.

"Hate to be the one to bring this up, but what are

we gonna do when we get back to New York?" Ace asked. "The boss might've figured somethin' out and might be waiting for us."

Ryker and I shared a matching glance. He was the only one that knew about the box of drugs. "Got it covered," I proclaimed.

Daniel's eyes widened in realization. "You didn't."

They stared at me for confirmation. "It was just one. He won't be botherin' us until next due date." They weren't upset, just surprised. "Not only did it save my hind-end, but yours too. I had to do what was best for the gang."

Olivia returned with a bowl of popcorn, plopping herself down in her so-called seat. She realized we were in the middle of a conversation. "Oh, did I interrupt?"

"Nah."

"So what'd I miss?"

"Nothing," we chorused.

She gave me a weird look. "Gang stuff," I informed.

"Oh. Yeah, I'm good with not knowing," she said.

I wasn't going to tell her anyways. She didn't need to know about the drugs. I'm not taking the chance of her becoming wary of my actions. I was a gang leader; I had to make dangerous choices and take risks.

It was a major part of my life. It wasn't something I could just avoid.

Grabbing the remote control, I turned on the TV to

ease the tension. "Let's watch something festive."

I was ambushed by several eager shouts of, "*Charlie Brown!*"

~~~

That night, I was lying wide awake with Olivia sleeping soundly beside me. My fingers were stroking up and down her spine as I stared at the ceiling, having nothing else better to do.

A chime distracted me from my thoughts. I turned my head to the screen of my phone gleaming with light. I removed myself from the warm sheets, checking the time on the clock: 3.24. Who'd be texting me this late at night? Picking up my phone, I tapped in the passcode, my eyes widening at the contact. The boss.

You may be one of the best gang leaders, but I do NOT tolerate my rules being abused and ignored. I do NOT appreciate the fact that you think you're better than me, and think you can run away... which is cowardly. I didn't think Sam Wayne ran away from his problems. I gritted my teeth. *I'll give you one last chance. Dump the girl, and she'll be safe. You have my word.*

Hitting the reply button, I typed in: *How can I trust you?*

I leaned against the wall, waiting.

Have I ever done anything to betray your trust?

You sent thugs after me.

I stared at the scar crossing my knuckles on my

right hand.

You betrayed me. I can't play favorites. The rules apply to everyone, including you.

I glanced over at Olivia who slept soundly.

How will I know she'll be safe?

I'll make sure of it.

I shook my head, even if he couldn't see me. The answer was plain and simple; I wasn't losing her again.

No.

I exited the message app, looking at my wallpaper that showed Olivia sitting on my bed, notebook open in front of her, pencil in hand; a beautiful smile on her face.

You're makin' a mistake, Wayne.

I smirked. *No, I'm not.*

Attaching the phone to its charger, I climbed back into bed. I wrapped an arm around my girlfriend's waist, dragging her until her back collided with my chest. Her nose scrunched up at the change of position, but she stayed fast asleep. I pressed a kiss to her temple, burying my nose in her hair and closing my eyes.

I would do everything in my power to keep him from touching her.

Even if that meant I had die to protect her.

Chapter 25: Sam

The next week went by slowly. We stayed inside, except the occasional outings for food and pharmacy stops. We had movies marathons, consisting of plenty of actions films and one romantic-thriller. The guys had ditched- what great friends they are- but if I'm being honest, it wasn't one of those stupid and cliché chick flicks. I was actually intrigued by the end. I was not expecting the secret that was exposed.

Mom and I haven't spoken since the phone-call that ended badly. I kept thinking that maybe something went wrong with her job and she was fired or our secret stash of money was stolen. I don't know why, but I could somehow feel that wasn't it. This had to do something with her and her only.

The day we had to go home came quick. That morning, after packing up the vehicles and stocking packs for the drive home and winning the last Coke of the twelve-pack, I found Olivia on the back porch, admiring the view. Her arms were crossed, hands covered with cozy gloves to keep the cool and windy air away.

Olivia sighed. "A part of me doesn't want to leave." She must have heard me come outside. "I absolutely love it here. I mean, we don't have to hide; I don't have to deal with drama, there's no pressuring parents or gang bosses coming after us..." I walked up behind her, placing my hands on her shoulders and began rubbing them. "I love

New York, but this cottage has always had a special place in my heart. It's so peaceful, and beauty is everywhere you look." She turned on the balls of her feet, facing me and I dropped my hands, keeping them by my sides. "I don't regret coming here, Sam; it just reminds me of the crap we're going back to."

Instead of telling her it's gonna be okay and I'm sorry or any of those other 'comforting' sayings and words, I said, "Tell you what. When all this stuff blows over with Boss and everything, we'll come back here on Spring Break. Just me and you," I smiled crookedly. "We'll go hiking and sightseeing and so much more."

"By ourselves?" Olivia quirked an eyebrow.

"Yeah," I answered, nodding, then I realized what she meant. By ourselves means non-supervised alone time. "If it'll make you feel better, I'll buy you an air-horn and if you get uncomfortable, blow it. I mean make my ears bleed babe!"

She bursts into laughter. "Oh, you so would!" she quipped.

"If it means coming here with you, I will," I grinned.

The right corner of her mouth elevated. She seemed to be warming up to the idea. "It sounds like it'd be fun, but… I don't know."

"We don't have to decide now, Liv. We'll talk about it when the time gets closer. And even if we don't go," I nudged her in the shoulder and winked, "I'll still find a way to whisk you away for another little vacation."

"Wouldn't doubt it," Olivia chortled.

"Hey, lovebirds!" Ryker called out and I looked in the direction his voice came from. "Everything's packed! Ready to go?"

Olivia squeezed my hand and intertwined our fingers as I replied, "Yeah."

~~~

Parking at the entrance of her wealthy neighborhood, my girlfriend didn't seem too ecstatic to jump out of the vehicle quite yet. Her hands were resting on her lap, gazing out the window.

I scratched at the back of my neck. "Need any help?"

She shook her head. "I don't want my parents becoming suspicious and wanting to know who's dropping me off, though I doubt they would, but thanks anyways."

"Well..." I cleared my throat, itching for an actual conversation instead of this awkward talk. "I think I should thank you..." I leaned over, our faces inches apart, "for coming up with this amazin' idea." Olivia gave an upbeat smile before our mouths met. "Thanks for a wonderful time."

"No problem. I had a great time too. You're a good cuddle partner," she winked.

I chuckled. "Ditto." I cocked my chin in the direction of her house. "Now get."

She stepped out of the truck, turning to look at me through the rolled down window. "Don't get into any trouble," Olivia warned.

"No promises," I grinned wickedly.

She removed her duffels from the bed, pulling them behind her with the straps. I kept an eye out until her silhouette disappeared from sight, and I sat there, wondering if I should head over to Ryker's or face the news Mom had for me. I had a feeling that her news would either ruin or make my night. "Ah, screw it," I muttered, accelerating and started on the familiar drive home.

Hope I'm choosing right.

~~~

Unlocking the deadbolt, I pushed open the door and trudged my stuff inside quietly and quickly so I wouldn't scare my dear mother. The lights from the kitchen reflected into the living area, notifying me she was still awake. I edged closer but stopped short when laughter echoed through my ears, hers and… a man's? *What?*

My left eyebrow rose as I dumped my luggage on the couch, barely making a sound with its loss of soft cushion. Stepping over the creaky parts of the floor- I snuck in and out plenty times without getting caught- my mom continued speaking to the dude, unaware of my whereabouts. I entered the kitchen, standing in the middle of the doorway, waiting for her to notice me. The guy, however, did and his voice drowned out to silence.

"Mom," I said carefully. She spun in her seat, looking surprised to see me and I recognized the look in her eyes. It was a familiar look. It was one I had hid from others and myself for years. Guilt. "Who is this and what is he doing here?"

"Welcome home, sweetie." She tried to wrap her arms around me, but I stopped her with a cold expression.

"Who. Is. This?" I repeated, saying one word at a time to make it known I wasn't in the mood for sugarcoating or lying.

She licked her lips, searching for an answer. I glanced at the guy, observing him. He had brown hair, almond-shaped eyes, and a full face. He seemed friendly and somewhat decent, but looks were deceiving. I should know; I've had tons of practice.

"Mom, tell me." I wanted- *deserved* an answer. Who was this guy?

"Sam," she said, "this is David Caldwell. He's a professor at Columbia University and we met- oh my gosh, it's actually a funny story-"

"Yeah, yeah, real funny," I interrupted harshly. "What's he doing *here*?"

"About that. Sam, we, uh-"

An icy shiver went down my spine. "Is this what you were hidin' from me?" Her eyes dropped to the floor and back at me, answering the question. I scoffed, a disbelieving knot forming in my stomach. "So you're in a relationship? What about our promise?" I asked bitterly.

"The promise you made when I was eleven-"

"Sam, I-"

"- that you'd tell me before you decided to date again!" I yelled.

It may seem like I was being selfish and unfair, but when all you have for twelve years was a mother, you become protective. I didn't want just any guy swooping in and grabbing a hold of my mother's heart and abusing it. She deserved more than that. She promised me at eleven years old that she'd talk to me about dating before actually getting back into it, but I guess I wasn't important enough because she went ahead and took charge.

David stood from his seat, pulling a sleeve over his arm. "Maybe I should go."

"Yeah, maybe you should!" I hissed.

Mom glared at me. "How dare you!

I stared at her incredulously. "No, *how dare you*? You didn't even think to tell me you were dating again! Why? Am I not important enough not to know?"

"Don't play that card, Samuel."

"Then what do you want me to say?!" I shouted, not caring at the moment this was my mother in front of me. "You didn't speak to me about it! Not once!"

She rolled her eyes. "I am old enough to make my own decisions. I don't need your permission to date."

I nodded, feeling nothing but worthless. She didn't care what I thought. She didn't care at all. "Whatever. I guess I'm not important. If I was, I would've already known."

"Sam-"

I began to walk out of the kitchen, not wanting to hear a stupid apology that meant nothing. "Don't bother. You've said enough."

Turning my back on her, I zipped up my leather jacket and headed out the door, slamming it loud behind me. I pounded down the stairs, fighting against the unmanly tears welding up in my eyes. Honestly, it wasn't her dating again bothering me; it was the fact she didn't care to mention it. She didn't care to tell me after years of it being just us. We were all each other had since Tyler.

After sliding inside my parked truck and locking the doors, I released a pained and angry yell, smacking the steering wheel with rage. I curled my fists into my hair, stopping myself from yanking bits of it out. Taking deep breaths to calm myself down, I leaned back in my seat and wiped at my wet face, not realizing my tears were let loose in the midst of it all.

I needed to be somewhere else tonight. I couldn't stay home.

I knew it would be a risk, but there was only person I needed in this situation. I put the key in the ignition, waking the engine, and drove off, making my way towards Olivia's house.

OLIVIA

I had just changed into sweatpants and mismatched socks and relaxed on my bed, a novel open when a loud plink against the glass of my window grabbed my attention. I marked the page and strolled over, taking a quick glance to identify who or whatever it was. A smile stretched across my lips and I slid the window open, leaning out for a better view. Sam stood a few inches from the garage with a lopsided grin.

"What are you doing, Wayne?" I whisper-shouted.

He smirked. "I came to sweep my beautiful princess from her tower."

"Don't go all *Rapunzel* on me!" I replied teasingly. "Not that I'm complaining or anything, but seriously, why are you here?"

His whole demeanor shifted and Sam stuffed his hands in his pockets, kicking at the dirt uncomfortably. "Uh, I'll- I'll tell you in a bit." There was no room for

argument because he quickly changed the subject. "Now come down."

"We have school tomorrow," I stated.

"*So?*"

I rolled my eyes. "My parents have super-hearing."

"Then be super quiet." I glared at him for his quick responses. "Olivia, come on. Be a little rebellious." I chewed on my bottom lip, contemplating the situation.

"You do remember that we just spent two weeks in North Carolina without parental consent? A late night bite with me isn't gonna hurt."

Point taken. I held a finger, gesturing for him to hold on. "Gimme a minute."

I turned away from the window and traded my sweatpants for a faded pair of jeans, slipping a black jacket on. I fingered the material, bringing it to my nose and inhaling the scent of Sam's cologne and musk. Two seconds later, I pinched myself at the girlish act. I am not girly.

One good thing about my bedroom's location, the garage was right below it, and it was an easy climb down and a large oak tree sat beside that.

"Hurry up. I'm hungry, babe!"

I shushed him, throwing one leg after the other over the windowsill and landed on the garage's roof, inwardly wincing at the sound of the metal making a sharp noise from the added weight. I hurriedly raced over to the tree and grabbed onto a branch, wrapping my legs around it and easily climbing down as I went.

"I'm takin' it you've done this a few times?" Sam asked.

I laughed. "Is it that obvious?"

Spoke too soon. I slipped on the tree sap seeping through the tree bark.

If it wasn't for Sam, I probably would've end up lying face down on the grass.

"Ow, seriously. Who slips on tree sap?" I muttered to nobody in particular, lifting my head from his chest.

"Apparently, someone by the name of 'Olivia Jenkins'," he answered.

I poked him in the cheek. "Punk."

Sam laughed and his emerald eyes flickered to our position. I had landed on top of him, his arms wrapped around my waist. "You wanna get up now or are we gonna stay here all night?"

"Oh, um, sorry," I apologized rolling off him.

He propped himself up by his elbows, looking at me like my rear end had dropped out from underneath me. I stifled a laugh at the thought. "Its fine, Liv." I used to hate my name being shortened; only Max had authorization to use it, but when Sam said it, I couldn't find any reason for him not to say it. "Ready for food?" His voice brought me back to reality.

"What'd you have in mind?"

"It's a surprise."

With a wide smile, I dragged him to his truck, answering his question.

~~~

At Mickey's, we chose a booth in the back, separating ourselves from the other customers. A family of four sat closest to us, enjoying their time together. The two kids were looking at us while finishing their meal and Sam waved at them, sending a quirky little smile. The daughter giggled and hid her face at the sight of a cute boy.

"I think you have a fan," I pointed out, stirring the contents of my drink then taking a sip.

Sam picked up a fry and dipped the end in barbeque sauce. "I have plenty of fans, but my favorite is this brown-eyed beauty who has one of the highest GPA's at our school," he said.

I didn't fight the smile wanting to show. "You're so incredibly cheesy."

"Oh, you thought I was talking about you. Sorry to disappoint, babe."

I gaped at him and threw my crumbled up napkin at him, but it lacked any weight. "That was cruel."

"It got a reaction outta you," Sam chuckled. He bit into his burger, swallowing. "So were your parents happy to see you?"

I shrugged, suddenly interested in the chicken strips laid out in front of me. "I wouldn't know."

"Wait, they weren't there?"

I tore apart a piece of chicken in the only way that I ate it. "They left me a note explaining they were out and won't be back until late and there were leftover meals in the fridge in case I got hungry. Around nine, I heard them downstairs and I waited in my room to see if they'd come up," I sighed loudly. "Parker came and saw me and asked a billion questions, but Melanie and Dad never did. I thought things would've changed after Melanie apologized, but I guess it was too good to be true. Maybe she was having a good day," I said sadly.

His eyes met mine across the table. "Are you okay?"

"Used to it, remember?" I muttered acrimoniously.

He frowned. "No one should be used to that."

I laughed, though nothing was funny. "I am."

"Olivia," Sam whispered gently yet seriously, "I know that it hurts you. Stop pretending it doesn't."

The ache of not being a perfect child and always being compared to an older brother and being neglected did hurt. A lot. "Yeah," I croaked admittedly. "It does hurt." Not wanting to stay on the topic for long, I changed the subject. "What about you? Was your mom happy to see you?" Again, his demeanor did a complete 360. He avoided eye-contact, staring at our half-eaten food. "She talked to you, didn't she?" By his silence, the answer was clear. "What was it?"

He looked up again, the color of his eyes a dark green; the shade when he's angry. "She's dating someone."

"That's great!"

Sam shook his head, bewildering me. What was so bad about his mom dating? "Olivia, don't get me wrong, I'm happy for her. It's been twelve years since she's been with anybody."

"I don't get it. What's the problem?"

"When I was eleven, she promised that she'd talk to me before dating again. She wanted to make sure I was ready, and if I was comfortable with it. I'm mad 'cause I went home and she was in the middle of a date so I figured out quickly what she wanted to talk about. She decided to start dating... but she didn't ask me. She didn't even bother to freaking tell me!" Sam crossed his arms and dropped back against the seat. "I know it might not seem like it's worth getting worked up on, but she broke her promise and acted like I had no right to know what her plans were. It's been me and her for so long. I don't want her ending up with just anybody."

I reached over and let out my hand, waiting for him to take it. His irises had returned to its beautiful emerald color. I didn't know what to say; I figured an action would be better. He eventually slipped his hand into mine. Sam's eyes flickered to something over my shoulder. I began to turn my head, but with the tight squeeze he inflicted, I stopped. With a quick nod in a *let's go* manner, he stood up and dumped our trash in the trashcan near the door, making a hasty exit.

His hands fished the keys out of his pocket, walking towards the truck. It sat in the only parking space available at the time, in the back of the restaurant.

"What was it?"

"It wasn't an it, it was a who. We need to get out of here. Fast."

Suddenly Sam stopped. I was about to ask why; however, two guys with buff, tattooed arms standing at his truck made the question halt in its tracks. A person appeared from behind them, clad in dark jeans and a brown leather jacket. He looked about early forties, had latte-colored skin and buzzed black hair with scruffy cheeks and tattoos peeking out from under his shirt. He was tall and muscular and walked like he held himself higher than others. The smirk directed at us bothered me, like an itch that I couldn't reach.

Sam pulled me behind him and I heard the echoes of steps. I glanced behind us to see two more guys show up. Sam kept a tight grip on me, keeping my body pressed against his back. I gripped his arm with my left hand and hooked two of my right fingers in the loops of his jeans.

"What do you want?" He sneered at the dark figure.

The person grinned. "I wanted to see how special this girl must be that you have to disobey my rules."

My eyes widened and a gasp escaped my mouth. This was the boss.

He saw me peering behind his shoulder. "Wow, she is a beauty."

Sam growled- a deep, masculine rumble in the back of his throat. "You touch her, I swear-"

"No need for violent words, Wayne," he retorted. I calmed my breathing as the two spat back and forth. "What's your name, gorgeous?"

I swallowed the large lump in my throat, clearing it

afterwards. How I kept my voice steady as a rock, it was a mystery to me. "Olivia."

"Olivia," the boss repeated. "That's a beautiful name."

"Enough with this. Why are you here?" Sam hissed.

"We have some unfinished business. Where are the rest of my supplies?"

My boyfriend shot him a look. "You got the-"

"Drugs. Yes, I did." Wait, drugs? I looked at Sam with questioning eyes. I thought he didn't do drug deals.

"Then we should be good."

"Not quite. You see, I need those supplies."

"We'll have them ready by Tuesday. We're behind on one run, but we'll be getting them tomorrow night."

"You're behind?"

"First one in years," Sam shot back. I pressed my mouth into his shoulder.

The boss didn't look too happy about waiting. "Hmm. Trevor, do me a favor. Put them in the van."

"No!" Sam snarled. "She's not a part of this."

The gang boss smirked insensitively. "Ever since you started dating her, she's been a part of this."

Surprising me, something hard hit me on the back of the head. I fell to the ground, and the last thing I saw was Sam being knocked out and collapsing.

Then everything turned black.

Chapter 26: Sam

A low groan slipped past my lips as I woke, and I touched the knot on the back of my head, becoming dizzy, and black spots dotted my vision. Sitting up, I took in my surroundings. By the uneasy glide underneath me, I could point out that I was in a vehicle- in the back of a large, black van to be specific.

On my right, I saw caramel-brown hair sprawled out on the floor. Olivia.

Everything came flooding back to me. Mom's news. Mickey's. The boss.

I clenched my fist to keep myself from hitting something. I crawled over to Olivia and flipped her over, checking for any signs of trauma or worse. The boss's men weren't very kind to the female species sometimes. She mumbled in her sleep, and I released a relieved breath.

I searched for anything that could be used against them, but it seemed to be empty. They must have cleaned out the back before shoving us inside. Smart. I could use dental floss as a weapon. The only thing I did find was a water bottle filled to the top, and I drunk a few swigs.

When the van went over a bump, my knees gave out and I crashed onto Olivia.

"Oof!" She gasped. "Wha-what happened?" She looked around frantically then brought a hand to her head, moaning about a headache.

"Yeah, don't sit up too fast or it'll pound more," I

informed her, handing over the water bottle. "What do you remember?"

"The boss told someone to put us in the back of a van... and you said something and next thing I knew, I blacked out."

I rubbed the back of my head, feeling the swollen knot. "It leaves a nasty bite."

"And a horrible headache," Olivia added, putting her head in between her knees. The van passed over another bump and we groaned simultaneously. "Do you think we'll get out of this alive?"

I didn't meet her eyes, focusing on the quiver in her hands. "I don't know."

She let out a shaky breath, bringing a hand to her mouth. I could tell she was trying to keep herself calm, trying not to scream or sob. The kind of situation we're in- a battle between life and death, not knowing if you're going to make it out alive- could shake anyone, independent or not.

"Olivia, listen to me," I began, "I'm going to do everything possible to save your life, to make sure you survive. I promise."

"I'll do the same," she replied unhesitatingly.

I drew my eyebrows together. "No. I'm not riskin' your life-"

"Sam, I'm not a damsel in distress. I'm not one of those girls that need a guy to fight her battles."

"I know that, but-" I fumbled over the words.

"But what?" She asked huffily, narrowing her eyes.

"These guys, Olivia, aren't the football players from school. They're men with real experience of torturing and killing," I explained through clenched teeth. My anger meter was about to reach its limit and I didn't want to blow up on her. Yet if she continues to act like a stubborn mule, I'll explode.

She crossed her arms, setting her jaw. "I think a kick in the groin will suffice."

"That's your brilliant plan? Kick them and run?" I asked incredulously. "Such a beautiful plan," I said sarcastically.

"Fine, what's yours?" Olivia snapped. "I mean, since you've dealt with these types of guys before!"

"Exactly, I've faced more danger than you! I know how to handle them!"

"Oh, and I don't?"

"You *don't!*" I slammed my fist into the wall of the van, probably bruising my knuckles. "You have no idea how to face these guys and you're too freaking stubborn to admit it!" I barked.

She threw the closest object she could find- the empty water bottle- at me and I let it hit me since it weighed nothing. "You're such a jerk!"

"Best you got?" I bellowed. "What happened to the

'I-can-take-on-anybody' Olivia Jenkins?" I hissed, red dots marking my vision.

I caught her wrist when she tried to slap me. I dodged her tries of hitting my face and torso, and before I knew it, I had tackled her, holding her wrists to the black carpeted floorboard, her right knee pressed to my abdomen. We were spitting threats and challenging each other's strength and howling insults. In the middle of the fight, our eyes locked and I noticed salty tears had welded up in her brown orbs.

Suddenly the dark emotion started to disappear from our bodies. Our minds weren't overcome with anger anymore. Her face softened, realization dawning on both of us.

All the crap that happened with Mom and the boss,

it hit me hard all at once, and everything happened so quickly, I didn't realize who I was taking it on. Olivia's stubbornness had provoked me at the wrong time. I closed my eyes in shame as the argument replayed in my thoughts and I realized I had said some pretty mean things. I hope she'd forgive me; I had been saying them out of rage.

I rested my forehead on hers and swallowed my pride. "Olivia, I'm sorry."

"I'm sorry too," she apologized. "Sam, what you said was true."

"It was wrong of me though."

She shook her head, stopping me. "No, I deserved

it. I was being stubborn. I have absolutely no idea what to do. I didn't want to admit it because I don't like being frightened. I don't like not knowing the outcome of a situation."

"Olivia, I-"

"I know you didn't mean it," she whispered.

"But still that doesn't give me the right to say hurtful things to you, out of anger or not."

She sighed. "Let's just forget about it."

"Liv-"

"Sam, please. I don't want our last moments together full of fighting and-"

"It's not gonna be our last moment," I declared.

The corner of her lips lifted to a smirk. "Stop interrupting me."

"Excuse me?" I raised an eyebrow. "You're the one interruptin' me."

Olivia laughed, her face breaking into a beautiful smile. "We're not supposed to be fighting, you idiot."

"It's not fighting, it's called innocent bickering," I corrected with a wink. She rolled her eyes playfully. It was amusing how we could go from yelling to flirting with each other within seconds.

"Hey, Wayne?" she murmured. "When are you gonna get off me?"

At her words, I glanced down at our position. I was

hovering above her, my hands wrapped around her wrists, holding them near her shoulders, and knees on either side of her. During our fight, I had somehow forced her down in the midst of dodging her physical attacks. I would never lay my hand on a girl, but I hadn't been in the mood to be punched and kicked.

"Oh, sorry," I grumbled yet made no effort to get up. I let her gain control of her hands again and she

cracked her fingers, relaxing the stiff joints then pushed me in the chest, causing me to laugh. "Vicious thing, aren't you?"

She shrugged. "I'll save them for the boss."

"I'll hold him," I said.

While looking at her, I had a sudden urge to kiss her so I leaned down and closed the aching gap. She threaded her fingers in my hair as I pressed my mouth harder against hers. All of our shared emotions- forgiveness, sadness, fear- was edged into the kiss. Olivia didn't hesitate in pulling me closer until there was no space between us.

I've never had feelings as strong as what I felt for Olivia. I mean, I've had plenty of girlfriends and there was Nikki, but it wasn't the same. When I was in a relationship with Nikki, I believed I was in love with her. The 'love' I had then couldn't even compare to the love I have for Olivia. I could live without the other girls, but not without Olivia. She's my rock, she's my best friend, and she's always been there. Even through those years of torment, she'd been there. I always picked on her, I loved making her blush, I loved getting under her skin and when she'd get defensive and fight with me. Even when Tyler died and I had turned my back on her, Olivia was still in my life.

No matter what relationship we had, she's always been there.

She knew the darkest patch of my life and every aspect, the bad and the good. She knew who I was behind the mask I'd put on for the world. She chose to be with me after all those years of bullying and rumors and insults. She chose to be with me even though there was a chance she could be killed.

Olivia pulled away from the kiss, both of us breathing heavily. I dropped my head in the crevice between her neck and shoulder, little wisps of her hair tickling my face.

That night, I made an important decision. There was no one in the world I rather be with besides her; my beautiful and smart, stubborn and argumentative, brown-eyed best friend, or otherwise known as the love of my life.

I brought my head back up and met her eyes, desperate to find the right words. "Olivia, if we get out of here..."

"Mm-hmm," she hummed.

"Remind me to give you somethin'."

She gave me a confused look. "What?"

"After we get out of here," I corrected my words

from earlier. We were both getting out of this alive. Cupping the side of her face and stroking her skin with my thumb, I repeated, "Remind me."

Out of nowhere, the van halted to a stop. Doors were slammed shut and I moved to sit on my knees, giving Olivia the space to get into a sitting position. We stared at each other, knowing we had to fight to make it out alive. The back doors opened and a hand stretched in, yanking me by the shirt. I was dragged out of the van roughly, dropping to the ground like a sack of potatoes. The boss's men brought me to my feet by the collar of my jacket and I struggled against them, hating their tight hold and hating the weak persona they gave me.

We were both thrown to our knees in the gravel. The boss stood with his hands clasped behind his back, facing the opposite direction. I scrutinized the area. We were on the roof of an abandoned parking garage. He turned around, staring at us with dark eyes, full of no remorse or emotion. One of the thugs grabbed a fistful of my hair, jerking my head back. I grunted, squeezing my teeth together.

Boss knelt down in front of me. "Sam, I'll be honest. You've been a great leader. One of the finest I've seen, especially at your age. You discipline your new recruits. You have somethin' unique. Why do you think I promoted you early?" He queried. "The boys listened to you, followed you. You had ideas no one else did. You're the one who made supply huntin' get as well as it is."

"Is that supposed to be a compliment?" I spat.

He slapped me. "I'm talkin'!" He tapped my temple, the crooked dip of his nose obvious. "Back to what we were discussing. Ah, yes, excellent leader, boys followed your every move. But what are they gonna think when they find out you disobeyed my most sacred law? I allow noncommittal dating 'cause the boys need a taste of freedom. I remember high school and its temptations and the girls. There are reasons why I don't allow serious relationships."

"Why is that?" Olivia asked. My head turned in her direction. What was she doing? Why was she talking to him?

"Well, my dear Olivia," he said brushing a strand of hair behind her ear, his cool fingertips touching her cheek. I shifted uncomfortably and resisted the urge to jump and attack him. The arms holding me back made it impossible too. He had no right to touch her. "A serious relationship, in our world, is a term we use when the boy becomes delusional and starts hangin' with the girl instead of doing his duties to the gang. And if things get extremely committed, he might try and leave... which is unacceptable."

"Don't you get new members regularly?" She inquired, arching her eyebrow. The way her voice sounded, she seemed actually interested why they're banned.

He didn't answer. Instead he glanced between us, back and forth. "You have some interesting questions. I thought your boy here explained the life of gangs."

"Yes, but he doesn't even know why they're not allowed. I was only wondering why," she assured him. "I mean, I don't see the problem in it, but I wanted to hear your side. I can understand your reasoning."

I don't freaking believe it. She's playing him.

The boss pursed his lips. "Okay, I told you. Now let's get down to business."

The hand holding my hair rammed the side of my face to my right, into the grey pavement. I winced at the impact and moaned lightly, knowing it was going to sport a bad bruise.

"What shall we do with the girl?" One of the gangsters questioned.

The boss smirked, a twinkle in his cold eyes. "Whatever you want." The guys chuckled predatorily, and

I wanted to smash my fist into their noses over and over again. Or better yet, kick them in a certain sensitive area repeatedly. They weren't going to touch her, not if I could help it. Olivia visibly shuddered, her jaw trembling at the thoughts of what they might do and what they're capable of. "But first, we should let her watch us torment her boyfriend."

He flicked his hand and I was picked up off the gravel and thrown against the body of the large van.

"SAM!" Olivia screeched.

I crumbled to the ground; the taste of blood layering my mouth. My ribs were on fire again, worse than the last time. I could barely breathe. It felt like the bone was protruding into my lung. It seemed impossible to get oxygen. I was hoisted up again and dropped in front of the boss. I watched as the man holding Olivia moved her closer for a better view of what was occurring. Fury filled every inch of my body. I wanted to bury each of them in the grave for this. The buff and tattooed man grinned mischievously. His fingers were busy unbuttoning her purple-and-black checkered button-up, exposing the white camisole underneath. I growled at the action, adrenaline bubbling in my veins.

Ignoring the agonizing pain in my torso, I pushed myself to my feet and was about to tackle him, but the boss interrupted, smashing his metal-toed boot into my knee. I crumbled and fell forwards, rolling onto my side. The boss threw his shoe into my stomach and I didn't even try to stop the blood from spurting. I buried my face in the rocks. My eyesight was blurry and the world was spinning. Olivia squirmed in the man's hold, but he held on tightly. The glint of a sharp blade against her neck penetrated my vision.

"Stop..." I grumbled weakly.

Her brown eyes met mine across the lot. "Please, please... STOP IT!" She cried out when they pulled me by my jacket and shoved me away. Not expecting the stabbing pain *everywhere*, my head spun rapidly and I collapsed.

I strained my neck to glimpse at the boss. "Stop. Don't make-" I spit the rotten taste out of my mouth and the crimson stain blended in with the sleekness of his large boots. "Don't hurt-"

"How sweet," he said examining the blood-stain with a deadly smile. "You're worried about her. Who knew the *great* Sam Wayne had weak spots?" He chuckled, throwing another kick to my side and I grunted in anguish, biting my lip hard to keep from screaming out.

I snapped my teeth together and slowly began to raise myself on my hands and elbows, getting a bewildered look from the big shot for a split second.

To keep Olivia from getting hurt and to guarantee her safety, I had to fight. I had to be the barrier between her and the boss. If it meant I had to die to protect her, then that's what I had to do.

Finally, I was able to stand at my full height, setting my jaw firm to retain a steady expression. To ensure him I wasn't quitting, I wasn't backing down. Olivia either saw the plan hidden in my eyes or somehow figured it out because the color drained from her face, the gleam in her eyes becoming soft and terrified.

I heard her whisper in the eerie silence, "No, Sam, no," but I ignored it, already deciding what route to take.

"That all you got?" I said vigorously.

He didn't like I was fighting back. I could see it edged in his features. The crinkle near his left eye, the twitching corner of his mouth- he wasn't use to opponents that'd challenged his authority, his strength, his rules. We circled each other, each step I took bringing on more pain, but I dismissed the temptation of admitting defeat. However that didn't stop the discomforting thoughts plaguing my head.

"You're fierce, Wayne. I'll give you that," the boss remarked. "Yet I don't like how you think you're better than me."

"I *am* better," I claimed. "I don't find pleasure in other people's misery. I don't prey on the innocent."

"Whether you believe it or not, we're alike," he said. "We've faced demons others couldn't imagine. I've seen the damage lurkin' in your eyes."

"You know nothing," I spit curtly.

He sighed, almost disappointingly. "I liked you, Sam. I really did. I even thought you'd continue on, growin' till you reached crime boss. Guess I was wrong."

Unexpectedly, someone seized my left arm from behind me, twisting it backwards to forcefully reach the middle of my back. The snap of the bone breaking thundered into my eardrums, and nothing- not embarrassment, not fear of being weak in front of the enemy- stopped the bloodcurdling scream leaving my mouth.

"SAM!" Olivia shrieked.

I dropped to the ground, the person moving out of the way just as fast as he got there, and landed hard on my back. Now it was excruciatingly difficult to breathe. My body was numb with distress. I didn't know how much more I could take. I faced the starry night, ebony spots dotting my vision. The idea of going to sleep was sounding delightful. I ached for the old and losing-its-cushion mattress than the rocks digging through the material of my jacket. I ached for the comfort of my home- the home I've lived in since I was seven. I needed sleep-

NO! Sam, stay awake. Fight for Olivia. Don't fail. Don't give up.

Feeling defeated, I watched the boss walk over to my girlfriend and take a hold of her chin, letting her have no choice but to look in his eyes. "She is a beauty."

"Let go... of...her," I wheezed straining the words.

He turned his coal-shaded eyes filled with evil towards me, his lips bending into a devilish smirk. "How about one last goodbye? What do you think, Trevor?" He directed the question to his member. "Shall I allow it?"

In the process of him doing that, my head lolled to the side and met Olivia's shaky brown eyes, her skin pale in the night. She slipped on her beautiful smile in a desperate attempt to get me to grin back, but my jaw and cheeks weren't up for it. If she was gonna be the last thing, person, subject I'd ever see, I'm ever-so-grateful for such a wonderful sight.

The boss abruptly snapped his fingers. I was heaved off the ground and one of the gangsters gripped my broken arm, making me cry out. They held me solidly while the boss reached inside his jacket and pulled out a Glock.

Olivia struggled against the man's grasp. "Let go!"

"Shut her up."

The guy placed his palm over her mouth. "OW!" He hissed, cursing loudly. "She freakin' bit me!"

The gang boss reached out his hand and she was thrown into his embrace. He wrapped a tight arm around her chest. She tried to break free though he didn't budge.

Knowing that maybe this was the end, I had to get these final words out. "Olivia, I love you. You're the best thing that's ever happened to me."

"I love you too, Sam. I've always loved you."

It went in slow motion with a line repeating over and over in my thoughts. *We have to fight. We have to fight. To beat him, we have to fight.* A plan swiftly formed in my head. He lifted the Glock, aiming the barrel at my chest. Olivia's eyes switched between the weapon and me, and I prayed that she would get the message.

I mouthed, "One."

She copied my actions. "Two."

He put his finger on the trigger.

"Three."

At the same time he pushed down on the trigger, Olivia shoved herself against his tattooed and muscular self. I moved to the right and the bullet went into the guy on the left. The other was surprised at the sudden change for too long. Adrenaline boiling through my veins, I punched him straight in the jaw and smashed my knee into his chest. He crumbled to the ground. I spun around to be knocked over, falling on my bad arm and being temporarily stunned. A few feet away, Olivia ran for the gun, lying on the pavement out of reach.

The boss tugged her back by her hair and wrestled her to the gravel and she blocked his fist flying towards her side with a knee to the crotch. He gasped in shock, but recovered quickly. She twisted under his weight and scratched at his face and torso, attempting another kick.

"Sam!" I perched up at the demanding tone in her voice. "The gun! Get the gun!"

Following her orders, I hauled myself up carefully in an effort to lessen my afflicted ribs and arm, and limped hurriedly to where it laid. Picking up the weapon, I cocked it open. There was only one bullet left, and it had to be perfect.

He pinned Olivia's arms to the ground, chuckling darkly, and she gave a frightened cry, not knowing what he'd do.

However, something stopped him from completing it.

The bullet lodging in his head.

Chapter 27: Olivia

The gunshot roared through the air. The boss collapsed on top of me, his dead hands weightless around my wrists. I frantically scrambled out from under him, the fresh blood caking my shirt. Sam was kneeling a few feet away, holding the gun in his right hand; cradling his broken arm to his chest. I met his eyes across the abandoned lot, the emerald color shining in the darkness.

"Sam," I whispered.

He trudged over, dropping the weapon, but I crossed the distance faster than he could. He wrapped an arm around me, obviously not caring at the moment about his injuries. I gripped his jacket tightly, a couple tears touching the surface of my face.

Oh thank God he was still here. We were still here.

"It's over," Sam muttered in my ear, sounding relieved and I could hear the pain in his voice. "Safe."

I leaned back, not breaking out of his embrace. I touched his face, smiling brokenly at the bruises and cuts. "I know, I know. We both are." Lifting up his shirt to examine his wounds, I brought a palm to my mouth. Dark bruising covered majority of his stomach, and- how was he standing? I wouldn't have been able to.

He opened his mouth to say something, but the adrenaline that carried him through our plan now crashed and would have brought him to his knees had I not been standing there. I helped him lay down, sitting down behind him and propping his head against my chest.

I had to be strong for the both of us. Sam had risked his life to protect me. He stood up to the boss and wasn't concerned about his well being, only mine.

"Call 911. Get an ambulance," he ordered faintly. I withdrew my phone and dialed the emergency number. "I'm in... a bad..." he trailed off. Sweat drenched his forehead and I brushed strands of hair out of his face.

After explaining a short version of the events to the police, they informed an ambulance was on its way and to hang tight, we'll be taken care of. Sam was shaking violently in my arms and I pressed my cheek against the top of his head. I couldn't lose him. Not now. Not after everything we've gone through. I never released his hand; I wasn't about to let him go. Sam convulsed; his entire body jerking, and tears streamed down my cheeks, my throat clogging up.

Two minutes later, I heard the shrill wails in the distance.

"Olivia-" His face scrunched up, a horrible sounding groan slipping past his lips. I chewed on the inside of my cheek, waiting patiently, wondering what he needed to say. "L-Liv, about earlier-"

"The fight? I've already forgiven you."

He attempted his lopsided smile and I let out a laughing sob, happy to see that adorable quirk of the mouth. "Uh, a-about the thing I wanted to give you..."

"What about it?" I asked hurriedly.

"I- UGH." His words were slurred and I knew there was maybe thirty seconds before he passed out. "B-baby, I w-wanna sleep."

"No, no, no, you can't sleep."

"But-"

An ambulance and plenty of police arrived at the scene, silencing the rest of his sentence. The bright lights on the roof of the vehicles blinded me and I hid my face in Sam's hair; he squeezed my hand tightly. EMTs scrambled out of the back of the medical van, running over with two gurneys. A paramedic asked politely if I'd allow them to take Sam out of my arms. I protested at first, but he knelt down, putting a gentle hand on my shoulder and assured me that they'd be careful and do everything humanly possible to help him. I reluctantly agreed.

I scooted back and gave them room to their job. They lifted him onto the gurney and stripped him of his clothing from the waist up, leaving him bare-chested in the January air, stabilizing his broken arm and ribs. In my peripheral vision, I saw the authorities scanning the scene, taking in the three bodies and writing down which ones were dead and in critical condition. The EMTs heaved Sam into the ambulance, and strapped an IV to his right wrist. Without asking, but somehow knowing I wanted to, the paramedic held out his hand and I took it gratefully, stepping in.

~~~

They rushed Sam through the emergency opening of the hospital and into a surgical room far down the hall. A nurse touched my arm gently and offered to treat the cuts and scrapes on my face. She cleaned them up and applied a few bandages to my forehead and chin. After checking my vitals and declaring me fine, a security officer escorted me to the waiting room. Walking through the automated doors, I stopped dead in my tracks at the sight of my family sitting in the lightly cushioned seats. Melanie was the only one awake, reading from a magazine the ER supplied. Parker was leaning against her shoulder and sleeping soundly. A part of me sunk because Dad wasn't there, but I didn't let it affect me. His work was always more important than anything else.

"Melanie?" It sounded awkwardly loud in the large empty room.

She looked up, relief spreading across face. I started walking towards her and my stepmother stood from her chair, pulling me in a bone-crushing hug. Instead of fighting it, I broke my hard exterior and wrapped my arms around her, relishing in the comforting embrace.

"Oh, Olivia!" She beamed. I shut my eyes, all tonight's events flooding my head. "I'm so glad you're okay!"

"You are?" I asked surprisingly.

Melanie brought me back to arm's length, nodding. "Yes. I was so worried when I got the call from the police. I dragged Parker out of bed and we've been waiting here since, waiting for any news." My heart swelled at the concern I've been starving for all these years. "Olivia, physically are you okay?"

"Yeah, but Sam-" My voice broke and her eyes softened, a look that wasn't never used when it applied to the gang leader. "He-he got beat up. I mean, picked up and thrown around beat up! Melanie, when they broke his arm, I-I-I can't get the sound of his bone snapping-" I stopped abruptly, swallowing the uncomfortable large lump in my throat. "I just want him to be okay. He has to be. He's everything to me."

She nodded again, listening to my rambling. "How long has this been going on?"

I paled for what seemed like the tenth time tonight. Deep down, I knew that one day, my family, friends, everyone would find out. I couldn't hide it. I couldn't be afraid anymore. "Since the beginning of November."

"You've been dating for almost two months?" Melanie inquired. I responded with a simple yes. "Why didn't you tell us?"

I gave her an incredulous look. "Are you kidding? Of course I couldn't say anything! For years we have judged him-"

"Olivia, he was your best friend! He turned his back on you!" Melanie argued. "How can we forgive him of that?"

"He's apologized. He's apologized for everything,"

I informed her. "And for all those years' worth of judgmental comments, something happened that summer. Something that made his change understandable. Something I'm not at liberty to share. Just know Sam isn't who everyone thinks he is," I said. "The boy we knew before high school is still there."

Even by my persuasive argument, I could tell she was still questioning the situation.

"Melanie, Sam loves me. Not that puppy-dog, middle school, I-have-a-crush love. I mean, *in love*. We're serious. He almost *died* for me. I think we could be on the road towards something more."

"Wait..." Her eyes widened. "Do you mean like- has he proposed?"

I shook my head. "No." Then I remembered our moment in the van and my heart skipped a beat. "Well, he did mention wanting to give me something before all heck broke loose. What if he was thinking about proposing?"

Melanie glanced behind her to where my brother was sleeping. I wondered what she was thinking. Or more importantly, was I about to be yelled at or congratulated, for him to even consider the idea of marriage- if that what he was talking about?

Surprising me, she asked the question I've been asking myself repeatedly.

"If he had proposed, what would you have said?"

My eyes drifted to my left hand and I imagined a ring resting on my third finger. After all we've been through, the good and the bad times, my love for him grew every passing second. I find something new to love every day. He was the only person I wanted to be with. No doubt, Sam has caused a great amount of heartache in my life- bullying me, abandoning me, and never being there in the moments I needed him most. Yet he's brought a greater deal of happiness, and honestly, no matter our relation, he was always there.

Right then and there, I found my answer.

SAM

The room was bright when I surfaced, my eyes staring at the plain white ceiling with little dubs of grey hovering over me. I moved my head slightly to the right only to be tackled in a bear hug, courtesy of my mother. She cried my name and I felt tears leaking onto my bare chest. I raised the hand that wasn't in a cast and patted her softly on the back, closing my eyes.

"Hey Mom," I greeted weakly.

"Oh, thank God!" She sobbed into my shoulder. "My heart dropped when I got that dreadful phone call." She released me gently and passed me a cup filled with water. I downed it, the cool liquid feeling wonderful against the dryness of my throat. My head relaxed against the hospital pillow, gazing at the colorless ceiling again. "Sam, I'm sorry," she said in the silence.

"What?"

"If I'd told you about David, maybe you wouldn't

have left and this wouldn't have happened-"

"Mom, stop. The boss had been planning that. He was tracking us the minute we got back from North Carolina," I explained taking her hand.

"Honey-"

"Mom, stop!" I begged indistinctly.

Tears pooled in her eyes. "Baby, I'm just so terribly sorry."

"I'm not mad anymore."

Even with watering eyes, she could pull off the 'don't try that with me' mom look. "Yes, you are. You're upset I didn't tell you."

"How else would you expect me to react?" I queried rhetorically. "I return home from being gone for two weeks and you're on a date with some guy!" I glanced at the bluish-grey sheets, feeling lightheaded. I breathed in and out of my nose slowly, calming myself down. Looking back at her, I met her eyes. "Mom... it's been me and you

for almost four years. I was six when Dad died. From that moment on, I took on the role of being the 'man of the house'. And after Tyler died, I had no choice but to join the gang to roll in some extra cash."

"Sam, do you honestly think I believe that? I know that's not the only reason you joined. Our financial problems might have had a little something to do with it, but that wasn't why." My attempt of trying to keep my expression straight must have given her the confirmation of her statement. "What's the real reason?"

I broke our gaze, finding sudden interest in my surroundings. There was a jacket strewn over the armrest of the chair, two Styrofoam coffee cups on the table next to it, and a book lying on the cushion. I recognized the brown spine, dented due to the numerous opening: her childhood Bible.

"Please talk to me," Mom pleaded.

"It should have been me," I murmured in a low voice. She watched as I had an inner turmoil, contemplating if I should tell her or not. "It should have been me, Mom! I'm the one who sent Tyler out. I'm the one who acted selfish and told him to go! It was supposed to be me. Not him!"

I started shaking, but I didn't know if it was from all the physical pain or the guilt clouding up in my chest.

"Sam..." Her voice was calm, squeezing my hand. "His death wasn't your fault. I promise you it wasn't."

"Then why does it hurt so much?" I asked.

"You've blamed yourself all these years," Mom said simply. "Sam, I'm not going to sit here and tell you it's not going to hurt, because it will. There'll be days where it hits you hard and there'll be days where it doesn't cross your mind. But honey, if you keep telling yourself it's your fault, it's going to eat you alive." She ran her fingers through my hair, a concerned look on her face. "Tyler doesn't blame you."

"How do you know?"

She smiled. "He loved you. You were his fearless big brother. You stood up to the bullies and always made a laugh in the worst moments. He'd go on and on about wanting to be just like you. Do you want him to look down here, and let him see you being someone you're not, blaming yourself for his death?"

"No."

"Then let it go!" Mom insisted. "Don't carry this unnecessary guilt around for your entire life. Start a new beginning. Leave the gang. Get married." I noted the glint

in her eyes, getting her hint. "And if it tries to sneak its way back, think of the good times. Think of the snowball fights and weird-looking snowmen."

I grinned. "We did make some ridiculous lookin' snowmen."

"Remember when Tyler tried to pee in the fountain at the mall?" She laughed, her eyes crinkling at the sides.

"Man that was embarrassing!"

"I had to pick him out of the water. You left me behind and hid yourself in the video game store."

I chuckled, but grunted at the harsh pinch in various places. "I wasn't about to be caught hangin' around you two."

"Great son you were."

"The best."

The hospital room turned silent, minus the whirring of machines and the *beep* of my heart monitor. She leaned back in her chair, crossing her legs. "Sam, I'm not gonna lie. He was taken from this world way too early for my liking, but I told myself there must be reason why, and I think I found that reason."

"What's that?"

"To help us become stronger. We've faced a lot of challenges in these past couple years. Yes, we've also made mistakes, including not telling you about David or about me dating in general. I should have told you. That was wrong of me."

"I forgive you," I told her. "I've made tons of mistakes. Too many to count. But all those errors are worth it. I have Olivia, and that's all that matters." She smiled widely, that little glint in her eye again. "So you like this guy? David?"

"He's very sweet and funny- you know I like a guy with a sense of humor. He's not arrogant and actually very bashful about his-"

"*Mom.*"

She nodded. "Yes, I do. I haven't been this happy since your father."

Knowing it'd make my mother happy, I decided to give the guy a chance. "How about after I'm doing better, we invite him for dinner?"

Her face brightened. "Really?"

"Yeah," I said grinning.

"You're amazing. Thank you."

I grabbed her hand. "It's the least I can do."

She smiled then reached over to grab her Bible. "I've been reading again. I've been slacking off a bit."

"Hmm."

"Honey, I know that you're not much a believer anymore-"

"And you know why," I interrupted shortly.

She squeezed my hand. "Yes, I do. I know after everything with Dad and Tyler, you lost faith, but I feel that if anything is gonna come out of this experience, I think it shows you the strength-"

"*Mom.*"

"I'm not trying to push you or pressure you into anything; I only want the best for you. I just think it'd do you a lot of good if you tried having a relationship again."

"I know you want what's best for me, but… that's not it." My stomach growled angrily so I asked, "Is there any way I can get some food? I'm hungry."

"Of course you are, my personal garbage disposal."

She stood up and left the room momentarily. Now alone, I glanced at the Bible again and sighed thoughtfully. I abandoned faith a long time ago, especially when my brother died and I entered the gang world. For me, it was a complete waste of time.

Sighing once more, I reached over and grabbed it out of curiosity. I opened the cover and flipped the first few pages until I was stopped with a blinding thought:

Bad things happen when you believe.

And at the sound of shoes squeaking against tile, I threw the Bible down and stared straight ahead like nothing had happened.

~~~

A knock on the door distracted me from the obnoxious cartoon playing on the TV screen. Olivia was leaning against the doorframe in jeans and a thick jacket zipped all the way- a normal look for her, but she never looked more beautiful. My mom must have figured that we'd want some alone time to talk, so she announced she'd get some snacks and drinks from the cafeteria. Olivia left the door cracked and walked over, sitting on the edge of the bed, facing me.

"Hey babe," I said taking her hand hostage.

She faked a smile. "Hey."

Reaching out, I held her chin with my fingers and stared at the Band-Aids on her chin and forehead. Her bottom lip was cut. I tucked a few strands of hair behind her ear, having a clear view of her face. "What's wrong?" I questioned.

"You seriously have to ask?" The gold swirls in her irises were almost animated; it was like a wave crashing into the rocks, spraying wisps of water everywhere. They reminded me of the set of eyes I stared at in the mirror every morning.

"I'm fine," I insisted. "I'm still here."

She sighed. "That's not the point. You could've died."

"I would've died protecting you." I touched my forehead to hers. "If that would've been the way I was supposed to leave, I'd never change it."

Olivia smiled for real, twisting her fingers in the fabric of my shirt. "Thank you," she whispered. "Thank you for saving me. Thank you for risking your life. Thank you for everything." I didn't need her thanks. All that mattered was that she was right in front of me. "What'd the doctor say?"

I shifted under the sheets, getting comfortable. They'd put me in a torso splint or whatever it was called to help steady my ribs. "I have five fractured ribs on the right side, and two fractured and three broken on the left. My arm is well, he used a bunch of fancy names that I barely grasped, but it's broken at the elbow, and the impact from that injury broke my collarbone; I also have a concussion," I explained. "I'm supposed to start physical therapy for both in a couple of weeks."

"I don't even know what to say," she said.

"I'm just grateful that I'm still here," I leaned back against the pillows.

Olivia pulled her knees to her chest and I held onto her ankle, rubbing little designs in the fabric of her jeans. "Me too." We sat in a moment of silence, letting our thoughts gather. "So... uh, I need to tell you something.

Melanie knows about us."

My eyebrows rose. "Seriously? What'd she say?"

"She wasn't on board with it and a little cautious at first, but I made it clear that you weren't gonna hurt me and you weren't the Sam from a few years ago. She took it, surprisingly, well."

"Wow." I scratched the back of my neck. "I mean, that's great and all, but... I think I'm more afraid of your father than Melanie."

She nodded, agreeing with me. "We'll leave that for another time. She promised she wouldn't mention to him and that I'd have to tell him, with you of course."

I sent her the stink eye. "Of course."

"Did you and your mom make up?"

"Yeah. I actually told her about Tyler and- yeah, you know. I even suggested she invite David over for dinner." She smiled proudly. "As long as you come. I don't know if I could be in a room with my mother's flirting attempts."

Olivia laughed, the melody bringing light into the room. "When are you going home?"

I rubbed my eyes with sleep. The pain medicine the doctor prescribed was making me drowsy. "Tomorrow, I think."

"That soon?"

"Not much they can do anymore. I have to keep this

splint-like thing on for a month or so. They've already done surgery on my arm. Just have to wait for therapy."

She took that into consideration. "I might come visit you after school."

"Yay," I said sarcastically, my brain whirling at the thought of classes and prying students and evil teachers.

"We have to go back sometime."

"Anyone bothers you and it's too overwhelming, tell Ryker or Ace. They'll see to it no one asks about the situation or me and you."

"I'll keep it in mind. It's Tammy I'm worried about. She's gonna strangle me."

"She's not the only one," I smirked. "Imagine all those girls' hearts being broken 'cause you took Lower Manhattan's hottest gang leader," I wiggled my eyebrows.

"I'll break it to them gently, but also make sure they know who you belong to."

I cocked my head. "Take lots of notes for me, Jenkins. I'm gonna need 'em."

"Don't worry. I'll write them in elementary terms."

I pushed her in the shoulder, glaring at her sassy smile. "Brat."

Olivia kissed me and I frowned when she pulled away too quick for my liking. She rolled her eyes at my expression. "I gotta go, Wayne." She stood from the hospital bed and headed towards the door, but stopped in her tracks.

"What?"

She looked back in my direction with an innocent smile. "Don't forget that you wanted to give me something."

And with one last smile, Olivia walked out of the room.

~~~

Sticking my head out from under the hut I made with my blankets last night, I glanced at the clock tiredly. Eleven. I had to take my first dose of medicine for the day.

I peeled the covers away and trudged off at the speed of a fat turtle. I trailed past the hallway and into the living room to see my girlfriend sitting at the table, chatting with my mom.

"The zombie lives," Olivia teased.

I shot her a dirty look. "Shut it." I ran my hand through my crazed hair, not even bothered by the knots. "Did school get out early?"

"I decided to take the day off. I'm using my time wisely by catching up with Leah and trading embarrassing stories about you."

"You're so lovely," I flicked her behind the ear. Not even thinking twice about it, I set myself down on her lap and bit into her toast. "You're comfy," I muttered grabbing her glass of water and drowning a few sips.

"Who gave you permission to eat my food and

drink my water?" I smirked, taking another bite. "My house. My food."

Mom sipped on her coffee, stifling her laughs. "Sam, get off your girlfriend's lap and stop eating her breakfast."

"Mom!" I whined purposely to aggravate her. She did the mom evil-eye. "I'm just kiddin', but I'm not moving. I'm comfy."

"Its fine, Leah. He barely weighs anything. You need more muscle, babe," Olivia crinkled her nose, grasping my right bicep.

I glanced over my shoulder and said, "Who gave you permission to touch me?"

"I'm your girlfriend, therefore-"

I smacked her on the leg, earning a laugh. "Terrible argument."

"Oh, shut up." She rested her head against my back, her arms wrapped loosely around my waist. The corner of my mouth lifted into a smile. "How you feeling?"

"Eh," I grumbled. "Speakin' of which, where's my meds?"

Mom pointed at the counter closest to the refrigerator. "Should be right there."

I stood from Olivia's lap and poured two pills into my palm, taking them with the last sips of her water. I followed Olivia to the living room, sitting next to her on the couch. She turned on the TV then yanked the blanket off the couch's back, spreading it across our laps. Our fingers interlocked like it was the most natural thing in the world. A random TV show played on the screen, and during a dramatic scene between the two main characters who were romantically involved, I used that moment as an advantage to *really* look at her.

Olivia wore dark skinny jeans and a white *Danskins* jacket with her high-top sneakers propped on the coffee table. She was playing with a loose thread on the blanket as her brown eyes stayed glued to the television. Her hair was down again; the waves falling over her shoulders and framing her face. While entranced with the show, she brushed strands behind her ear- a habit she's had her whole life. The cuts on her face were healing. Her tannish skin seemed to glow from the sun reflecting from the kitchen.

Every girl I've dated for the past two years, it wasn't real. There were no feelings. I only dated them for the part. I was a player; I wasn't the guy that'd put everything he had in a relationship only to get heartbroken. I used to think if I kept my distance and buried those little suckers called feelings, I'd keep myself from getting hurt again. I would date whoever showed interest and dump them without a care.

Everything changed when Olivia and I were assigned partners in math class.

"Sam?" Her voice broke into my thoughts.

I blinked a few times before saying something intelligent like, "Uh, what?"

"Did you decide to zone out on my face?" she asked.

"Maybe." Adapting a devilish smirk, I moved closer until our faces were inches apart. "That okay with you?"

Olivia looked at me with an enticing smile. "It might be." I felt myself being drawn closer to her. "As long as I... get to do this." Thinking something entirely different, I was expecting a kiss or two. What I wasn't expecting was a cupcake being smashed on my cheek. She burst into laughter. "I can't believe you fell for that!"

I wiped at the icing, looking at the globs of blue on my fingers. "Mm-hmm, yeah. I gotta admit that was good. But this is better." I smeared it on her face, grinning. "Now we're both Smurfs."

"Sam," Mom entered the living room, interrupting our playful banter. She glanced up from rummaging in her purse and stopped. "I thought I wouldn't have to tell you guys to keep food off of each other!"

"We didn't get it on the couch. We're all good."

"Anyways, I have to stop by the bank and I'm meeting David for lunch. He finally has one off. I'll probably be back by two, the latest. I don't have to tell you two to behave yourselves." Mom pointed at me. "Don't burn my house down. Money's on the table if you wanna order something."

"Thanks. Love you," I called as she pulled on her

coat and shouldered her purse.

"Love you both!"

Olivia handed me a napkin to clean off my face. After doing so, I relaxed against the back of the couch and closed my eyes.

"You're such a Mama's boy."

"Nothin' wrong with that," I replied. "Besides it's been me and her for a long time. I'm all she has left."

"Maybe her and this David guy will get serious."

I draped my good arm over my face, closing in the darkness. "Maybe."

Olivia grabbed the remote that rested on my thigh and turned the volume up on the TV. I lifted my elbow and cracked open an eye. "Am I being too loud for you?"

"Yes." She stuck her tongue out.

"I'm so sorry, dearest."

Her nose crinkled at the term of endearment. "Don't start calling me those ridiculous nicknames couples use."

"I've called you babe plenty of times and you've never seemed to mind," I pointed out.

"That might be because I *actually* like it. You've always called me that, even before dating," Olivia smiled.

It was at that exact moment I had a feeling in my gut saying this was the perfect time. We were alone and safe and there was no one to ruin it. We were being ourselves in the comfort of my home, in the place where my buried crush from sixth grade resurged. In the place where I was confused about how I felt, and where I was afraid about how real they were becoming. In the place where I told Olivia I loved her.

"Can you come with me?"

She slid her hand into mine. "Sure."

We traveled to my bedroom and I stopped her at the doorway. She raised her eyebrows, but I shook my head and asked if she could close her eyes. When she did, I opened my dresser drawer. Picking up the small velvet box from inside, I flipped it open and stared at the promise ring. It was fairly simple. It was a twisted silver heart with a tiny emerald in the middle.

I took Olivia's hand and guided her to my bed. I couldn't exactly kneel so I sat beside her, fumbling with the words and licking my lips to moist them. I couldn't screw this up. She seemed anxious by her nervous wiping on her jeans and thumbs fiddling with each other. Opening the palm of her right hand, I set the box there.

"Wayne, what is this?" she whispered, admiring the ring.

I tilted her chin up and we locked eyes; emerald green on chocolate brown. "This is a promise to you that I'll never treat you the way I did all these past years. A promise that you'll always have me, no matter how hard life gets. A promise that one day we will be married." I pressed my forehead against hers. "I love you and I want to have you as my wife someday, Jenkins," I said, meaning every word.

"Sam… this is amazing," Olivia told me, taking the ring and sliding it onto her finger. It fit perfectly. She wound an arm around my neck and pulled me in for a kiss. I kissed her back with joy. "I love you so much, Samuel Wayne."

"I love you too, Olivia Jenkins."

Epilogue: Santiago

My boots were silent on the floor, leaving blood-stained and cocaine-dusted footprints behind me. I had just returned from another deal, basking myself in the glory of victory, smell of money, and bags of drugs I had taken.

Wayne was wrong; I made a great leader. Way better than he could ever be.

When I returned to my appointed office, I deposited each of the goods in their differing cycling bins. After doing so, I fell back in my seat and kicked my feet on the table, twirling my blade on the edge of the oak desk and stared at the handful of notes and photographs laid out. The photos were of a murder scene. The notes were plans already prepped and ready.

I dug the tip of my blade into the most important photo of them all; a shot of U20's favorite gang leader, Sam Wayne.

I let out a sweet, low chuckle of revenge, "He won't even see what's coming."

I ripped the knife out of the wood angrily, tearing the picture with it.

ACKNOWLEDGMENTS

First and foremost, the biggest thank you possible to Jesus, my constant best friend and rock, for choosing me to write this story. Honestly, without Him, none of these words would be written. "I can do all things through Christ who gives me strength" is indeed truth.

To Sarah, my wonderful Mom and guidepost. Thank you for being the best role model a girl could ever want. You never fail to amaze me and make me proud. You're the person I'll always want next to me when my dreams come true. To James, my dork of a dad. Thanks for being one in a minion and coming back into my life when you did. I'm so thankful for our relationship. To both of my parents, thank you for not letting me give up on my dreams and always chasing after God's will even when we had to follow blindly. To my little sister Katie, aka my Buggles. Thank you for being my best friend. I'm so freaking blessed to have you. You've helped me in so many ways whether it was holding my hand while I was in pain or listening to my rants and the many ideas I had for this book. I can't wait to see who you grow up to be. To my amazing grandparents: Craig and Cheryl. Thank you for the memories of bouncing on MaMa's knee and collecting softballs in an old field. Thank you for always standing tall in your faith and love. To my other set of grandparents, Jack and Linda. To my family in Florida, Washington, and Heaven- all of you hold a special place in my heart.

To the friends that never left. Thank you for standing beside me and never letting me doubt my ability and talent. Thank you for holding my hand and offering your shoulder to lean on. Thank you for loving me despite my flaws and challenges.

To my church family and support team. Thank you for your love, prayers, encouragement, and appreciation. To my youth pastor, Aaron, for teaching that light can shine in a dark world. To my RSD life coach, Jennifer, for being a great mentor and becoming a lifelong friend. To my Plexus ambassador, Erin, for sharing your amazing testimony. Thank you both for being a constant reminder that RSD doesn't have to run your life. Thank you Sarah Kathrin Biser for creating The Stranger Within's amazing cover. You took my idea and turned it into something better.

To my fellow chronic pain warriors- Hannah, Abby, Gabe, Daniella, Cameron, Alden, Samantha, Patrick, and the several others I have met personally and online. To any RSD/CRPS, POTS/Dysautonomia, Gastroparesis, Fibromyalgia, EDS, Crohn's, MS, Lou Gehrig's/ALS, Lupus, Lyme Disease, Hepatitis, Diabetes, Cancer, etc. warriors reading this- let's show the doubters and non-believers that we are strong, ferocious, and we CAN achieve our goals and live our dreams. To the parents of warriors- thank you for everything you do.

To the best teachers I've ever had: Mr. Reed and Mr. Luisi. The lessons in your classrooms and the love you expressed for your students, I will cherish forever. Thank you for acknowledging my talent and pushing me

.orward to live it out.

And last but not least, to you- the reader. Thank you for picking up this book and joining me in Sam and Olivia's journey.

About the Author

Although The Stranger Within is her first novel, Gabby Johnson has been a writer since 2006, coming a long way from scribbling away at notebooks in class. She now writes at her laptop and slowly yet surely works on her novels. Not only is she a book nerd and a Ravenclaw, she's also a Ferocious Fighter, battling the chronic pain disorder RSD/CRPS every day for the last four years. She can be seen browsing the aisles of Barnes and Noble or with a McDonald's drink in her hand.

COMING FALL 2018

The Stranger Within:

Lovely Vengeance

Printed in Great
Britain
by Amazon